# THE SHROUD OF TORRINGTON

# THE SHROUD OF TORRINGTON

Jeffrey J. Messenger

iUniverse, Inc.
New York  Lincoln  Shanghai

# THE SHROUD OF TORRINGTON

iUniverse books may be ordered through booksellers or by contacting:

iUniverse
2021 Pine Lake Road, Suite 100
Lincoln, NE 68512
www.iuniverse.com
1-800-Authors (1-800-288-4677)

ISBN-13: 978-0-595-35533-4 (pbk)
ISBN-13: 978-0-595-80016-2 (ebk)
ISBN-10: 0-595-35533-1 (pbk)
ISBN-10: 0-595-80016-5 (ebk)

Printed in the United States of America

This book is dedicated to my parents, whose support made this project possible.

"For now we are looking in a mirror that gives only a dim reflection, but then we shall see in reality and face to face! Now I know in part, but then I shall know fully and clearly, even in the same manner as I have been fully known and understood (by God)."

1 Corinthians 13:12, Amplified Bible

# A Note from the Author

*The Shroud of Torrington* is a story that incorporates both real and fictional Connecticut locations within its narrative.

The events of September 11, 2001, are also dramatized. It is my hope that this reference will not demean the reality of this tragic day, or offend those directly impacted by the attacks.

The right to life and dignity for the developmentally challenged is a subject near to my heart. When considering a person's worth, issues such as deformity, awareness, and impairment are irrelevant. Their vulnerability puts our humanity to the test. Let us beware of code words such as choice, quality of life, and the right to die. They are road signs, posted on a highway of rationalization. Ultimately, the vulnerable can be terminated due to how they inconvenience us, the so-called healthy.

The character of Dr. Ray Boyington is portrayed as having direct contact with the real Shroud of Turin Research Project of 1978. This is simply a literary device. Other organizations, researchers, and publications within the story are fictional.

All historic Jesus and Shroud of Turin research included in my story come from published books. A recommended reading list is included at the end of this story.

This fictional narrative takes the position that the Shroud of Turin was created through a miraculous process. While viable, this position is simply one of many that may explain the mysterious Shroud image. If other explanations for the Shroud image are validated in the future, this shouldn't detract from the broader messages this story attempts to convey.

Many political and religious positions offered by the protagonist early in the story do not reflect my opinions. They represent a cultural schism in modern America, and a popular bias against mainstream Christianity.

# CHAPTER 1

▼

# THE NEW MANAGER

Why am I, David Paul, writing this story? Probably because it's safer than telling anyone about it. How I tire of that look: the expression of concern as if I just started to bark like a dog and lifted my leg toward them. Still, I can understand their reaction. I used to be judgmental as well. Despite the skepticism of anyone reading this, I stand by my account. I swear by my faith in Jesus Christ—this is a true story.

It was September 1995.

My drive to work this particular Friday was more pleasant than usual. The leaves were just starting to turn, painting the landscape red, orange, and yellow. It would be this day that I met someone. Someone who forever changed my perception of reality.

I lived in a small studio apartment in Winsted and drove down to Torrington for work. The apartment was in a renovated factory, the famed Gilbert Clock Shop that went out of business before I was born. Red brick walls and high ceilings defined the decor. My particular apartment was an efficiency. It basically had one room and a kitchenette. This suited my needs, since I didn't own many possessions.

Winsted was a thriving mill town before it was devastated by a nasty flood in the 1950s. It was a village of curiosities, thanks to the popular writings of Winsted resident Lou Stone. Mr. Stone liked to write of things such as local witches and hairy wild men who roamed the woods. One *Life* magazine cartoon during the '20s called Winsted "Home of the freak news story."

Back to the 1990s. I was then employed by a Torrington day program for developmentally challenged adults, an organization that cared for and taught people with profound disabilities. My job title was program instructor, but the job encompassed more than instructing. I and the other program instructors lifted people out of wheelchairs and positioned them onto beds, mats, and foam wedges. We lifted them onto toilets. We occasionally cleaned up their vomit, urine, and excrement. We drove them to jobs in large vans built to accommodate several wheelchairs. We accompanied them to doctor and hospital visits. We dispensed medications, took vital signs, and monitored their general health. We utilized various "range of motion" exercises with their restricted limbs. On rare occasions, we restrained them when they sought to harm themselves or other people. Rarer still, we were required to resuscitate those at death's door. Yes, the six of us program instructors had all this responsibility—for ten dollars an hour. Most of us lacked a college education. The company trained us.

Those in our care had various disabilities. Some had autism, others had severe birth defects. Most had cerebral palsy and were confined to wheelchairs. The organization I worked for was named Residential Associates Incorporated, and my particular day program was labeled an intermediate care facility. We worked with twelve people with diverse personalities and needs. I grew to care for each resident. It was a parental feeling, a bond one forms when someone depends on you for everything. Most of these residents were elderly, but at the young age of twenty-eight, I considered them my foster children. Oh sure, my shift was a mere seven hours a day, five days a week. Still, they were the closest thing to a family I had.

Yes, I never knew my biological family. I grew up an orphan. I suspected that my mother was a teen with an unwanted pregnancy. I bounced from institutes to foster homes to group homes. I considered myself an outcast, an outsider. My teen years were uncontrolled. I was arrested for shoplifting and vandalism on several occasions. Not many foster homes had sponsored me more than a few months.

I met the residents at RAI around the age of twenty-two. I started to work for the company when I was still an immature rebel. The population my employers serviced was deformed. They were unloved. Their families had abandoned them. Most of them had grown up in institutions. They were moved into group homes. Unlike me, they didn't have their health. They lacked independence. They had employed caregivers. We were their true lifelines. On a personal level, I identified with them. My self-absorption and hostility faded away. I started to appreciate what I had in life. Another factor for this newly formed maturity was the friendship I had with two coworkers. Marcus Pattyson and Jessica Kim made me feel welcome from the start. They provided me with a sense of belonging.

Marcus was an outgoing, charismatic guy. He was in his late thirties and recently married. Being the first African-American friend I ever had, he helped me shed some residual racism I carried from my bitter youth. Articulate, intelligent, and usually smiling, Marcus made me feel comfortable.

Then we have Jessica Kim. I didn't warm up to Jessica at first. She was just, well, too gorgeous for an ordinary guy like me to talk to. She stood at five feet eleven—two inches taller than me. She was slender. Her hair was long and shimmering, brown with silver and red highlights. Her mother was French and her father was half-Japanese. This unique blending of heritage added an exotic flair to her beauty. Her eyes were blue green, a brilliant shade of turquoise. They were so bright and lively, people wondered if she was wearing artificially colored contact lenses. I knew she wasn't. Jessica was oblivious to how beautiful she was. She routinely wore jeans and T-shirts, and her makeup was at a minimum. She was just Jessica, or "Jess." In my initial intimidation of her, I failed to recognize that she was down to earth.

After several months of working with Jessica, I discovered we had some things in common. We were history buffs. We held socially liberal views. I was very attracted to her, but this sentiment wasn't reciprocated. I was a mere friend. She pursued friendships with multiple men, preferring the platonic company of the opposite sex to other women. Jess was the only woman I was close to or had ever been close to. She was a joyous, flirtatious woman full of energy and warmth.

During a company Christmas party in 1993, Jessica and I allowed our flirtation to go a step beyond. I was slightly buzzed on beer and she was technically intoxicated. A playful game of "keep away" with her cell phone turned into a long, passionate kiss with several coworkers "whoooing" the performance. I assumed that the lip lock was a prelude to a relationship until Marcus pointed at mistletoe hanging above the doorway. Jessica had kissed three other men in like fashion before I arrived at the party.

The next day, Jess didn't remember kissing anyone. She was embarrassed about being drunk. I was in love with her. I couldn't shake the feeling, as much as I tried.

Anyway, back to September 1995. As I pulled into the parking lot of the day program that morning, I momentarily panicked. Where was Jess's car? Was she out sick today? Oh man, to go three days without seeing her seemed as harsh to me as it would be for an alcoholic being dry for three days. Yes, I knew this emotional dependency wasn't healthy, yet I was unable to overcome its intensity. Finally, I spotted her blue Ford Escort; it was blocked by an SUV. I breathed a sigh of relief.

My workplace was a one-floor facility. It comprised two large rooms and a kitchenette. A few small offices were situated in the back—tight spaces where management typed reports and filed documentation.

Inside, the first person I encountered was Jess, her eyes beaming.

"Hey, handsome! You're two minutes late. Ya better shape up, slacker."

"Okay, okay. It's Friday. Cut me some slack," I said, blushing.

"Maybe I will, maybe I won't," she teased.

Marcus walked in. His eyes dark, his mouth stretched in an intense yawn.

"Hi, Marcus."

"Hey, David," Marcus replied. "Tell me, is it Thursday or Friday?"

"Friday. TGIF, Marcus!"

"TGIF my butt," he sneered. "The ball-and-chain has me installing a panel wood floor. Oh, my aching back. I need to come to work to rest!"

"Poor baby," I answered. I didn't have much sympathy, considering that I was a lonely bachelor.

Marcus signed into the work log and pointed out a fact that had somehow missed my attention.

"Hey, Dave!" He grinned, while looking around to make sure no one was within earshot. "I see Jess signed you up to do transport to Elm Street with her this morning. Since you both will have at least ten minutes alone, how about finally asking her out?"

Morning transport was a duty in which a pair of RAI workers drove a van to one of three particular group homes then brought the residents back to the day-program facility.

"Shh!" I reprimanded. "Keep your voice down! You want everyone to hear?"

"Oh right," Marcus chided. "Perhaps we can pass notes in third period."

"You know as well as I do that Jess is still dating that steroid poster boy."

"Aw man," Marcus rolled his eyes. "You need to listen to the gossip mill more. Jess broke up with him a few days back."

"Again?"

"Yes, 'again.' This is your opportunity man. Strike while the iron is hot!"

"You know, she has been more flirtatious than usual these last few days."

"Exactly. If you don't ask that fox out soon, some other dude is going to snatch her up. Get your gonads in gear and do it already!"

"Gonads?"

"Yeah, gonads! My wife loves that word. I hate it."

I contemplated Marcus's suggestion. Why not ask Jessica out? Must I continue to pine away for her from afar like some lovesick schoolboy? Wasn't the lady sending me enough signals?

I felt a hand on my back. I turned to see the eyes that captivated me from the moment I first saw them.

"Hope you don't mind me signing you up for Elm transport today, Dave."

"Mind? Uh—naw. It's my job to do these things."

When it came to the fine art of flirting, I was a pure amateur.

"Let's go a few minutes early," Jessica prompted.

Soon we were on the road. The company vans were spacious. Seat belts and chair straps were hinged on the floor. They rattled and jingled as I drove. The vehicle interiors were tinged with a faint smell of urine and vomit. After a few months of working in the field, I was able to ignore such olfactory sensations.

Jess sat to my right as I drove. We engaged in small talk. We discussed the weather and touched on the OJ Simpson murder trial. Finally, I mustered enough courage to start a personal conversation.

"Jess. How's Kyle?"

"Guess what? That muscle-bound Neanderthal stood me up again! He claimed he was ill Monday night, then I saw him with one of those Gold's Gym aerobics instructors later that evening. This time, it's finished."

I marveled. How could he treat her like this, when someone like me would give his right kidney to be in his position? Anyway, in the three years that I had known Jessica, she had broken up with Kyle at least five times.

"You're sure about that?" I asked.

"Yeah, I know. You've heard this song and dance before, right Dave?"

"Well, I didn't want to put it that way."

"Please do. I know I can be an airhead."

"C'mon, Jess. You're no 'airhead.'"

"That's sweet of you to say, but facts are facts," she sighed. Actually, she was partially correct. Her romantic affections seemed as fickle as the New England weather.

After a few minutes of awkward silence, Jessica reinitiated the conversation. "Uh, you know David," she paused. "I can tell you that my eyes are now open. You know, I'm open to finding someone new."

"Really?"

"Yes, really." She sat quietly before adding an addendum. "Except for one person. I know he likes me, but I can't see him as more than a friend."

*Ouch.* This was the type of mixed signals, the type of ambiguity Jess routinely hit me with. On the one hand, an attractive, flirtatious, single woman just told me she is available. Then she has to ruin it all by informing me that one of her male friends doesn't have a chance with her. Was I that guy? Was I the one she liked, but wasn't attracted to? Was she sending me a warning? The mere prospect made my blood run cold. I knew it was preferable to pretend that I had a romantic chance with her.

We arrived at the Elm Street group home. The house was a one-story building. Modern. A large wheelchair ramp with high wooden rails led to the front door. White aluminum siding covered the structure.

This was my favorite house of the three group homes because "Huey" lived here. Huey was an elderly gentleman of about sixty-five. His arms had good range of motion, but he was unable to walk. Huey was "profoundly retarded," the term we used during those years to describe those with severe developmental challenges. Repeated grand mal seizures contributed to his condition. His intelligence was that of a three-year-old, which placed him ahead of most we took care of. His face had a few deformities. Yet when he smiled, it was contagious. His speech was muffled and slurred. It took a familiarity with his verbal patterns to interpret what he said. While his language was childlike, he often came out with little pearls of wisdom that impressed me.

Jess and I walked into the house, having had another awkward silence due to her commentary.

I broke the silence. "I wonder who's filling in for house manager today?"

This group home had been without a manager for three weeks due to the unexpected departure of the last one. The job was a tenuous one. If anything went wrong or was mishandled, the manager took the fall.

Jess looked around.

"I don't know, Dave. I think the new guy is supposed to start today."

"New guy? They hired someone already?"

"Indeed they have," a deep voice sounded behind me. "And I'm mighty grateful to have this job!"

I turned around to look at the man behind the voice. I was immediately intimidated. This guy stood at six foot four, with broad shoulders and a thick neck. His three-piece suit was without a wrinkle; his swept-back hair was silver.

He wore a black beard and mustache, which along with dark eyebrows, made a startling contrast to his premature gray hair. He held out a huge, beefy hand.

"How do you do, friend. My name is Brad Ramsey."

I took his hand, at which he squeezed my fingers with a strength I couldn't match.

"Uh, hi. I'm Dave Paul."

"Pleased to meet you, Dave. And who is this?"

I turned to see Jessica blushing, her head tilted to one side and her eyes dancing on our new acquaintance. She advanced toward us, momentarily losing her balance.

"Hi, Mr. Ramsey. I'm Jessica. Jessica Kim."

"Please, Jessica. Call me Brad."

"Okay, Brad. You can call me Jess."

I seethed internally. It took me four weeks to get close enough with Jessica to call her "Jess!" I knew this meeting was bad news for my closely guarded pipe dream.

Brad turned toward me and flashed a brilliant white-toothed grin.

"You too, Dave. Call me Brad."

He started to walk to his cubbyhole, but thought for a moment and turned around. "I look forward to getting to know you both. If either of you have future suggestions regarding the home, you know where to reach me."

With a wink, he began to walk back to his office—a walk-in closet converted for managerial privacy. "Back to the paperwork. God, I hate Microsoft Windows."

"That makes two of us," Jessica giggled.

"Have a fine day, Dave, Jess."

Jessica and I silently attired the six residents in their autumn jackets and walked them to the van. A group home employee dutifully helped us secure the wheelchairs with the custom clamps and belts.

Finally, it was time to wheel Huey out. He greeted me with that contagious smile.

"Avey!" Huey yelled, whenever he saw me. "Avey! Avey!"

"Hey, Huey. Ready for another adventure-filled day?"

He laughed on cue at all my little jokes. I think he responded more to the tone of my voice than to the words themselves.

"Ewy goo boy ay. Ewy goo boy ay."

This was one of Huey's favorite phrases, which he often repeated to the impatience of all around him. It was translated as "Huey is a good boy today."

"Yes, Huey," I answered. "You're a good man. Remember Huey, you're a man, not a boy."

"Ewy boy."

"No. Both Davey and Huey are men."

"Avey goo."

"Thank you, bud. Too bad more women didn't think so."

Huey laughed again.

Jessica was within earshot of my comment. She walked over and gave me a side hug.

"Don't fret, cutie. Some lucky woman will snatch you up."

Huey nodded vigorously at Jessica's observation.

"Ess goo! Ess goo!"

She then gave Huey his morning hug. "Huey, you sweetie. You brighten my morning."

As she walked to the front of the van, Huey pointed at her.

"Ess goo!"

I watched every graceful movement Jessica made and sighed with longing.

Soon, all were secured in the van and headed for the day program. Huey kept chanting his familiar refrain, "Ewy goo boy. Ewy goo boy." Other residents made variable sounds. Rich liked to make "raspberry" noises with his tongue. A few rocked nervously back and forth. Erica, a woman with autistic mannerisms, frequently let loose a piercing shriek.

A few minutes into our ride, Jessica turned to smile at Huey. "What about Brad, Huey? Your new friend back at the house? Brad is a good man, isn't he?"

Huey remained silent. Jessica pushed on.

"Right, Huey? Isn't Brad a good man?"

Huey repeated, "Bad man, bad man, bad man, bad man."

# CHAPTER 2

▼

# A DINNER CONVERSATION

I awoke from a Saturday afternoon nap and realized I was late. Marcus was good enough to invite his dispirited friend and coworker for dinner, and here I was with bed-head hair and rumpled clothes. I dashed around my cramped efficiency in a mad rush to become presentable. With a quick wash and change of clothes, I was on my way to the Pattyson residence.

The previous day's conversation with Marcus replayed in my head as I drove along the country road. He approached me at the end of our shift.

"Hey! I didn't get a chance to ask you today!" Marcus smiled. "So-o-o?"

"So?"

"So, did you finally ask her out?"

"Oh, yeah. You see...uh. Well, it's like this—"

"*Oh, man!*" my friend yelled. "You do have a serious gonad deficiency!"

"True as that may be," I said, "the magic eight ball was telling me to wait. Our favorite supermodel was distracted."

"Distracted? What discouraged you now?"

"I don't know. Perhaps it was her gushing over that new guy."

"New guy?"

"Yeah, you know, the new manager at Elm. Some slick Don Juan."

"Haven't met him yet."

"Well, Jessica and I did. Oh sure, the guy was likable, but he was a bit too perfect. You know…the perfectly pressed suit. Perfect swept-back hair. A face Michelangelo could have sculpted. Ugh."

"Okay. So why do you think Jessica was taken in by Mr. GQ?"

"Well, she seemed to actually lose her balance when she met him. Her face was in a perpetual blush for the rest of the day! I also heard Jessica whispering with Rose and Angela about 'the new guy.'"

"Hmm. That doesn't sound good, friend."

"No, it doesn't. You know what really got to me?"

"What?"

"Even Huey didn't like him!"

"Care for a suggestion, Dave?"

"Uh-oh, here it comes."

"Forget about Jessica, man! No forward momentum is to be found with her. She's one of those sweet, but fickle, types who bounces from stud to stud. She's in love with being infatuated. She's always looking for that new charmer who will make her heart go pitter-patter."

"*What?* I don't get it. Weren't you the one who told me to ask her out, to 'strike while the iron was hot?'"

"Sure was. I wanted her to turn you down once and for all, so you would finally end this schoolboy crush of yours. Sometimes, a person has to be cruel to be kind."

"Aw man, what a cliché."

"Sorry, but you're just a reliable friend to her. She takes those roller-coaster rides with her multiple boyfriends, then talks to you when she needs to feel grounded again. You're too reliable, too nice, and too comfortable. You'll never make her heart go pitter-patter."

"B-but," I stammered, as I tried to keep hope alive. "There was that kiss!"

"Aw gawd, not the kiss story again. Dave, my man, Jess was feelin' no pain that evening. She kissed several guys at the party."

A deep ache grew in my stomach. Marcus was right. I knew I had no chance with this woman who haunted my dreams. She was wired for excitement, for romantic adventure. I was a person who needed stability, affirmation, and approval. Jessica and I had an odd, dysfunctional friendship that was destined to stagnate.

I gave Marcus a shoulder pat and slowly walked across the parking lot.

"Dave! Dave!" I heard Marcus behind me. I turned and waved good-bye.

"Yo, Dave!" Marcus jogged to catch up to me.

"Sorry. Really, I am."

"Never be sorry for telling the truth," I smiled.

"Tamika is cooking my favorite dinner tomorrow, a reward for working on that panel wood floor she wanted. Come on over and eat with us."

"What's she cooking?"

"Beef stroganoff."

"Hmm. That does sound good."

"C'mon over. Don't sit around and brood this weekend. Come enjoy the company of friends."

Although the sour stomachache continued, I mustered a smile for my good friend.

"Okay. I'll be there."

"Outstanding! See ya at five sharp?"

"Sure will."

Here it was, five-thirty. I had so few friends in life that the thought of offending Marcus sent me into a panic. My foot lay heavy on the gas pedal, and squirrels that ran in front of me did so at their peril.

Finally, I reached their home on Torringford West Street. I checked my watch and saw I was forty minutes late. With a deep breath, I calmed myself and walked to the front door. On the first knock, the door opened.

"Dave! Good to see you! I just called your apartment to see if you had forgotten."

Marcus was a jovial soul. It was hard to picture him ever being offended or angry.

"Hi, Marcus. No, no…I wasn't…I mean, I didn't forget. I was napping and overslept."

"No problem! Tamika usually takes her time with cooking and tonight is no exception. Come in and relax!"

Tamika greeted me. She was a heavyset woman with bright eyes and an outspoken demeanor.

"Hello, Dave! Good to see ya again!"

She gave me a crushing bear hug. Her strength was incredible, and she never held back when offering one of her famous embraces.

"Hi, Tamika. Good to see you too," I wheezed through the pain.

"Now you two go sit and talk about football or whatever. Dinner will be ready in a few minutes."

Marcus's living room was beautiful with a plush white carpet and tan furniture. It was obvious the main breadwinner was Tamika, considering Marcus and

I earned less than twenty thousand dollars a year. Tamika was a registered nurse. Her income easily doubled Marcus's. This would have bothered some husbands, but not Marcus. Always easygoing, always secure, the man had a rock-solid ego. I envied his strength.

I sat in an easy chair, momentarily shocked at its exceptional comfort. Marcus sat on the couch opposite me.

"So how are you doing, Dave?"

"I'm okay."

"Feeling better today?"

"I suppose."

"I remember before I met Tamika, I was burned. Aw man! I must have been rejected about a billion times!"

"You, Marcus? No way."

"No lie! I did that personal ad thing in the *Foothills Trader*! I went to singles clubs, bars, dance clubs, and libraries. I approached strangers with pick-up lines. Yeow! The stories I could tell!"

"What's this?" Tamika's voice echoed from the kitchen. "You better not be boring our guest with your memories as a 'playah!'"

"Me? Never!" Marcus yelled back. Then he leaned forward and whispered, "You aren't bored, are ya, Dave?"

"Me? Never."

"Anyway, I used to work with this girl—Lord! She'd walk into a room and cause the wallpaper to peel! She was solely responsible for global warming! Anyway, I left little notes on her windshield, and—"

"Your new bride can hear you!" the voice from the kitchen intoned.

Marcus lowered his volume.

"And I attached long-stem roses to her timecard. She was intrigued and would constantly talk about her secret admirer. One day, I left an invitation on her car inviting her to meet her 'secret admirer' at the Patriot Diner. She walked in, looked at me, and *wham!*"

"Wham?"

"Wham! She blasted my ego with both barrels. She looked at me and said 'You? I knew this was too good to be true.'"

"Ouch!"

"Darn right, 'ouch.' I still have psychic wounds from that."

"Well, Marcus, at least you had the courage to act on your feelings. Perhaps you can donate a gonad?"

"I can't," he sighed. "My wife has them in her coat pocket."

"Oh brother," the voice from the kitchen retorted.

"Dave, Dave," Marcus patted my leg. "You're a young, semi-attractive dude. You're thin. You've got all your hair. Go out there and live!"

"You mean, go get the type of reaction you received at the Patriot Diner?"

"That's all part of the game, my man. If you play the slots, you lose and lose before you hit the jackpot."

"You mean, *if* you hit the jackpot."

"No man, when. It's all about attitude! Women smell insecurity like animals smell fear! Once they get a whiff of your self-doubt, the game is lost."

"Isn't that ironic? Self-doubt causes rejection, and rejection causes self-doubt."

"Yeah, it's ironic. But to break that cycle is an act of willpower. You look at yourself in the mirror and tell yourself you are 'the man!' You tell yourself you deserve any woman you set eyes on! You tell yourself only the blind or the ignorant would pass you by! You tell yourself you are God's gift to the opposite sex!"

Tamika walked back into the living room, a look of displeasure on her face.

"Do you realize, Marcus, that the first segment of floorboard is already warped in the middle? I told you not to leave the new panels in that dank basement! As usual, you do your own thing. Anyway, the meal is ready. I hope you enjoy it, Dave, 'cause Mr. Home Improvement here doesn't deserve it."

"Ahh, marital bliss," Marcus murmured.

As we walked into the dining room, I heard him repeat under his breath, "I am 'the man.' I am God's gift to women." I couldn't help but erupt into loud laughter.

The meal was the best I had smelled in years. As a single man, I ate mostly deli food. I didn't have a mother to visit; a parent to show me what home cooking was about. Eating was eating—something to be done, not experienced.

Tamika had a flair for decor. Her table was immaculately arranged with two slender candles flanking a central floral arrangement. Her best china was set and silverware polished to a shine. I didn't want to touch anything, for fear of spoiling something that took so much effort.

As we sat, Tamika bowed her head and started to pray.

"We thank you, Lord, for this bounty we are about to receive. We thank you for your blessings and praise your name now and forever. Praise Jesus! Amen!"

Marcus replied with an enthusiastic "Amen." I simply mouthed the word. At this stage in my life, I had a palatable distaste for all religions. Especially Christianity.

During the meal, Marcus and Tamika had engaged me in small talk, but the most they got out of me was an occasional grunt or nod. My mouth was too busy consuming the divine edibles presented before me. I always thought Tamika was a nag and wondered how Marcus put up with her personality. Yet, as chauvinistic as this may sound, the thought of eating this well seemed worth any perpetual conflict.

With a protruding stomach and a satisfied stretch, I welcomed the after-dinner coffee. I was now available for conversation.

Tamika leaned in, dying to ask something she had hinted at during the meal.

"Okay, Dave, point blank: Would you like to meet a wonderful, single friend of mine?"

"Aw, 'Mika," Marcus groaned. "I thought we agreed you wouldn't do this."

"I'm violating the terms of that treaty, love."

Tamika leaned closer. "Well, David?"

I was stunned. Being that I was lonely, part of me wanted to take any assistance she could give. Another part of me resisted the idea of dating anyone other than my fantasy love, Jessica.

"W…well," I stammered.

Tamika flew out of her seat and went to grab a photo off the nearby buffet. With an energetic leap, she presented me the picture. The woman was pleasant looking with short, dark hair and pale skin. She had an inviting smile.

"This is Doris," Tamika continued. "She goes to the First Pentecostal Church that Marcus and I attend. The one on Hayden Street. She is a good woman. Virtuous. She walks closely with the Lord. She's looking for a good man, a man who loves the Lord as well."

I knitted my brow. "Loves the Lord?"

"Uh, 'Mika," Marcus warned.

Tamika sat down and leaned away from me. "What's amatter, Davey-boy? Don't you love the Lord?"

I loosened the collar around my neck, which felt rather tight at that moment. "Uh, well, sure. I guess. If there is a God, I suppose he deserves some emotion from me."

*"If there is a God?"* Tamika exclaimed.

"Oh man!" Marcus interrupted. "Look 'Mika, I told you that I wasn't sure how religious Dave was. Don't push this on him."

"Some friend you are!" Tamika became louder. "What if the Rapture occurred tomorrow? We'd be with the Lord, enjoying paradise. Dave would be…stuck on this dung hill of a planet."

"The Rapture?" I inquired.

Tamika leaned in again. "The Rapture is an event that precedes the Last Days and rule of Antichrist. The Lord Jesus is going to come from the heavens with a shout, and all that belong to him will be gathered in the clouds to be forever with the Lord!"

I sat dumbfounded. Was this woman serious?

Tamika started to tear up. She reached in and grabbed my arm.

"David. Haven't you accepted Jesus as your personal Lord and Savior?"

"Uh…no," I replied through a giggle.

"So, why not? Certain sins ya don't want to give up, pray tell?"

"Well," I started reluctantly, "I haven't seen any evidence that Jesus is a Lord or a Savior. As far as my sins go, they're not even interesting enough to brag about."

Marcus looked uncomfortable as he retreated into the bathroom.

"Evidence of the Lord?" Tamika laughed. "This is about faith, man! If you accept him with faith, only then will he speak to your heart!"

"My heart?"

"Yes, your heart."

"Sorry, Tamika. I live by my brain, not my heart."

The woman paused at this comment.

"Okay, Dave. What does your brain say about the universe? Didn't something create all this?"

"Maybe," I nodded. "Or maybe the universe is a fluke. An unplanned happening. I recently read about some cosmologist who reasoned that a natural process called Inflation Theory set all that quantum stuff into action and set off a big bang."

*"Yeah, right!"* Tamika snorted. "Let me tell ya, honey, inflation means something else to us ordinary folks."

I continued on the subject. "Let's say that a god did create everything. Who is to say it's Jesus, or Jesus' father, or whatever you believe? Maybe it was Allah. Or Buddha. Or Vishnu. Or some pagan deity worshiped at Stonehenge."

Tamika looked angry.

"All I'm saying is that I need proof. If Jesus walked into this room, showed me his wounds, and disappeared in a puff of smoke, maybe then I'd believe this fairy tale."

*"Fairy tale?"* Tamika winced.

"Uh, sorry. Bad choice of words," I quickly added.

"You bet it was a poor choice of words."

"Sorry. All I'm saying is—that for me—me personally, I need proof. It's okay if you believe in Jesus and all that jazz. I'm not attacking you or anything."

"Let me tell ya, honey. If you attack Jesus, you attack me."

"I didn't attack Jesus."

*"Yes, you did!"*

I started to get angry. "When did I do that?"

"When you said that he was no more real than some make-believe voodoo!"

"Well, can you prove to me that he is?"

"You said that Jesus was an outright fairy tale!"

"Can you prove to me he isn't?"

"Prove to you? Man, Dave. I never knew you were one of those scoffers."

"I'm not a scoffer. I'm a thinker."

"Are you saying I'm not a thinker?"

"No, I'm saying that you can't prove that some man named Jesus, who scholars disagree about, is God of the universe."

"What scholars disagree?"

"Well, there's a scholar who appeared on the *History Channel* last week. He said that Jesus was most likely a Jewish rebel, an insurgent who had problems with Rome. Jesus wasn't any Messiah, miracle worker or such nonsense. He was crucified. His body was thrown in a common grave for criminals. Roaming dogs and crows ate his remains. All this was the likely scenario."

*"Dogs and crows?"* Tamika sprang out of her chair.

"Yeah, he said something like that."

Tamika stood there vibrating like a spring wound too tight. I became afraid. What did I do? This woman was obviously a religious fanatic, and I pushed her sensitive buttons.

*"Marcus!"* Her shrill voice shot through me like an electric shock. *"Marcus!"*

My friend reluctantly walked back into the room. "Yeah. You two okay?"

"Your good friend here said that our risen Lord and Savior can be found in *dog poop and crow dung!*"

"I…uh, no. That's not what I said. I said there was this guy. Yeah, this historian I saw on the *History Channel*, and he said—"

Marcus walked up to me and grabbed my shoulder. "It's all right, David. Really."

He then turned to Tamika. "Look 'Mika, didn't I warn you not to Holy Roller over this poor guy?"

"Well, Marcus, you never told me he was an unbeliever."

"I didn't know what David believed. I just like him, okay?"

"Well, the man you like doesn't respect the Lord!"

"I respect Jesus," I responded. "I'm sure he was a good and wise teacher and all. What I'm saying is that…well…I need a reason to—"

Marcus interrupted. "Don't sweat it, Dave. One doesn't need to be Christian to be our friend and have dinner with us. Right, Tamika?"

The woman paused, then relaxed. "Of course not. Dave, sorry if I came on too strong."

"That's okay, Tamika. I'm sorry if I offended you and your beliefs."

"Apology accepted. All I ask is…well, you try Jesus out. Pray to him. Ask him to come into your heart. You'll be very surprised, believe me."

I smiled and held back a sudden urge to laugh at Tamika for promoting a magic formula.

"Okay, Tamika. Maybe I'll try that sometime."

After an awkward silence, the intense woman started toward the kitchen. "You two sit tight. We have pecan pie to indulge in. One scoop or two of ice cream, David?"

"Uh, one please," I responded.

"One it is!" Then I heard Tamika murmur "heathen" under her breath.

Small-talk dominated the rest of the evening. Religious topics were avoided; Tamika's friend Doris was forgotten. After that holy war, it seemed I wasn't good enough for the blind date anymore. Not that I cared. I would just constantly compare her to Jessica.

Marcus walked me out to my car. A fine, misty rain started to fall through the air, mixing with autumn leaves. The feel of the cool, fresh air awakened me from a political-theological haze. Marcus was a good friend. Did I really have to have that particular battle with his wife? Shouldn't I have simply humored my host and her apparent delusions?

"See you Monday, Dave. I apologize again for Tamika. She's fiery, let me tell you. Sometimes that's good and sometimes not so good. But she does care."

"No problem, Marcus. See ya Monday."

# CHAPTER 3

▼

# A TRIP TO THE SHRINE

After the residents were brought to the day program on Monday, something seemed alien. Work had somehow changed. Marcus was cheerful as ever, although he was rather embarrassed by my debate with Tamika on Saturday. Jessica was also upbeat. Still, something felt wrong.

One contributing factor was Huey. The man was usually happy. Yet this day, he arrived at day program with his head hung low. Even my lame jokes failed to solicit a chuckle. His eyes were pained. Drool ran out the corner of his mouth.

As I sat down to chart his range of motion exercises, Jessica came over and sat beside me.

"So, Dave, what's with Huey? Do you know why he seems so down?"

"No. It's odd, isn't it?"

"Sure is. Did you take his vitals?"

"Yes. Pupil dilation, pulse, respiration, blood pressure, and temp are all normal. When I ask if he feels sick, he just shakes his head no."

"Hmm. Perhaps a petit mal seizure, one that passed unnoticed?"

"I think he's just sad. For what reason, who knows? He's incapable of telling us."

Jessica quietly thought about the situation.

"Dave, you know what? No one has an outing planned. It's Indian summer outside and the colors are beautiful. Why don't we take a group out for lunch? Perhaps to a park?"

"Good idea. I know just the place to cheer Huey up."

I approached Huey who was positioned on a foam wedge. Velcro straps held him secure. This positioning allowed a small pressure ulcer on his right butt cheek to heal. A welcome relief for Huey, I'm sure, since his significant weight bore down on his bedsore. It must have been very uncomfortable after a few hours.

"Hey, Huey! Would you like to eat lunch somewhere else today?"

He shook his head no.

"You sure?"

Again, his head signaled no.

"Not even to the shrine?"

Huey's eyes brightened. He looked at me.

"Well? How about a trip to the shrine?"

For the first time all day, Huey smiled. He nodded his head vigorously.

"All right! We'll leave in an hour. How's that?"

Huey's grin grew larger. He finally spoke. He said, "Good Avey."

"You're welcome, buddy."

Jessica was standing nearby. Her smile outdid Huey's. "How well you know him, Dave."

"Well, yeah. I suppose."

"You two have a great friendship. It's so sweet! I wish I could just get it all on videotape."

"Lord, Jess! Don't do that! Those state inspectors would have documented evidence of all my mistakes!"

"Well, in my book, you do everything right."

As I looked at her, Jess tilted her head to the side. She gave me a smile before walking away. My heart skipped a beat.

"Exhale. You're turning blue," Marcus whispered.

I let out a slow, labored breath, which concluded with Marcus's laughter.

"I hate to ruin this moment for you, Dave, but I have a situation," he murmured.

"Situation?"

"Uh, yeah."

Marcus looked sheepish. This was uncharacteristic of him.

"Dave, when I went to lift Richard off the toilet, he had something stuck to his private member."

*"Stuck to his member?"*

"Yeah."

"Jeez, what would be stuck to that?"

"A sticker from his underwear. Are you aware of that commercial where a certain brand of underwear brags about how its garments are 'inspected by number twelve?' An old battle-ax of a woman stretches those 'tightie whities' in all directions. Well, all these briefs come with stickers, claiming 'this product was inspected by number twelve.'"

"Are you saying that Richard's genitalia has a sticker claiming that this product was inspected by number twelve?"

"Yeah."

I started to chuckle.

"This isn't funny!" Marcus exclaimed. "If we don't remove the sticker, the group home staff will think one of us put it on intentionally! This type of humor could get someone fired!"

"Okay," I composed myself. "Okay. What do you want me to do about it?"

"Could you remove the sticker for me?"

"What? Why me?"

"Richard doesn't like me. He starts yelling as soon as I reach for it."

"Who can blame him!" I laughed.

"I think the parents who abandoned him were clansmen," Marcus sighed.

"BS, he just doesn't like your tobacco breath."

"Yeah, yeah, whatever. Will you do it?"

"Only if you protect me. I don't want him to start flaying his arms. Last year, I ended up with a black eye when Rich had his foot wedged behind his footrest."

"Sure. Okay. But don't think having my ethnic face nearby is going to help matters."

We walked into the bathroom. I opened the stall. There was Richard, oblivious to the situation.

"Hi, Rich," I soothed as I knelt in front of him. "I need to do something here. Real quick." Richard couldn't understand what I was saying, due to his severe autism. Still, it made me feel more comfortable to speak.

Marcus moved to the side of the poor fellow as I put on latex gloves. Slowly, reluctantly, I reached for Richard's penis.

"*Arrrgggghhh!*" he yelled. I jerked back.

"Sometimes, I hate this job."

I saw the sticker had one corner raised. With a quick, precise movement, I reached down and peeled the label off.

"*Ahhhhhh!*" Rich yelled, while swinging his arm spasmodically. Marcus blocked his hand before it clocked me in the chin.

"Thank you, Kato," I sighed with relief.

"Don't mention it, Captain Gonads."

One hour later, Jess and I packed their lunches and their afternoon meds. We were taking four residents, Huey being the only one with verbal ability. The other three had varying degrees of autism. Their mannerisms were unique and compulsive. Erica continually stared at her right hand, which she would repeatedly rotate toward her eyes. Alice rocked her body with vigor. Her wheelchair would sometimes rock as well. Manuel sat motionless, but his perpetual, monotone vocalizing of *"dum de dum de dum de dum"* had the unfortunate effect of his exclusion from planned field trips. Jessica and I made a point to include him this time.

Soon, all four were secured in the van. Huey beamed a smile and his earlier mood was now forgotten. Jess tossed me the keys. A whirlwind of leaves blew past as we drove out of the day program parking lot. With Jess beside me and Huey happy, all seemed normal.

Our destination was the Lourdes Shrine in Litchfield. This shrine was a replica of the famous one in France. There was an outdoor grotto, and a long path honoring the stations of the cross. Statues were everywhere. A lazy brook ran through a grove of trees. Picnic tables sat nearby. The place was custom-made for a group with our needs. The religious trappings were irrelevant to everyone save Huey. He seemed fascinated by the statues and the sights. I figured it was Huey's attraction to statues and stained glass that compelled his group home staff to bring him to Saint Andrew's church every Saturday evening. Huey's mind wasn't equipped for theological abstractions.

Upon arrival, Jess and I went to work positioning Erica, Alice, and Manuel around a picnic table. Huey was different. I was expected to first walk him to the grotto. There he could look at the statues and the burning candles. This routine seemed to give him pleasure.

Soon, Huey and I approached the statue of a young Bernadette, bowing to a Virgin Mary icon perched on a ledge. These figures were the focal point of the shrine, along with a facsimile rock face and cave. Dozens of devotional candles glowed within the cave. My friend studied the statue of the young woman.

"Ess," he replied. "Ess!"

"No, Huey," I laughed. "That's not Ess. This girl was less worldly. Her name was Bernadette."

"Ette!" he yelled. "Ette!"

"That's right."

Huey looked up. "Mary," he said with clear pronunciation.

I was impressed. It was the first time Huey properly identified a statue.

"That's right! That's Mary!"

"Mary goo."

"Yes. Mary is good."

"Mary eetty."

"Yes, Mary is very pretty."

"Handmaiden."

I was stunned. Did Huey just say handmaiden? A complicated, multi-syllable word? Did he actually pronounce it correctly?

*"Huey! Say that again!"*

He grinned.

*"Please!* Say that again!" He laughed loudly. His grin grew larger.

"Can you say that again? *Try!"*

"Avey goo. Ewy goo boy."

I sighed. Perhaps I was hearing things. "Uh, yeah. I'm good, you're good. Remember Huey, you're a man, not a boy."

"Ewy boy."

"Okay, Huey. Okay."

I often dreamt that my friend was fully functional and articulate. The two of us would sit and discuss current events. For a brief moment, it seemed my dreams had a foothold in reality. But the moment passed. I brought Huey back to the picnic table.

Jessica had all the processed food set out. Some of the food was pureed because Manuel and Huey had trouble chewing and swallowing. Whenever either man started coughing or wheezing, all of us would hold our breath. Choking incidents were common.

"So, Dave," Jessica inquired, "did you two have a pleasant walk?"

"I think we did. At the very least, I made Huey laugh. Although that wasn't my intention."

"I think he just enjoys your company. We all do."

Once again, Jessica made me blush.

"Careful, Jess," I warned. "Flattery will get you nowhere."

"Aw," she stamped her foot. "You tease."

After assisting the two men with their food, Jess and I ate our own bagged lunches. It was also our chance for some small talk.

"You know something, Jess? I can't help but feel odd with all these religious trappings around us."

"Tell me about it. I went to Catholic school, remember?"

I then tried to be as bold with my flirtation as Jess was.

"That's right! If you ever wish to wear your old school uniform to work one day, I wouldn't complain."

The risky comment had the desired effect. Jessica broke out into hysterical laughter.

"*You pervert!*" she yelled, and birds took flight from a nearby tree. She punched my left arm and giggled. "Anyway," Jessica continued, "my mother wishes I went to Mass more often. But I can't. Too many sour memories."

"You mean the traditional Sister Mary Discipline stuff?"

"Not exactly."

"Oh. What do you mean?"

Jessica looked uncomfortable. This was rare. I took the signal.

"If it's too personal, I understand."

"No, no. Just give me a moment."

After a few seconds, she started reluctantly.

"When I was nine years old, a Father Valdi worked at St. Andrew's."

"Yes?"

"Well, he walked into the girl's bathroom one day. He opened the stall I was sitting in and accused me of smoking. Scared and embarrassed, I quickly pulled up my skirt. I denied the accusation. He told me to pull down my skirt again. He said I was hiding a pack of cigarettes in my panties."

My blood pressure raised and I felt a throbbing in my head. This story was headed in a bad direction.

"Well, I did as he asked. After looking at me for an uncomfortable length of time, he said, 'What do you have down there? Pull down your panties.' I was scared. I didn't know what to do. He then reached in and yanked down my underwear. He…fondled me."

I listened with anger.

"And…well, he then said, 'Sorry, Jess. I see you have nothing to hide.' I was paralyzed. As he left the bathroom, he said, 'I wouldn't tell anyone about this. After all, you did pull down your skirt. You wanted me to touch you.'"

"God, Jess."

"For years I felt ashamed," she continued. "I wondered if I did want him to touch me. I was embarrassed by my willingness to pull down my skirt. I was ashamed. Needless to say, I never told anyone about it."

I sat silently.

After a few minutes of cricket and bird sounds, I reached out and took her hand.

"Do you know whatever happened to this Father Valdi?"

I had an ulterior motive in asking the question. I hoped he was still in the area, so I could find him and introduce him to "the fear of God."

"I think he moved to California. He died a few years back. And guess how I know this?"

"How?"

"Because the pervert became a famous author! He wrote a book about sexual morality! He promoted the virtues of celibacy and monogamy!"

I shook my head in disbelief.

"This pedophile became a spokesman for sexual purity. His obituary was on the news. I couldn't believe it."

I stood up and started pacing. I let loose.

*"This stuff is so typical!"* I maniacally ranted. "*These holy hypocrites! These sanctimonious Christians!* That's the type of men they receive direction from! They make me sick! I recently had a run-in with this type of moron. A woman who tried to save my soul. Why are they so sure of their superstitions? Why are they so arrogant to believe that they alone are headed to heaven and everyone else is headed to hell? You know what hell is? Hell is suffering through their pious, sanctimonious platitudes!"

"You tell 'em, brother," Jessica smiled through tears.

"And who dwells in the midst of these saintly pretenders? Yeah, people like this Valdi. His type is celebrated and defended. Meanwhile, someone like me expresses honest doubts and I'm considered a bad guy. I'm called a heathen. Well, it's better to be a heathen than to be counted in the ranks of the *self-righteous!*"

My rant was overboard. I shook with rage.

Jessica reached out and took my arm. "Dave, you're absolutely right. I do appreciate your empathy. But I think you're upsetting Huey."

I looked over at Huey. His face was contorted with tears.

"Oh my God. He must have been shocked by the volume of my voice. *Oh God.*"

I walked over and put my arm around him. I tried to comfort him.

"Hey, Huey. Hey, buddy. It's okay. Really, I'm not mad at you. It's okay, buddy."

Huey's tears lessened. He kept saying, "Avey. Avey. Avey."

"Dave's not mad at you, buddy. Really. It's okay."

After Huey stopped crying, I returned to the previous conversation, minus the emotionalism and volume.

"Oh, Jess, I'm so sorry for what happened to you."

"I appreciate that, Dave. I didn't mean to shed this all on you."

"Would you believe that you're not the first person I've known with this story? When I was in the orphanage, I knew someone with a similar account. A boy by the name of Gary. A Methodist minister and his wife adopted him. Well, soon Gary was returned to the orphanage. The good minister and his wife not only abused him sexually, they filmed it with their super-eight camera."

"Oh Lord."

"It was back in the late seventies. A big news story of the day. I'll never forget how this guy's parishioners continued to rally in his defense. They said the tape was a fake."

"Typical," Jessica responded. "Those people care little about fact. They only care about their little mythological fantasies."

"Funny you say that! Just this past weekend, I was telling a Christian holier-than-thou about recent scholarship involving Jesus. That he was merely a Jewish revolutionary magnified by his followers. Magnified generations after his time."

"The *History Channel*?"

"Hey, Jess! You saw that too?"

"Sure did. Excellent program!"

"It certainly was! But was Ms. Christian impressed by what I presented to her? No way. She just got angry."

Jessica chuckled.

"And what about cosmology? Evolution? No wonder the zealots think a fetus is a human being."

"That's right. Since they don't believe in evolution, it follows that they don't recognize that the fetus is not a person. It just evolves into one!"

"Not only that, look at what the medieval church did to all who disagreed with them! Remember what happened to Galileo? Remember the Puritans? The—"

"—the Salem witch trials?"

Jessica once again finished one of my sentences, something she did routinely. Whether we talked about the OJ murder trial or about the foolishness of Christians, it was like we had one mind.

"There you go again," I chuckled. "Stop finishing my comments!"

"Sorry," Jess smiled back.

"On the subject of the religious right," I continued, "did you hear about that abortion clinic bombing? It happened again, just a few days ago."

"I did. What do you think can be done to defend people from these fanatics?"

"For starters, these fundamentalists need deprogramming."

"Deprogramming?"

"Yes, you know the process of liberating dupes from cults and mind control."

"How would anyone deprogram a fundamentalist Christian?"

"Good question. Perhaps they should be educated."

"Good luck with that. I wouldn't define them as an intellectual crowd."

"True," I laughed. "Yet, I would expose the misguided to what the research scholars have done on Jesus and early Christianity. Jesus, if he existed at all, was a Jewish zealot. It's likely that his followers, in the centuries following his ministry, transformed Jesus into a mythological 'man god.' They borrowed 'man god' stories from the Greeks, the Romans, the Babylonians, and the Egyptians. The weavers of this New Testament 'Christ' myth made it up for their personal ambitions. After all, the first Christians were rejects of society. The Judaic aristocracy despised them, as did the Romans. They were underdogs who needed to feel important."

"How do you know so much about this subject?"

"I read. One particular book I just finished is called *The Christian Lie*. Do you know about the Jesus think tank that meets in Britain once a year? The Christ Convention? Well, several members have put out books as well. They are frequent guests on the *History Channel* and *PBS*."

"I mean, why are you interested in the subject?"

I paused. I never analyzed why I was interested in the historical Jesus, I just was. Something about this larger-than-life person intrigued me.

"I don't know why. I just am."

"Most guys your age are simply into booze, babes, and any sport with a ball."

"That's true, Jess. Do you think I should be more like most guys? Should I concentrate on the three b's?"

"*No!*" she yelled. "God, *no!* Most guys should be like you! Intelligent and sweet."

I paused. Was this the time to ask the woman out? How many positive signs did I need? After all, she hadn't mentioned Brad Ramsey all day. Perhaps Marcus's assessment of my relationship with Jessica was wrong! Then on cue, the woman deflated my temporary balloon.

"Dave, let me tell you. RAI is the best place I've ever worked. Men like you, Marcus, and Brad. Well, it's a real pleasure to know some intelligent men. Men who talk to me, not to my chest. Men who don't make some inane pass at me every day of the week. I like you three guys, you know how to be friends with women."

Yeah. A real good time to ask her out, I mused. Was this woman psychic? Was God teasing me? Did I hear laughing from beyond the pearly gates? Well, at the very least, Brad was cast into the 'friends' category along with Marcus and myself.

"You…you're already friends with Brad? We just met the man last Friday," I observed.

"That's right. But Friday evening, I had an unexpected phone call. Brad wanted to know about the various phone extension numbers at the day program. We ended up having the greatest conversation! You know, you really should get to know him, Dave. He's a sweetie, just like you. I think you two would really get along."

"Okaayy. As long as a managerial guy wouldn't mind associating with a grunt."

"Oh, c'mon! He's not like that. He's down to earth."

"I'll take your word for it."

"As you should. And, thanks for listening to me today. You're a true friend."

"Anytime, Jess."

In unison, Jess and I turned to look at Huey again. Even though we had been talking to each other in whispers, in calm tones, he was crying again.

"I wonder what set Huey off this time? Is he just depressed?"

"I think he is, Dave. The poor dear! If only we could get inside his head."

I noticed Huey had slid in his wheelchair, his torso was too far forward. He sat on a bubble cushion combined with a donut pillow. These pads alleviated the pressure on his wound. But the cushions had the unfortunate tendency to slide forward and come off the seat of the wheelchair. In the manner which I was trained, I got behind Huey, crossed my arms in front of him and held his forearms. I elevated him into a better position.

"There. Maybe that will make him more comfortable," I said to myself.

As I turned to help Jessica pick garbage off the picnic table, I froze. My lower back was paralyzed in a muscle spasm. The tightness hit like a sledgehammer. I groaned in pain.

Jessica heard me.

"Dave, you okay?"

"Uh, yeah. Sure."

I tried to play tough. When I stepped forward, the spasm grew more intense. I grabbed the table for support. "Aw damn!" I winced.

Jessica rushed over. She took my arm and helped me into a sitting position. I held the corner of the table for stability.

"I knew it," Jessica sighed. "First, Marcus and Henry threw their backs out a few months ago, and now you. You guys do too much manual lifting."

"Can't disagree with that," I gasped.

Jessica finished the work of that day. She secured everyone into the van and drove us back. I sat at the day program for the rest of the afternoon, stiff with pain. Jessica arranged to drive me home at quitting time, with Marcus following. They helped me climb the stairs to my apartment and urged me to call if I needed further assistance. Marcus ordered a pizza for my meal. I thanked them both. I laid out on my couch and wallowed in self-pity.

# CHAPTER 4

▼

# AN AFTERNOON WITH BRAD

The ensuing week was misery. I used a cane to hobble around my small apartment. All the muscles to the left of my spine would spasm at the slightest misstep. I ate delivery food. I watched talk shows.

One particular show was breaking down all conventional network standards. It regularly featured strippers, adultery, and incest. As much as I disliked the religious right, the permissive voyeurism of this new pop culture annoyed me more.

The highlights of the week featured phone calls from Jessica and Marcus. The two helped me stay connected to life outside the four walls of my apartment. They picked up my paycheck that Friday. They arranged for the proper worker's compensation forms to be delivered. Marcus drove me to my doctor. The diagnosis was a severe muscle strain. During one phone call with Jessica, I detected a tear in her voice as she said how much everyone missed me.

Marcus offered his usual gift of humor. He shared some news that made my back muscles stiffen, however. He warned me that Jessica was speaking more about Brad. The two of them were growing close. Work was ablaze with gossip, and many found the Jessica-Brad relationship more entertaining than their favorite television soap opera.

Was it friendship? Was it a passionate fling? Was it love? I ruminated. At least when Jess was involved with her past beau Kyle, it was outside of RAI. It was beyond the eyes and ears of our coworkers. Now, I would be forced to digest this bitter meal every day. Worst of all, I recognized that Brad was a much better fit for Jessica than me. He was tall, stunning, and muscular. I was short, skinny, and ordinary. If Jess and I were a couple, I could imagine people asking themselves, "What's she doing with him?"

After two weeks of inactivity, my back healed. I could lift again. I could bend again. Soon, I was to witness for myself the blooming relationship between Jessica and Brad.

A Friday marked my return to work. As I approached RAI that morning, it seemed as if I had been absent for a year. Again, I checked for my beautiful coworker's car. Again, it was there. Would she be at work, all aglow about her new-found relationship? Would she gush about Ramsey all day? I prepared myself.

Jessica was the first to greet me, as usual.

*"Davey-Avey!"* she exclaimed, giving me a tight hug. "'Bout time you stopped faking! Welcome back!"

"Good to be back. You and Marcus have been godsends these past two weeks."

"Oh pish-aw!" Jessica waved off the observation.

I noticed her new hairstyle. It was shorter with more wave. Was this for Brad, I wondered?

Jess grabbed my arm. "*Oh!* By the way, Davey, you better not have any plans after work."

My heart jumped. "Uh, why is that?"

"I made plans for you this evening, and don't you dare say no."

Time froze. Was this woman asking me out?

"What do you have in mind, Jess?"

"I told Brad Ramsey about your back injury and how it's happened to you before. It just so happens that Brad has some experience with physical therapy. He's also worked as a personal trainer. He's agreed to work with you Mondays, Wednesdays, and Fridays, starting today! If you can, of course."

"Ahh, I see," I managed to say through disappointment.

"Brad will be here at quitting time, if you want. He'll start you off slowly. Hopefully, you'll never have an injury like this again."

"Well, thanks. That was nice of you to arrange. And it was nice of Brad."

"Don't mention it. You'll grow to like him as much as I do."

"I doubt that."

"Come again?" Jessica asked with confusion.

"Well, I'm not a woman and I'm straight. I can't possibly like Brad as much as you do."

"You nerd," she giggled. "Oh sure, Brad is gorgeous and all. But we're just friends. Where it goes, who can say? I think he's involved with someone else."

"I see," I offered with a pseudo-casual tone.

Marcus was happy to see me back. He presented me with a loaf of banana bread Tamika had baked. I expressed appreciation, all the while fearing that Tamika may have poisoned it somehow.

Huey arrived at the day program in a depressed slouch, but did perk up a tad when he saw I had returned. The rest of the workday went well. My back didn't protest when I reintroduced it to lifting.

After the shift ended, the day program staff used the last minutes to clean and straighten up the worksite. This time, the usually active Jessica waited by the front entrance, eyes glued to the parking lot. I knew who she was waiting for, as did Marcus. He noticed my concern.

"Don't sweat it," he whispered.

Suddenly, Jessica's body stiffened. She bolted out the door.

"Ladies and gentlemen, Elvis has entered the building," I murmured.

The late afternoon sun glared through the door, making all figures in that direction dark forms. First, I made out Jessica's svelte silhouette. Like an acolyte of some Egyptian Pharaoh, she opened the glass door for the looming hulk behind her. He stood and shed the jacket draped over his shoulders. As he folded it over his left arm, Jess took the same arm and led him in my direction. My stomach sickened at the choreography of the scene.

Jessica beamed. "Dave, I just told Brad you are willing to give this a try."

"Uh, yes, that's right, Mr. Hamsey. Thanks for the offer," I replied.

"My name is Ramsey, and don't mention it."

"Sorry, Mr. Ramsey."

"Hey now, never mind this Mr. stuff! It's Brad! I'm a manager, not some dignitary."

"Okay, Brad. You can call me Dave."

The giant broke out in a loud, raucous laugh.

"Dave…Dave…no. That won't do. I'm going to give you a nickname. I have a talent for nicknames, wouldn't you say, Legs?" he said looking at Jessica.

"Oh, Brad, you're terrible!" Jessica giggled.

Brad rewrapped the jacket over his shoulders, the jacket's sleeves hanging down his chest. "Well, Dave, shall we hit the road?"

"I'm ready."

I held his gaze, which dwelled uncomfortably on my face.

Jessica gave me a quick hug.

"You take it easy, Dave. We don't need to experience another two weeks without you."

"I'll go easy on him, hon."

I flinched. Brad called her hon. Worse still, Jess gave him a quick kiss on the cheek for his send-off. The man motioned to the door and we proceeded to the parking lot. The thought of spending the next hour with this character filled me with revulsion. Why? I couldn't put my finger on it. Sure, he was all politeness and humor, but something seethed under the surface of his charm.

"Ahh, that Legs. She's a sweet girl. Don't you think so, Dave?"

"Yes, Jessica is as sweet as they come," I retorted.

Brad's chest heaved with laughter.

"Hey now. You're not hot for Legs, are you?"

I felt my face burn. I worried how visible the blushing was.

"Not at all. Jess and I have been friends for years."

"Who defined this as a friendship? You or her?"

"Doesn't the woman always define the relationship?" I asked.

Again, Brad's bulk shook with laughter.

"That's very astute, Dave! Very good indeed."

He entered his brand new Jaguar and rolled down the window. "Meet you at the gym," he yelled. I gave him a polite nod, then rolled my eyes as I entered my 1988 Chevy Citation. Part of me wanted to drive home, but I didn't want to offend Jessica. Brad burned rubber as he squealed out of the parking lot. I turned on my signal light and waited four minutes before I saw a suitable opening in the traffic. Our driving was indicative of our contrasting personalities. By the time I reached the gym, Ramsey was waiting by the front door and chatting with two women. Brad gestured toward me as I approached.

"Monica. Angelica. This is the new guy I was talking about. David Paul."

"Hiiiiiii," both girls singsonged at me.

I nodded in return.

One of the girls grabbed my upper arm. "Looks like you got him here just in time," she observed.

The other girl spoke up. "Shush now, Mon! With Brad baby training him, he'll be bench pressing both of us in a week!"

"A reliable back is all I'm aiming for," I responded.

"And a reliable back you shall have, Dave. Move aside, angels. We've got some serious work to do." The women didn't take offense at Brad's order. Instead, they parted to either side as if he was Moses and they were the Red Sea.

We proceeded to the locker room where Brad presented me with a pair of brand new shorts and a T-shirt.

"Don't bother thanking me. Legs has an unusual power over me and I'll do any philanthropy to win her approval," Brad confessed.

"I don't think you have to work too hard for it," I offered.

"No?"

"No. She's very impressed with you."

"Really?" he pondered, knitting his brow.

As Brad removed his shirt to change into his workout clothes, I was amazed. The guy had no body fat. His muscles were taunt and defined. Veins protruded everywhere. His stomach was a washboard. Biceps strained to break free of his skin. In return, I looked down at my featureless build, soft and undefined. What was I doing here?

The gym was filled with jocks and jockettes. Clanging Nautilus equipment made for background noise. Women wearing spandex ran on treadmills and climbed stair machines. The whole building seemed flooded with hormones and pheromones. Laughing, flirting, and leering occurred in all directions.

The workout began. Stretches were first, followed by stomach exercises.

"Firm up that gut! Your back will thank you for it."

A sweaty hour later, we sat on a mat to rest. Brad pointed at Monica and Angelica as they looked in our direction. He waved. The two bobbed up and down on stair machines.

"Now, Dave, there's a fringe benefit to coming here. Those two haven't stopped staring."

"You think so?" I asked, wiping sweat off my forehead.

"I know so. Which one of them do you prefer?"

"No, Brad. The question is, which one will settle for me?"

"Aw, c'mon! Don't sell yourself short. Women don't always go for jocks like me. Believe me."

"Yeah, sure," I snorted.

"Case in point. We have Jessica."

I perked up. "Yeah? What about her?"

"Let's say there is an uncertainty to her. She spends more time talking about you than anyone else."

*"You're kidding!"* I exclaimed.

"Yes, indeed. She has this odd fascination with you."

Warmth filled my body. Was this rival for Jessica's affection giving me hope?

"So once again, Dave. Which one strikes your fancy? Monica or Angelica?"

"If I had to choose, I'd go with Angelica. She stuck up for me in a way, when Monica critiqued my lack of muscle."

"Yeah, right," Brad observed. "You sure that's the reason? Her chest just happens to be larger than Monica's."

"I'm not that way, Brad. As a matter of fact, I try not to judge women by their appearance at all. If there was a body type I would gravitate toward, it would probably be one that's tall and slender."

"That so? Then Jessica is indeed your type!"

"I suppose," I covered with a casual demeanor.

"Now," Brad continued, "I don't discriminate by body type at all. For example, you see that woman in the right corner? Most men would be repulsed by her obesity, but not me."

"Really! Muscle guys like you usually want their dates to be buff."

"Not at all. I don't require that any of my lovers be fit. I don't even demand that they be women!"

I paused. Did this jock just say what I thought he said?

"Come again?"

"Yes, that's right, Dave. I'm bisexual. Surprised?"

"Uh, yeah. I would have never suspected," I admitted.

"You mean I'm too macho to swing both ways?"

"Uh, you know, Brad, I don't know what I mean. You took me by surprise."

"Relax, sport. I suspect you suffer from a common illness. Most people define sexuality in narrow terms and gift wrap it in some little box. 'This is right, that is wrong.' 'This is moral, that is immoral.'"

"Not at all!" I flustered. "You're talking to a modern liberal. I'm very broad minded."

"Is that so?"

*"Yes!"*

"Then you would be free for dinner? Sometime soon?"

I hesitated. Was I leading this huge guy on?

"Personally, uh, I'm not interested. But, you know, it's okay if you like men. I'm not judging you or anything."

Brad laughed loudly. "Dave—Daavvee—your homophobia is coming out of your ears like smoke!"

"I am not homophobic."

"Yes, you are. But don't worry, I don't blame you. Our culture, our religious institutions, they are the boundary setters. They are the mental oppressors."

"As an enlightened humanist, I can't argue with that," I nodded.

"The way I see it," Brad continued, "human flesh is human flesh. What difference does it make what gender it wears? Who cares what shape it assumes? It is universally understood that human touch is pleasurable. In this world of misery, why do so many wish to restrict the small experiences of pleasure available to us?"

Ramsey was both articulate and logical. Still, I was wary.

At that point, I noticed something came over Brad. The air felt colder. Brad's expression changed, his eyes flashed. He looked like a different person.

"David, if you knew for yourself how hot sodomy is. Especially with children or the retarded. The more upset they get, the tighter they get!"

I winced at his vulgar observation. *What? What did he just say?*

Immediately, his expression returned to normal. He laughed.

"What's wrong, Dave? Have I offended your moral sensibilities? Children and the retarded are not supposed to have sexual experiences, are they? That would be all too threatening to your little social code, am I correct?"

"Well, yeah! Are you a pedophile? Someone preying on children or the mentally challenged?"

"See? That's the point I was trying to make! Pedophile, smedaphile. What if children or the retarded happen to enjoy this contact? What if their eyes are opened to the wonderful world of sexuality? This is wrong? Why is it seen as preying on anyone?"

"Molesting people who don't have the tools or maturity to give consent—this is what you're promoting?"

"Consent? Once they feel the pleasure of this type of contact, that's when they have the information needed to give consent. Oh sure, at first some may resist. Soon, they'll ask for it."

"Don't you believe consent is an issue of maturity and intelligence?"

"No I don't, Dave. Capability to experience the pleasure of sexual contact—that should be the standard. Children are just as sexual as we are."

At this point, I was speechless. In most conversations, I was considered the liberal and permissive participant. What Brad was saying was beyond belief. "Consenting adults" was the standard for sexual activity both liberals and conservatives agreed upon, yet even this was too restrictive for Ramsey.

"Brad, remind me to ask your house staff to never leave you alone with the residents," I murmured.

"Relax, Mr. Falwell," he sneered. "I'm talking about sexual liberation…in general. No, I don't target children or the retarded. I'm too busy with my many male and female friends."

"Yeah, sure." My mind still could hear him saying how tight children and the retarded are when they're upset. Now he was denying that he engaged in such activity? This man was bizarre. I had no difficulty believing him a molester and a rapist. And he had authority at a group home?

Brad stood up and threw a towel at me.

"Okay, Sparky. Yeah, your new nickname is Sparky. You can hit the showers. We're done."

*"Thank God,"* I murmured at him. "I've suffered your company long enough."

He looked stunned. I proceeded to the locker room. To my relief, he didn't follow.

I showered quickly. As I wrapped a towel around my midsection, the hairs on my neck stood on end. A cold blast of air blew in. I turned and there was Brad. He looked wild. A feral grin dominated his face.

"Sure you don't want to explore your feminine side, Dave?"

*"Get away from me,"* I hissed. Brad broke into a giggle as I quickly walked back to the locker room.

"I'll cure you of your homophobia yet, Sparky."

Within minutes I was dressed and headed for the parking lot, all the while looking over my shoulder, fearful Brad was following.

Sunset was approaching; the parking lot was dark. Where did I park? My frantic search began. At one point, I thought I spotted my lime green Chevy, but it was just another old vehicle. It seemed a miracle when I finally found my car. Brad's flashy Jaguar was parked nearby, which motivated me to move faster.

"What? No kiss goodnight?"

I turned. Where did he come from? It was as if Brad appeared through magic. I yelled at him, adrenaline pumping.

"Give it a rest, pedophile!"

Again, he cackled sadistically.

As I entered my car, Ramsey ran toward me. I quickly locked the door and started to roll up the window. He stuck his hand in the crack remaining. Holding up his other hand, he stopped giggling.

"Dave, I'm sorry. Really. All that I said about sex with children and the retarded, well, I was yanking your chain. I wanted to see how you'd react since Jessica told me how liberal you were. I like playing devil's advocate. I'm bi, but don't fear, you're not my type for more reasons than you know! Neither are children, or the mentally challenged."

"Sure, Brad, whatever. See ya."

I started the engine.

"Meet you next Monday? Here at the gym?" he asked.

"No way."

Brad's face turned red. He looked sincerely insulted.

"Legs told me how easygoing you were. Man, was she off base. Oh well, say 'hi' for me when Jess calls you at seven-sixteen this evening."

I burned rubber as his hand left my window. I needed to escape and quick. Who was this guy? How could Jessica like such a psycho?

Later that night, I was watching *Jeopardy* on television. The phone rang. As predicted by Brad, it was Jessica. The clock read seven-sixteen. Much to my beautiful friend's disappointment, I decided not to undergo any future workouts with Brad. I didn't tell her why.

# CHAPTER 5

▼

# SUSPICION

I arrived at work early that Monday. The clouds were thick. Rain fell with frigid lethargy. Most leaves had been shed by now, leaving bare branches that resembled bony fingers. Mid-October was upon us.

Halloween decorations graced the day program, yet nothing seemed as creepy as the new manager at the Elm Street group home.

Jessica was going to interrogate me about my afternoon with Brad. I didn't know how to handle her curiosity. Perhaps this was something Marcus could help with. My confidant greeted me as I entered the workplace. After some small talk, I told him about my afternoon with Ramsey. His reaction was memorable.

He stood still a moment then grabbed his mouth and ducked down. He straightened up and looked me in the eye.

*"The hell you say! Get outta here!"*

"No lie!"

"You mean Mr. GQ, every woman's fantasy here at RAI, is homosexual?" he asked.

"Technically, I wouldn't say he's conventionally gay, like our manager Tim. Brad's 'omni-sexual.' He'll target anyone, any age."

"Oh, God. Dave. What about the Elm Street residents? Some are unable to move or resist. Others are nonverbal."

"I know. Sometimes Brad fills in for absent third-shift workers. The potential for abuse in that house is high. And, afterward, the guy said he was yanking my chain, but I don't buy it."

The front door opened and I immediately lowered my voice.

"To be continued," I whispered.

Jessica quietly marched past me to sign the day program logbook. I leaned on the table next to her.

"Morning, Jess. How are you?"

"Fine," she replied in monotone. Again, she walked past me.

"Jess, you're not angry with me, are you?"

"No, just disappointed."

"Disappointed?"

"Brad told me about the argument you guys had."

"He did?"

"Yeah. He said you turned on him when he admitted to being bisexual. You pushed him away and didn't want his help anymore."

"It wasn't that. His personal life is his business."

"Of course it is! I never thought you were a bigot, Dave."

That comment hurt.

"Jess! In the years you have known me, have I ever seemed intolerant?"

"You told me on Friday night how you discontinued the therapy. What other reason is there?"

"Let's just say…Brad made several comments that have me concerned."

"Like what?"

I hesitated. Jessica had already formed a connection to Brad. If the potential molester knew I was blabbing our private conversation around the workplace, he would plan a defensive strategy.

"At this time, it wouldn't be right to share my suspicions."

"What's the matter? Do you need time to make up some excuse for why you hate those with alternative lifestyles?"

"Not at all. I've always got along well with Tim, haven't I?"

"Then give me a good reason, here and now, why Brad isn't fit to be your physical therapist."

"I can't."

Jessica lowered her head. "Dave, you disappoint me. I hoped you would have accepted Brad's friendship. I had hoped you would join our new discussion group."

"Discussion group?"

"Since Brad is the organizer, you're going to prejudge it. Anyway, it's like a book club where several friends talk about what they've read. Books pertaining to spiritual pursuits."

"Really, Jess? Tell me more."

"I'll tell you more on one condition. Reconsider your attitude toward Brad. You hardly know him."

"Okay, I'll try," I lied. "What kind of discussions does this group have?"

"It's a philosophic group, a place where people engage in conversations like we always have. We try to blend world religions into one viewpoint. Brad happens to be well-versed in comparative religions. Considering all that research you did on the historical Jesus, I thought you would add to the dialogue. When Brad talks about the dangers and pitfalls of mainstream Christianity, he sounds exactly like you!"

"I'm not very religious. Neither is the historical Jesus I have researched."

"Many of the philosophical practices we discuss aren't religious either! They don't involve intolerance, hatred, fear, and bigotry like the big three offenders do."

"Big three offenders?"

"Yeah. Judaism, Christianity, and Islam. Three patriarchal religions that promote a judgmental male deity. A god who enjoys punishing his creation for being flawed."

As bizarre as Brad's group sounded, they were on my philosophical wavelength. I was curious.

At this point, my manager Tim Gould called me into his office. I gave Jessica a nod and she smiled. It seemed I ironed out the schism between us.

Feeling more relaxed, I jogged over to the burly manager. Tim handed me Huey's medical book, a thick pile of records and an envelope of insurance cards. "Apparently, we were supposed to bring Huey to Dr. Wilkes, the proctologist who replaced Dr. DeAngelis, five days ago. I forgot all about it and the quarterlies are due. Take the red van, pick up Huey at Elm, and take him straight to Bloomfield. The appointment is at nine-thirty. Go to DeAngelis' old office. Make sure he renews Huey's 'as needed' PRN order for Preparation H."

I laughed. "A doctor's order for Preparation H?"

"You know the drill. We need doctors' orders for sunblock! The bureaucratic processes must be obeyed."

"Yeah, I know. Do you think Huey will need a Xanax for this visit?"

"There are no invasive examinations planned. He should be calm."

I heaved the five-pound notebook onto my shoulder and waved to Marcus and Jessica.

"Huey has a proctology appointment. See you guys at noon."

Marcus gave me a nod as Jessica walked over.

"Sorry I was hard on you, Dave. I trust you'll be fair with Brad," she whispered.

Ramsey was absent when I picked up Huey. I thanked whatever deity existed for small favors. Soon, Huey and I were on the road. My friend was depressed again. Even my presence didn't inspire him to lift his head. I turned on a classic rock station. The upbeat tempo usually energized Huey to a degree. Alas, not this day.

The drive to Bloomfield was fifty minutes long. Half the drive was amid scenic wilderness, half was stop-and-go through commercial districts. The road was slick with rain, so I drove extra slow. Drivers would pass, exhibiting various hand gestures. Most involved a single finger.

When I reached the designated medical building in Bloomfield, the parking lot was full. Even the handicapped spaces. I pushed Huey's cumbersome wheelchair an obscene distance and then maneuvered him into a crowded elevator. Dr. Wilkes was on the fifth floor of the health care facility.

I squeezed the huge wheelchair through the narrow office door. After handing the receptionist Huey's insurance card, I sat down for the customary wait. A young boy stared at Huey, confused by Huey's deformities.

"Mom, why is that man ugly?" The child asked his mother, who quickly hid her face behind the latest issue of *Time* magazine.

"Mom," the child became louder. "Why does that man look like that?"

"Be quiet!" The mother hissed from behind a picture of Bill Clinton.

Normally, Huey would have waved to the tot. Yet this day, he sat with his head hung low. No familiar refrains of "Ewy goo boy ay" were spoken. No laughing at my jokes. That month was the first time I witnessed these mood swings.

I picked up an issue of *US News and World Report*. OJ Simpson was on the cover. I resigned myself to reading articles about the Republican-led Congress. About an influx of frog mutations in the northeastern U.S.

"Mr. Hubert Riiska, you're next," a nurse announced thirty minutes later.

I wheeled Huey through a series of awkward doors and corridors. On occasion, the footrest would bang against a wall or a door. I'd murmur an embarrassed apology to the scowling nurse each time. We squeezed into a tight room and I locked Huey's chair next to the examination table. Hopefully, I wouldn't have to lift him onto the thing.

Another long wait ensued. I studied a diagram of the lower digestive system on the wall.

"Well, how are 'we' doing today?" the new proctologist asked as he entered the room.

"Hi, doctor. My name is David Paul, and this is Huey Riiska. Huey is all right of late, except for his mood. He needs a new order for Preparation H, however."

Wilkes flipped through Huey's records.

"Hmm. Is Lou capable of speaking to me?"

"His name is Hubert or Huey. It takes some practice to understand him. He's not in a speaking mood anyhow."

"I see, I see," the short, bald man responded. "His chart indicates that his hemorrhoids haven't been a problem for a few years. Has Mr. Riiska been experiencing frequent episodes of loose stools?"

"Not at the day program. His movements have been regular and well formed."

"Has Louie been taking his daily dose of Metamucil?"

"Yes, he has." If the doctor insisted on calling him Lou, I decided to let him.

"I see. Can you get Mr. Riiska on the table?"

"Oh," I grimaced. "Could you help me with that?"

The man sighed with impatience.

"Wait here," he snapped as he left the room.

"Sorry that I'm not a human Arjo lift," I murmured under my breath.

Wilkes returned with a frail, short nurse in tow.

"Help Mr. Saul here get the patient on the table," he ordered. I wasn't about to tell this strutting mass of impatience that my last name was Paul, not Saul.

The nurse bent low, hooked under Huey's left arm and I hooked under his right. Together, we grabbed the back of Huey's pants and hoisted him onto the table. My back fared well through the strain. The woman wasn't very strong and she nearly dropped him during the lift.

"Be more careful!" the doctor snapped at her.

I gave him a dirty look. This guy looked twice as strong as his nurse.

He then instructed me to lower Huey's pants and underwear. I comforted my friend, telling him it would only take a few minutes. Huey had a few marks on his buttocks. Discolorations I never saw before. Wilkes looked at them closely. They were different than the nearby pressure ulcer.

"Has Lou been lying near anything hot? A radiator vent?"

"No."

"These marks appear to be surface burns."

"Really? How could that have happened?"

"When examining members of this population, I'm seldom surprised by anything out of the ordinary. The whole lot of these unfortunates should have been aborted the moment they were conceived," the clod chuckled.

I hated this man.

He spread Huey's butt cheeks and took a better look at the anus. It appeared inflamed with exterior hemorrhoids.

*"Ahh! No! No! No! No!"* Huey finally spoke, apparently distressed by the examination of the sensitive area.

I took Huey's hand.

"Hey, it's okay buddy. We're almost done."

"No! No—bad. Bad," Huey continued.

"Calm him down, will you?" the doctor snapped.

"Do I look like one of your nurses?" I snapped back.

"Excuse me, Mr. Saul?" the arrogant physician raised his eyebrows at me.

I bit my lip. The jerk had a great bedside manner.

"Can Mr. Riiska reach his anus with either arm?"

"He can with his left. Why?"

"I thought so. Lou here has been doing some anal digging and scratching."

"I've never seen Huey do that," I responded.

"Regardless, that's my assessment. There are fingernail marks present. Some fissures."

"No…no…no," Huey was still murmuring.

A horrifying thought flashed through my mind. I shuddered at the possibility. I noticed Brad puffing on cigarettes before, and those burn marks matched the size of a cigarette butt. Were the burns linked to a sadomasochistic fetish of Ramsey's? My stomach turned over.

"Uh, doctor. Could those marks be indicative of abuse?"

The man actually laughed at my question. "What's the matter, Mr. Saul. You have something to hide?"

"Excuse me, Dr. *Filkes?*" I mispronounced his name on purpose. A surge of rage coursed through me and I resisted the temptation to throw a punch.

"Relax, kid," he retorted. "The type of irritations Mr. Riiska has are not consistent with sexual abuse."

"Don't you think that the safe course is for you to report the possibility of abuse?"

"There isn't enough evidence, Mr. Saul. And the paperwork involved! The legalities!"

"What about the burn marks?"

"Inconsequential," Wilkes responded. "Wait here. I'm going to give you a few free samples of a new hemorrhoid cream. Also Louie should take a dose of mineral oil every evening. This will allow his feces to pass easily, as his anus heals. I recommend that Lou's left arm be restrained from reaching his buttocks. Tie it down if you have to."

"We have restraint procedures, doctor. We aren't allowed to arbitrarily tie down Huey's arm. That's abusive."

"Oh brother," Wilkes rolled his eyes. "Okay, this is what I recommend. A kitchen hot mitt. The padded type, with one thumb and no fingers. Velcro strap this on Huey's left hand each time he's supine."

"Technically, even that's a restraint. But if you write it out as a doctor's order, we can implement your recommendation."

"Group homes," the guy sneered. "You people need a doctor's order to lift a toilet seat."

He left the room, returned with the samples and departed again. His frail nurse walked up to me and murmured, "Charming, isn't he?"

The nurse and I assisted Huey back into the chair. This time, she positioned herself better. Both my back and her body did well. Huey had stopped talking by now and was hanging his head again.

I clenched my fist. This Dr. Wilkes may not have any concern for Huey, but I did. The cigarette burns, the anal trauma, Brad's bizarre comments, all combined to make a solid case. I would approach Tim Gould about my suspicion. He was a good manager. I had faith in him.

With samples and doctor's orders in hand, Huey and I rushed back to the day program. The rain had stopped; no one gave me the finger on this trip. The other residents were eating lunch when we arrived. Marcus and Jessica greeted us with their customary smiles. The other workers took little notice of our return. I wheeled Huey past everyone and made a beeline to the manager's office. Luckily, Tim was in.

"Hey, Dave. How'd the appointment go?"

"Can Huey and I speak to you in private?"

"Certainly! Come on in."

We entered the office. I didn't know how to begin. It was such a horrible allegation to make! But I owed it to my friend.

"Tim, I believe Huey has been abused."

"What makes you think this?"

"Today's appointment. It confirmed a suspicion I had."

"Tell me."

"Huey had a few mysterious burns on his left butt cheek. I believe they are consistent with cigarette burns. Also, his hemorrhoids aren't just inflamed. There's evidence of trauma. Evidence of fingernail marks or cuts."

"What's the new proctologist say?"

"Tim, I'm going to be blunt. The guy is a prick. He didn't seem concerned about anything. He couldn't retain Huey's name. The guy even recommended that we tie his arm down in bed!"

"You're kidding. What would make him suggest such a thing?"

"He believes that Huey has been doing some anal scratching."

"Oh…" Tim's face indicated knowledge. "Dave, I've been manager here for nine years. Well before you started, Huey engaged in habitual scratching. His whole rectum used to be inflamed."

"Really? I haven't seen any record of it."

"As you know, records of five years or more are filed away. I can pull them for you, if you don't believe me."

"No, Tim. I believe you. But there's one other thing. Someone who works at Elm made a comment to me. He suggested how children and retarded people should be targeted for sodomy. He later said he was just kidding, but still—"

"That is certainly of concern!" interrupted Tim. "Who is this individual?"

"Brad Ramsey. The new manager."

At this, Tim started laughing. He slapped his left leg repeatedly. I was dumbfounded. What was this all about?

"Aw, man! Brad screwed with your head, didn't he? Relax, Dave. Brad and I are old frat brothers. I recommended him for the job. He is a jokester. But not in the conventional sense. He is a vicious prankster. He only does this stuff with people he likes, so you should be honored!"

"Should I?"

"Yeah, I know. He's hard to take. In college, he pulled a vicious prank on me. I hated Brad for days. Eventually, I realized what a caring heart he has. The man is the salt of the earth! It just takes a while to know the clown."

"So…you don't think there's evidence of abuse here?"

"I know there isn't. But you did the right thing in coming to me. We'll keep an eye on Huey's marks."

Tim then leaned down in front of Huey. "Hey, how are you, Huey? Has anyone hurt you, Huey?"

My sad friend didn't respond. His head continued to hang low.

"Okay, Dave," Tim continued. "Let's check those burn marks…after we get him on the wedge."

Following a quick maneuver with an Arjo lift, Huey was lying on his side. I set up privacy screens and pulled down Huey's pants and underwear. I stepped back in shock! Tim leaned in closer. The burn marks were *gone!* It was as if they were never there.

# CHAPTER 6

▼

# PERCEPTIONS

The work shift ended. As I turned the key in the ignition of my car, I heard a knock on the passenger side window. It was Marcus. His curiosity concerning the day's events must have overcome him.

"Hey, Dave. Now that no sensitive ears are hovering nearby, we're free to talk. Are you busy, or in a rush to be somewhere?"

"Not at all. Why don't you meet me for coffee at the Patriot Diner?"

"Good plan. See you in a few."

As usual, I waited for a huge gap in traffic before entering Main Street. I looked in my rearview window and saw Marcus laughing at my timidity. His mouth formed the word "go-nads."

After a few minutes, we were on East Main Street. As I turned on the radio and adjusted it to the classic rock station, a man who appeared homeless wandered into the street in front of me. I slammed on my brakes just in time! He stood in front of my car and stared. It was bizarre. Deep set eyes and jutting cheekbones gave his face a skeletal look. White whiskers grew in all directions from his chin. I looked in my rearview mirror and saw Marcus stopped behind me, his brow knit with concern. Impatient horns blared amid the line of cars accumulating. I opened my car door to prompt the character out of my way.

"Yoouu," the frail, tattered individual pointed at me. "Yoouu will see. He'll take care of you. You'll see. He knows what you're saying about him!" His shaky voice wailed at me. He then lowered his bony arm and walked slowly to the opposite sidewalk. I settled back into the driver's seat and made a turn and shrug gesture to Marcus. My friend shook his head side to side, acknowledging the fact that an obvious paranoid schizophrenic was meandering around Torrington. It was a sad situation.

Soon, we were sitting in the diner, cradling our coffee cups. The crowd was light, but we made certain our booth was beyond all ears. The planned conversation was not fit for public consumption. A booth of giggling teenagers also gave us cover. In comparison, our discussion involving confidential information and suspicion was a mere whisper. Marcus still looked anxious, however. His anxiety turned to concern, when I informed him of the appointment and subsequent conversation with Tim.

"Man, that's bogus!" Marcus exclaimed. "Tim said Ramsey's just a vicious prankster?"

"You know the deal. We're bottom feeders."

"Oh man! Do you think Tim is protecting Brad just because they both have…alternative lifestyles?"

"No way! Tim is a good guy. He would protect Huey, even if it meant going against an old friend. He sincerely believes Brad is innocent."

"Was the doctor sure the marks on Huey were burns?"

"He seemed to be. They looked like burns at the time. But you know, not only was this doctor rude and insensitive to the mentally challenged, he did not seem competent. Maybe the group home staff didn't wash Huey well that morning."

"Wouldn't be the first time," Marcus sighed.

"No, it wouldn't."

We both sat in silence for a few minutes. All this was a lot to digest.

"Marcus, what if Brad was pulling my leg, as vulgar as he was?"

"Even if it was humor, it was horribly inappropriate."

"True."

"What does Jessica have to say about Brad? She has been spending time with him."

"Well, Jessica admits that he is bisexual. She thinks I'm some right-wing bigot for avoiding him."

"You? You're the most liberal guy I know!"

"As liberal as I am, I'm not about to defend the Pedophile Rights Association. Brad on the other hand—"

"*Dave, please!*" Marcus held out his hand. "I'm eating a donut here, you know."

"Sorry."

"You know, Dave, Jessica is a good person. Too bad her taste in men is in the gutter."

"Well, Jessica is a woman with a healthy libido. Her hormones may interfere with her objectivity. After all, look at her last boyfriend Kyle. The guy was an insensitive buffoon."

"Good point."

"Speaking of Jessica, she wants me to join a group that Brad formed."

"A group?"

"Yeah, some spiritual discussion group."

"Ookkaayy," Marcus laughed.

"Yeah, I know. Strange, all strange."

"No stranger than Tamika's zeal," my friend admitted.

"Hey, Marcus, that's okay. Really."

"Also, I hope you don't have a negative view of Christians. I'm Christian too, you know."

"I know, Marcus. The difference is that you don't try to ram it down anyone's throat."

"No, but I do share my faith with anyone interested."

"That's a fair enough approach. You have to be the exception to the norm with these people. I'm offended by their pious superiority, by their 'our way is the only way' theology, and by their rampant hypocrisy."

"Yes, many so-called Christians are hypocrites. But the 'one way' theology isn't something to condemn out of hand."

"No? Are you saying that you also believe Jesus is the one way to heaven?"

"Yes I do."

"How can you believe that?"

"Because the gospels and the epistles teach that."

"Oh yeah, the gospels. Don't you know the gospels were written more than a century after the events they supposedly describe? Do some research, Marcus. Your faith is distorted and corrupted."

"Not true. Have you heard of the uh…what was that university again? Oh yes. Have you heard of the John Rylands Papyrus? It's a fragment of the Gospel according to John. It was discovered in Egypt and has been dated to around the year 120."

"Okay. That would date it ninety years after Jesus' time, wouldn't it?"

"You're forgetting one thing. That fragment isn't a piece of the original transcript. It was a copy being circulated in Egypt—far from where its author lived. The original gospel transcript was most likely written a good twenty years prior."

"And that author was the Apostle John?"

"Either the elderly apostle, living in exile on Patmos, or an apostle of the apostle. The Ryland fragment is the oldest existing papyrus that relates to Jesus. Others are under dispute. Something called the Magdalen Papyrus may be dated AD 55. Another fragment found with the Dead Sea Scrolls may be part of the Gospel of Mark and dated around that time as well. Scholars are still debating the legitimacy of these two."

"Very interesting. But all you have done is succeeded in dating the Gospel of John to seventy years after Jesus' time. That's still not very close."

"Okay, Dave. In your research, which gospel account is the earliest?"

"Not counting the hypothetical Q?"

"No, not counting Q. That gospel is but a theory, a book based on the similarities between Matthew and Luke. Similarities not found in Mark."

"Touché. Not counting Q, Mark is probably the earliest gospel."

"Did you know that early church elder Papias stated that Matthew wrote the first gospel in Aramaic? Papias lived AD 60 to 130, so he would certainly be in a position to know."

"Most serious researchers don't pay too much attention to those nutty church fathers, Marcus," I chuckled.

At that point in the conversation, a waitress came by to offer coffee refills. She was a tall, middle-aged woman with salt and pepper hair. Her glasses with thick plastic rims weighed heavily on her nose. She just happened to hear words like Papias and Aramaic in our conversation and knitted her brow with curiosity.

"Hey! Are you two guys professors at our UConn branch?" she asked.

"No, we're just two ordinary, blue-collar workers," Marcus smiled.

"Uh-huh," she responded, looking at us like we were from Mars. "More coffee?"

"No thanks," Marcus answered. "We're set for now."

"Okey dokey."

My friend continued, in a slightly lower voice. "Guess our conversation is rather odd, at least to most people. Okay, let's say the earliest gospel is a toss-up between Mark and Matthew."

"Fair enough. But who's to say that those gospels we now know are the originals? Isn't it generally accepted that after Constantine and the Council of Nicea, Roman officials confiscated all Christian scriptures in the fourth century and revised them? Heresy wasn't tolerated. The sect called the Gnostics were persecuted and censored. Accounts that described Jesus in merely mortal terms were excluded."

"Bull-spit," Marcus smiled.

"Bull-spit? Bud, you have the greatest ability to avoid profanity I've ever seen!"

"Thank you, Dave. Anyway, this idea that Constantine reinvented Christianity is en vogue, but it's unsupported by history. Not one early scripture discovered alters Christian doctrine, save for the Gnostic scriptures that discounted both Judaism and the physical universe as evil.

"All the early scriptures call Jesus Kyrios; a term used in the Septuagint Old Testament as a designation for Jehovah, the one Lord.

"The earliest Gnostic scriptures are dated to the second century; mostly coming from a heretical ringleader called Marcion.

"Legitimate Christian scribes were often fearful that a particular verse of scripture could be misinterpreted. They wrote margin footnotes to prevent this.

"Regardless," I interjected, "We still don't have any *complete* gospel accounts dated to the first century."

"In Paul's letters," Marcus continued, "some gospel messages predate the actual gospel documents. Creeds found in Romans, First Corinthians, and so on. Creeds that specifically list the Last Supper, the crucifixion, Christ's divinity, the atonement of the cross, the resurrection and the order of resurrection appearances."

I leaned back in my chair, and rubbed my temples.

"These creeds are dated anywhere between AD 30 and 50!" Marcus exclaimed. "Church elders such as Justin Martyr and Irenaeus speak of four gospels, or refer to all four. The Didache, a summary of the teachings of the twelve apostles, is dated late first to early second century. These teachings are harmonious with the canonical gospels as we now know them."

"So the early Christian scribes agreed with each other. No surprise there. Are there any non-Christian sources indicating that Jesus was considered divine early in church history?"

"Roman historian Pliny the Younger wrote about Christians and how they sang a hymn to Christ, as to a god," Marcus answered. "He wrote this in AD 112. All these information sources predate the Council of Nicea by two centuries or more!"

I shook my head. "Wow, you're quite the Christian encyclopedia, Marcus. What about the fact that Mark is the earliest gospel narrative, and that his narrative is the least supernatural of them all? Nowhere in this gospel is Jesus called Son of God, he is simply Son of Man. Even the Resurrection story isn't included in the earliest transcripts of Mark!"

"The Resurrection is included; it's just reliant on the testimony of angels. Concerning messianic titles, in the Old Testament book of Daniel, and the apocryphal Old Testament book of Enoch, the Son of Man is a Heavenly Judge. A judge who arrives on earth with the clouds of heaven. Consistently through the Old Testament, the Jews consider God their only Heavenly Judge. Also, Mark chapter two, verse five has Jesus forgive the sins of a paralyzed man."

"So what? Catholic priests dish out absolution as well. They're not claiming to be God."

"A couple of differences here. Catholics forgive according to the authority given to the apostles—in scripture—by Jesus. But beyond that, the Jewish culture Jesus belonged to didn't allow mere men to grant heavenly forgiveness. To earn divine forgiveness, they had to provide burnt offerings to God. If Jesus bypassed Judaic ritual and forgave someone on the spot, he would be claiming to be that Heavenly Judge mentioned by Daniel and Enoch. Those who witnessed his act of forgiveness called it blasphemy! They knew he was claiming to be God."

"Well, someone probably added that account to the Gospel of Mark. Probably at a later date."

"There you go, Dave. That's the arbitrary approach. As with the Christ Convention, they dismiss the parts of the gospels they don't approve of and accept the least theological passages. They judge according to twentieth-century standards. According to political bias."

"Marcus, the Christ Convention are learned men. PhDs all! They know their stuff."

"Perhaps they do. But like our friends Tim and Jessica, they are biased."

"Biased?"

"Think about it. Regardless of what you say about Brad, Tim and Jessica will assume you are wrong. In this same way, certain people have preconceived notions about a humanistic Jesus. A Jesus divorced from his Jewish culture and religion."

"C'mon, Marcus," I chuckled. "Christians are just as academically prejudiced as humanistic scholars."

"True, all people have prejudices. Christians as well. But we aren't the ones arbitrarily accepting one gospel verse and throwing away the next. We may be prejudiced, but at least we're consistent. A reliable source is a reliable source! Not something considered having a grain of truth recovered through the filter of modern enlightenment."

"Modern men do know better, Marcus. We *are* enlightened! We've evolved! We look less to supernatural hooey and more to fact."

"We have evolved, Dave? Modern men never lie or distort? Watch the evening news! And what if Huey is being molested? How evolved is that?"

"Where are you getting all this Bible trivia, Marcus?"

"From Dr. Jonah Rubenstein, a guest speaker who frequents the Bible study I attend."

"Jonah Rubenstein? A Jewish name?"

"He's also a Christian. He's a social worker affiliated with our church. The guy knows his stuff. Anyway, let's chill out the conversation. Religion is controversial. You know what they say, 'Never talk about religion or politics.'"

"I could always talk about anything with Jess—no matter how touchy the conversation. We're of one mind. Man, I wish she were attracted to me. But of course, she's not obligated to date me. I'm not attracted to every nice woman I know."

"Of course, Dave. I think she has led you on, but that's neither here nor there. Anyway, let's keep our eyes open for any suspicious marks or burns on the Elm Street residents."

"So Marcus, you distrust Brad as much as I do?"

"Probably more. Even before you gave me the lowdown on Brad's behavior at the gym, this guy—man. How do I say this? The guy gave me the heebie-jeebies."

"Heebie-jeebies? That's even a better expression than gonads!"

"I do my best to entertain," Marcus chuckled. "And, Dave, have you noticed Ramsey's eyes? Man, they are wild. They often look like a cat—you know, with the pupils long and vertical."

"My God, you've seen that too? Have you noticed that they even flash red?"

"I thought it was just me!" Marcus exclaimed.

We both sat in stunned silence. Outside the front window, the sun was sinking low in the western horizon. An autumn breeze made everything clear. Vehicle emissions and humidity were absent. Above the bleak view of East Main Street, the sky was turning a pink-violet color. I stared at the scene.

"You know, Marcus, when I see a sunset like this, I often think I could believe in a loving, personal God."

"And, when I see Brad Ramsey's eyes, I can believe in something else," Marcus whispered.

# CHAPTER 7

▼

# BRAD'S DISCUSSION GROUP

As I waited outside the Clock Shop Apartments the next evening, I reprimanded myself. How could I have agreed to this? Oh sure, when Jessica flashed those big green eyes at me, I would do anything she asked. Yet this went against every fiber of my being.

Still, I owed it more to myself than to Jessica. For Huey's sake, I should learn all the ins and outs of his suspected molester. If only I had evidence to back up my nagging suspicion concerning this manager at Elm.

Soon, I saw Jessica's blue Escort approach. I sucked in my small gut.

She parked next to me and opened the passenger's side door.

"Dave!" she squealed. "Glad you're going through with this! You're going to enjoy yourself, I know it!"

"Yeah," I offered. "I'll try."

"Oh brother," Jessica sighed. "What a 'tude you have."

"Well, Jess, it can't be that much of a 'tude. I'm here, aren't I?"

"Can't deny that!" she beamed. "Belt yourself in, let's get going!"

I agreed to let Jessica drive me to this social event, due to the fact that I didn't know where Brad lived and Jess was horrible with directions. She tried to scribble me a road map at the day program, but finally exclaimed, "Forget it! I'll drive you!" An experience I appreciate because when a man and woman ride together in a car, it feels intimate.

For the majority of the drive we talked about work. It was comfortable. A rude awakening hit when Jess pulled up to Brad's house. A line of cars filled his spacious driveway. Apparently this group was bigger than I had imagined.

Brad's house was small. A brown Cape Cod cottage. Two concrete gargoyles guarded his front door. "How appropriate," I murmured under my breath. Jessica rang the bell and a gorgeous, blonde woman greeted us. She hugged Jessica and shot me a suspicious glance—the look schoolchildren give newcomers. She was dressed all in black. First two gargoyles, then this vampire-like woman. What next?

All heads immediately turned toward someone descending the staircase. It was Brad in all his glory. He was dressed in a black silk shirt and beige Dockers. His silver hair was combed back, not one follicle strayed. Muscles bulged under the smooth fabric.

"Jessica! David! Glad you could come!" he exclaimed, flashing perfectly white teeth.

"Hi, Brad!" Jess smiled. "I told ya I'd wear down Mr. Gloom, here!"

Ramsey walked up to me and offered his hand. I took it.

"Once again David, I do apologize for my inappropriate behavior that afternoon. I teased you like an old friend, not realizing my unique sense of humor could put you off."

"You did have me worried," I admitted.

"You're here! That's all that matters!" Brad laughed. "Come into the living room and meet my motley crew!"

Including Jessica, I counted twelve people seated on easy chairs, folding chairs, and a sofa. I pondered the number. Apparently, Brad had gathered twelve disciples for himself? Or perhaps a witch's coven? In either case, I was the unlucky thirteenth visitor.

"Gang, this is David Paul. A workmate and friend of Jess and I."

The group gave silent nods and smiles, or indifferent glances. Ten of them were women, attractive and young. Black garments were the norm. Of the two men, one sported a goatee and another featured purple hair. I was horribly normal looking—my little-boy haircut, T-shirt and jeans—compared to this group. Again, I asked myself what I was doing there.

Jessica had found a folding chair and was deep in conversation with Mr. Purple Hair. I found a spot to sit on the sofa, but was pressed uncomfortably close to the beautiful blonde dressed in black. As my leg touched hers, she scowled with revulsion and shuffled her body away.

"I was saving this spot for Brad," she monotoned.

"That's okay, Donica," the Elm manager replied. "I'm going to stay near the blackboard tonight."

Brad unveiled a small blackboard that was set on an easel near the television. He also had different colored chalks.

Ramsey stood by his stool. It was as if the national anthem *Hail to the Chief* started to play. Everyone snapped to attention.

"Shall we begin with a prayer, friends?" Brad suggested with authority. Immediately, all heads bowed. I reluctantly went along, even though prayer was repugnant to me.

"We are gathered here, before you—the greatest of mysteries. Creator and light bringer, we care not what gender, race or mask you wear. We will not limit you to our petty expectations. We simply ask whoever or whatever you are, that you bring enlightenment and revelation to all here. May all preconceptions be shed. So be it."

"So be it!" the group replied.

I was impressed by the words. Non-denominational and non-specific, it was more like announcing a frame of mind than asking for divine favors. I liked it.

"Okay," Brad started. "Last week we were trying to separate the wheat from the chaff, as it were. We were in agreement that all religion had something of value. Transversely, they all have negatives as well."

"Some more than others," Donica stated.

"Agreed. Who can remember the negatives we were speaking about last time?" Ramsey raised one eyebrow, anticipating a response.

"We agreed that attributing a masculine gender to a god was destructive. It results in the oppression of women," Jessica commented.

"Good," Brad complimented as he wrote 'sexism' on the board with red chalk. "Anyone else?"

"The identifying of a particular race as a chosen people," the goatee man added.

"Excellent," Ramsey smiled as he wrote 'racism' under 'sexism.'

"The destructive idea that a god or goddess is a moral judge, one who weighs human behavior with divine scales," an obese woman offered from the far end of the couch.

"You would be against the concept of scales," a skinny friend next to her teased. With a laugh, the heavyset woman snatched a throw pillow and whacked her buddy on the head. All had a laugh, including myself. I started to enjoy the camaraderie.

"The idea that one's religion or theology is the only true theology," a tall brunette added to the list.

"Good, good, good," Brad replied as he wrote 'moral certitude' and 'one-way-ism' on the blackboard.

I smiled. These were all views I agreed with; things I've been critical of in regard to organized religion. Just as John Lennon visualized the song *Imagine*, I believed an earth free of religious superstition would be an earth united and tolerant.

"And who can think of how history demonstrates the dangers of these narrow-minded concepts?" Brad asked.

I quickly jumped in. "The Crusades, the Inquisition, the persecution of European heretics, the Salem witch trials, the anti-choicers attempting to limit reproductive freedom, gay bashing, the persecution of—"

"Whoa, whoa!" Brad laughed, as he sat down on his stool. "Dave, you just mentioned several things I thought would be brought up on a gradual basis!"

The group gave me smiles of approval. For the first time that evening, I felt a wave of warmth and acceptance wash over me. Even Donica shuffled her body closer. The side of her leg settled against mine once again.

"Oh—maybe one at a time would be better," I said.

"See?" Jessica directed at Brad. "Didn't I tell you about Dave's astute observations?"

"Yes you did, Jess. I can see I was selling Dave short," Brad grinned.

All this flattery was alien to me. I sat there, red-faced. I felt Donica's hand drift slowly over my knee as she reached for a handful of peanuts. The room started to feel very warm.

"Well, friends," Brad continued. "Dave here touched on what was covered at our last discussion group and he wasn't even privy to it. The name David means 'beloved one' in Hebrew and unlike that militant chieftain in ancient Israel, this David is a welcome addition to our club. Back on topic, I think we had covered the holy wars through the centuries and were on the subject of sexual mores. Dave had mentioned how the antiabortion movement is trying to cast women back into their oppressed roles as housewives. How does patriarchal religion view female sexuality?"

"It doesn't," the guy with the purple hair chuckled.

"Sure it does," the oldest woman with gray hair spoke up. "It realizes that women have sexual desires, but work to impose any limitation they can on those desires."

"These fundamentalist men also try to limit their own desires," the heavyset woman added. "Just look at most Muslim nations. They cloak their women from head to foot for fear that any show of skin would solicit lust on their part."

"Yeah, that's right!" the goatee fellow added. "When I was in high school, a group of kids from that community in Goshen attended our classes. They were called freaks by the kids. I think their Amish-like village was called The Huemmel Brethren. They were mostly German. The girls were weighed down by their old-country religion. They were like Puritans. They came to school with their heads wrapped in scarves and God forbid any boys should touch their hair. They wore baggy, plaid dresses and God forbid any boys should see their breasts or their curves! They were forbidden to shave their legs. God forbid any boys would stare at smooth legs."

"Interesting, Scott," Brad responded. "But who can tell me how Scott is falling into a Christian mindset with his criticism of the sexual oppression of those girls?"

Silence fell over the room. Many knitted their brow.

"I know!" Donica broke the silence. "Scott is assuming that only boys would have desired those girls!"

"Exactly!" Brad replied. "He is limiting the sexuality of that school to heterosexual boundaries. Those girls might have learned much about themselves if any lesbian opportunity presented itself."

Scott slapped his forehead.

"*Ahh!* I should have known better!"

"No, you shouldn't have known better," Brad corrected him. Everyone looked surprised by his comment. Brad then walked to the other side of the blackboard.

"Friends," Brad continued. "Do not be surprised when an unenlightened Christian frame of mind takes over now and then. This is the culture you were brought up in. This culture has indoctrinated you with a 'good' category and a 'bad' category. The moral concepts of good and evil become a cross on our backs. Didn't your parents lay this burden on your souls? 'Clean your plate,' 'clean your room,' and most importantly, 'clean your thoughts?' How many here hid pornographic magazines under your mattress when you were young? I hid both *Playboy* and *Playgirl* under my mattress back in the seventies. I knew I liked both men and women. What were we ashamed of? Of being normal humans with normal sexual impulses? When my mother found them, let's just say her shock was only outdone by the shock of my father. 'Are ya a fairy, boy?' I can still hear him asking. Never mind the fact that the old man had a bizarre collection of foot fetish magazines in his closet—his repressed homosexuality notwithstanding."

The room laughed.

"Indeed," Brad continued. "Mr. Darwin proved to us that we are merely animals. Because of our opposing thumb, we happen to have a huge leg up on our animal cousins. That being said, many of our first cousins, monkeys and chimpanzees willingly partake in unrestrained sexual practices. Do they get criticized, chastised, demonized or simonized over that?"

"You go, Reverend Jackson!" Donica yelled.

The gathering broke out into a sprinkle of giggles.

"You'll have to forgive us, Dave," Brad sighed. "We get silly at times."

"Hey, don't apologize," I replied. "This is refreshing."

At that moment, a subtle wind hit my right ear. I turned. Did Donica blow in my ear?

"Anyway," Brad started again, "here we are. Humans who evolved from animals, only we enjoy less liberation and freedom than chimpanzees. Where is the logic in that?"

I felt the devil's advocate in me start to rise.

"Well," I offered, "that sex stuff is mostly true. Anyway, we humans can't kill as indiscriminately as a chimp does. Some chimps kill less dominant chimps. They also eat smaller breeds of monkey. That's not a freedom we should have."

"Excellent, David. Very good. But consider…do chimps fight in world wars, or partake in attempted genocide? Do chimps discriminate according to coloration? I would suggest that humans are far more murderous, more violent than any wild animal. And why is this? Because of our beloved, blessed morality. Our abstract truths. Our vital lies; things we delude ourselves with like heaven and hell, like right and wrong. We do this to bring order to a natural universe that has no need of it. Nature has all the order it needs."

Brad beamed. His eyes looked red again. My earlier distrust came flooding back. What was happening here? Did I lose sight of the suspicion that this guy was abusing Huey? If I stayed much longer, this charismatic force of nature would have me believing there was no such thing as sexual abuse. The guy was powerful—one could feel his presence like electricity.

Brad walked closer to me, staring intensely.

"*Dave!* Let's not lose you now. Consider the chimps of the jungle! They do not sow or reap. They do not elect presidents, attend Sunday services, pay taxes. Yet the greatest of all mysteries—the light bringer—feeds them! He or She cares for them through the natural processes of the earth, our Mother Gia. They do whatever they desire, yet our heavenly Father-Mother who brings light to all loves them."

His pupils literally vibrated. They pulled vertical and long, then snapped back into circles. Was I seeing things?

Donica was rocking back and forth. I glanced over and saw her eyes had rolled back. She let out subtle moans as if lost in an erotic dream. I blushed and looked around the room. No one noticed her. Or they didn't care. All sat still and silent, eyes glued on Brad. Even Jessica seemed like a statue.

"Whatever they desire, Brad?" I then choked out. "Do they sodomize without the consent of the recipient? What do you say about consent, Brad?"

"Consent?" Brad acted confused by the question. He knew what I was implying.

"Yeah. You know the term consenting adults. Or as you would have it, consenting people."

I regained my clarity of thought. The group dynamic was no longer controlling me with approval or flattery. I wanted to strike at the heart of this guy and his beliefs. I wanted to bring his pedophilia to the surface.

Brad looked annoyed.

"Dave, the term consenting adult is fine by me."

"Then you don't believe that adults should engage in sexual acts with children?"

"Of course not, unless we are talking about older teenagers who have achieved physical maturity," Brad laughed uncomfortably.

"So hypothetically," I pressed on, "a child or a mentally challenged person shouldn't be introduced to sexual behavior by the more experienced adult?"

Here, by repeating Brad's opinion, I was hoping he would incriminate himself in front of the group. Jessica looked at me with concern.

*"Certainly not!"* Brad retorted. I sat back realizing Ramsey was smarter than to say something in a large group that he might later regret.

"I believe that as humans, we are to honor one social boundary with sexual behavior, and that boundary is set at adult consent. This is a boundary free of theological origins. Children and the mentally challenged are easily manipulated. I'm surprised to hear you express confusion in this matter, Dave," Brad concluded with confidence. I sighed at his duplicity.

"Wouldn't you agree, Scott?" the Elm manager asked, his grin so large I thought it would tear the skin on his face.

"Not only do I agree," Scott responded, "but I drafted that exact sentiment in our RAI employee handbook. The mentally challenged, in most cases, do not have the tools needed to give consent. Especially since people are willing to manipulate them on that level. Sexual contact between residents of equal mental capabilities is acceptable. Any employee found engaging in sexual activity with a resident at RAI will be terminated. They will be prosecuted to the fullest extent of the law."

I froze. I squirmed.

"Uh, Scott…you drafted the RAI handbook?"

Brad laughed.

"Come now, David! Don't you recognize the president of Residential Associates Incorporated? Dr. Scott Fullman?"

"N-no, I had no idea," I stuttered.

Dr. Fullman looked at me with a raised eyebrow.

"And where do you work, Mr. Paul?"

"At the Intermediate Care day program."

"Indeed!" he continued. "I know this is a philosophic discussion group, but I'm not comfortable that you had questions concerning sexual consent. Are you confused with this standard, Mr. Paul?"

Jessica looked worried.

"*No!* Not at all! The only reason I brought it up is because Brad led me to believe that *he* had confusion with this standard!"

Many groaned at my defensive comment, being that they were so enamored with Brad Ramsey.

"That may be possible Scott," Brad offered magnanimously. "Dave and I had a conversation sometime back where he misconstrued much of what I was saying."

"Still!" Dr. Fullman lamented. "Just six years ago, RAI had a sexual abuse case at one of our group homes. The media scrutiny was unbearable. We are sniffing out potential threats now, believe me."

"Scott!" Jessica spoke up. "I work with Dave at the day program. I can promise you, he is not a molester or potential molester!"

"I have to agree with Jess," Brad nodded.

"Well," Dr. Fullman concluded. "If Jess and Brad vouch for your character, David, who am I to question it? After all, hypothetical discussions about moral boundaries is what this group is all about."

Sweat poured off my brow. I smiled sheepishly back. Here I sought to burn Brad and instead the blowtorch came at me.

The rest of the group discussion went smoothly. I didn't speak up again. Donica stopped rocking, her trance was broken. Jessica kept giving me reassuring smiles, but I was a beaten man. Large, wet stains formed under my arms.

Soon it was coffee time. I hid in the bathroom during most of the socializing. People had looked at me like they had darts emerging from their pupils. Despite my efforts to be elusive, Brad caught me alone as I emerged from my hideout. He pushed me against the wall and hissed. His tongue flickered out of his mouth like a snake. I was paralyzed.

"I hope this evening taught you about me, 'Avey,'" Brad whispered. "I am not someone to 'f' with. Now, go home to your little beddy bye. No cookies for you."

Jessica walked into the hallway at that moment. Brad's demeanor immediately changed. His arm settled around my shoulder and he continued to whisper. "The genius just jumped with my backpack and lunch."

"You aren't telling Dave that awful joke, are you?"

I felt Brad's fingernails cut into my neck.

"Uh, yeah! It was hilarious," I lied.

"Wasn't it nice of Brad to vouch for you like that?" she asked.

"Yes. Very nice," I replied.

As Jessica left the hallway, Ramsey patted me on the head.

"Good boy," he giggled.

The rest of the meeting was quiet. The warmth I felt early in the evening was now a memory. As the women socialized and sipped their coffee, they longingly looked in Brad's direction. His hold on them was undeniable. The moment Jessica left a circular formation of chatting friends, I told her I was tired and wanted to leave. She seemed to understand, considering the social snafu I was involved in earlier.

Soon, Jessica was driving us back home. The moon was full. The air was still. The constellation Orion climbed the horizon. The three-star belt pointed the way home. I meditated, stunned by my stupidity during the group discussion. Jessica was energized. She talked on about how great the group was.

"You really didn't think Brad was molesting children or the mentally challenged, did you?" she asked.

"No...I guess it was a misunderstanding," I responded.

# C H A P T E R  8

▼

# D ISCOVERY

Normally, I avoided the group homes when they needed last minute staffing. The hours were bizarre, and the work was different than one would experience at the day program. Young and inexperienced workers would call in sick at the last minute, mostly on Friday or Saturday nights. Their timing was suspect.

When the assistant manager at Elm Street called me this particular Friday, I shocked him when I agreed to work third shift. Oh sure, I had been awake since six a.m., and now I would have to work straight from twelve midnight to eight a.m. I was primed, however. I was ready. I was willing to risk seeing Brad early the next day as he arrived at the house to perform his managerial shift. Why would I subject myself to such misery? I needed to find evidence that Huey was being abused. Ramsey would not intimidate me into silence.

The sky was clear as I drove to Elm Street that night. Halloween decorations and pumpkins graced the middle-income homes on the way to Torrington. Everything was lit in a bluish glow as the moon approached last quarter phase. White sheets hung off trees, seasonal decorations that flapped in the wind. They pointed the way to the bizarre group home. No, no, it wasn't the special needs residents that were bizarre; it was the staff—from the evil manager down to the stoned employees.

The moment I walked up to the group home's door, two second-shift workers bolted by me and ran to their cars. They didn't acknowledge my arrival.

"Think we're too late to meet Christie at Water Street?" The eighteen-year-old blonde asked her companion.

"No way," the pierced and tattooed guy responded. "The party is just starting, if I know Christie."

I murmured "bye" to the human blurs as I entered the house.

"Yo, man," Ross, a regular third-shifter greeted me. "Don't be too bummed, but the second shift ate up all the munchies."

"That's okay," I said. "I'm not hungry at night."

"That's good," Ross responded. With a big yawn, he claimed his favorite easy chair in the living room and turned on *Cinemax*. Some lewd erotica was playing out as Ross quickly drifted into a dose. In a mere ten minutes, he was fast asleep, despite the moaning coming from the television.

"Perfect," I whispered to myself. I made my way through the messy kitchen and located Huey's bedroom. My friend didn't like the dark. A bright nightlight illuminated his room.

The gentle soul was asleep. His snoring was raspy and loud. Somehow, his stiff body managed to curl into a fetal position. I started to search through the sparse room. Huey had a few religious paintings. One was of Jesus touching his heart; his heart radiating two shafts of light, one red and the other blue.

I shook my head at the image and smiled.

A cumbersome Arjo lift blocked my access to Huey's closet. I quietly moved it to open the sliding door. Again, nothing seemed out of the ordinary. At least not in low light.

As I walked to the far side of Huey's large bed with its side rails up, something caught my eye. It was under the bed. His bedpan?

I carefully pulled out the pan just in case some lazy second-shift worker had left any stools or urine. Sure enough, there was a dark, rectangular object.

The open doorway provided some light, allowing me to identify the object. Was it a book? I walked into the hallway. Yes, it was a book. It was *Huey's Bible!*

I picked the Bible out of the bedpan not expecting to see the puddle of loose stools underneath. The back cover and pages were stained brown from the runny fluid.

My fingers were soiled! I was shocked at the blatant disregard for Huey's possessions. I walked into the bathroom and thoroughly rinsed my hands under hot running water. I scrubbed with anti-bacterial soap. As I put on latex gloves and started to rinse off Huey's book, I paused. Wait a minute! This could have been intentional! Was this Brad's doing, considering his animosity toward Judaism and Christianity? Yes, it was an animosity I shared, but I would never desecrate someone else's objects of faith, especially when the person in question was inno-cent, like Huey. He owned the Bible for the religious illustrations it included. After further consideration, I placed the book into a white garbage bag. This could be evidence of Ramsey's behavior.

Now I walked back into the bedroom with purpose. If someone desecrated the Bible intentionally, it was time to look at Huey's other Catholic collectibles. His posters and paintings checked out. No marks, no stains. Then I noticed two stat-uettes on Huey's dresser.

I carried them into the hallway. One was of the Virgin Mary, her hands clasped in prayer, her robe flowing. The other was of Jesus on the cross, his blood and wounds represented with accuracy. I continued to study the figurines. Was something on top of the cross? Just above the INRI sign? There was a discolora-tion, specks of red and brown. One spot of brown was large, so I smudged a little on my latex finger and took a sniff. Sure enough, it smelled like fecal matter. The red spots may have been—blood?

It started to all add up. *Brad sodomized Huey with his treasured statuettes!* With his precious icons! The rough edges made cuts that appeared as fingernail marks.

Adrenaline surged through my body. How could someone do this to Huey? Poor Huey, he wouldn't harm a fly if it landed on his tray table. If there were such things as saints, this childlike individual would qualify. My hands trembled with fury. My vision was colored red. I pictured myself wrapping my fingers around Brad's throat. Strangling him right there in the driveway before he came into the house. Perhaps I could lay in wait for his arrival and stab him with one of Huey's icons—right through the chest.

You may ask me at this point, how did I know with certainty that Brad was the one doing these things? Why not one of the young, undisciplined group home workers? Other than the fact that Brad was a liar who made vulgar, sexual commentaries; other than the fact that Brad was on a campaign to accumulate spiritual followers and attack Huey's misguided religion; other than the fact that Brad had threatened me, my gut told me it was Brad's doing. I smelled his foul order. While most smelled musk deodorant and Old Spice aftershave, I smelled all that was wrong with the world.

Thinking ahead, I gathered Huey's Bible and his statuettes and put them in a bag. I placed them in my car while Ross slept. I spent the rest of the shift doing some silent cleaning, trying to calm my rage. Slowly, the hours passed. Three o'clock. Four. Five. Come seven, Ross woke on cue and started some busy work as well. He knew managerial types could drop in anytime from this hour on. Res-idents slowly started to awaken. Rich came shuffling into the kitchen nude, making his customary raspberry noises. I escorted him to the shower, washed him, got him dressed. While I was doing this, Erica let loose a few of her famous screeches. Ross started her morning routine. I was done with Rich when I heard Huey chanting from his room.

"Ewy goo boy ay. Ewy goo boy ay. Ewy goo boy ay."

I immediately went into Huey's room, to get him up and bathe him in the modified sauna bath. As I walked in, he seemed pleasantly surprised.

"Avey! Avey! Goo!"

"Hey, Huey, how are you feeling today?"

"Avey goo! Ewy goo boy ay."

I turned him on his side and placed a rolled-up lift harness under his right side. I took a good look at Huey's butt. It was worse than before with raw red marks and cuts surrounding his rectum. All these new marks, even when Huey had those accursed kitchen mitts velcroed onto his hands? Didn't anyone notice this? Didn't anyone get suspicious? I figured no one cared enough.

As I lowered the poor soul into his wheelchair with the help of the Arjo lift, I couldn't help but ask him a few questions.

"Tell me, Huey, has anyone hurt you recently? Has anyone caused you pain?"

He just sat there. No response.

"Has Brad hurt you, Huey?"

Again, no response.

"What do you think about Brad?"

"Baaad man, bad man," he whispered.

"Why is Brad bad? What bad things has Brad done?"

Silence. An expression of distress overtook his features.

"Brad did something bad, didn't he?" I pushed on.

Huey bowed his head. "No, no, no Avey."

I puzzled at his reaction. Why wouldn't he share any of this with me? Was he afraid that Brad would know?

"Okay, Huey. No more questions."

"Avey goo. Ewy goo boy."

"Yes, Huey, you are a very good man," I responded.

I started to prepare him for the sauna bath. I wept silently.

Within twenty minutes, Huey was bathed, dressed, and ready for breakfast. Most of the residents were up by now. Ross was busy bathing Teddy.

A first shift worker walked through the front door. I became anxious. Was it Brad? Thankfully, it was Carissa, a cute and young residential counselor.

"Oh, Dave," she startled. "I didn't expect to see a day programmer here. Where's Ross?"

"He's busy with Teddy."

"I see," she smiled. "Well, anything interesting to report?"

"Just the usual," I replied. "Huey's rectum is looking worse; however, I noted it in the log and also in the cardex file. I applied a PRN of Bacitracian to his raw area."

"Oh! That's funny. Yesterday during second shift, his rectum appeared better." Carissa looked at me with suspicion.

"Well, apparently it wasn't 'better,'" I shot back.

"Uh-huh," she replied in a doubting tone.

My anger resurfaced. My hands trembled with adrenaline. Brad apparently succeeded in shifting the suspicion of abuse onto me. He biased the minds of his staff just as he had done at the group discussion. Apparently, this suspicion wasn't enough concern to prevent Brad's assistant manager from getting me to fill in. Better a suspected molester work that night, than any of them miss a weekend party.

Eight o'clock arrived. My eyes were heavy with fatigue. I bid the house staff adieu and started out to my car. I almost made it. I almost avoided Brad.

But no, Brad was there. He was standing in the driveway. Odd. Why didn't he just walk in and start his shift?

"Well, well, well," Brad directed a sneer at me. "Finally, a day programmer humbles himself and fills in at the house."

"That's right, Brad. No thank-yous are needed. See ya."

I went to open my driver's side door, but Ramsey rushed over and forced it shut. I turned toward him, adrenaline filling my veins.

"You think I'll let you simply leave? Like this?" Brad hissed.

"Well, the shift is over," I answered.

"That's not what I meant, boy."

"Then what did you mean, 'sir?'" I responded with sarcasm.

"Give it to me."

"Give what to you?" My body froze.

"The bag in your backseat. Give it to me."

"You want my dirty laundry?" I bluffed with a laugh.

"No, I want that sickening book and those two icons."

I tried to keep the innocent act going. How could he possibly know what I had in the bag? My car was locked! He didn't have x-ray vision!

"Icons, Brad?"

"You test my patience, flea. The ceramic representations of that Nazarene whore and her deified bastard! Give them to me now! You wouldn't want to deny Huey his hour of anal gratification, would you?"

I shoved the hulking manager away from my car.

"*Go to hell, Brad!* You're about to be found out, crud."

I opened my car door. As quickly as I moved, it wasn't fast enough. Brad grabbed my right arm and spun my whole body around. He then landed a jab to my midsection! His strength was incredible. The force of the blow paralyzed my diaphragm. I crumbled to the ground trying to catch my breath. He calmly reached into my car and took the bag.

"Trying to cover-up something, Sparky? Seems to me like you were busy last night! First you soiled Huey's book of lies, then you sodomized the poor soul with his own graven images? My, my, my!"

I charged toward him. This time, Brad reached down and grabbed my belt. What happened next was so fast, I couldn't tell what occurred until after. Ramsey had lifted me off the ground, high over his head then body slammed me onto the hood of my car! I blacked out. By the time my vision cleared, the powerhouse had already entered the house—with the bag.

Injured and infuriated, I didn't know what to do. I couldn't charge into the house like a lunatic, confirming the suspicions that Brad had planted in the minds of his staff. With tears of frustration, I entered my car and slammed the door.

I drove home experiencing severe neck pain. Insane, violent thoughts filled my head. I would get this guy. I would buy a gun or I would get a long, bladed knife—I would get something. For the first time in my life, I felt capable of murder.

Sunday, the next day, my phone rang around noon. It was Tim Gould.

"I hear you filled in at Elm, Friday, third shift?"

"Yes, Tim. That's right."

"I'm sorry to tell you this, but Brad Ramsey has lodged several complaints about you. These could result in a written warning, or perhaps suspension. He claims you attempted to steal religious items from Huey's bedroom and that…well, I'm not sure I believe my old friend with this. But he claims that you physically attacked him in the driveway."

I knew I had to choose my words carefully. As fair as Tim was, Brad was more persuasive with people than I could ever be.

"Uh…yeah, Tim. That's how those events occurred. I suspected someone was using Huey's statuettes as…well, let's just say I found fecal matter and blood spots on them."

"You did? Did you fill out the appropriate paperwork and submit it to Brad?"

"No, Tim. I still don't trust Brad. I believe he may be the abuser or that he is covering for someone on his staff."

I didn't believe Brad was covering. I said that to appear more fair to Tim.

"I see," Tim paused. "Hmm, what about that driveway incident?"

"Yeah. Well, it happened like this. Brad got angry when I tried to take those items from the group home. I attempted to get by him, but he's the one who attacked first. He landed a blow to my gut, which knocked the wind out of me for a solid minute."

"I see, I see," Tim responded.

"The rest of the fight was a blur. One thing should be obvious. I'm a twerp compared to Brad, and he won in no time."

"Yes, I can see that. No offense, Dave."

"No offense taken. So, what happens next?"

"I've already arranged a meeting concerning this. It will involve you, me, Brad, and Scott Fullman."

"Scott Fullman? Oh no. Did you realize that our president at RAI is a friend of Brad's and he's a member of Ramsey's religious study group?"

"Really? That's interesting."

"Yeah, interesting!" I scoffed. "My side of the argument is already down in flames."

"Dave," Tim assured me, "you will be heard. I know you to be an honest man and a hard worker. I will be there for you."

# CHAPTER 9

▼

# THE MEETING

The drive to work on Monday was tense. My sweaty hands grabbed the steering wheel with force. My heart raced, my legs trembled. Everything could come to a head this morning. Either Brad or I would emerge victorious. Foreboding filled me. I knew the odds were with Brad. I tried to concentrate on the highway before me. Route 8 south. The cars in front maintained an equal distance. The generic scenery rolled on by. Cedar trees. Exit signs. It didn't work; nothing could distract me from my anxiety.

Suddenly, I remembered Tamika's recommendation. "Pray to Jesus, give Him a try." I laughed. Why not? What did I have to lose? On the slim chance that Christians were right—about the Nazarene, about His power to intervene into our little lives—I murmured a prayer request while driving.

"Jesus," I started off, "I don't know who you are, or what God is. I always believed that you were a misunderstood revolutionary, but in case you're more than that, here goes. If you are divine, please come into my life. Help me now, please."

I felt embarrassed by the words, even though I was alone. I continued the prayer.

"Jesus, just don't intervene for my sake. Do it for Huey. He is innocent. He has an attraction to your religion. He has very little in life. Brad Ramsey is abusing him in vulgar ways. Please, Jesus, let Brad be found out. Let Huey and I win this battle."

My embarrassment continued, but my nerves did calm a little. Okay, the test was on. Would Jesus fly in like Tamika implied—a super hero to save the day?

I arrived at the day program an hour early as Tim had asked. Several cars were in the parking lot. As I approached the entrance, I felt like an inmate walking death row. A bird cheerfully chirped by the front door. I waved at it, making it fly away. With foreboding, I reached for the doorknob and entered the building.

Sure enough, there they were. My judge and jury. They sat in a semicircle in the main recreation room. Brad greeted me with a harsh look. Tim gestured to a chair next to him. I sat down. Scott Fullman was there, along with Brad, Brad's house staff Carissa, Tim, and myself. Then the door to the room opened. Who else would be included in this? My heart skipped a beat. It was Jessica! Jess sat on my side of the group. A positive sign.

"Hello, people," Scott started. "This meeting is to get to the bottom of a serious dispute between Mr. Ramsey and Mr. Paul. Each accuses the other of vulgar misconduct. We shall see who has the most credible claim. I am the arbiter of this decision, but I welcome any observations. Let's begin."

The president of RAI sat down and gestured toward me.

"Mr. Paul? Please share with us your complaint concerning Mr. Ramsey."

I tried to tone down my accusations. I tried to be conservative with my words. I was dying to say that Brad was a cruel, abusive molester with a sick attraction to the helpless. But I knew I couldn't be blunt.

"Thanks, Scott…uh, I mean Dr. Fullman. First, I'd like to say that I don't have a personal hatred for Brad. I have even spent some free time in his company. Yet Mr. Ramsey has said many things to me. Things that disturb me."

The company president leaned forward.

"Okay, let's hear these comments."

"Well, one afternoon, Brad and I were at a gym. Mr. Ramsey here insinuated that he was interested in sodomizing children and the mentally challenged. Uh…specifically, he said they were 'tight when upset.'"

Dr. Fullman grimaced.

"Go on."

"Brad claimed that the naiveté and innocence of children and the mentally challenged didn't concern him. At first, their resistance to intercourse was irrelevant, due to the fact that they didn't know exactly what they were resisting. It was supposedly their 'right' to be introduced to sexual contact by the more experienced."

"Lies," Ramsey interrupted.

"Relax, Brad," Dr. Fullman interjected. "Your turn is next."

"At the evening discussion group you attended, Dr. Fullman, Brad grabbed me by the neck and threatened me. He told me to never cross him."

The molester snickered. Jessica looked concerned. Was this look for Brad or for me?

"Then recently," I continued, "I was working third shift at Elm. I discovered fecal matter and bloodstains on Huey Riiska's religious statuettes and I took them, along with Huey's Bible I found soiled in his bedpan. I wanted an impartial manager like Tim to test the evidence. Combined with the fact that Huey had anal cuts, it was all very suspicious."

"What makes you think the spots on the statues were fecal material?" Scott asked.

"I didn't know for sure. They smelled like feces," I added. "When Mr. Ramsey here discovered that I had these items in my car, he became enraged. He delivered a blow to my stomach. As I tried to fight back, he lifted me off the ground and body slammed me on the hood of my car. The dent is still on my vehicle. Brad made a comment about how I was 'denying Huey his hour of anal gratification' by taking the statuettes."

"Uh-huh." Scott then pointed to Brad and monotoned, "Your turn."

Ramsey stood and straightened his silk shirt. He slowly walked in front of the group like a defense attorney giving his final summation.

"Thank you, Scott, for allowing me to voice my complaints here. And with Mr. Paul, my complaints are many. Where to begin?"

He grabbed an empty chair and placed one foot on it. His leg became an armrest as he spoke.

"First of all, I offered my services as a physical therapist to Mr. Paul here, when he was experiencing back problems. This is how we ended up in a gym. During the workout, I admitted to Mr. Paul that I was bisexual. Apparently, this threatened David. His demeanor changed. He labeled me a 'pervert.'"

I knew Brad would lie, and here was the first instance.

"Mr. Paul then ran away from me, fearful I was sexually interested in him. I tried to belay such fears with no success. I believe Mr. Paul is intolerant and homophobic."

Scott listened intently.

"As most of you here know, I am independently wealthy. I have a solid inheritance from my father, who was once a media mogul and magazine owner. I work here at RAI for humanitarian reasons, for I wish to give back to society. I do not stake out children and the mentally challenged for sexual purposes! Such an accusation horrifies me! In fact, those of you here know that I have a very active love life. The idea that I would prey on the vulnerable—like some desperate, lonely loser—this defies logic."

Brad faced me.

"David, how many dates have you been on this past year? Please, be specific."

"I really don't see how this is relevant," I blushed.

"Please, Mr. Paul, answer him," Scott urged.

"Well, no dates this past year," I murmured.

"Well, well," Brad grinned. "It appears that the accuser himself is defined by sexual frustration, instead of the one he suspects."

"Brad," Tim scolded, "That's below the belt!"

"My next point is that Huey Riiska's icons have drips of brown paint on them. This inadvertently happened when my house staff painted the trim in Huey's bedroom," Brad continued, as he pulled out some papers from his briefcase. "It's all documented here. Two months ago, a second-shift worker admitted that a few drips got away from him. He thought he cleaned all of it, but apparently, he didn't. Also, I have the statues here—paint spots are on them."

Brad handed the figurines to Dr. Fullman who studied them. He passed them around.

"*But,*" I protested. "Brad has had access to those icons since I made the charge to him on Saturday!"

"That doesn't explain away the fact that a painter, working with brown paint, confessed his sloppiness. The paperwork proves this," Scott interjected. "You yourself said you weren't sure what the spots were, David."

When the ceramic figures were passed to me, I saw obvious paint spots that were not on them before.

"With the Bible," Brad continued. "Carissa here worked the second shift before David filled in, and the first shift after. Carissa admits that Huey's Bible accidentally fell off his bedside dresser and into the mess."

"Is this true?" Scott asked her.

Carissa looked affectionately at Ramsey.

"Yes, it is," she blushed. "When Teddy started having a temper tantrum in the living room, I ran…like, to investigate. I forgot all about Huey's bedpan I placed on the floor."

"Those things happen," Scott smiled.

"And this Dave guy, like…he gives me the creeps," Carissa continued. "He looks at my chest, my butt…he makes all the girls uncomfortable. He sure ain't getting any!"

Dr. Fullman giggled at the observation.

*"Come on now!"* I exclaimed.

"I concur," Tim added. "This is an investigation, not a character assassination!"

"Oh, Tim?" Brad interjected. "I wonder what the worse charge is…that Dave isn't getting any, or that I'm some sort of pedophile predator?"

Tim rubbed his forehead.

"Okay people," Dr. Fullman spoke. "Let's calm it down. Brad, go on."

"Thank you, Scott. As I was saying, I will not have my character assaulted by these baseless charges. I have worked in the Peace Corps, I have worked for the Red Cross. I've always labored for the greater good. My humanitarianism is on public record. Meanwhile, my accuser here has a criminal record. So what is more likely? That I attacked Dave in the driveway on Saturday or that he attacked me?"

*"Liar!"* I sprang out of my chair.

"Relax, Dave." Tim grabbed me by the arm.

"Criminal record?" Scott asked.

"I was arrested a few times for vandalism when I was eighteen. A lifetime ago!"

"Hey, folks! I've worked with Dave for years now. He is not a criminal, just as Brad is not a molester," Jessica offered.

"Well, Tim and Jess both know," I spoke again. "I'm not in the habit of stirring up trouble. I'm not that type. I wouldn't make these things up—that's not my nature."

"Maybe that's true," Dr. Fullman observed. "But I just can't take your word for it."

"I'll vouch for Dave," Tim added. "He's reliable and honest. He expressed concerns about Brad a few weeks back."

"Perhaps I've been too defensive here, regarding Dave," Brad softened. "I do overreact when people falsely accuse me of things. He's not unreliable or criminal. He's just biased."

"Biased?" Tim and Scott asked in unison.

"Yes. Dave isn't motivated by malice. He's jealous."

*"Brad!"* Jess yelled out. "We agreed that you wouldn't!"

"I'm sorry, hon," Ramsey sighed. "I must speak the truth."

I stiffened. My legs cramped with tension.

"Go on," Dr. Fullman prompted.

"Mr. Paul here is jealous. Jessica and I have grown close. We have dated. Dave has been infatuated with Jessica for a long time."

I sat motionless. Horrified.

"Is this true?" Scott asked.

I tried to gather my thoughts.

"It's okay, Dave. Really…it's okay," Jess tried to comfort me.

"This is all irrelevant," I replied in a low voice. "I've never propositioned Jess. I've never behaved inappropriately."

"He's right, Scott," Jess responded. "Dave has always been a good friend."

"Regardless," Brad added, "David has a motive for believing the worst where I am concerned. He accused me of being a pedophile, knowing that such a monster once molested Jess. He wanted to turn her against me."

I was speechless.

Scott Fullman stood up. He looked angry.

"People, I can't believe what I've heard here. This situation is more of a soap opera than a criminal investigation. Why am I wasting my time on this?"

He then looked at me, fire in his eyes.

"Mr. Paul, regardless of whether you like to stir up trouble or not, you have done just that! What evidence do you have of abuse? Mr. Riiska has a history of rectal scratching. Those statuettes are paint stained. We know how the Bible got soiled. None of these things have anything to do with Mr. Ramsey! All we are left with are comments you claim Mr. Ramsey has made. Not once has anyone else heard such comments. Not one other person has complained of Mr. Ramsey's behavior. Yet the woman you are infatuated with is dating the man you routinely attack? Your behavior is suspect. No, it's more than suspect…your behavior is deplorable! I am therefore suspending you for one week, starting today. A week suspension without pay."

"*Scott!*" Tim objected. "There hasn't been any evidence of wrongdoing! If anything, David had legitimate suspicions. He was trying to protect Huey and RAI! Don't punish him for being conscientious!"

"Normally, I'd agree," he replied. "Yet this man was competing for the affections of a woman by cutting down the competition. I've made my decision. Meeting over."

Everyone stood and stretched. Carissa gave Brad a high five. My entire body trembled with tension. I felt humiliated. A hand settled on my arm. I turned and saw it was Jessica. Her eyes were teary.

"Dave, I'm so sorry. I know you weren't trying to scandalize Brad. I know your suspicions were sincere."

I looked at her. What could I say?

"I…also know how you feel about me," she continued. "I am…so flattered. You and I have a special friendship, one we should never risk."

"Yeah, sure," I murmured.

Brad stood at a distance.

"Jess, let's go," he commanded.

Jessica then gave me a friendship hug—the type of hug that avoids full frontal contact.

"I'll call you, Davey," she whispered.

As special as our friendship may have been, it took but one sentence for Brad to take her from my side.

The two of them left with a company van to do morning transport, since the molester graciously agreed to fill in my shift. Tim apologized for the tone of the meeting.

"It's okay, Tim," I responded. "That's what I get for praying to some fictitious god."

I started my drive home in a daze. While on Route 8 north, my head started to spin. I was infatuated with Jessica for years and it was revealed in one fell swoop! As I feared, my feelings were obvious. As I feared, Jessica didn't reciprocate. As I feared, my entire universe was a house of cards. One built by delusion. I was pathetic. Tears streaked down my face as I contemplated the unthinkable. I worked out scenarios for Brad Ramsey's murder. My life was worthless, but at least I could save Huey from his abuser.

Suddenly, my chest became tight. What was happening? My heart rhythm went from a forceful beat to a fluttering, rapid machine gun. I had trouble catching my breath! I quickly pulled over.

A sensation of dread filled me.

*"Holy!"* I gasped. "I'm having a heart attack! I'm dying! *Oh god! Oh god!"*

My hands tingled. My body erupted into a cold sweat. I tried to take deep breaths.

I started driving up the highway again. I averaged about thirty miles an hour toward Winsted, listening to various motorists blare their horns at me. My heart would go from a rapid flutter to an uneven hiccup sensation. Those few miles remaining seemed to last forever. Suddenly, the life I believed worthless was in danger of slipping away. I wasn't ready to die! There was so much to do. Ramsey had to be brought to justice! As I reached the end of the highway, I turned into Winsted. Driving in a panic, I ran every red light. The hospital was on the west end of town, and that final stretch felt like the end of a marathon. Finally, gratefully, I reached the Winsted Memorial Hospital. I stumbled into the emergency room and grabbed the reception desk.

*"I—I think I'm having a heart attack!"* I told the woman sitting there. *"Please, help!"*

She walked over to a nurse and said something, then sat at her computer.

"Do you have an insurance card?" she asked calmly.

"*God!*" I exclaimed. With shaky hands I found the right card.

"Okay, Mr. Paul," she responded after studying the card. "The doctor will be right with you. Try to relax."

Sure enough, a nurse immediately came out and led me to an examination room. She put sticky, round sensor pads on my chest and stomach. A blood pressure cuff was attached to my arm. Soon a heart monitor was beeping at me, rapid and uneven. I worked at breathing deep. All my body wanted to do was take shallow and rapid breaths.

After a humming sound, the nurse took a long strip of paper into her hands.

"Try to relax, Mr. Paul," she said. "I'll bring this EKG to the doctor and we'll have some answers shortly."

I started to relax some. If I was having a heart attack, at least I was now in the right place. Yet why save my miserable life? My friend Huey was being molested and I was powerless to protect him. The evil monster doing this had succeeded in seducing the woman I loved. This same woman saw me as a mere buddy. Not since I was a lonely kid in an orphanage had I felt this way. All that made my life worthwhile was slipping away.

Soon, a doctor entered the room. He had a nurse with him who proceeded to insert an intravenous needle in my arm.

"Don't be alarmed, Mr. Paul," the gentle doctor said. "This IV will help your heart rate slow down. After analyzing your EKG, I can safely say you are not having a heart attack. Instead, you are experiencing supraventricular tachycardia. Do you have a history of heart rhythm problems?"

"No," I replied.

"Are you taking any medications?"

"No. None."

"How about your stress levels? Any unusual stress of late?"

"*Hah!*" I laughed. "I should say so! *My whole life is coming apart!*"

"I see, I see," the doctor said. "Okay. Try to relax. Take deep breaths. We'll slow down your heart rate and then work from there."

"What's happening to me, doctor? Am I ill, or am I losing my mind?"

"None of the above. I believe you are having a severe panic attack. It is a very common disorder. Apparently this is your first. Don't despair, it is a treatable condition."

"Panic attack? No way. This is more than mere nerves."

"You would be surprised at what mere nerves can do," the doctor replied.

"Not anymore," I answered. I continued to take deep breaths as the monitor made annoying beeps at me. After twenty-five minutes, a rate of one hundred and thirty beats per minute had slowed to ninety beats a minute. I breathed easier.

I heard the doctor and nurse whispering outside the examination room door. Finally, the doctor walked in and took off my sensors.

"Okay, you've responded well to the IV," he said. "Get dressed. I'm writing you a prescription for Xanax. Take three pills a day, morning, noon, and evening. This will last a week during which you should make an appointment with your regular doctor. Share with him your stress, your problems. He'll decide if further cardiac tests are warranted. We've already called his office concerning you."

"Okay, no problem," I answered. "I've been suspended from work this week."

"I see," the elderly gent nodded. "Try to keep yourself occupied. Stay busy."

"I'll do that," I answered.

A vision of me buying a rifle flashed into my head. As my rage continued to burn, I realized that I couldn't let my dark impulses control me. I couldn't allow myself to become like Ramsey. There had to be a better way. I prided myself on being an intellectual. I had to think my way through this.

# CHAPTER 10

▼

# DEATH AND DISAPPEARANCE

The week of my suspension was tedious. I broke the promise to keep myself occupied. I lived on my couch, sedated by tranquilizers. When I slept, I had nightmares. Jessica was taunting and cruel. My parents watched in the background, without faces. While awake, the television was my only companion.

With the exception of Marcus. Good ol' Marcus would call me every few days. He was enraged at the way RAI took Brad's side. He even threatened to quit his job. I reminded him that his new house was an expensive venture and both he and Tamika needed the income. My friend conceded to the logic. He had volunteered to drive me to my scheduled doctor's appointment. I appreciated his support.

When the doctor's visit did occur, it went as I expected. He tried to get me into therapy. He suggested a few social workers and mental health clinics for me to visit. I resisted. It had been several days since my panic attack and I didn't see the need to start treating myself like a basket case. I lived my whole life independent and alone. I hardly needed some quack draining my wallet just to tell me how my absent parents are to blame for all my problems. The doctor ended up writing me a prescription for Prozac. He believed that depression was a contributor to my anxiety. I filled the prescription, but never took them. I also stopped the Xanax, but kept a pill in my wallet just in case I felt out of control again.

Halloween night arrived. I dutifully handed out bite-size candy bars to trick-or-treaters and watched horror movies on television. My suspension was almost over. I mentally prepared myself to see Jessica again. Our friendship would be forever changed. I didn't know if I could overcome the hurt of her preferring Brad over me. Any normal feeling of jealousy was dwarfed by my intense hatred for Elm's perverted abuser, however.

Was there any way to prove that Brad had been abusing Huey? The OJ Simpson murder trial came to mind. DNA. DNA. What if Brad left semen evidence on Huey's sheets? Did Brad bring the abuse to that level? Did he inflict his molestations as a cruelty and a perversion? I decided to somehow get Huey's sheets analyzed. My opportunity came about in the most horrible way.

It was midnight. Trees outside my apartment building were draped in toilet paper. They looked like macabre skeletons emerging from their burial wrappings. I was startled when my phone rang. Who would call at such an hour? I picked up the receiver.

A weak voice choked out my name.

"Dave?"

"Yes, this is David Paul. Who's this?"

"Dave, this is…Jess."

"Oh," I replied coldly. "What can I do for you?"

"Dave, please. Please."

"What do you want?"

"Dave, it's Huey. I thought you should know."

My blood ran cold. "What about Huey?"

"I'm sorry Dave, but Huey…died tonight. Just a short time ago."

"Wha—I'm sorry, *what did you say?*" I heard, but my brain refused to accept it.

"Huey's dead, Dave. Brad told me just now, on the phone. It was a grand mal seizure. By the time the ambulance arrived…it was too late. CPR was used…but that didn't help."

Jessica started sobbing. She took a brief moment to compose herself.

"Dave, what is happening? Why is everything falling apart? Why can't life be like it was just a short time ago?"

"You mean, why can't it be like it was before Brad Ramsey entered the scene?"

I was cold, numb, and angry. I didn't care at that moment if Jessica liked me or not.

"Oh, please Dave! *Don't do this!* Please, not now. Not now."

"Was Brad there with Huey, tonight?"

"No! His staff called him as soon as Huey's seizure was discovered."

"Was Brad at Elm today?"

"*Dave!* Will you put your jealousy aside? We just lost a friend tonight!"

"Yes, I did lose a friend tonight. And I lost your friendship when you allied yourself with Huey's abuser!"

"Dave…how could you say that?"

Jessica hung up. I didn't care. I now considered her Brad's toadie. Huey was miserable since Brad came into his life, and now he was dead. Perhaps stress had something to do with it. Whatever the reason, I never had the opportunity to see Huey that week. Maybe I would have noticed whether Huey was in need of a med adjustment. Perhaps I would have noted those subtle, petit mal seizures that others routinely missed.

"*That bastard Ramsey!*" I murmured, as I entered my small kitchenette and took a sharp peeling knife from its holder. I stuck the knife in my back pocket, threw on my jacket and left the building. My car was covered with shaving cream, but I didn't care. I cleared the windshield and started driving to Elm. Ramsey was probably there now—soon to come face to face with his mortality.

It was eerie, how calm I felt. Calm and numb. I was on autopilot, as if it was all a dream. Along the drive, lawns and porches flickered with dying jack-o'-lanterns, their candles reduced to late night puddles. I believed that like Huey, these lights were falling into the abyss of nothingness. I believed death was annihilation.

In a mere fifteen minutes, I saw strobes flashing in the distance. The ambulance was still there, at Elm. I didn't care. I would send Ramsey to the abyss while they watched. I almost preferred an audience.

I pulled into the spacious driveway. Immediately, a police officer held up his hand for me to stop approaching. That's when it dawned on me—not only an ambulance, but a police car? What was this all about? I parked my car and approached the cop.

"What business do you have here?" the officer asked.

"My name is David Paul. I'm a worker with RAI and a friend of Huey Riiska."

"Okay. And what business do you have here?"

"I just wanted to see Huey one last time. Even if it's just…his remains."

"Uh-huh," the guy said with skepticism. "Okay, you stay right here."

The officer entered the house and soon emerged with Brad. I smiled and reached for the back pocket of my jeans. The knife was gone! It must have slipped out.

Brad approached me. A pretend somberness and sympathy shaped his features.

"David, Jess told me she called you. I'm so sorry for the loss of your friend. *Our friend.*"

"Sure you are you bastard," I hissed. I then wrapped my hands around his throat. The officer quickly jumped between us and put me into a physical restraint.

*"Calm down!"* he ordered. "Calm it down! What's all this about?"

*"Ask him, officer!"* I gasped. "He's been sexually abusing Huey for weeks now!"

Brad smiled. "Don't listen to him, officer. This man has recently been suspended from RAI due to his wild accusations and fantasies."

"Is this true?" the cop asked.

"Did the imbeciles at RAI believe his story over mine? Yeah, that's true," I shot back.

The officer pushed me to the other side of the driveway and instructed Brad to stay where he was. Brad nodded. A subtle look of concern came over his face.

"Okay you," the tough cop hissed. "Calm it down right now, or I'll put you in restraints. I have a few questions."

"You want to hear from me?" I laughed. "Here's a first! I'll tell you anything you want to know."

"Very good. First, tell me straight up, did you take the body?"

"Excuse me?"

"Did you take the body of Hubert Riiska from his bedroom? The window was open, and…"

"I'm sorry, I don't get you. Somebody *took* Huey's body?"

"That's right. The staff reported Mr. Riiska's seizure and an ambulance crew came and worked on him. After resuscitation attempts failed, the staff and paramedics went into the kitchen to sign some paperwork. When they returned to the bedroom to retrieve the body, it was gone."

*"What? My God!"* I gasped.

"You apparently have some invested interest in Mr. Riiska, and claim that this poor soul was sexually abused by Mr. Ramsey over there. Did you take the body in order to personally protect the evidence? Just admit it now, and—"

*"You!"* I yelled at Brad. "You disposed of Huey's body, didn't you? You don't want anyone to know—through forensics—what you've been doing! Admit it!"

"That's enough!" the cop shot back. "Get a grip! Mr. Ramsey didn't arrive on the scene until after the body disappeared!"

"And you think I did it?"

"Right now, I don't know what to think, Mr. Paul."

I stood there and thought about the situation. Then a realization came to me.

"Between what times did Huey's body disappear?"

"Twelve and twelve fifteen."

"Okay, well, I was on the phone at my Winsted apartment, in the old 'Gilbert Clock Shop,' around ten after. My coworker, Jessica Kim, called to tell me that Huey had died."

"And how did this Jessica know about it so quickly?"

"Brad Ramsey called her as soon as Huey died."

"Okay, okay." The officer scribbled facts in his little notebook. "Is that Jessica K-i-m?"

"Yes."

"If this checks out with her," the cop sighed, "both you and Ramsey have an alibi. The phone records should confirm that you were both elsewhere at the time in question."

I nodded. All this was happening so fast, the bizarre nature of it all didn't hit me until after. It was unreal.

The officer leaned in closer.

"And now, between you and me, what's all this about sexual abuse?"

"I heard Brad admit it from his own lips," I whispered. "But everyone in this crappy little company is so charmed by Ramsey, they don't believe a word I say."

"Ahh," the man nodded. "This could all factor in."

"Officer, could I suggest something?" I felt a small tinge of hope.

"Shoot."

"Test Huey's bed sheets for semen. Upper and lower sheets."

"Semen? Are you serious?" The guy grimaced.

"Completely serious."

"Well, we do have his sheets. I was hoping to test them for hair follicles, perhaps shed from whoever stole the body. It's Halloween. Mr. Riiska's window was open. Sick teenagers or cultists or someone could have stolen the corpse after they saw the ambulance. A sick, sick gag, if it is one."

"This could get sicker, officer."

"Okay, Mr. Paul. I'll see what I can do. But no promises. The department may be reluctant to spend much on this investigation. Mr. Riiska was confirmed dead. He has no immediate family. No loved ones."

"I'm Huey's family!" I shouted back.

"I'm talking about legal relations. I may get someone to look for hair follicles on the sheets—hair not identified as an Elm employee. Mr. Riiska was between two sheets when someone took his remains. I'm not sure if I could get more involved tests, like for semen stains. But I'll see what I can do."

"I'd appreciate that, officer."

"Mr. Paul, I believe you're a good person. A friend to this poor guy Huey. Here's my card and number. You call me in two days. Ask for Officer Mullady."

"Thank you."

"Hey! What exactly are you two conferring about over there?" Brad shouted from across the driveway.

"Nothing that concerns you, Ramsey!" Mullady shouted back.

I knew there was something about this guy I liked.

I left the group home before the officer did, knowing that Ramsey would taunt or attack me in the guy's absence. My insanity was now on hold. Perhaps there was a way to legally pin Ramsey to the wall. I would do it to honor Huey and all innocents who were victimized in like manner. The ride home was long. My emotional numbness wore off and waves of grief hit me.

Two days later Marcus called and we shared our outrage and grief concerning Huey. I told him about Mullady. Marcus became hopeful as well. I never heard back from Jessica, I imagined her seeking solace in Ramsey's arms.

The last day of my suspension came. I was extremely anxious to learn about the tests on Huey's sheets. As five p.m. approached, I gave in and reached for the phone. As I touched it, it rang. I quickly picked up the receiver.

"Hello."

"David Paul?"

"Yes! Is this Officer Mullady? I was just about—"

"Yeah, it is. What's the joke? Why exactly did you want us to analyze these sheets?"

"Joke? I don't understand! Didn't you find any hair? Any semen stains?"

"Nothing of that nature. But what the hell is that imprint?"

"Imprint?"

"Don't play dumb with me, Mr. Paul. Are you and Mr. Ramsey in on this together? Because if you are, I'm not amused!"

"I don't get you. What are you—?"

"How did you guys do it? How did you discolor those sheets in such a perfect way? It's photographic!"

"What's photographic? Start making sense!"

"Okay, Mr. Paul—as if you didn't know—there are two imprints of your friend, Mr. Riiska. One image on the upper sheet, one on the lower. They are discolorations. Yellow shades, which depict a man lying in bed. Arms to his side.

If I find that you and Brad Ramsey created this, to sell a mystery to the *National Inquisitor* or such, I swear to god, I'll run you both in."

I put the phone down in stunned silence.

# CHAPTER 11

▼

# THE SHEETS

I returned to work the next day. Jessica avoided my company and didn't speak to me. Nor did I say anything to her. Marcus was curious about the mysterious sheets, and what was being done to find Huey's remains. I had nothing to quench his curiosity. Officer Mullady went from ally to foe, although his suspicions were understandable. Tim Gould was happy to have me back. He didn't believe that jealousy motivated my accusations about Brad. As much as Tim liked his old friend, he knew the man was an acquired taste. Ramsey had poor judgment.

For several days, work went on as usual with the exception of Jessica and I avoiding each other. My emotions fluctuated between sadness and anger. Huey's absence was glaring. I missed him.

When the group home hosted a small memorial service for Huey, Marcus and I went together. Jess attended with Brad and wept on his shoulder. Huey's Catholic priest gave a generic eulogy. The event took place in a large cemetery located on the Winsted end of Torringford Street. RAI purchased a marker and a gravesite, in case Huey's remains were found. The isolated stone depressed me. Gray clouds cloaked the sky. A bitter wind penetrated my coat. My bones.

A few days after the memorial, Tim called me into his office. To my surprise, there sat Officer Mullady.

"Mr. Paul. I thought you should know that the investigation regarding Mr. Riiska's disappearance has been terminated. There is no evidence for us to work with. No eyewitnesses noted anything unusual around Elm Street that night. The group home had two trick-or-treaters, both of whom were preschool age and accompanied by their parents. They visited at eight o'clock. No others were seen near the house. No teens with toilet paper, no late trick-or-treaters. Nobody."

"That's because the neighbors on Elm avoid contact with the group home," I added.

"Perhaps," Mullady replied. "Anyway, all we're left with are these bizarre sheets, and the feud between you and Mr. Ramsey. Ms. Kim provided a solid alibi for both of you. The sheets had nothing to offer in the way of incrimination. But the body image left on them is unexplainable. It is a yellow image, invisible to the naked eye unless one stands a good seven feet from it. It's a photographic negative. It's a stain that resists most cleansing methods. Other than that, we have nothing."

I nodded.

"Mr. Paul, is there anything you want to admit to me now?"

My patience fuse was very short. Sarcasm took hold.

"Yes, officer, there is. I admit that I took Huey's body from his room while a talented voice double I had hired talked to Jessica on my apartment phone. Then just to 'f' with everyone's head, I imprinted Huey's sheets with a bizarre image and planted them in the room in the mere minutes between Huey's death and the discovery of his missing body. Aren't I clever? And of course, my master plan was for you to discover the image! Haha!"

"Look here, you—" Mullady stood up.

"Hey! Let's all simmer down," Tim suggested. "Officer, subtract David's sarcastic tone from his confession and you can see the logic. There's no way he could had been responsible for any of this."

"Well, someone is responsible," the police officer grumbled.

"Not necessarily," Tim replied. "Maybe this is one of those unexplainable mysteries. The world's full of them."

"BS," the cop retorted. "I investigate things. Everything has an explanation."

"Then explain this mystery, Sherlock," I challenged.

"With or without my revolver up your butt?"

"Much like the way your head is up yours?"

"David!" Tim exclaimed. "Let's not try to antagonize the police here, okay?"

I lowered my head.

Mullady grabbed a large brown package and tossed it on Tim's desk.

"Despite your attitudes," the officer murmured, "I dislike that Ramsey all the more. I don't doubt what you told me about him, Mr. Paul, so I thought you guys would like to have these. And don't let me see these in the *Inquirer*," he warned as he left the office.

"Are those—?" I asked.

"Only one way to find out," my manager responded.

I stood at the far end of the office as Tim opened the package. He then unfolded the sheets. Sure enough, there it was. An imprint of Huey's body, so faint one could barely see it. His entire body was imprinted, minus where his underwear was worn. If Huey's underwear had been left behind, it must have been lost in the mix. It was bizarre.

Tim tacked the sheet to the wall and went to get the rest of the day program staff. Soon all six of us were in the room staring silently at the sheet. Jessica wiped her eyes.

Marcus spoke first.

"Strange. Looks like the Shroud of Turin."

"What?" I asked.

"The Shroud of Turin. You know—the supposed burial shroud of Jesus, kept in Italy under close watch by the Vatican."

"Oh, you mean that medieval painting?" I asked.

"Painting? No man, it isn't a painting. I don't know what it is. I never was interested in it. But that social worker and author I told you about, Jonah Rubenstein, well, he's really into the relic. He calls himself a Shroudie."

"Shroudie?" Tim laughed. "Is that like being a Trekkie?"

Another worker named Henry joined in.

"Shroudie, Trekkie—they're all in orbit. Didn't 'Bones' from *Star Trek* lean over that Shroud years ago and say 'It's dead, Jim?'"

"Yeah, that's how the media treated it," Marcus said.

Tim rubbed his temples before speaking.

"Can you give these sheets to this Rubenstein guy? Perhaps he'll have a few explanations, considering his interest in that Turin Shroud."

"Sure can! I'm going to see him tonight at my church, as a matter of fact. He's giving a lecture. He's just returned from a trip to Israel. He has some prestige as an amateur archeologist."

Henry sighed with impatience.

"Why should Rubenstein be interested? Are you guys implying that Huey is like some Jesus, and that both shrouds are miraculous?"

"Not at all," Tim replied. "I'm just curious about this thing. Aren't you?"

"Not really," Henry snickered.

"From what I know of the Turin Shroud, scientists in the late eighties proved it was medieval. What possible relevance could it have for us now?" I asked.

"You're over thinking, Dave," Marcus answered. "Just open your eyes and look! You don't see any similarities between the two?"

"Well, yeah—they're visually similar."

"That's a starting point," my friend said while starting out the office door.

"Tim!" Jessica finally spoke up. "Brad Ramsey is an expert on almost everything. He writes for the *Humanist Inquirer* magazine. Why don't we let him look this over?"

I felt a dry heave coming on.

"Perhaps we will," Tim replied. "But first I want to give this guy Rubenstein access to the sheets."

Tim cupped his hand around his mouth and yelled. "Marcus! Hey, Marcus!"

My friend ducked his head back into the office.

"Yeah?"

Tim pulled the two sheets off the wall, folded them, and gave them to Marcus. As he handed them over, he hesitated.

"Can you promise me that this friend of yours won't speak of this to anyone, or try to sensationalize this in any way? Some years back, Residential Associates had that sex abuse scandal, and the last thing this company needs is media attention. We're not a sideshow here, we're providing a necessary service."

"You can trust Jonah. If anything leaks out, you can fire me on the spot."

"If anything leaks out, I'll be joining you in the unemployment line," Tim chortled.

We all started to file out of the office. Jessica gave me a quick, sideward glance as she walked by. Tim suddenly grabbed my arm.

"Not so fast, David."

"Yes?"

"What was this the cop said about 'not doubting you' in regard to Brad?"

"Oh," I hesitated.

"Damn right 'oh.' What did you say to him?"

"I uh…well, it was Halloween, and I was a bit crazy after hearing about Huey's death and disappearance. As you know, I immediately drove over to Elm. I kind of told the officer that night that Brad had been molesting Huey."

"You what?"

"Now, before you blow a gasket, try to understand. I had just heard that someone stole Huey's body."

"I can't believe this!" Tim stood up and grabbed his head. "Do you realize what a type of rumor like this could do to this company, especially after that scandal?"

"Yeah," I nodded.

"When will you show some restraint? Do you know what slander is?"

The rotund manager started to pace.

I laughed to myself. Brad was still alive—this was evidence of my restraint.

After an awkward minute or so, Tim sat back down. His face grim.

"Dave, I have gone to bat for you many times. Even when I knew you were wrong about Brad, even then I bent over backward to justify your behavior. I have made myself unpopular with my old frat buddy and with Dr. Fullman. All the while I'm doing this, you're telling some law enforcement official that an RAI manager is a sexual predator?"

"Well, I—"

"*Good God!* I just realized why you and this Officer Mullady are now hostile to each other. Aw gawd…this keeps getting worse."

"I know. It wasn't very professional of me. But please try to understand my state of mind…"

"Enough! Really, Dave, enough. You're going to eventually get *me* fired. I have to look out for my interests and for the company's interests."

"What are you saying?"

"I'm sorry. I have to fire you."

"What?"

"Put yourself in my position! Here I give you a new life. Stick up for you after the bleeping company president reams you out, and here we go again. You're a loose cannon, friend. I'm sorry."

Tim's logic was sound. Yet here I was, being punished again and again for speaking the truth. Meanwhile, that lying Ramsey was sitting pretty with his managerial position and with the affection of Jessica. The irony was rich.

"You know, Tim, that's all right. I was too uncomfortable working with Jess and Ramsey as it was. But when the feces hits the fan, you just remember. I was right about Brad. You morons will learn soon enough."

I marched through the day program recreation room and grabbed my jacket. Marcus noticed and came running over.

"Yo Dave! Dave! Where are you going?"

"I'm off to the unemployment office."

"What?"

"That's right. I'm fired. Fired for telling Mullady my suspicions about Brad."

"Bogus!" Marcus yelled. *"That's total BS!"*

"It's okay," I offered. "I was too uncomfortable around Jess anyway. You keep an eye on Ramsey. You keep a watch for future evidence of abuse with the other Elm residents."

"You can count on it! But you and I…we'll still be in touch, right?"

"You kidding? You're the only friend I have left, Marcus."

"Then come with me tonight. To Dr. Rubenstein's presentation."

"I'm not in the mood to hear some Christian apologist promote his reliijjiinn."

"But, on the other hand, you'll be with me when I give Huey's sheets to him. I want you in on this, man."

I sighed. Why not? Marcus' friendship—and those sheets—were important considerations.

"Okay," I smiled. "But no one had better try to save my soul, or get me to attend some potluck supper and bingo night."

"I promise. No recruiting," my friend laughed.

# CHAPTER 12

▼

# MEETING JONAH

Marcus told me to meet him in front of the First Pentecostal Church on Hayden Street. I hoped his bride wouldn't be with him. Sure enough, there she was standing with him as I pulled into the parking lot. Tamika gave me a big wave.

"Now I know there's no God," I hissed to myself. "Could this bloody day get any worse?"

I put on a smile as one would put on a tie. I exited my Chevy and walked slowly over to the couple.

*"Davey!"* Tamika squealed. "Here you are at church! Miracles do happen!"

"Miikkaa," Marcus groaned. Under his arm was a brown paper bag that held the mysterious sheets.

"No miracles happen with me, Tamika," I murmured.

She crushed me with her customary bear hug. "Yes, I heard about your job. I'm sorry."

As much as I disliked the woman, her sympathy did seem sincere.

"That's all right, Tamika. I'll get another job soon, I'm sure."

The woman took my arm.

"How are you financially? If unemployment doesn't help ya out, Marcus and I are here. Any money you need."

I looked at Marcus who was shaking his head in the affirmative.

"That's right. Even if you need a place to stay, we're here for you. Both 'Mika and I agreed on this during the ride over."

I was inwardly embarrassed by my initial reaction at seeing Tamika.

"Thank you both," I smiled.

The three of us walked into the church. It was a classic looking Protestant church, New England in flavor. The edifice was white and the windows, clear. A plush, red carpet welcomed our feet. The wood grain of the pews was polished to a shine. A basic cross hung over the altar.

A small crowd accumulated. About twenty-five eventually sat down. A few teenagers set up a screen and a slide projector was perched in the middle isle.

"Don't worry, Dave," Marcus leaned past his wife to whisper to me. "There's no praying, preaching or singing tonight. This is simply a lecture, open to members and non-members."

"I'll sing and pray with you in the parking lot afterward," Tamika teased.

"Don't put yourself out on my expense," I laughed.

An elderly man wearing a floppy safari hat walked in. Under his arm was a loose-leaf binder, complete with dog-eared papers seeking escape. His Western windbreaker flapped loudly as he walked. His face was weather-beaten and a trimmed white mustache and beard contrasted with his dark complexion. He had a long nose and deep set eyes.

"He's finally here!" Marcus whispered with enthusiasm.

The old gent walked to the front of the sanctuary and laid his notes on a small podium.

"Good turnout I see," he commented.

I thought he was being sarcastic.

"Last time I did this," he continued, "only about ten people showed up. Mostly from this church. It's good to see some new faces tonight. Some of you from the UConn branch?"

"Yo!" a kid from the back pew yelled out.

"Yo to you," Rubenstein responded.

A few people chuckled.

"Shalom to the rest of you. My name is Jonah Rubenstein and I am a social worker affiliated with several churches in this area. I work with Christian Family Services. Psychology was my minor at Yale, but my PhD is in theology. I'm an author. A few of my books can be found gathering dust at flea markets. One of my passions is the field of biblical archeology, and I've had the pleasure of working with several prominent archeologists in the Middle East. My trip last month was to the excavation of Jericho, where new discoveries are being found each day."

I sat forward, starting to take interest.

"Since the dating of Jericho continues to be a hotbed of controversy, I really don't have anything definitive to share with you about that site. Yes, the city at one point had a protective wall; parts of which collapsed, and grain reserves were discovered within a dark, charred layer. Still, the minimalist scholars working there claim that the dating of these finds don't reinforce the biblical account. Many are disputing the timetables. For now, I'll reserve comment about Jericho."

I was impressed. I thought that like other Christian apologists, Rubenstein would leap to the conclusion that the excavated Jericho was proof of Old Testament accuracy. Instead, he was waiting for more facts to present themselves.

"But I do have so much to share, some of which I photographed. These particular finds all reinforce the history recorded by the New Testament. Lights!"

Rubenstein's deep voice echoed and his excitement felt contagious. Each slide was presented with an explanation and history behind it.

One interesting photo showed an excavated inscription. It was a Roman decree found in Nazareth. A dire warning of capital punishment against grave robbing.

"I believe this decree was issued by Claudius," Jonah offered. "Around AD 41 to 54. Its intended target was the tiny, rural village of Nazareth. Nazareth was so small, some biblical scholars and archeologists don't believe it actually existed at the time of Jesus. They assume the gospel accounts were written after the first century, and Nazareth was inserted into the supposed fiction. Even in the gospels, one disciple had the audacity to ask, 'Can anything good come from Nazareth?'"

The audience laughed.

"Well, this discovery is another good thing to have come from Nazareth. This Caesar had an ax to grind with the growing Christian community, called The Way. A Roman record of Claudius tells us of his expulsion of the entire Jewish community from Rome. Why did he do this? Cryptically, he said that they were fomenting a malady common to the world."

My interest increased.

"Some scholars, myself among them, believe this malady was The Way, the earliest Christian movement."

Rubenstein sipped some water before continuing.

"The Christian faith was spreading fast. At the base of each growing Christian branch, there was an evangelizing Jew. By the time Nero took charge, there were literally thousands of Christians in Roman territory for the new Caesar to scapegoat, torture, and execute. How obnoxious this new superstition must have seemed to Claudius. Regarding the resurrection, there was an established explanation for Claudius to cling to. Perhaps the scheming followers of Jesus stole their master's remains and invented a resurrection story to validate their status as leaders."

The elderly scholar then leaned forward on his podium before continuing.

"The Gospel according to Matthew tells us that the high priests who condemned Jesus paid off the guard who witnessed the Resurrection. They were instructed to tell all who inquired that the disciples stole the body while they slept. Even at face value, that claim was silly, for if one is asleep, one doesn't know who stole the body. If they awoke during such a theft, they would have slain the grave robbers. Matthew writes that this stolen body explanation was still circulating at the time he wrote his gospel account, between the years AD 40 and 80."

"Excuse me, Dr. Rubenstein," the young guy operating the slide projector interrupted. "Why would Claudius post that warning in obscure Nazareth?"

"Claudius must have had very few facts at his disposal," Jonah continued. "An insurgent was executed under Roman authority. His followers claimed that he returned to life and was divine. He was a Nazarene. The disciples were rumored to have stolen the body. This new cult was seeping into Rome, and Jewish evangelists were on the prowl across the known territories. First, Claudius expelled the whole Jewish community from Rome, regardless of whether they were Christian or not. Then to prevent future messiahs from being smuggled from their tombs, he posted a warning in the hometown of the Nazarene. A warning against future grave robbings. In Claudius's mind, Nazareth was probably a focal point for Jesus followers. He was wrong, for Jesus specifically lamented over Nazareth when he said that a prophet is never accepted in his own community. This Claudius inscription proves that Jesus' grave was empty, that his gospel was spreading rapidly, and that Matthew accurately reported the lies and opposition the early church encountered."

"That's a stretch," I interrupted. "That warning against grave robbing was probably standard policy, posted everywhere. It's coincidence that it was excavated in Nazareth."

"*Dave!*" Marcus gasped.

Jonah smiled. "A challenge! I like this! What is your name, young man?"

"David Paul."

"Okay, Mr. Paul," the elderly explorer chuckled. "You bring up an interesting alternative. Yes, this inscription doesn't definitively prove that Claudius was solely concerned with the new malady when this decree was sent out to Nazareth or possibly elsewhere. Yet the Jewish community was hardly in the habit of grave robbing, or other violation of sepulcher. They painted the sepulchers of the recently deceased white, warning their community of the decomposition occurring inside. Physical corruption was believed to make whoever came in contact with it ritually unclean."

"If occupied tombs were considered unclean, how did the Jews gather the bones of deseased loved ones in bone boxes, or ossuaries?" I pressed on.

"Only after enough time passed, and decomposition was complete…only then would faithful Jews reenter the tomb and gather the bones of the deceased. Remember in the gospels, when Jesus called the Pharisees whited sepulchers? This was a loaded insult. He claimed that inside their souls, they were full of all corruption. He also warned the crowds to stay away from them. Listening to the Pharisees would be like becoming ritually unclean. To follow the guidance of those Pharisees was compared to embracing a decomposing corpse. So Mr. Paul, is there a logical explanation for this warning being found in tiny, obscure Nazareth?"

"None I can think of."

"Also keep in mind that the standard punishment against grave robbing usually wasn't that severe. Yes, even with an empire as brutal as Rome."

I was glad the lights were low. My face must have been dark red at that moment.

"Well, the interpretation I hold to with this Nazareth inscription—that it was a new policy inspired by the spread of Christianity—is logical, if not definitive," Jonah laughed. "Keep me on my toes, Mr. Paul. There's more to come."

The slide projector clicked.

"Speaking of ossuaries, I have two compelling finds to present.

This inscription, photographed in a tomb near Jerusalem, mentions an Alexander, son of Simon. The abbreviation QRNYT seen here may be interpreted as Cyrenian. As many of you know, Mark's gospel account tells us that a man named Simon the Cyrenian was enlisted to carry Jesus' cross for him. The gospel even notes that he had two sons who were apparently well-known during the time of the gospel's authorship. They were named Rufus and Alexander. And here we have the tomb of a Cyrenian, named Alexander, son of Simon. Coincidence? Even if the tomb isn't of this particular Alexander, it is certainly evidence of the common names during the first century. Names specific to certain regions. Names found routinely in the New Testament, which bolsters the fact that the Christian scriptures are indeed first century in origin."

I felt Marcus's glance as if he had actually tapped my cheek. I didn't return the look. This alluded to the debate we had at the diner.

"The second slide I have here is a spectacular find," Rubenstein continued. "It's the ossuary of the high priest Caiaphas. The man who tore his robe at Jesus' perceived blasphemy; the man who sent Jesus to Pilate. The Aramaic inscription on this ornate ossuary is 'Joseph, son of Caiaphas.' It was discovered in the Peace Forest section of Jerusalem during December of 1990, and is now on display at the Israel museum."

I was grudgingly impressed with this man's presentation.

The slides clicked forward. One first century inscription mentioned the same man named 'Erastus' referred to in Paul's letter to the Romans. Another inscription listed a Publius, the Chief Man of Malta, who is referred to in the book of Acts. A Herod's temple inscription was found, warning Gentiles not to enter—corresponding with the story also found in Acts. Another slide was of a first century inscription mentioning Pontius Pilate by name. Another showed the actual Pool of Bethesda excavated in Jerusalem, the pool described in John's gospel account. Slides of the Corinthian Synagogue of the Hebrews, another of the theater in Ephesus—both mentioned in Acts, both excavated.

Pictures of a first century fisherman's dwelling in Capernaum were shown. Over this excavated house a primitive church was built, thus it is thought to be the home of some original disciples. Including Simon Peter.

"On the subject of Simon Peter," Jonah continued. "Here is an ancient inscription found above one tomb underneath Saint Peter's Basilica in Rome. Located directly under the altar, this partial inscription reads 'Peter is buried here.' The medium-size bones of a sixty something man was interred below the inscription, along with other random bone fragments. Tradition records that Peter was crucified upside down in Rome, and he was probably in his sixties at the time of his execution. This find is controversial and debated heavily. But it remains of interest."

Rubenstein's discussion went on to include the Dead Sea Scrolls. He stated that phrases found within the Essene scrolls support the fact that John's Gospel was more Judaic than Gentile with its terminology. Phrases such as "spirit of truth," "children of light," "walking in darkness," and "eternal life" were believed to be Gnostic—belonging to a sect influenced by Gentile and Far Eastern philosophy. These Jewish writings proved that the author of John's Gospel was a faithful Jew, nothing more.

The presentation included a discussion of a few Dead Sea Scroll fragments, each containing certain phrases or words that could be traced to New Testament documents. An ongoing debate was taking place in the scholarly community concerning these fragments, and whether they actually could be from New Testament writings. If they were Christian, it would dramatically push up the dating of the New Testament.

Jonah wrapped up his lecture with a tease, suggesting possible new locations for the biblical Mt. Sinai. Upon his "thank you for coming," the small audience gave him a standing ovation. Immediately, about ten people surrounded the elderly man, with books to sign and questions to answer.

The presentation was impressive. The skeptic in me kept dwelling on the obvious; none of these finds could convince anyone that the New Testament was factual. Nothing presented made the miraculous possible. All the evidence established is that Christian scriptures were earlier than most skeptics believe, and that they had a basis in actual history. Whether early Christians magnified things into mythological exaggerations wasn't only a matter of faith, but a matter of logic. Obviously, men can't walk on water, or rise from the dead. If I debated Jonah Rubenstein, the strength of reason alone would shatter his presuppositions, I mused.

Tamika, Marcus, and I waited for the small crowd around Dr. Rubenstein to lessen. That evening's audience may have been small, but they were engrossed. Marcus impatiently held the brown paper bag containing the sheets in his left hand, his Styrofoam coffee cup trembled in his right.

Tamika started to ask questions concerning the status of my belief, or lack thereof.

"What did you think of the overall lecture, Davey?" she probed.

"I thought it was fascinating," I conceded.

She raised one eyebrow at me. "Oh? You comin' around? Is the Lord tugging at your heart?"

"No."

"Uh-huh."

"By the way, Tamika, I tried praying to your Jesus as you suggested. I asked for his help. What happened immediately thereafter? As you know, Brad Ramsey got away with his crime. I had a severe attack of palpitations. The woman I love is currently hooked up with that Ramsey pervert. Poor, innocent Huey died. His body disappeared. I lost my job. If this is your Lord's idea of answering prayers, then I'm better off on my own!"

"You must have prayed wrong," she chided.

"I'm sorry?"

"The Lord can see into your heart, Dave. You can't pray for selfish reasons, like getting one-up on your enemies, or impressing some babe you're gushing over. First and foremost, you need to confess your sins and repent."

"'Miikkaa," Marcus moaned.

"Tamika, I resent that. I prayed mostly for Huey's protection."

"Hon, you can't fool me. I have a gift from the Holy Spirit, the gift of discernment. I have proven my worthiness by speaking in tongues and interpreting tongues. I'm a perfected apostle, and you'd do well to listen to me."

"Tamika!" Marcus exclaimed. "That's uncalled for!"

"Ahh…I must have prayed *wrong*? I'm not worthy of divine favors, like you are? Of course. It has *nothing* to do with that heavenly *Wizard of Oz you worship!*" I exclaimed.

"That's also uncalled for Dave," Marcus sighed. "God doesn't always deliver what we want, or hope, or expect. His ways are not man's ways. I'm sure you didn't pray out of selfishness, it's just that God's will is beyond our comprehension."

"That's your interpretation, babe," Tamika sighed.

"So God doesn't want justice for Huey? Huey didn't even live to see a better day, or to have his abuser brought to justice. That's how much God cares."

"I know. It's that when evil things happen to good people dilemma. Tough pill for all of us to swallow. But that Ramsey will get his, I have no doubt," Marcus hissed.

"When would that be, Marcus? At the 'end of days?' At the 'final judgment?'"

Marcus looked down.

"Well, Huey got his much faster. A fate he didn't deserve."

"I believe Huey is with the Lord as we speak," Marcus murmured.

"I envy you, Marcus. I believe Huey is in an abyss of nothingness, and God knows who is doing what to his remains."

Tamika flinched.

"David, I'll continue to pray for you," she condescended.

"And your prayers will be as effective as mine were," I sighed.

Jonah's conversation circle was breaking up. As soon as the elderly scholar's eyes met mine, he excused himself from his groupies and made a beeline toward me. I braced myself for what was to come. Was he going to witness to me? Was he going to save my soul?

"Mr. Paul!" he laughed as he approached. His hand was outstretched in greeting. "I just wanted to thank you for your challenge tonight. Frankly, I was hoping you were going to continue the behavior. I love it when my audience is skeptical."

"Are you being sarcastic?" I asked. My combative agnosticism was now in full throttle.

"Not at all," he answered. "In my Judaic heritage, young rabbinical students do not simply sit around, memorizing phrases and catechisms. We challenge our teachers. We probe, question, ask, argue, and engage. One can even see this in the pages of the gospels—the disciples don't sit around taking notes. They even appear to argue with their 'Master' at times. Jesus himself stimulates thought by meeting questions with questions."

"Well, I do like to debate," I nodded. My hostility was fading.

"As do I," Rubenstein grinned.

"Great lecture, Jonah! I loved it, as always," Marcus gushed.

"Marcus, Tamika! A pleasure to see the two of you, as always. Is Mr. Paul here a friend of yours?"

"He's a friend and…formally, a coworker," Marcus answered.

"Thanks for reminding me," I murmured.

"Oh? You've recently lost your job, Mr. Paul?"

"Just today, Dr. Rubenstein."

"Oh dear! You have my sympathy."

"That's okay," I nodded with a red face. This was getting embarrassing.

"Just today, I had to fire my personal assistant. He arrived for his shift hung-over for the last time. How are you with Microsoft Windows?" the elderly author asked, staring at me intensely.

Was this guy actually thinking about hiring me?

"I get by," I responded. "But I'm not sure you want me working for you, if that's what you're thinking. I don't have much office experience, my typing is slow, and I'm not a Christian."

Jonah smiled.

"I'm not hiring a lapdog, or a chorus who will shout 'amen' at my every opinion. I'm looking for a man who can transfer my notes to CD-ROM. Who can take phone calls at the office where I do some individual counseling. Normal, nine to five hours. On rare occasion, I may ask you to assist at lectures, or with travel preparations. You may have an opportunity for field work, if you want it."

"Well, that's a generous offer," I sidetracked, "but I really don't think—"

"I'll pay you twenty an hour, thirty-five hours a week," Rubenstein interrupted.

"Yo Dave!" Marcus yelled. "That's two times what you made at RAI!"

I paused. Where else in northwest Connecticut was I going to make this kind of money? I had to think this through.

"Well, Mr. Paul?" Jonah's stare was intense. It made me uncomfortable. I squirmed. My skin felt itchy.

"Okay, Dr. Rubenstein. On one condition—you will not try to convert me, save me, evangelize me, and so on."

The gray-haired gentleman laughed.

"No worries, Mr. Paul. I will not actively try to introduce you to the Lord."

"Uh-huh," I answered with suspicion. "May I ask, why would you want to hire me? A stranger. A non-Christian. A person who heckled you during your presentation. A person without polished office skills."

"Yes, that is rather odd, isn't it David? May I call you David?"

I nodded.

"Let's just say, I trust my instincts. You had the fortitude to challenge me, to speak your mind. You have a spark."

"You mean, 'da boy has gonads?'" Marcus teased. I poked his shoulder, while he grinned.

"Exactly," Jonah smiled. "He has 'gonads.' Just don't ever show up to work intoxicated or under the influence of any illegal drug."

"Don't worry about that with Dave," Marcus interjected. "He only had one beer at my bachelor party. I've never seen a nonbeliever as straight arrowed."

"Just as I suspected," Rubenstein nodded. "How about it? Will I see you at my office at the Exchange building, West Hartford, this Monday morning? Nine a.m.? I'll write down the address for you."

Although suspicious of Jonah's impulsive behavior, the money was too good for me to ignore.

"Okay, Dr. Rubenstein. I accept your offer."

"Excellent!" The doctor bent down to write. Marcus placed the bag next to his scrap paper on the podium.

"Marcus? What's this?" Rubenstein looked up.

"The Shroud of Torrington," Marcus replied.

"Excuse me?"

"I thought that would grab you. These sheets are imprinted with the image of Huey Riiska, a special needs resident who recently died at a RAI group home. We couldn't make sense of them and neither could police investigators. Since you have shared your research concerning the Shroud of Turin with me, I thought you might have some insights."

Rubenstein silently took the top sheet out of the bag and held it up.

"I don't see any image."

"You have to stand at least seven feet back from it," I responded.

Jonah handed the top corners of the sheet to Marcus who held it high as the scholar stepped back. About ten feet away, Jonah bent forward, his hands on his knees.

"Remarkable!" he exclaimed. He rubbed his eyes and looked again.

Marcus laughed. "Remind you of anything, doc?"

"All the observable qualities of the Shroud of Turin seem to be here! The pale, sepia-colored imaging. The subtlety. The negative image. Just who was this Huey Riiska?"

"Huey was a person with profound physical challenges," I offered. "His verbal skills were limited. His development was that of a child around three. He was mobile only with the assistance of a wheelchair. Yet he had a warm personality and a good sense of humor."

Jonah stared uncomfortably at my face once again.

"You were close to Mr. Riiska, David?"

"Dave and Huey had a bond, like they were family," Marcus responded.

"Tell me, David," the doctor asked as he started to analyze the sheets up close. "Did Mr. Riiska ever express any form of—spirituality?"

"Not really. Just an attraction to religious imagery," I replied.

"I see, I see," Rubenstein nodded while looking at the underside of the top sheet.

"They couldn't find Huey's body after he was pronounced dead," Marcus stated.

The elderly man slowly lowered the sheet and looked at Marcus with amazement.

"What did you say, Marcus? What was that?"

"Huey's body just—disappeared."

"My word!" Jonah's face turned white. "And…was Mr. Riiska under this very sheet when he disappeared?"

"Yes," my friend replied.

"Why is that significant?" I asked.

"I don't know if it is…yet," the scholar murmured.

He continued to flip the sheet over, from image side to under side.

"The discolorations are superficial. They don't seem to penetrate the cloth. No perceivable powders or pigments. Marcus, would you mind very much if I kept these sheets for a few weeks? I have some friends who participated with the Shroud of Turin Research Project back in seventy-eight. They have the experience and equipment I lack."

"That's why I brought the sheets here, Jonah. So you could get to the bottom of this."

The crowd had dispersed. Marcus, Tamika, and I gathered up Jonah's equipment and helped him pack his sports utility vehicle. The elderly social worker extended his hand to me once again.

"I look forward to working with you, David. I'll see you this Monday."

"Thanks. I look forward to it too."

I lied. My distrust of him nagged at me.

"Marcus, Tamika, as always—thanks for coming to my lecture. I hope to see you next month at Bible study."

"Sure thing, doc. Take care," Marcus smiled.


I was exhausted when I entered my apartment. In the darkness, I saw the blinking red light of my answering machine. I pressed the message button.

A long period of taped silence ensued. Then, "David? Dave, you there?"

It was Jessica.

"David, I was…so shocked to hear that you lost your job. I…still can't believe it. Let's not become strangers, Dave. We've been friends for too long. Please?" I could hear her hold back a sob then she hung up.

It broke my heart to know that I was hurting her, but it was more painful to remain in contact with her. For her safety, my mission in life was to expose Ramsey's crime.

# Chapter 13

▼

# Psychotherapy

Some people handle change well. They marry, join the military, travel the world, go from job to job with ease. I wasn't this type of person. My life needed to feel familiar, otherwise its seams might unravel and I would be lost in an alien realm. Change felt like chaos.

My first week of employment under Jonah Rubenstein went well, all things considered. The man was kind. We got the new employment paperwork out of the way that Monday. He greeted me with a smile each morning thereafter. He allowed me several breaks during my shift. I dutifully typed his notes and downloaded them into his computer. I stored his information on CD-ROM. Most of his notes involved the scholarly defense of conservative Christianity. I felt like adding rebuttals to each of his positions.

The office was tight. My desk, phone, and computer were crammed into a small greeting room. Wood panel walls were adorned with prints. Da Vinci's *Last Supper*. Caravaggio's *Conversion of Saint Paul*. A cross and a plaque with some Bible verse hung over my desk.

I answered the phone and called to verify appointments. Rubenstein's patients were mostly Christians referred by priests and ministers. He counseled couples and adolescents. A few families would come to his office as a group; one even arrived with a shaggy dog in tow. Most people would have felt comfortable in this casual environment, yet I didn't.

I woke up dreading daylight. The sun assaulted me. I despised its cheery glare. Rain felt more natural. Yet that week, the sun ruled, birds chirped. Everything was happy around me, including Jonah. I had no joy. I ate very little, slept less. The only time I didn't despair were the times I burned with rage. Brad Ramsey was going to pay somehow.

How I missed my old life, the belonging I felt at RAI. The work environment that was untouched by Brad Ramsey. Deep down, I knew Jessica and I had zero chance as a couple, yet her flirtatious friendship soothed my lonely heart. Huey was a pleasure to be around. Marcus provided the needed comedy. Now here I was, surrounded by pious Christians with all their trappings. These religious types sickened me with their "God bless yous" and broad smiles. They seemed all doped up on what Karl Marx called the "opiate of the masses."

The doctor was always polite, yet he stood for what I despised. My distrust of him lingered. It was with reservation that I accepted an invitation. A visit with a professor at Yale the following week. The idea of driving him to New Haven was unpleasant, but the mission was worthy. We were going to deliver Huey's sheets to a researcher who participated with the Shroud of Turin Research Project.

Toward the end of my shift that Friday, Jonah called me into his inner sanctum. The room he did most of his counseling. The couch I sat on was plush and cushy. Jonah sat in an easy chair.

"So, David," he began, "how has the job been for you? Are you happy so far?"

"Yes," I lied.

"May I be frank with you?"

"Of course." I tightened. What was this guy going to say?

"I don't think you're doing well. The rings under your eyes appear darker each day. You are noticeably thinner. Is something bothering you? Are you ill?"

"No. I'm not ill."

"Then you are stressed?"

"No more than usual, Mr. Rubenstein."

"Remember, David, call me Jonah. My father was 'Mr. Rubenstein.' You're making me feel ancient!"

"Oh. Sorry."

"Is there anything you'd like to get off your chest? I'm a professional listener, you know."

"No. Thanks for the offer, but no."

Jonah sat back into his chair.

"If you are worried that I'm going to quote Bible verses at you and get you to pray, you can relax. I have counseled many non-Christians in my day."

"No, it's not that."

"Oh?"

"It's just that I'm a very private person, that's all."

"I see! Would you call yourself a loner?"

"I guess."

"Yet you are friends with Marcus and Tamika, correct?"

"With Marcus, yes."

With that answer, Rubenstein erupted into a belly laugh.

"I take it that Tamika's assertiveness doesn't agree with you?"

"No," I smiled. "It doesn't."

"Don't worry, most who know Tamika have to adjust to her personality. Once she called me 'girlfriend.' 'What is this?' I asked. 'Are you questioning my gender?' She hit me in the arm and told me it was just an expression."

I laughed. The first laugh I had all week.

"And does she ever crush you in a bear hug?" I asked.

"Ahh, don't even mention the bear hugs. The pain. The horror."

I laughed some more.

"Yet," Jonah continued, "When one gets beneath her Mike Tyson demeanor, one finds a heart of gold."

"Perhaps you're right…Mister…ahh, Jonah. Still, she's always accusing me of something. I'm supposedly not a Christian because there's a sin I can't give up. My prayer wasn't answered because I prayed with self-interest. I don't like being accused of being sinful or selfish."

"She said those things to you? This combative and superior attitude of hers is the sole reason why I didn't hire her sister for the job you currently hold. She and her sister are identical in demeanor."

"Her sister wanted this job?"

"After I told Tamika I was thinking about firing my receptionist, she had expressed interest on her sister's behalf…yes."

"Wow! She wasn't angry after you gave it to me…right in front of her and Marcus?"

"Yes, she has since expressed some anger. She'll eventually let it go."

"For your sake, I hope so!"

"I am sure of it," the elderly gent nodded. "Now, what's this about an unanswered prayer?"

"Oh. Did I mention that?"

"Yes."

"Well, let's just say I took Tamika up on a challenge. Her side lost."

"Did you pray for your friend Huey?"

I hesitated. How did this guy guess that?

"Well, yes. I did."

"I see. Huey died, even though you prayed for his healing."

"Not exactly."

"No?"

"Huey was being abused. I prayed for the truth to be revealed during an inquiry."

"Abused? Oh my, that's dreadful. I have counseled many former residents of mental health institutions. Oh, the abuse those poor folks endured, at the hands of the so-called healthy."

"Especially those who were most helpless, right doctor?"

"Yes, especially those. Oh my…you don't suppose Mr. Riiska's death had anything to do with the abuse you speak of, do you?"

"Well, technically…Huey's death was caused by a grand mal seizure. Behind it all, a man was sodomizing Huey with his religious figurines for more than a month. The man who did these things admitted it to my face. That sort of stress wouldn't help Huey's general health, would it?"

"Mr. Riiska was being…sodomized with his religious icons?"

"Yes."

"*My word!* You are certain of this?"

"Yes I am."

Jonah removed his glasses and wiped his eyes. The man actually teared up. He cleared his throat.

"And, you mentioned to me that Mr. Riiska, in his limited way, was a Catholic believer. Am I correct?"

"Uh…yeah, I suppose. He certainly was fascinated with the trappings."

"Oh, the shame the man must have felt. He was a vessel for blasphemy."

"I don't know, doctor. I'm sure he felt violated. Felt hurt. But I doubt Huey would have concerned himself with the abstract concept of blasphemy and such."

"Yet he was attracted to icons? Shrines and the like?"

"Yes, that is undeniable."

Jonah's brow furrowed. He actually looked angry.

"And who is this monster who admitted to performing such vile acts?"

"Blabbing his name is the very thing that got me fired, Jonah."

"Between the two of us, David. Who is this man?"

"Brad Ramsey, an RAI manager at a Torrington group home."

"Brad…Ramsey?"

"That's right."

"Is he the son of the late Julius Ramsey, the media mogul? The publisher of *Truth* magazine? I know Julius was from Torrington, originally."

"I don't know. Brad mentioned being the heir to some family fortune. Wait…yeah! Brad did mention a family-owned magazine. What is *Truth* magazine?"

"The magazine was discontinued when you were but a young child. But from the forties through the early sixties, *Truth* magazine was popular. It was considered avant-garde, a champion of freedom. A forum for trendy artists. It was slanted toward attacking traditional values. It was liberal long before liberalism became popular in the west. Ramsey was even investigated by Joseph McCarthy for one particular article that sympathized with Marxism."

"Really! What became of that?"

"Not much. McCarthy was hoping to learn about possible Soviet spies Ramsey knew. He wasn't interested in Ramsey and the magazine itself. Certain groups boycotted the magazine, certain stores wouldn't carry it. Yet it continued to thrive through the turbulent sixties."

"How about that!" I exclaimed. "Why did it fold?"

"It didn't fold. Julius Ramsey claimed he converted to Christianity and no longer embraced the views the magazine promoted. He discontinued the publication himself. He remained a radical though—just under a different banner."

"Hmm."

"Rumor has it that Julius learned his wife had a back alley abortion when she was dating him in high school. He murdered her and the media covered his trial with zeal. Julius' own explanation for the murder was 'an eye for an eye.'"

"This all took place where?"

"In New York City, where I lived most of my life."

"If Brad is the son of this Julius, I suppose that would partially explain his criminality."

"Especially if this Brad is excited by the desecration of Christian symbols."

"Not only that, doctor! He is the leader of some club that meets weekly to discuss the errors of organized religion. Wait, club isn't a good enough word. Let's just say that the shepherd Brad has a flock of his own."

"I see," Rubenstein nodded.

"Brad Ramsey is a charismatic person. He controls people. Other than being good looking, I really don't know how he does it."

"Controls people? In what way?"

"Well, people look to him as a guide. An oracle."

"Indeed? A man with a vile need to abuse the helpless? You must be exaggerating. Most people can sense that type of evil."

"Jonah," I said while leaning forward. "If that were true, I wouldn't be here right now. I presented an inquiry with Brad's own words, with indirect evidences. RAI administrators wouldn't have anything to do with it. Even a woman I was very close to didn't believe me."

"Oh? Was this a woman you had a romantic relationship with?"

"Not really. We were close friends. I was…am…in love with her, but that's neither here or there."

"On the contrary, your feelings aren't irrelevant. They are valid!"

"Psshh! If they were valid, they wouldn't be so contrary to reality."

"David, feelings are neither right nor wrong. They just are."

"'Nobody knows the trouble I see, Doc."

"You know what, David? I'll grant you that. Your friend died. His abuser was believed over you. The woman you love doesn't believe you. I knew you were carrying a heavy burden this week."

"How about adding this straw to the camel's back? This woman I care for is most likely in love with Brad."

"*My!* David, you may not know this, but you are a strong person."

"Not me. I even had a panic attack a few weeks back."

"Take my word as a mental health professional. Having a panic attack is not a sign of weakness. All people, when stressed to a certain degree, react the same way. Strength comes from journeying through these experiences, not from avoiding them."

"That's all fine, doc. Still…I'm a shell. My porch light's on, but nobody's home."

"No, David, you're not a shell. Your mind is coping the best way it knows how. More about this in a minute. Concerning Brad Ramsey, I have a few more questions."

"Uh, okay. Shoot."

"Does this man ever seem to change while you're in his company? His mannerisms? His appearance?"

"Funny you should mention that! One moment, he's this sophisticated GQ man, and the next…he's like an animal in a bear trap."

"Intriguing."

"Do you think he's schizophrenic, doctor?"

"I don't know. Does Ramsey do anything else out of the ordinary?"

"Hmm."

"Does he seem to know things—facts that he would have no access to?"

"Oh, wait a minute. Yeah! Now that you mention it, he once told me when a friend was going to call later that evening. To the minute! Another time, he knew what I had hidden in my locked car. He had no way of knowing these things."

"Uh-huh. I see."

"That's an odd inquiry to make, Jonah. Where are you going with this?"

"It's way out there, something you would have trouble believing."

"Just as well you keep it to yourself then," I snickered.

"Is there a possibility that I could meet this man?"

"I wouldn't recommend it. This guy is dangerous."

"I'm a big boy, David. But thanks for the warning. As far as danger goes, you're talking to someone who has spent much time in the Middle East."

"Touché."

"Would Mr. Ramsey be receptive to a public debate?"

"Public?"

"Yes. I have a discussion show on community access television each week. It's called *Christian Café*. Usually, it involves the discussion of social issues. Just local community leaders and clergy. If Mr. Ramsey leads a group discussion of his own, it may be the type of forum he'd be attracted to."

"Jonah, his group is only about twelve people."

"Twelve? Like in twelve apostles?"

"Bingo."

"Well, twelve is a decent following here in northwest Connecticut. An Episcopal minister friend has about twelve regular parishioners. My television show has a viewership of about twelve, I'm sure."

I laughed. "Anyway, Jonah, I'm sure he'd love to publicly challenge you. You can reach him at this Elm Street group home phone number."

I quickly scribbled the number on some notepaper.

"Just do me a favor, Jonah. Tell him you heard of his club incidentally. Don't mention my name."

"I didn't plan to," the doctor winked. "Now, back to more important things—your stress. I can provide you with some stress relieving exercises and suggest a few other things."

"That's okay. I'll be fine," I replied. I had no intention of sharing any of this stuff with Jonah, and here he had me spilling my guts. This guy was good.

"Okay. But keep in mind, I've helped many people through broken hearts. Through mourning. I'm here for you. Anytime you need to share, vent, and talk—I'm here."

"That's very kind of you doctor, but I'll survive. I've been on my own my whole life; I know how to rely on myself. I need no one else."

"Hopefully, you'll do more than survive, David. I want you to live well."

"Please. How many people actually live well?"

"Admittedly, not many. Now, you say you've been on your own all of your life...don't you have any close relatives?"

"Nope. I grew up an orphan."

Rubenstein looked as if he was going to tear up again.

"Hey now, doc. Don't worry. I grew up streetwise. There's a silver lining here. No one pulls the wool over my eyes, which is probably why Brad couldn't con me like everyone else."

"That, plus the fact that Ramsey revealed his sinister side to you. Curious...why only you?"

"Everyone else makes excuses for him. They say he has an inappropriate sense of humor."

"I see," Jonah nodded. He walked over to his desk and pulled a few papers and pamphlets from the top drawer. He handed them to me.

"Now, concerning your depression, David. These are stress reducing exercises and techniques. Tips for better sleep. And if you experience anxiety attacks again, one technique called masterly inactivity is quite effective. You'll find it detailed in one of these pamphlets. If your symptoms worsen, please, tell me about them."

My mouth really dug a hole for myself this time. Jonah was now my therapist, whether I liked it or not. Still, I needed to talk. To get things off my chest. It felt good.

# CHAPTER 14

▼

# SHROUD OF TURIN, 101

I managed to get some quality sleep that weekend. I was still trapped within a cloud of despair, but the relaxation exercises Dr. Rubenstein gave me did help. As much as I hated myself for spilling my guts, the rap session had a lightening effect. A hundred-pound burden became a fifty-pound burden. I still had dreams that involved Huey, Jessica, and Brad, but I managed to cope.

Marcus called to see how my first week with Jonah went. I kept upbeat. I didn't tell him how being around so many devout Christians sickened me. My friend wasn't like the Christian stereotype I held—he was actually fun to be with. As real as his faith was, he didn't inflict people with chapter and verse quotations and prayer demonstrations. Tamika, on the other hand, represented all the pious behavior that annoyed me.

Marcus said that Jess was asking about me. I felt a temptation to call her. Whenever the thought crossed my mind, a sudden image of Brad Ramsey shot into my head. That was enough to end all temptation.

I told my friend about the Monday trip to Yale. That excited him, to know how Huey's sheets would be given scholarly attention. I was wary. I told Marcus I believed the Shroud of Turin Research Project wasn't a feather for any scholar's cap. The findings of the 1988 carbon dating proved their conclusion wrong—the conclusion that the Shroud was not a painting or man-made relic. Even the Vatican accepted the dating. The Shroud would be honored as a medieval depiction of Christ's passion—nothing more.

I told my friend about Jonah's idea of debating Ramsey on community television. He squealed with delight. He was certain that Jonah would bury Brad in an avalanche of logic. I was divided. I loathed Ramsey, and was starting to like Jonah. Still, I agreed with Brad and disagreed with Jonah concerning Christian belief. It was a bizarre conflict.

Monday morning came. I felt fairly refreshed, having slept a good deal that weekend. I was calmer. The doctor greeted me with his customary cheer.

"Good morning, David! You're looking better this morning!"

"Those relaxation techniques helped."

"Glad to hear it. My docket is clear today and New Haven is a two-hour drive. Shall we get going?"

"Sure thing. Your car or mine?"

"We'll take my SUV. The traffic on I-84 and I-91 seems to respect the size of one's vehicle."

After a few tasks, we were on the road. Jonah didn't drive like an elderly man. He sped down the highway weaving through traffic with precision. Heading south on Route 8, the traffic became steadily thicker. At the junction of I-84, construction had closed all but one lane. The bottleneck slowed everyone to a crawl. Jonah and I sat in silence. The doctor took the opportunity to inform me of his friend and the relic he studied.

"Are you at all familiar with Dr. Boyington's work? He is a prominent biochemist who was recently featured in *The New England Journal of Medicine*."

"I'm not a scholar, or one who reads medical journals," I laughed.

"Well, his work on protein crystallization is ground breaking."

"If the guy is at Yale, I knew he'd have some prominence. Still, was he one of those nutty Shroud of Turin Research Project advocates who were promoting the relic's probable authenticity?"

"Yes, he was. And is. And you can refer to the project as STURP, Dave. It's easier on the tongue."

"Hmm. He was…and is…a shroud advocate? That must be embarrassing for him professionally."

"Why is that, David?"

"Well, you know. The carbon dating shot their work out of the water."

"Ahh, I see! You must have read the *Hartford Courant*, back in eighty-eight."

"The *Hartford Courant*?"

"Yes. It proclaimed, along with most of the news media, that the Shroud of Turin was proven to be a medieval forgery. In headlines!"

"Wasn't that true?"

"No, David. That conclusion was far from true."

"Are you just saying that because you are a Christian apologist?"

"Not at all. Some non-Christian scholars still favor authenticity. Yes, even now, after the dating fiasco. The carbon dating was far from definitive."

"From what I remember, three different universities tested Shroud samples, and all three came up with the same medieval date range. What could be more definitive?"

"It's not that simple. First, the test was horribly mishandled and second, a multitude of external variables are casting legitimate doubts on the dating."

"How was the dating mishandled?"

"You want to hear about this? It can be dry and technical. As a matter of fact, I can first summarize most of the Shroud controversy for you, then address the dating issue."

"I'm game. Especially since your radio is broken."

"I'm more interesting than Howard Stern, young man. First of all, STURP was a gathering of agnostics, atheists, Jews, and Protestants—only a couple identified themselves as Catholic. The majority of them weren't religious. They were simply researchers intrigued by a mystery and challenged to solve it.

"When STURP announced the results of their nineteen seventy-eight study, they held a press conference here in New London, Connecticut. Reporters wanted a comment to sensationalize; a definitive yea or nay as to whether the Shroud was that of Jesus of Nazareth. As professional scientists, they didn't make any sensational claims. Team leader Ray Rogers told the gathering that science had no 'test' for Jesus. They were there to present their findings—not confirm or deny authenticity.

"When they proclaimed the Shroud image was a surface dehydration of the linen—not a painting, powder rubbing or scorch—no one was prepared to deal with the implications. Obviously, nowhere in human history has any other relic or artwork exhibited a surface dehydration image with three-dimensional characteristics and accurate forensic information. It's unprecedented! Even with modern technology, researchers struggle to imitate its delicate image. Keep in mind, the Turin linen is at least six hundred years old!"

"So, Jonah, why isn't there a scholarly consensus concerning the relic? They certainly studied it enough."

"Well, the Shroud is the subject of many theories, books, and allegations. It rivals the JFK assassination at times. STURP were comprehensive, considering their marathon session with the Shroud. They collected fiber samples lifted off the linen by Mylar tape. One researcher, and an eventual Shroud debunker, was given the entire collection to study. The critic took the tape samples, sealed them sticky-side down on microscope slides, and covered them with glass cover slips. He then identified random paint and iron oxide particles on the tape samples.

"Another Shroud researcher wrote of how he begged the critic to send some tape samples. His job was to verify if actual blood was on the linen. The critic was aloof. An academic tug of war ensued. STURP eventually identified the blood particles as real, through studies such as microspectrophotometric scans, reflective scans, hemochromogen and cyanomethemoglobin tests, bile pigment tests, protein tests, albumin tests, protease tests, and immunological tests for human albumin."

"Whoa, Jonah! Those are some million dollar words there."

"Yeah," Jonah laughed. "Just don't ask me to describe the science behind the terms. I memorized the names, just to answer critical questions at my lectures."

"I see."

The traffic started to proceed more quickly. Another lane had opened up and within a few minutes we were moving fast again. The task of driving the busy interstate didn't distract Jonah from his conversation.

"Anyway, to get back to my main point," Jonah continued. "The Shroud critic was unimpressed with STURP's findings. The debunker went on to say that the Shroud image was created by iron oxide, either in powder form or suspended in a gelatin base. He concluded that the Shroud blood was vermilion paint. His suspected paint particles were observed to be birefringent, meaning that they were capable of splitting a light wave in two directions. Unfortunately, Mylar tape makes all particles stuck to it appear birefringent, a fact reportedly unacknowledged by the critic. Science is dependent on various control information. More often than not, these controls come from peers with whom an individual can either heed or dismiss. The rebuttal of other team members was disregarded by the skeptic."

"Hmm. I can buy that. It reminds me of when I presented my case against Brad Ramsey. Ramsey and the company president portrayed me as an agenda-driven lunatic."

"That's the modus operandi for dismissing unwanted information. One dismisses the person or people delivering it."

"Okay, Jonah. We're in agreement on that. But can you dismiss the paint theory without dismissing the critic personally?"

"STURP did just that. They reported that what the debunker visually discovered is authentic, but his interpretation of the evidence is in error."

"In error? Did they prove that through scientific methodology?"

"Yes. Let's see…the critic claimed that an 'Amido Black' test proved a gelatin protein was on the image fibers. Amido Black was an inappropriate test to use because it reportedly stains oxidized cellulose fibers whether they possess protein or not! STURP researchers used the more sensitive Biuret-Lowry test to look for such protein, but didn't find it. Ultraviolet florescence studies, proteolytic enzyme tests, and fluorescamine tests reinforced these results. All concurred—no gelatin protein on the Shroud.

"STURP uncovered the fact that linen fibers act as an iron exchanger during the 'rhetting' process of manufacture. The linen absorbs calcium, strontium, and iron from the water. These very particles are spread evenly over the entire surface of the Shroud without concentration in the image area. The critic did note the real presence of iron and the like, but seemed to misinterpret its reason for being present on the cloth. It was also found that the iron oxide particles were too chemically pure to be from paint. They were most likely the result of rhetting. Other iron rich particles flaked off the bloodstains and were scattered throughout the Shroud due to its repeated foldings.

"The detractor claimed to find nine particles of vermilion paint on the Mylar samples. STURP later found only one. Neither one nor nine particles of vermilion are of sufficient concentration to create any image. Odd particles are all over the linen, even pink nylon! The Shroud was in medieval artist studios, and devout copyists would press their finished work on the linen as a 'blessing.'

"STURP confirmed that the straw yellow fibers of the body image were caused by 'conjugated carbonyl,' the end result of dehydration, of acid oxidation.

"Also, the painting theory contradicts itself. For example, some claim that the DNA and blood type indicators found in the Shroud's bloodstains couldn't have survived the intense heat of the fifteen thirty-two fire. This is the fire that melted parts of the silver casket that held the linen and caused the lateral burn holes and scorch strips running down each side of the Shroud. Yet they maintain that a gelatin based powder painting survived intense heat, flame and water unaltered? That's one magic painting!

"Personally, David, I trust the forty STURP scientists and their direct access findings more than a couple of critics. Skeptics who merely studied the Mylar tape fiber samples."

I was at a loss. This guy was a true Shroudie, to be sure. I didn't have enough research on the topic to debate his view. This didn't stop me from trying.

"Come on Jonah. If paint didn't create the image, what did?"

"One theory has the image formation occurring through strict vertical motion due to a type of radiation. Some energy field created the image. If direct body contact created the image, the sides of the face, arms, and body would be widened like a fun house mirror. If heat or vapor created the image, diffusion factors would prevent the focused and detailed imaging found on the Shroud. Another compelling fact is that no image fibers were found underneath the bloodstains. The bloodstains were on the cloth before the image! Very illogical, if the image is a forgery. Very logical, if the leftover, postmortem blood oozed from a corpse before the image was imprinted. The image shows no signs of bodily decomposition.

"Certain anatomical and forensic features also convince me of the Shroud's authenticity. The anatomy demonstrates foreshortening that wasn't utilized in medieval art. Nor did medieval depictions of the crucified Christ include nail wounds in the wrist, nudity, hair gathered in a ponytail or crown of thorn wounds in the shape of a cap rather than a wreath. The scourging wounds are also tragically compelling. There are numerous welts, lacerations, and blisters made by dumbbell-shaped pellets at the tips of a Roman flagellum. Some scars oozed a clear serum border. The wounds occur at two different angles. The scourger on the right side of the victim was of a different height than the one at his left. It is evident that two different men whipped the victim.

"The side wound is stained by postmortem fluid, a combination of serum and blood. The Gospel according to John refers to the flow as blood and water. The wound oozes toward the victim's back and pools across the small of his back. It's a medical reality that those who die torturous deaths will continue to ooze through their wounds postmortem. The bloodstains are redder than normal, causing critics to dismiss them as paint. Actually, the blood contains high amounts of bilirubin, which binds with hemolyzed hemoglobin in the liver of those enduring torture. This would redden the blood. Another prominent bloodstain is on the victim's forehead. It assumes the shape of a three. There's even a physiological reason for this! The three stain gathers in the recesses of a furrowed brow with precision. The blood thickened and clotted in that position."

"Jonah, I always believed that the Jews washed their dead and anointed them for burial."

"Good point. Apparently, certain deaths could supersede this, according to some ancient Jewish writings. A violent and torturous death was a special circumstance and all the blood had to be gathered—as much as possible, anyway—for a proper burial. The blood was to be interred with the body, in hopes that the final resurrection of God's faithful would restore it all within the corpse. The Shroud man was probably washed, in regard to most of the blood. The traumatized corpse would continue to ooze through the wounds.

"Yet hypothetically, let's say they wanted to fully prepare Jesus for burial. Joseph of Arimathea received permission from Pilate to spare Jesus the common grave, where Roman victims had their remains openly consumed by dogs and carrion crows. He arranged the rare honor of burial for a culturally disgraced crucified person. But sunset was fast approaching. The festival Sabbath was to begin at nightfall. So Jesus' burial *was* incomplete. The women arriving to the tomb that Sunday had ointments and spices to complete Jesus' interment ritual."

"Okay, but weren't Jews routinely wrapped in strips of cloth?"

"Not necessarily. John's Gospel speaks of burial clothes that bound the body, indicating that there was more than one long cloth. Yet a jaw band, a wristband, an ankle band, and a face napkin used prior to burial may all account for the multiple linens that John alludes to. Even if mummy style was the norm, we're still referring to an incomplete, partial burial with Jesus. Mark's and Luke's accounts allude to the fact that the women visiting Jesus' tomb that Sunday were there with a purpose—to assist with the completion of Jesus' burial. They brought ointments and spices.

"A few more things link the Shroud of Turin with the gospel narrative. The long Turin Shroud had a rare weave—three to one herringbone. It was linen of high quality. One the reportedly wealthy and influential Joseph of Arimathea could afford. This could explain how and why a crucified prisoner—disgraced by the hanging on a tree, being that the tree symbolized man's fall in the garden of Eden—could and would be wrapped in fine, expensive linen! This man on the Shroud had a few friends in high places. Similar, high quality fabrics have been excavated with the same invisible seaming that the Shroud has. Specifically, they were excavated at the first century Jewish site, Masada. Textile expert Gilbert Raes has stated that the Shroud's herringbone twill was a pattern very common to the Middle East in the first century.

"The anatomy of the Shroud image is horribly compelling. The shoulders look as if the arms were forced down from their elevated posture. The chest is tense with rigor mortis. The stomach is distended. The face, nose, shoulders, and knees appear to be swollen, consistent with the reported beatings Jesus endured. Some beard hair may have been pulled out, also consistent with the gospel accounts. Yet amid all the gore, pain, and humiliation one finds on the Shroud image, the face has an odd look of peace.

"A VP-8 analysis of the face, a computerized three-dimensional relief, showed what appeared to be pottery shards or coins on the image's eyes. Or very swollen eyelids. Further still, some believe they can make out a few letters and a staff on one coin, conforming to a Pontius Pilate lepton circulating during the time of Jesus.

"Others say the coarse nature of the linen couldn't contain the resolution needed for this fine detail. I am undecided about this issue. Likewise, faint outlines of a sponge, a spear, flowers, and so on have been analyzed on the linen. These too are in question. Hypothetically, Jesus' followers would have wanted to bury all items that were available and stained with his blood."

"Man, it's a wonder you Shroudies haven't found a profile of Elvis on that cloth."

Jonah erupted in a belly laugh. "Good one, David! Yes, very good! Amazingly, the Shroud also has cotton traces found within its weave identified as Gossypium Herbaceum. This cotton makes it likely that the Shroud's place of manufacture was the Middle East. Also significant is the fact that no wool traces were detected in the Shroud, conforming to the Judaic regulation against mixing linen and wool found in Deuteronomy, Leviticus, and the Mishnah.

"Spectrographic chemical analysis done on dust particles collected on the Shroud's backside identifies them as travertine aragonite calcium, uncommon limestone found exclusively within Jerusalem's caves and tombs. Certain pollen samples found on the Shroud come from plants native to Palestine and Jerusalem, and even more specifically, these pollens were active in springtime! Other pollens trace the Shroud's movements through Turkey and much of Europe, following a trail of legend and art history. It is probable that the Shroud was once folded to reveal only its face, and that European murals, icons, and coins started to copy its unique features in the sixth century. Prior to the sixth century, Jesus was depicted in Roman style, beardless and resembling the god Apollo.

"The Shroud is fourteen feet, three inches by three feet, seven inches. At first analysis, its measurements are arbitrary. Yet the ancient Israeli method of measurement would have the Shroud measuring eight by two cubits.

"Also of interest is the relic called 'the Sudarium of Oviedo,' a cloth with a traceable history back to the eighth century. The towel-size cloth has a massive, postmortem blood flow. The bloodstains indicate the dimensions of a face similar to the man on the Shroud, with a similar beard. The stain is also type AB. Many believe that this cloth was draped over Jesus' head when he was removed from the cross and carried to Joseph of Arimathea's tomb. The cloth would have been buried next to him, in the spirit of preserving the victim's blood."

"Man, you're a machine gun of Shroud facts, aren't you, Jonah? This is really bizarre. STURP must have used faulty science. The carbon dating is rather definitive, isn't it?"

"Ahh yes, my opinion about the 1988 dating. A spokesman for that test would publish his approval concerning the exclusion of STURP scholars with the dating. As with skeptics today, many saw STURP as a team of forty zealous Christians who set out to validate the Shroud as a real Christian relic, even though most STURP researchers concluded that they didn't know whether the Shroud was legitimate. They just knew they couldn't disprove the Shroud's claim to authenticity.

"The dating sample was taken from a poor site, a darkened corner of the linen. If only STURP researchers had a say as to which location the one sample would be taken from! Some researchers chosen for the testing seemed embarrassingly unfamiliar with the Shroud. Thus, they settled for an inappropriate site to test.

"A corner that was discolored and charred from heat—and water-stained— possibly from the fire of fifteen thirty-two. A corner shown to have medieval reweave near and possibly within the sample area. A corner that was handled by countless human hands, as the etchings of past Shroud exhibitions demonstrates. A corner with multiple contaminants, as certain STURP scientists would later point out. A few STURP affiliates conducted an unofficial carbon dating of a single thread from the Shroud. One end of the thread dated to two hundred AD, the other end dated to one thousand AD. This was evidence of contamination, involving single thread reweaves, or other external factors like starch or bacteria growth.

"One STURP researcher did a microspectrophotometry test of the area that was dated and he determined that the sample had a gross enrichment of inorganic mineral elements. The sample was an exaggerated composite of water stain and scorch fibers. Both factors can alter the carbon content of linen.

"Furthermore, I sigh at how many individuals believe that the nineteen eighty-eight dating of the Shroud was its death nail. As if the test was infallible, definitive, and all other research is irrelevant. Well, carbon dating is far from the perfect method most believe it is. In *New Scientist,* in 1989, Britain's Science and Engineering Research Council put the accuracy of carbon dating to the test. They had thirty-eight different dating labs test artifact samples of known age and origin. Of the thirty-eight, only seven produced satisfactory conclusions and measurements! One university with its famous Accelerator Mass Spectrometry method that it had used just a year before on the Shroud, failed its test."

"Wow. You sure take this all seriously."

"As it should be taken, David. Seriously. This relic could be the most significant revelation of all time, forcing humanity to merge the supernatural, religion, and science into one observable phenomenon. When religion and science debate issues like evolution versus creationism, it's impossible for anyone to step into a time machine and prove one view once and for all. They can appeal to clues within geology, paleontology, genetics, even scripture, but they cannot definitively end the controversy. With the Shroud, a time machine isn't needed."

"No, Jonah, it's not. Three universities dated the Shroud to medieval times."

"David, it's unfortunate that the original protocols for dating the Shroud weren't followed. The dating was compromised. One early protocol was the need for various samples to be tested from different locations of the cloth. Seven was the proposed number, for samples and sample sites. This was horribly reduced to three samples, from one sample site. One reason for their limited test was to preserve the cloth. Did they accomplish even this? No. They ended up extracting seventy-five milligrams more than what was needed for the seven lab protocol.

"Another protocol abandoned was the need for a blind test. Researchers at each lab would not know which samples were control samples and which samples were from the Shroud. Unfortunately, the control samples had different weave patterns than the Shroud. Researchers also sent the labs certificates identifying the dates of the control samples! This not needed information could help the labs identify which sample was from where and possibly bias any findings.

"After the three labs finished their dating procedures, certain people involved in the project leaked the results to the British press. This violated their agreement to first inform the Vatican, then release their findings at an organized venue. The researcher's anti-authenticity bias also showed itself at their official press conference. Organizers wrote the dates 1260-1390 with an exclamation mark on the blackboard behind their seats. It was a supposedly definitive conclusion to the Shroud's mystery. All other evidence, all other studies were now deemed irrelevant.

"STURP scholars were shunned. Protocol after protocol was dumped. Agreements of conduct were ignored. Sorry, Dave, I remain thoroughly unimpressed with the 1988 carbon dating."

"Gawd, Jonah. Let's not beat around the bush anymore. What exactly do you believe the Shroud of Turin represents?"

"Ahem, okay. Point blank. My opinion only, not proven science. I believe the Shroud image was created by a quantum level event. Some form of holographic, biophysical radiation encompassed and dematerialized a crucifixion victim. That victim was Jesus of Nazareth, Lord Messiah. When he appeared resurrected to his followers, he was reported to materialize and dematerialize at will. Yet he was solid enough for them to touch."

"Jonah, beam me up! Are you serious? You're an educated man!"

"Thank you, David. And as an educated man, I believe the uncovered facts fit this scenario.

"Fact one: The image is distance sensitive. More linen fibrils at the tip of the victim's nose were dehydrated than linen fibrils near his right cheek, and so on. It's mathematical—the number of image pixels correlates to how far the cloth was from his body. Also, the hands and head appear to have x-ray image qualities, suggesting a release of radiation. Some researchers believe in a collapse theory—that the linen fell through the energy of the dematerialized body. The distance sensitivity and x-ray features make sense with such a scenario.

"Fact two: Only the very top linen fibrils are affected. This type of subtlety probably came from an energy field. An energy with vertical directionality.

"Fact three: The bloodstains soak through, yet remain unsmeared and unbroken. They are perfect exudate bloodstains with separate serum borders. Obviously, the sheet was removed from the body before decomposition set in, but after the blood and fluid that caused the stains completely dried or disappeared.

"Fact four: This type of flash radiation could account for the outlines of objects buried with the victim and seen on the image. Suspected objects such as flowers, coins on the eyes, a phylactery, a spearhead, a sponge, and a crown of thorns. This fact is a bit more subjective than the first three. The jury is out concerning these burial objects."

"Jonah, this is like science fiction!"

"No, I consider it more like science theory. Researchers have long believed that quantum level energies make the universe cohesive. Some have called the universe a quantum hologram. I'm not a physics expert, so forgive my simplifications here. I do know how this ties in with scripture. The Transfiguration account describes Jesus as turning radiant and white. The apostle Paul was converted when he saw a vision of Christ as a radiant light from heaven. The Old Testament describes the energy of God's presence as the Shekinah, a light, cloud or fire from heaven. Even those with modern near death experiences speak of a brilliant light that they associate with God and love. I believe the Shekinah itself imprinted the Shroud of Turin, just as light imprints a sensitive frame of film."

This guy was making sense. This scared me. I tried to find logical objections.

"But your own Bible makes no mention of a shroud image."

"This is true. Jesus' burial clothes are left behind and they impress the disciples Peter and John. How they impress them is not clear. It could be that the disciples, overcoming their Judaic objection to burial corruption, gathered his clothes as an act of reverence. After all, no physical decomposition occurred here, and not one of them would consider bloodstains left by their master to be unclean.

Quite the opposite. Some believe that the Shroud is the source of the Holy Grail legend. Others believe it became known as the image of Edessa, or Veronica's veil."

"Okaayy," I smiled. "What about Huey? Are you saying that he is—Jesus?"

"Of course not. It may not be as similar to the Turin Shroud as I suspect. But if it is, I believe your friend is a member of a very select club. The club of translated saints."

"Translated saints?"

"Yes. The Old Testament prophet Elijah is an example. He was brought to heaven in physical form, in a fiery chariot. Catholics and some Protestants believe that Jesus' mother was translated into heaven in physical form, an event they call the 'assumption.' These saints, now existing in both spiritual and physical bodies, were transformed by God. Protestant scholars call this being 'translated,' something Paul alluded to implying that God's people would be changed in a flash. Some call this the Rapture. In any event, God himself would transform these people and his power may manifest at a quantum level—as it did with the Messiah Jesus. Jesus was called the 'first fruits' of the final resurrection, where all of God's faithful will be given incorruptible bodies."

I sat dumbfounded. Apparently, grown men can believe in fairy tales. Even those with academic prestige. As I-91 unfolded before us, New Haven came into view. Our destination was a welcome sight. This conversation was giving me a headache.

# CHAPTER 15

▼

# THE ANALYSIS

Ironically, Dr. Boyington was a boyish man. He had youthful features. Large glasses dominated his face. The man gave the impression of intelligence personified.

Jonah and I sat in his office, waiting for the doctor to return from an errand. The room was efficient. All hardcovers on his bookshelves were lined up. Not one edition leaned or laid flat. His plants were watered, his goldfish tank was clean. It didn't take Sherlock Holmes to notice the man's attention to detail. His perfectionism was obvious.

My elderly companion held Huey's two bedsheets with obvious anxiety, his hands and feet fidgeting in anticipation. After about three minutes, I grabbed Rubenstein's right foot, crossed over his left knee. It's quick up and down movements became too much to bear.

"Sorry about that, David," he smiled.

"That's okay. Your fidgeting wouldn't bother me so much, if my head wasn't splitting in half from that Shroud conversation."

Jonah laughed. "Brace yourself, what we find with this sheet may compound your misery."

"Oh joy. Say, where is your buddy anyway? He said he would be with us in ten minutes."

"Ray's a busy man. He'll be back. He's just as anxious to explore this sheet as I am."

"God save us from Shroudies," I murmured.

"I see you're praying more every day, my agnostic friend," Jonah chuckled.

"Just a figure of speech."

"Ahh. A figure of speech. My focus is on a 'figure of sheet.'"

I turned toward Jonah who had a wry smile on his face. "Jonah! That is probably the most corny, most pathetic attempt at humor I've ever heard!" I wheezed out through laughter.

"Pathetic? Perhaps. But look at you laugh."

"I'm an easy audience. Don't book any HBO comedy specials."

On that note, the door to Boyington's office swung open.

"Sorry for the wait," the scientist offered. "Would you two accompany me to lab thirty-two, down the hall?"

Jonah jumped to his feet like a coiled spring. The two of us dutifully followed the white coat into a small and cluttered lab. Several tables were adorned with microscopes and test tubes.

As we entered, Boyington offered Jonah four thumbtacks.

"Please mount the sheet with the frontal image on the wall, Jonah. Let's have a look-see."

My friend did as he was asked. Boyington stood for a few moments, then slowly backed up to the far end of the lab.

"Remarkable!" he exclaimed. "Just as with the Turin Shroud, the image is only visibly discernible from several feet away. A faint, sepia image!"

Jonah handed him some photographs.

"As with the Turin Shroud, it's a true photographic negative. More details and features can be seen with the negative image of the sheet, transforming the imprint into a white positive," Jonah told his friend.

"Amazing. Did you test for the distance sensitive quality?"

"Yes. My PC was able to render the image into a low relief, just as with the Turin Shroud. The nose rises higher than the cheeks, the chest rises higher than the throat, et cetera."

"Impressive. Are some image fibers darker, or does the number of fiber pixels determine image intensity?"

"It's the number of fiber pixels."

Boyington then walked up close to the sheet and looked intensely at the image area.

"How deep does the image penetrate?"

"No more than two fibrils, and with these fibrils, only their crest is discolored."

The scientist shook his head and then offered Jonah his hand.

"Congratulations! You've done it! No one has been able to replicate all of those Turin Shroud features, only a few at the most. How did you do it?"

"Excuse me?" Jonah responded.

"C'mon, old friend! How did you make this?"

"I didn't."

"Jonah, Jonah," Boyington shook his head. "Here you've obviously found the 'Rosetta Stone' of Shroud research. You know the secret! What method did you use to create this?"

I spoke up. "Dr. Boyington, Jonah has nothing to do with this sheet, or where it came from. My friend and I brought it to him."

"Okay, Mr. Paul. How did you and your friend create this?"

"We didn't. Neither of us is into that Shroud of Turin mystery, and wouldn't even be able to list those relic features as you just had. This sheet is the last clue for me regarding the disappearance of my friend's body."

"Your friend's body?"

"Yes. A profoundly retarded man who I cared for at one of the Residential Associates group homes. He died last Halloween night. These two sheets are all that's left to where his body was last seen."

"Somebody stole his body?"

"Apparently."

"Mr. Riiska was a man of simple, childlike faith," Jonah interjected. "He held an attraction to Christianity. I believe we may be looking at a quantum level event here."

"Oh no, Jonah," Boyington exclaimed while rubbing his neck. "Not this radioactive dematerialization collapse theory again."

"Oh?" I interrupted. "You don't go along with that dematerialization resurrection stuff, doctor?"

"No I don't, Mr. Paul. Jonah here is used to thinking in theological terms, but I am a scientist. All I know about the Turin Shroud is what it is not. It is not a painting, a powder rubbing or transfer, a burn, a scorch or any image caused by direct contact with a human body. Nor did sweat, oils, or chemicals create its image. I know it's not the work of some medieval forger. While Jonah's thinking is theoretically possible, it doesn't jibe with my grounded, scientific approach."

"Here comes that 'Occam's razor,'" Jonah laughed.

"What's wrong, Jonah, don't you want a free shave today?"

"No thanks, Ray."

"In case you don't know, Mr. Paul," Boyington said, "Occam's razor is a philosophy that dictates that the simplest explanation is usually the best explanation."

"Okay, Ray," Jonah added. "And what is your simple explanation for the Turin Shroud's image?"

"You know very well, I don't have one as of yet. This doesn't mean it's not out there."

"Exactly. You don't have any theory. Well, the collapse theory explains all the odd Turin image features, like the unbroken and unsmudged bloodstains and the vertical, distance sensitive imaging."

"Just because a theory fits, doesn't mean it's valid, Jonah. After all, how many dead human beings dematerialize in a burst of radiation that you know of?"

"History records just one resurrection, Ray. Maybe a few others were physically 'translated.' We may have another such occurrence with Mr. Riiska here."

"Oh? Mr. Paul, did your friend appear to you 'risen?'"

*"Ray!"* Jonah exclaimed.

"Watch what you say," I hissed. "We're talking about a friend of mine who died and disappeared under mysterious circumstances. He didn't appear to me 'risen,' as you say, nor do I believe that Christian claim that Jesus is risen."

Dr. Boyington held his hand up in a knowing gesture.

"My sincere apologies, Jonah…David. Sometimes when a debate gets rolling, my analytical side ignores all social etiquette. I am very sorry."

"I understand, Ray," Jonah added. "Your hostility toward Christianity is hardly a rare thing in today's academia."

"Come now. If I were that hostile to Christianity, I would never risk my professional reputation by declaring the Turin Shroud an unsolved mystery."

"This is true," Rubenstein smiled. "Now back to Mr. Riiska's sheet. Is there any test we can do to see just how similar it is…chemically…to the Turin Shroud? If, in fact, the image fibers are discolored in an identical manner?"

"You're reading my mind, Jonah," Boyington nodded. "It will involve small samples of the image fibers. Can I remove such samples?"

"That's what we're here for, doc," I responded.

Soon, the scientist had a small collection of fibers, some of which were in a petri dish. Others were stuck on Mylar tape.

"The STURP team discovered that the Turin Shroud image was created by an oxidation of the linen fibers. The same seems to be true with this sheet. First, we'll make sure there isn't any other cause for this discoloration," Ray Boyington explained.

The doctor proceeded. He introduced concentrated hydrochloric acid to the yellowed fibers. Nothing happened. He tried concentrated sulfuric acid. Still no effect.

"Let's try some alkaline solutions," Boyington said.

He introduced concentrated ammonium hydroxide and strong potassium hydroxide. No change in the fibers. He tried a few powerful oxidants. No effect. Next, he tested for organic compounds. The yellow imaging remained, just as stubborn as the Turin Shroud fibers were.

"Déjà vu," Ray whispered. "I'm going to bypass most of those tests that rule out human forgery and get right to the one test STURP used to prove the Turin Shroud image was an end product of dehydrating acid oxidation."

Ray then introduced reductant solutions to the image fibers. Ascorbate was tried and, as with the Turin Shroud, the yellowing remained on the linen fibers. The scientist commented on how the solution wasn't strong enough. He then introduced Diimide and immediately the fibers went white. As white as the sheet that was around the image.

"Remarkable!" Ray shouted. "Incredible! So far, the Turin Shroud has a modern twin! Now I'll look through the oxidative intermediate reactions."

Time passed. When Dr. Boyington finally finished his tests, he just smiled and shook his head.

"Jonah, I can't believe this. I just wound up with an 'aldol condensation that on dehydration, gave an alpha, beta unsaturated carbonyl, which in turn went to a conjugated carbonyl.' This is the result STURP researchers reported."

"Ray, this is more than I hoped for. This is astounding."

"Yes, it is. Not proof of dematerialization though. Remember that."

"I know, my friend, there is no need to condescend. You are a scientist. I am a theologian. As a theologian, I don't require clinical proof staring at me from a petri dish. I weigh evidence and ponder possibilities. Just as a historian does. As a court of law does. Is there room for doubt in any historical or legal conclusion? Of course! Just as with any theological conclusion! If evidence points me toward the miraculous, I venture in. Scientists dare not approach such ground."

"This is why modern people want scientific verification with most things, Jonah. They don't want to be medieval."

"So, if one believes something is unconfirmed by clinical science, one is medieval, Ray?"

"That's right."

I listened with rapt interest. These two men reminded me of Marcus and I. One, a pragmatic agnostic, the other, a supernaturally minded idealist. Yet both men held a liking for the other.

"I couldn't disagree more," Jonah continued. "For example, do you believe that several people accused of witchcraft were hung in Salem, Massachusetts?"

"Of course."

"Okay, Ray. Prove to me scientifically that the Salem witch trials took place."

"Scientifically? Well, there's the written history. The artifacts and documents of the era. The traditions that evolved from this tragic history."

"Exactly. Just as there are written histories, documents, artifacts, and historical movements that grew from the life, death and Resurrection of Jesus."

"Come on, Jonah! Religious zealots murdering innocents here and abroad, that's within the normal realm of experience. People walking on water, healing the blind, and rising from the dead—that's not the norm."

"Regardless. Supernatural events occur. Even in this modern era! One risks academic stigma if one investigates, records, and validates such occurrences. Academic and journalistic embarrassment is heaped on all who dare contemplate such things. The religion of Post-Modernism shall never be defied."

"Baloney. If evidence of the supernatural was available, the scientific and journalistic communities would be all over it."

"Oh, Ray?"

"Of course!"

"Then explain the manner in which the Turin Shroud was covered after that sloppy carbon dating! The media embraced that silly painting theory. The majority of your scientific peers embraced it!"

"That's true. It's just that those individuals failed to study the topic in depth."

"They didn't fail to study the topic, they *refused* to study the topic! They read a few articles in the *Humanist Inquirer* and considered that information sufficient. It was a choice, not a failure, Ray."

"Okay, I'll grant you that."

"And what about how you are treated, Ray? You were kicked out of several committees and think tanks, simply because you were labeled a Shroudie. How terrible it is for you to know the actual science behind the Turin Shroud."

"Yes, I know. But this is where you and David here can help me."

"Help you?" I asked.

"Yes. If I were allowed to keep your sheet and study it in depth, I could crack the Shroud mystery once and for all. With verifiable evidence that a natural process can produce a photographic dehydration of linen fibers—well, imagine the fallout! Once I publish this study in peer reviewed journals, the *Humanist Inquirer* and all other debunkers would be embarrassed. Their snobbery would be exposed."

"*Jonah!* We agreed tha—" I started to say. Jonah grabbed my arm.

"I'm sorry, Ray," Jonah took over for me. "This is out of the question. The sheet is the possession of Residential Associates Incorporated, a private human service provider based in Torrington. A friend and RAI employee named Marcus Pattyson was entrusted with this sheet. I promised him it would be kept from all media attention."

"This includes academic attention, Jonah?" Boyington asked.

"I'm afraid so."

"So, here you present me with the key to the Turin Shroud, only to tell me that I can't try the key in any lock? Am I supposed to just forget all this?"

"Perhaps you and I can speak to the execs at RAI," Jonah commented to his friend.

"Won't happen," I replied. "The RAI execs are too embarrassed about the circumstances involving Huey's disappearance. They're lucky their organization was the legal guardian of this man, otherwise there would be an investigation and lawsuit that could cripple them."

"If they were Huey's executors and guardians, then indeed it's within their purview to allow the study of this sheet," Ray commented.

"Don't get your hopes up, Dr. Boyington. This man disappeared on their watch. He may have been abused in unspeakable ways. They want to bury Huey, Huey's memory, and Huey's mystery so deep, nothing will ever resurface."

"They may want that. Let's do an 'end run.'"

"How's that?"

"It wouldn't be difficult to get this bedsheet and the man who disappeared beneath it vast media attention. First, we could attract the usual mind numbing tabloid coverage and eventually I could do a respectable paper about the sheet."

I pondered. RAI had protected Huey's abuser. They fired me for exposing the truth. Brad Ramsey was obviously involved with Huey's disappearance. The police were disinterested. Still, I didn't want Marcus or Jessica to get caught in the grinder.

"I don't trust the mainstream media," Jonah responded.

"Okay," Boyington sighed. "What about the paper? What about giving this sheet the attention it deserves?"

"I'll see what I can do," Jonah responded. "I want this find to be compared and contrasted to the Turin Shroud as much as you do, Ray."

"Don't let me down, Jonah. Both of our professional reputations could depend on this sheet."

# CHAPTER 16

▼

# THE PRODIGAL SON

I had Monday off. It was an opportunity to return the sheets to Tim. Yet as I stood at the entrance to the day program, my heart raced. Inside was the man who fired me, the woman who broke my heart, and my best friend. I hoped Brad wasn't there. The hairs on my neck weren't standing—that was a good sign.

With a deep breath, I walked in. Various coworkers caught a glimpse of me and did double takes. Marcus yelled with enthusiasm.

"Davey! Hey, man, git your butt over here!"

With Marcus's announcement, Jessica paused and turned.

"David!" she smiled. "Hi!"

I nodded politely and smiled back. Unfortunately, the left corner of my mouth twitched with nervous tension.

"Hi, everyone."

Marcus jabbed me in the shoulder with his fist.

"Dave, I can't begin to tell you what a drag it's been here at day program. People are walkin' on eggshells."

"As they should," I responded.

"Not that you're any worse for wear, my man. Better hours, more money, and a boss who is nicer than nice."

"That's true. Jonah is very likable."

Marcus pointed down at the brown bag.

"Is that what I think it is?"

"Yes."

"Phew! I was gettin' worried. Let's see if Tim is busy—he's been nagging at me every day. 'Where's David and that sheet? He wouldn't get revenge, would he?'"

"Well, I was tempted," I admitted.

Marcus knocked on the office door. Tim's familiar voice murmured "Come in."

As we entered, Tim's face went white. He stood up and gave me a hug. "David! I'm so glad to see you. I've felt horrible about letting you go. Terrible."

"That's okay, Tim. I have a job now."

"Yes, Marcus told me. You work for that 'Shroudie,' Rubenstein. This is another reason I'm happy to see you. You have the sheets?"

"Of course! True to my word."

The manager took the bag from my outstretched arm and sighed with relief.

"So, Dave! What did the Yale dude have to say?" Marcus asked.

"He determined that the sheets have a dehydrated image, identical in nature to the Shroud of Turin."

"You're kidding," Tim murmured. "Where does that leave us?"

"Absolutely nowhere. Jonah thinks Huey physically dematerialized. Spiritually transformed in the manner Jesus was."

Tim erupted into hysterical laughter. "Shut up!" he shrieked. "Does this Yale scientist attend the same church of science fiction that Rubenstein does?"

"Not at all. The Yale Shroudie isn't even a Christian."

"Finally, some sanity. What does he think of the image?"

"He knew it wasn't a gimmick or a prank. As for me, I'm just concerned with what happened to Huey's body. I want to explain this image. Find more clues."

"Then let me have the sheets," Jessica said, as she entered the office. "Brad Ramsey has friends at the *Humanist Inquirer*, a magazine affiliated with his father's."

"A magazine? Journalists? Out of the question," Tim replied.

"So Brad *is* the son of that guy who ran *Truth* magazine?" I asked.

Jessica nodded in the affirmative.

"The *Humanist Inquirer* doesn't just feature a collection of scientists and journalists, they also have a good number of illusionists on staff," she continued. "They have debunked everything from Bigfoot to UFOs. They have explained away that Turin Shroud. We all want to get to the bottom of what happened to Huey, Brad and I most of all."

I snickered briefly. Jess glared before continuing.

"I can't see this image coming from a prankster. This happened at Elm Street! Some sort of natural functioning did this. Shouldn't we try all avenues of inquiry?"

"Again Jess, no," Tim sighed. "No one affiliated with a magazine, a Web site, a television show—no media people can come within walking distance of these sheets."

*"Censorship!"* Jessica exclaimed.

"See?" Marcus whispered in my ear. "Our calm day program is no more. Could Jonah use another staffer?"

"Well, you can expect a call from Brad this evening. He'll talk you into this, I'm sure," Jessica said, addressing Tim.

"Brad is a good friend, but my mind is made up. Sorry, Jess."

"Ramsey may not get his way? Imagine that!" I whispered to Marcus.

"Ancient sign of the apocalypse," Marcus whispered back.

Jessica left the office with her head down. I'm sure the whispering between Marcus and I made her uncomfortable. Part of me wanted to run after Jess. Assure her that we weren't whispering about her. Another part of me wanted to hurt her. Just as I was hurt.

Tim locked the sheets in the bottom drawer of his wooden desk.

"Okay, Marcus, David," Tim conceded. "I'll talk to Scott Fullman. I'll recommend an in-depth study of these sheets. I do this with reservations, though. I suspect this Yale scientist is more interested in comparing Huey's sheets to the Turin Shroud than with the mystery of Huey's disappearance."

"That's true," I admitted. "But beggars can't be choosers here. The police have abandoned the investigation. If these Shroudies find anything that provides answers, it's worth tolerating ulterior motives."

Tim nodded. "Again, David, I'm very sorry about firing you. The place hasn't been the same."

"I would have probably quit RAI anyhow. After all, look how humiliating that investigation was for me."

"That was a travesty, Dave. Digging into your past, profiling you as a lonely loser. It was shameful. I am shocked with Brad for resorting to such tactics."

"I'm not."

At that note, an awkward silence took hold. Marcus finally broke it.

"Well, thanks for your efforts, Tim."

Marcus and I walked into the main room of the day program. To my dismay, I saw Jess walking toward us. I forced a casual smile.

"Hey, Dave," she started. "You work for that Rubenstein shrink, right?"

"That's right."

"He called us last night. Apparently, he got wind of Brad's little discussion group and invited him to appear on his community access television show. Do you know anything about this?"

"He did? No, I don't know anything about that," I lied.

"Really? Isn't it coincidental that the man you're working for is challenging Brad to a public debate?"

"Look, Jess!" I said in an abrupt tone. "I really don't care what Jonah or Brad do or don't do. I'm trying to start a new life for myself."

"And that means erasing your old friendships, eh David?"

"I'm not the one who's erased anything here."

"Oh?" she replied with sarcasm "And who has, pray tell?"

"You're the one who used that erasing term, not me."

"I just call 'em as I see them," she muttered.

"Did Brad take Jonah up on his offer?" Marcus interrupted.

"Yes he did, Marcus. He's on Rubenstein's show tomorrow night."

"Whoa! That's quick," Marcus commented.

"Brad's always up for a challenge," Jessica replied. "But what I want to know, Dave, is whether this Jonah guy will mention Huey or Huey's sheets? Is he going to publicly accuse Brad of molesting, or of necrophilia?"

"Jess!" Marcus exclaimed. "That's not what Jonah is like!"

"Don't worry," I added. "Rubenstein is a professional, he never gets personal in a debate. Unlike other people."

"Look," Jess sighed. "What Brad did to you was wrong. I was the first to tell him so. But you have to understand, if someone accused you of something as distasteful as molesting a resident here, you would take your defensive posture to the extreme as well."

"Uh-huh," I murmured.

"When does this debate take place?" Marcus asked.

"Tomorrow at seven in the evening. Rubenstein and Brad will face off at the community TV station on Maple Street."

"Any studio audience allowed?" I asked.

"I don't know," Jess answered while marching away. "I'll be there just the same. I've got work to do guys, I'll see you around."

Marcus took me by the arm and walked me toward the exit. When we reached the parking lot, he put his arm around my shoulder.

"So, what time do I come over tomorrow night, Dave?"

"Huh?"

"To watch Jonah and Brad face off! I'll bring the pizza and beer."

"I don't want to watch. All that religious mumbo-jumbo. Don't put me in the position of rooting for Brad."

"I don't think you'd ever do that, Dave."

"A debate should be weighed on facts, not personality."

"Tell that to Washington," Marcus laughed.

"Okay," I nodded. "Be at my place by 6:30. Make sure the pizza has pepperoni. And, bring some Ruffles. Pizza, chips, and beer are my holy trinity."

"I knew you had some form of religious belief! I'll tell Tamika."

"Oh. That's right. Are you bringing Tamika along?"

"Relax, Dave," Marcus laughed. "I also need a break from her at times. See ya."

As my car exited the day program parking lot, I turned to look at the building. In one of the windows, Jessica's face peered out. Her expression appeared pained.

# Chapter 17

▼

# The Debate

Tuesday evening, six-forty. Marcus arrived at my apartment. He struggled with the two pizza boxes, the bag of chips, and a twelve pack of beer. I grabbed the chips and beer from his loosening grip and placed them on the counter of my kitchenette. Marcus followed suit.

"Let's eat!" Marcus exclaimed. "Smelling that pizza in my car drove me nuts."

"I'm all for that," I replied. "That show may take my appetite away. Let's eat while we can."

After loading our plates, we settled on my couch. We engaged in small talk. We discussed college basketball. Talked about the weather. Several minutes passed before Marcus mentioned what weighed on us both.

"I tell ya, Davey, I'm nervous. Jonah doesn't know who he's facing tonight."

"I know. Poor Jonah."

"One thing is certain. We won't see the animal. We'll see smooth Brad," said Marcus.

"I don't know. Do you think Brad can control his animal side?"

"Yes, I do. I think he unleashes wild behavior only when he deems it safe to do so."

"Like when he's one-on-one with me."

"Exactly!" exclaimed Marcus.

"What about after the show? Will Jonah be safe in the parking lot?"

"He leaves the studio with his small production crew."

"That's good."

"So, how are you holding up after that little face-off with Jess yesterday?"

"I won't lie, Marcus. It bothered me. I had trouble sleeping last night."

"Yeah, I know, maybe we should set Brad up. Get him to publicly unleash 'Mr. Red Eyes,' so Jess can see what we've been talking about."

"No. The guy's psychic, or something. He's always two steps ahead of me."

"You think he's psychic?"

"You know me, Marcus. I'm not into that supernatural hooey. But if there's anyone alive who could be called psychic, it would be Brad."

"Hmm. Do you think he blames you for tonight's debate?"

"Jess knew I had some involvement."

"But you didn't want Jonah to do this."

"Not at all!"

"Well, maybe we're taking this too seriously. Friends surround Jonah. Only about twenty people probably watch community television with regularity."

"Let's make that thirty-two. I'm sure Brad's disciples will tune in."

"Including Jess."

"Including Jess and Scott Fullman."

"Ugh," Marcus murmured.

"Well, it's getting near broadcast time."

I grabbed the remote and turned on the television. Within a few minutes, Jonah's show started. The title *Christian Café* stretched across the screen. Jonah and Brad sat in armchairs, facing the camera and angled toward each other. The background had a facsimile of a stained glass window.

Jonah started the dialogue.

"Good evening and welcome to *Christian Café*—a show dedicated to exploring Christian issues here in northwestern Connecticut. I'm Dr. Jonah Rubenstein. Tonight, we're fortunate to have Torrington's own Mr. Brad Ramsey as our guest. Mr. Ramsey leads a study group that explores the religious and political trends in our country. Mr. Ramsey is also a contributing editorialist to the *Humanist Inquirer* magazine. Thank you for coming, Mr. Ramsey, and welcome to *Christian Café*."

"Thank you very much, Dr. Rubenstein. Thank you for inviting me."

"So, Mr. Ramsey, you have a regular feature in the *Humanist Inquirer* magazine," Jonah commented.

"Yes, I do. I used to be involved with journalism and publishing. Now I work in human services. Working with the mentally challenged is my current way of giving back to society. My friends at the *Humanist Inquirer* were kind enough to allow me to keep a toehold with the print media. Each month, I analyze the destructive religious trends that threaten to undermine our global community."

"Could you summarize for us how you view religion and Christianity in particular?"

"Be happy to, doctor. Christianity, along with other world religions, has some good to offer. It promotes love, brotherhood, and charity. It has a social consciousness the enlightenment brought to fruition. Unfortunately, the chaff often overwhelms the wheat."

"How so?"

"Christianity has departed from the social consciousness that a simple rabbi named Jesus taught. The first departure occurred with the teachings of a Hellenized Jew and Roman citizen designated as Saint Paul. Paul's insistence that salvation was only acquired through an active faith in Jesus as God was—and is—a destructive concept. What vile crop grows from such a narrow, exclusive salvation concept? History tells us. We have the Inquisitions, the Dark Ages, the witch trials, and so on. Even today we are infested with anti-choice radicals, with abortion clinic bombers. The Fundamentalists and Evangelicals would have all school children praying to a Christian god, all of America bowing to the cross. Intolerance is the end result of any religion that dares to call itself 'the true faith.'"

"So in other words, you are saying the concept of salvation through Jesus results in the violent oppression of nonbelievers?"

"Yes."

"Isn't that a generalization, Mr. Ramsey? Isn't that overreaching?"

"It's not just the conclusion of small Brad Ramsey. It's the verdict of time."

"Not all history supports your conclusion."

"How so?"

"Take World War Two, for example. There were numerous Christian movements and individuals who sought to rescue oppressed Jews suffering under Nazi occupation."

"The allied defeat of Nazi Germany wasn't inspired by the plight of the European Jews."

"No, it wasn't. There was denial concerning the holocaust. Yet if your hypothesis about religious intolerance were valid, it would manifest in an active Christian support for the persecution of Jews during that era. As it is, Hitler was despised en masse in most nations with Christian majorities."

"Hitler himself was a Christian, Mr. Rubenstein."

"That's not true. Adolph Hitler embraced an esoteric occultism, one which held anti-Semitism as a tenant."

"So, doctor, you are denying that religious intolerance is the end result of Christian fundamentalism?"

"Yes, I am. Intolerance never results from Christianity proper. It sometimes stems from Christianity perverted. You claim that the Christian salvation tenant is the cause of religious oppression and violence. Yet this myopia excludes the very foundation of Christian teaching. The teaching that loving one's neighbor is equated with the love of God. These are the two greatest commandments! Jesus taught that we should actively love our enemies, our neighbors—love all."

"That humanitarianism came from the Rabbi Jesus—*not* from the founders of Christianity. People like Paul created an 'us versus them' psychology. The medieval torture chambers were located under a Christian banner."

"I'm not concerned with robes, churches, banners, and flags, Mr. Ramsey. Most of that is political. Like Jesus, I'd rather look at an individual's 'fruits.' Individual faith actively demonstrating the spirit of Christ."

"So, like the failed communists of Russia, you disown your own historic brethren when they embarrass you."

"On the contrary! I simply set a decency standard for the qualification of the title 'Christian brethren.'"

"Very convenient, doctor. Humanitarianism and true faith doctrines never go together."

"Then according to you, the Rabbi Jesus contradicted himself when he claimed that 'No man can come to the Father, but by me.' Or when he called himself 'the resurrection and the life.' That all 'who believed' in him would never die."

"It's doubtful that Jesus ever said those things."

"Only according to modern scholarship, Mr. Ramsey. Modern, enlightened scholars who know better what Jesus said and did than the very people who walked with him—including his apostles."

"Well…yes."

"Let's say I wanted to know about someone like yourself, after your passing, Mr. Ramsey. Wouldn't the most advantageous avenue involve interviewing your coworkers, friends, and family?"

"That would be the logical approach, yes. Unless my coworkers, friends, and claimed that I worked miracles and rose from the dead. If that were the case, I would be exploring the reasons why these people were promoting absurd stories."

"So, you hold a naturalistic worldview?"

"Yes. Nothing can ever bend or break the natural laws of the universe."

"I am glad that you used the word 'bend,' Mr. Ramsey. Within the realm of physics, universal laws that are assumed unbendable can be manipulated at the quantum level. Hypothetically speaking."

"Yes, hypothetically speaking."

"You don't approve of hypothetical thinking?"

"No."

"Except, when a twentieth century academic determines who Jesus of Nazareth was and what he did, to the exclusion of the first century testimony. Isn't that scholarship also hypothetical, Mr. Ramsey?"

"Uh well, I wouldn't say that."

"So, hypothetical thinking is only allowed with your presuppositions."

"Well, uh…"

Beads of sweat started to form on Brad's forehead. It was the first time I ever saw a person get a verbal advantage over the devious Elm Street manager.

"Okay, Rubenstein, okay! What about you?" Brad gestured wildly. "Obviously, you embrace the hypothetical possibility of the supernatural, but scoff at the modern reinterpretation of Jesus!"

"That is correct. Unlike you, I never expressed an aversion to hypothetical thinking. I simply maintain that certain hypotheses are stronger than others."

"As do I, Rubenstein!"

"Notice, Marcus, Brad's getting huffy. He's no longer respecting Jonah by calling him doctor, now he's just calling him Rubenstein," I observed.

"Yeah. He's starting to lose it," Marcus replied.

"So, you do approve of some hypothetical thinking, Mr. Ramsey?" Jonah asked.

"Well…yes."

"Okay. I'm glad we got that straight."

Brad's face was flushed. The foot crossed over his left knee started to twitch.

"Let me ask you something, Rubenstein. Do you believe that God created the universe in six earth days, then rested on the seventh?"

"Yes. The creation-evolution controversy. This is a contentious subject, one that divides Christians from other Christians. From the secular world in general. This topic isn't my expertise. I believe God created the universe. I'm unclear about the timetable."

"So, you don't accept the book of Genesis as literal?" asked Brad.

"Perhaps not the two creation narratives. It's my understanding that the creation narratives were the songs of Middle Eastern people of prehistory."

Brad was regaining his composure. He felt the advantage returning to him.

"So, doctor, you reject the biblical creation story!"

"I wouldn't say that, Mr. Ramsey. Have you ever heard of Dr. Hugh Ross?"

"No."

"Dr. Ross is an astronomer and an evangelist. He does a great job of interpreting the chronology of scriptural creation, in cosmological terms, within his book *The Fingerprint of God.*

"First, we have the Bible imply a big bang, and the creation of the physical universe. Afterward, we have the transformation of the earth's atmosphere from opaque to translucent. Next, a stable water cycle. Then the establishment of continent and ocean. Then the appearance of plants. Next, the atmosphere becomes transparent, allowing the sun, moon, and stars to become visible for the first time, implying their creation from an earthly perspective. The order of life then proceeds, going from sea organisms, to sea mammals, to birds, to land mammals, to man himself. Apparently, the creation narrative was an inspired vision."

"Well," Brad laughed. "That was certainly imaginative."

"Thank you, Mr. Ramsey. All knowledge begins with imagination, after all."

"You do realize, Rubenstein, that all the fundamentalist Christians watching you were just offended by your interpretation of Genesis?"

"That's possible. All I can say is that I don't begrudge literal creationism. With God, all things are possible."

"Even the evolution of man from monkey?"

"That hypothesis is a possibility, yes. The mistake that evolutionists make is that they think the theory of evolution removes all need for a Creator. They think that natural processes are random, meaningless, and a replacement for God."

"Yes, doctor. Natural selection knocked God off his throne."

"Unfortunately, it did seem to undermine our respect for life. Do you support a woman's right to abort a fetus, Mr. Ramsey? Even late term abortions?"

"Of course. A woman's body is her domain, not ours."

"And that organism within her womb—the developing human with it's own DNA and characteristics—is merely 'part' of her body?"

"Yes."

"Tell me, Mr. Ramsey, I recently read of your efforts to save the spotted owl from environmental threats in the Northwest. Does an owl have a greater sanctity, a greater right to life than an embryo, fetus, or baby?"

"That's apples and oranges. Evolution renders the fetus irrelevant. It's a mere growth. An unviable life form."

"It may be unviable, as you say, but it is human! Within its genetic code, lies a blueprint of his or her future. It has potentiality, it has humanity. Yet the same people who would risk their lives to save a redwood tree assert the right to throw these human organisms in the garbage like banana peels."

"Rubenstein, your real problem isn't abortion. Your problem is with the universe itself. Humanity isn't the sacred organism you think. It's but another offspring of an indifferent universe. A universe born of meaninglessness, of random chance."

"In a meaningless universe, where random chance reigns, why should life come into existence? Evolve with purpose? Why does life promote life?"

"Well…just because. That's how the universe governs itself."

"Mr. Ramsey, you say 'universe,' I say 'God.' Toe-may-toe, toe-mah-toe."

"Do you actually believe in miracles, Rubenstein? Do you believe in the supernatural?"

"Not only do I believe in such things, I've witnessed them first hand."

"You have?" Brad questioned, while looking out of the corners of his eyes.

"Yes. I have witnessed the faith healing of a child with a fatal brain tumor. It's on record. The girl's doctors still can't explain it. I've witnessed people speaking in tongues, with others interpreting the foreign language. I've been present at an exorcism, where a seven-year-old boy levitated out of the chair he was sitting in."

"An exorcism? Levitation? Surely you jest, good doctor!"

"I am very serious, Mr. Ramsey. There wasn't any head spinning or pea soup. Instead, this child spoke Aramaic to me. He knew details concerning my childhood. His strength was disproportionate to his age and size. It took two men to restrain him during his rages. Fortunately, the exorcism worked and the boy now leads a normal life."

"Have you ever heard of schizophrenia, doctor? Tourette's syndrome? Epilepsy? Attention deficit disorder? Oppositional defiance disorder?"

"Of course. I am a licensed social worker. All somatic causes were ruled out with this boy. And as far as I know, speaking in foreign languages and levitating are not symptoms of any of those disorders."

"Do you have any video of this boy levitating, doctor?"

"No. I was compelled to honor the child's privacy. The family's privacy."

"That's very convenient."

"This doesn't mean that there are no evidences of the supernatural out there for you to study, Mr. Ramsey. Perhaps you've heard of Connecticut's own ghost hunter and religious demonologist, Ms. Claire Monroe? She has been doing the college lecture circuit for a few decades. This woman has many videos, photographs, and recordings to share."

"Yes, I've heard of her. She made quite a profit on her book *Principalities and Powers*. Her coauthor admitted to the media that they imagined most of the stories."

"She and her coauthor had a falling out. He enacted revenge."

"So she says."

"Okay, so you don't approve of Claire Monroe. All you have to do, Mr. Ramsey, is explore what evidences of the supernatural are out there. Perhaps on the Internet. You should start with the Shroud of Turin."

"Ahh, yes! I heard you're a Shroudie, Dr. Rubenstein. I came with some literature explaining your so-called Shroud as a masterful forgery. Successfully carbon dated to the thirteenth century."

"I am well versed with various Shroud explanations, so 'sock it to me,'" Rubenstein smiled confidently.

"Okay! Here I have an article from the *Humanist Inquirer,* which subscribes to the view that the Turin Shroud is a proto-photographic experiment. An experiment conducted by none other than Leonardo da Vinci himself!"

"Yes, I am familiar with this theory. First, perhaps you can fill the viewers in about this hypothesis."

"I'd love to! Some historians believe that Leonardo was hostile to the church and Christianity in general. In his Last Supper painting, certain clues can be found that indicate his true beliefs.

"For example, the Holy Grail or chalice is missing from the table. The face of John is very feminine, perhaps portraying the face of Mary Magdalene. The positioning of the figures creates an 'M,' which certain people believe represents Mary Magdalene. Many sects believed, and still believe, that Jesus and Mary Magdalene were married. They had a secret lineage symbolized by the Holy Grail, a living ancestry that holds Jesus' bloodline. This is why the Last Supper omits the grail from the table. Such beliefs were deemed heresy by the medieval church and were not tolerated.

"The Shroud of Turin was probably the greatest 'middle finger' that Leonardo could have flicked at the church. The artist and inventor was the forensics expert of his time. He diagramed the internal structures of the human body. He had access to cadavers. He possessed a basic knowledge of the 'camera obscura,' the projection of an image through a pinhole or small lens into a dark room. The face of the Shroud resembles the mature Leonardo. The head of the Shroud image is smaller than it should be. This is because Leonardo exposed his face on the sensitized linen and superimposed it on the body of a cadaver. He then added the bloodstains, and we now have the world's first photograph!"

"Thank you, Mr. Ramsey," Jonah nodded. "This is indeed an intriguing theory. If anyone had the genius to create the Shroud, it would have been Leonardo da Vinci. Unfortunately, the facts don't reinforce your theory. Fact number one: The Shroud's known history predates the adult Leonardo by more than a century!"

"If I may interrupt, Rubenstein. I forgot to mention that it is believed that Leonardo switched an inferior Shroud with his more advanced work."

"This scenario is unlikely. A crude Shroud was suddenly replaced with a superior one? This would discredit both linens. A pilgrim's medallion from thirteen fifty-five represents the double Shroud image exactly as it is now. There were exhibitions of the Shroud prior to Leonardo's birth.

"Now, on to fact number two. Leonardo did include wine tumblers in his Last Supper painting, easily noticed in an early Gianpetrino copy of the masterpiece. The deterioration of Leonardo's original makes it difficult to see the cups. It's not proven that Leonardo held to any secret societies or heresies.

"Number three: If Leonardo or any other forger found the secret of photography—the imprinting of light upon a sensitized surface—it's beyond belief that he would sit on such a discovery. For fear that some forged icon would be exposed? Nonsense. The knowledge of photography would have gotten out!"

"That's just speculation," Brad added.

"Yes it is, Mr. Ramsey. A more logical speculation than the concept that Leonardo belonged to a secret society, held a secret theology, or suppressed the discovery of photography.

"On to number four. Modern linen photographs fail to imitate the Shroud of Turin successfully! One professor created linen photographs by projecting the image of a white plaster statue into a dark, 'camera obscura' room. Hanging in this room, he draped a chemically sensitized linen sheet. Sure enough, an interesting image was imprinted on the cloth! It was subtle. It was a negative image. It didn't penetrate far into the linen.

"So far so good, right? But unfortunately for him, the image was not three-dimensional. It was not encoded with distance-sensitive information. This is because the plaster statue was lit by an exterior light source, such as the sun. It had shadowing and outlining. The Shroud has neither; it just records the parts of the body closest to the cloth. Photographs record whatever happens to catch the most light. Put through a VP-8 image analyzer, the professor's image fails the three-dimension accuracy test.

"This leads me to number five. The Shroud of Turin Research Project found that the bloodstains were on the Shroud before the body image. Hardly the succession a forger would choose. Imagine his grief at lining up the projected image of a man to some random blood streaks!"

"That may explain why the Turin Shroud has blood streaks in the hair image alongside his head," Brad responded.

"Good point, Mr. Ramsey. Shroud researchers had found that the bloodstains match the dimensions of the face if the cloth was in contact with the sides of the face. The image was recorded only at right angles from the body, so the sides of the face were foreshortened into darkness. Those bloodstains were on the sides of the face, not in the hair."

"Uh-huh," Brad smiled. He then turned to the camera, with an incredulous expression.

"Tell me, Rubenstein. Have you ever seen a dead body?"

Jonah became pale.

"Excuse me? What does this have to do…?"

"Well, doctor, you claim that this Turin Shroud records the image of an actual dead body. Have you ever seen one? I don't mean embalmed, lying in a casket. I mean a dead body…someone recently killed."

"Well…yes, I have. But it's not my testimony that the forensic analysis of the Shroud relies on. It's the testimony of multiple scholars, doctors, and—"

"Where have you seen a dead body, may I ask?" Brad interrupted.

"That's irrelevant. I'd rather stick to…"

"Ahh, okay, doctor. Perhaps we can speak of this later, over a hot coffee. Perhaps we can bring your *Christian Cafe* to a sidewalk café?"

The doctor's body visibly shook.

*"You will not fluster me, Mr. Ramsey."*

"Fluster you? Why would coffee and conversation fluster you, doctor? I'm thinking of a charming place, where children and parents alike partake in excellent food and drink."

Jonah glared at Brad. Brad innocently shrugged.

"Maybe you hate the idea of having coffee and conversation with an unbeliever?"

Jonah's face was white. His hands trembled. Whatever Brad had just done hit home. The elderly scholar started coughing. Eventually, Jonah cleared his throat. "I…I see that we're out of time for…this week. Please join us again next week for *Christian Café*. I'm Jonah Rubenstein."

"What the hell was that?" I asked, as Jonah's show concluded with music and credits.

"That slimy bastard," Marcus hissed. His fists were clenched, his knuckles white.

"What? Do you know what just happened?"

"I sure do. Ten years ago, Jonah was involved in a dig near Jerusalem. He and his colleagues were resting at a roadside café in the city, drinking coffee. They heard an Israeli soldier yelling. They all took the clue and ducked for cover. A Palestinian suicide bomber blew himself up. Jonah remembered lying there, splattered in blood. He thought it was his own blood, until he noticed that there was a weight on his legs. It was a little girl. Four years old. Impaled with nails and glass, bleeding profusely. Some suicide bombers are very proficient. They sometimes pack their bombs with homemade shrapnel, treated with an anticoagulant that prevents the victim's wounds from clotting. Her parents were killed instantly. Jonah held the child while they waited for an ambulance. She hemorrhaged and died in his arms."

*"My God, Marcus!"*

"The worst part of it is, Jonah remembers seeing her standing near him as he ducked for cover. He knew he could have pulled her down with him. But in the panic of the moment, he just grabbed his head with both hands. For two years, he was diagnosed with post-traumatic stress disorder."

"Marcus, do you think Brad knew about this?"

"Of course he did! First, Ramsey asked Jonah if he had ever seen a dead body. Then he immediately mentioned a roadside café, having coffee, and then mentioning children with their parents! Did you hear him emphasize the word 'children?'"

"How would he know?"

"I don't know. Jonah shared his story with a select few. The news coverage at that time didn't mention any names."

"Unbelievable."

"I'm going to that station, Dave."

I grabbed Marcus' coat and then my own.

"Count me in."


Marcus drove us to the community television studio. The building was about three minutes from the Clock Shop Apartments. The evening was windy. Leaves and litter blew against the windshield as we drove. Anxiety overtook both Marcus and me. We were convinced that Jonah was in danger.

As we pulled into the parking lot, I noticed that Jonah's SUV and Ramsey's Jaguar were still there. As Marcus and I ran into the studio, the wind rushed in behind us. Marcus's baseball cap blew off his head and tumbled along the floor toward a few people. It caught the attention of Jonah's staffers. Some of the production crew were standing in a circle around Jonah. Brad was with Jessica, separate from the group and talking on his cell phone. When Jessica noticed our entrance, she quickly jogged over to us.

"Marcus! Dave! Your friend Jonah isn't well! We think it may be his heart."

At this point Brad approached. He smiled malevolently, then quickly assumed the more appropriate look of concern as he laid his hand on Jessica's shoulder.

"The paramedics are on their way, hon," Brad assured her in a soothing voice.

"Why did Jonah freak out on you?" Jessica asked.

"Good question, babe. I knew our broadcast time was running out and I was just thinking of how and where we could continue this fascinating discussion. I never knew Jonah had such a problem with coffee!"

"Bull crap," Marcus murmured, as he shoved Brad aside and walked over to Jonah.

"Wha—what the hell was that?" Jessica directed at me.

"Ask your lover here, Jess. Ask him if he knew anything about a sidewalk café that Jonah was almost killed at."

"I really have no idea what you're talking about," Brad protested.

"I'm sick of this attitude, David. Brad is not out to hurt anyone! He was the first person to call for help when Jonah grabbed his chest. And what's with Marcus?"

"Forget it, hon," Brad sighed, as he put his arm around Jessica. "Their friend is having trouble and they're just concerned. I'm not taking it personally."

"Well, I do," Jessica fumed.

"Whatever," I murmured, as I walked past the couple to check on Jonah. Brad and Jessica left the studio, mumbling among themselves. I saw the station manager go running out the door after them.

Eight men and women were standing around Jonah as he sipped a cup of water with his shaky hands. He seemed pale and sweaty. When his eyes met mine, he gestured for me to come close.

"Jonah, you just take it easy, the paramedics are on their way."

"Brad Ramsey is more formidable than you suggested, David. His abilities go beyond natural boundaries."

"Rest easy, Jonah. Don't think about it."

"Now, now people, don't fawn over me like I'm some sort of an old man. I just had a brief attack of palpitations. Believe me, friends, this is not what has affected me."

Marcus came closer and knelt down next to me.

"What do you mean, Jonah?" he asked.

"I saw her."

"Who?"

"The young girl I watched die in Jerusalem. She walked up next to Brad's chair when he invited me out for coffee."

"What?"

Jonah coughed vigorously before continuing.

"Yes. It was her. Bloody, with pale blue skin. Her eyes were empty sockets. Maggots were twisting out of her skin. She stood there facing me. Then she faded away."

I looked at Marcus. Was Jonah having another nervous breakdown?

"Did anyone else see anything?" Marcus asked the gathering.

They silently shook their heads in denial.

"As soon as I met Ramsey, a weight settled on me. Waves of confusion and fear swept through me during the broadcast. Only one other time in my life have I felt this way."

Marcus looked concerned.

"You mean—?"

"That's right, Marcus. This reminded me of the exorcism of young Timmy Walston. I'm telling you, *there are diabolical forces empowering Brad Ramsey!*"

# CHAPTER 18

▼

# CLAIRE MONROE

Jonah rested a few days after the incident. The doctors at Winsted Memorial told him he experienced a panic attack, complete with supraventricular tachycardia. How familiar those words were. Anyway, Dr. Rubenstein was kind enough to pay me for those two days he closed his office. I returned to work Friday, wondering what to expect. I thought that Jonah was losing his mind. Marcus believed the whole diabolical forces explanation. I considered that medieval superstition.

I was at my desk when Jonah arrived. He still looked rather pale.

"Good morning. How are you feeling?"

"Much better. Thank you, David."

"Any palpitations these past few days?"

"No. But…"

Jonah hesitated. He wasn't his usual, confident self.

"What Jonah?"

"Let's just say…I feel him. Brad Ramsey is targeting us. You and I. It's as if an icy towel has been wrapped around my neck."

"Look, if any man could qualify as 'the devil,' it's Ramsey. Yet you're talking about pointy tails and pitchforks. Jonah, you're an educated man!"

He ignored the comment.

"The Mulligans are coming in for a ten o'clock session and the Parkers at eleven. Oh yes…Dave, I took the liberty of clearing my docket from one to three.

Ms. Claire Monroe will be visiting. I'd like you to join the meeting. Listen to what she has to say."

"You mean the Catholic-ghost hunting-demonologist lady?"

"The same."

"Jonah! You're a social worker. You're educated in abnormal psychology. Don't you think other explanations are more viable?"

"I'd like you there," the elderly counselor said as he disappeared behind his office door.

I spent the morning thinking about the doc's request. I typed up his notes concerning the Caiaphas Ossuary and saved them on CD-ROMs. I decided to attend the meeting to make sure Jonah didn't completely loose the cheese off his cracker. To insure that Claire Monroe didn't exploit his condition.

At one o'clock sharp, Claire Monroe arrived. I estimated her to be around fifty years of age. She wore a floral print dress. Her white gloves harkened back to the 1950s, her string of pearls looked tight on her throat. She was overweight. Graying hair framed her round face.

"Good afternoon, young man," she said, with a hint of a British accent. "Please inform Dr. Rubenstein that Ms. Claire is here to see him."

"Jonah's expecting you, Ms. Monroe. I'll be joining you both. Follow me," I said.

"Very good! The more, the merrier."

As we walked into the office, Jonah appeared to be kneeling in prayer. He looked up and laughed.

"Ms. Claire! You came! How great it is to see you!"

They embraced.

"Jonah, my dear. The past years haven't aged you a day!"

"And you…you must have lost fifty pounds!"

"Fifty? Why, I am offended, doctor. I have lost precisely fifty-two and one half pounds!"

"My apologies! You have met young David here?"

"Yes and no. We haven't been formally introduced."

"Well then. Ms. Claire Monroe, I'd like you to meet David Paul. This is one of the young men who brought the imprinted linen for us to analyze. The man who has been in direct conflict with Brad Ramsey."

I grimaced. "Jonah! You shared all this with her? How do we know that she's not going to want press coverage on that linen, and—"

"Put your fears to rest!" Claire interrupted. "I am not here to write a book. I'm here to assist a friend."

"I'm sorry, Ms. Monroe. But considering the books and media attention that defines your career, I—"

"Look here, young man. I will not tolerate this Ms. Monroe business. You are to address me as Claire. Is that understood?"

"You better make that Ms. Claire!" Jonah laughed.

"Here's an odd phenomenon to consider," Claire responded while leaning close to me. "Men are intimidated by me. Do you believe that?"

"Uh well, you seem very nice," I observed.

"And you, dear David, are adorable! Are you romantically attached, pray tell?"

"Ahh, well, I—"

"Yes, David," Jonah chuckled. "I forgot to tell you that Ms. Claire has an eye for younger men."

"Wow. I mean, thanks for the compliment, Ms. Mon—I mean Ms. Claire."

The demonologist laughed.

"Relax, honey! I'm not going to bite you! I'm just an old-fashioned lady, with good Catholic values."

Jonah settled in his chair, which forced me to sit beside Ms. Monroe on the sofa. As I settled into the cushion, she patted my knee three times, then kept her hand there. I squirmed. After about ten seconds, she withdrew with a chuckle.

"So, Jonah dear!" Claire started. "I understand you had a most dreadful experience with this Brad Ramsey fellow."

"Yes, I did. I haven't felt this much evil—this much hatred—since little Timmy Walston."

"Oh yes. Timmy Walston. I understand he recently married."

"Is that so? Thank the Lord for his blessings," Jonah smiled.

"So, what precisely did this Ramsey fellow do?"

"By all outward appearances, not much. We debated as Christian believer and humanist skeptic. I felt the same weight, the same confusion that came over me during Timmy's exorcism."

"I see," Claire nodded. "Go on."

"My prayers helped me here. I seemed to get the verbal advantage at times, about which anger radiated off Ramsey like a furnace. Toward the end of our contest, he asked me if I ever saw a dead body…as it appears before embalming. I thought he asked this in relation to our Turin Shroud debate. Then he invited me for coffee and suggested a roadside café."

Claire knitted her brow.

"More than that, he suggested a roadside café popular with parents and children. It was around this time that I saw her. A little girl who appeared to be Ruth Goldman. Precious little Ruth, who died in my arms so many years ago. Brad turned to look at her as she stood by his chair. It was Ruth's face, but it was decomposed…vile."

"Did anyone else witness this manifestation?"

"No."

"I see. Tell me about the girl's eyes."

"She didn't have any eyes, Claire. They were just empty sockets. Bordered with…hanging veins."

"Oh dear, oh dear. That's not good. Typically, inhuman spirits manifest with incomplete forms, faces, or eyes. They also exploit our weaknesses. Such as the guilt you've had concerning poor Ruth."

"Ms. Claire," I interjected. "Isn't it possible that Jonah was overcome with emotion? Fatigue? Isn't it possible that he let his imagination get the better of him? After all, only he saw this macabre vision."

"Yes, those things are possible. Yet they are not typical of dear Jonah. When he struggled with post-traumatic stress disorder, hallucinations and delusions were not part of his illness. As a paranormal researcher, I know that spirits can manifest to an individual, but remain invisible to a group."

"Friends," Jonah sighed. "Try not to speak about me like I am not present."

"Sorry, hon," Claire apologized. "As I was saying, inhuman spirits existed under—"

"What is this inhuman spirit stuff?" I interrupted.

Claire sighed. "David, inhuman spirits are entities that have never lived in human form. They can be angelic, but they're more common as demons and devils. These are spirits older than the universe itself. The demonic once bathed in God's presence. The chief angel among them, Lucifer—the 'morning star' and 'light bringer'—"

"Wait a minute," I interrupted again. "What was that term again?"

"What? Morning star? Light bringer?"

"Yeah! Light bringer! I've heard that term before! Back when I attended Brad's discussion group, he prayed to God as Creator and light bringer. That last term stuck in my head and I believed he was being allegorical and non-denominational."

"Honey," Claire sighed, "there's nothing non-denominational about his choice of words. Light bringer is the definition of Lucifer. Lucifer exceeded all other angels in outward perfection. He allowed himself to become arrogant. Prideful. He was jealous of the very God who created him. He wanted to become

God himself. A third of heaven's angels followed him, in active rebellion. Their banishment from heaven was prompt. Jesus described Lucifer 'falling like lightning.' Now separate from God, beings who were once mirrors—reflecting God's light—became dark as night. They mourn. They rage. The abyss they were confined to became hell. A realm of their own construct."

"C'mon," I laughed. "Isn't this all rather medieval?"

"Not everything medieval is false, David. These fallen angels are now the personification of darkness. They are the antithesis of anything life-affirming. They are powerful, shrewd, and cunning. Humanity's only defense in their presence is an active and reliant faith in God."

"Ms. Claire, if God is good and loving, why would he allow such entities to even have access to humanity?"

"That's a good question. I believe that God wants to fill the vacancy in heaven. He wants humanity to become part of his staff. First, he provided humanity with free will. With this freedom, we actively choose to be in God's presence and are therefore less likely to rebel against him. The presence of the diabolical forces the issue. Who will you side with? God or his enemies? There is no neutral ground."

"What about those humans who don't choose God, ma'am?"

"These people choose their own destiny. I'm not a big hellfire and brimstone preacher, Mr. Paul. I don't believe God desires any of his creation to be in torment. Yet torment is the emotional ramification of being excluded from God's presence. Jesus described those who reject God as 'crying' and 'gnashing their teeth.' God requires his angels and people to be loving, trusting, and faithful. Even on earth, a marriage or family without love and trust is destined for failure. Love, trust and faith are the very keys that open heaven."

"Well, Ms. Claire, you certainly have your theological ducks in a row, don't you?"

"You better believe it, cutie. Now don't you take any shots at them. This isn't a carnival game here. This is the eternal battle of the ages!"

More sarcasm came to mind, but I stayed silent.

"Ms. Claire, there are a few other facts concerning Brad Ramsey that you should know about," Jonah interjected.

"Okay, shoot."

"He is the son of Julius Ramsey, the man behind *Truth* magazine."

"Julius Ramsey? The atheist turned religious zealot who murdered his wife?"

"The same."

"Oh my."

"Brad has exhibited extrasensory abilities with David and me."

"That would fit the pattern."

"So here we have a man with psychic ability, who knows our private vulnerabilities, who desecrates Christian symbols, who engaged in the sexual abuse of a mentally challenged man, and who assaulted me with a macabre vision," Jonah sighed.

"Let me put it this way. I would be shocked if this man wasn't possessed," Claire responded.

"Possessed?" I exclaimed. "You two can't be serious! Brad is a twisted human being, not Linda Blair!"

"Not all possession mimics the William Peter Blatty story," Claire answered. "Some people willingly give themselves to the diabolical. They coexist in a symbiotic relationship. These willing hosts are called the perfectly possessed. It is the diabolical counterpart to the indwelling of the Holy Spirit."

"Please," I whispered, while shaking my head.

"My friend David is very agnostic," Jonah explained.

"Then he is in greater danger than you," Claire responded.

"Now don't talk about *me* like I'm not here!" I laughed.

"I'll need to meet this Brad myself," Claire continued. "I'll try to use religious provocation, perhaps the covert holding of a blessed item. We'll see how he reacts."

"Do you know where Claire can meet Brad, perhaps in a public forum?" Jonah asked me.

"She can join his discussion group," I joked.

"No thank you," Claire responded.

"I didn't want to tell you this, Jonah, but you're bound to find out. Marcus called me last night and told me that your station manager offered Brad his own community access broadcast."

"He what?" Jonah shrieked.

"He said he wanted to bring balance to your Christian editorials."

"As distasteful as that is," Claire observed, "it does present me with a public forum in which I can meet Mr. Ramsey. These community shows usually offer five or so seats for whoever wishes to watch."

"Brad is bound to have his followers with him," Jonah responded. "You be careful, Ms. Claire. The danger transcends the paranormal. There is an earthly threat here."

Jonah's cell phone rang. He answered it.

"Hello? Hi, Marcus, are you okay? You sound winded."

A long silence followed. Jonah's face dropped. He looked down.

"Okay, Marcus. Thanks for telling me. Yes, David is right here. I'll tell him." The doctor rubbed his face, then took a deep breath before speaking.

"Well," he sighed. "Your ex-manager Tim met with Brad last night. He told Mr. Ramsey that both he and Scott Fullman agreed to deny the *Humanist Inquirer* access to Huey's sheets. They wanted to give Dr. Boyington more opportunity to study the image."

"Scott Fullman actually went against Brad's wishes? Hey, that's great news!"

"I wish the story ended here, Dave. During the work shift today, Tim's office caught on fire."

"What?"

"Everyone at the day program got out. But Tim's office was destroyed, along with his wooden desk. Along with Huey's sheets."

I sat down. The news hit me hard. It was as if Huey had died again. How would we find out who took his body now? Despair filled me.

"Your friend Tim said that he was doing some paperwork on his desk and the papers spontaneously ignited! The flame reportedly spread as if the whole desk was soaked in gasoline."

"Good Lord!" Claire exclaimed. "Does this Tim fellow smoke?"

"No, he doesn't," I murmured.

"Possible spontaneous combustion," Claire whispered. "Mr. Ramsey was unhappy with the decision regarding those sheets. Through natural or unnatural means, he assured that the world will never learn that God translated your departed friend."

"Well, Ramsey may be shrewd and devious, but he is not all-knowing," Jonah added.

"What do you mean, Jonah?" I asked.

"Brad Ramsey doesn't know that Ray Boyington has two dozen Mylar tapes and linen patch samples lifted from Huey's sheets. The study will be published!"

# CHAPTER 19

▼

# A SHOWDOWN

I dropped by Marcus's home after work. To my relief, Tamika's SUV was absent from their driveway. Marcus heard me arrive and walked into his front yard to greet me. He only wore a sweater for warmth and the November air made him shudder.

"David! Hello."

"Hi, Marcus. You must know why I'm here."

"Of course. I've already called your apartment twice."

"So, what the hell happened?"

"I wish I knew. I asked the fire chief to look for evidence of arson. Our old friend, Officer Mullady, is also investigating."

"I hope they find some evidence. After all, who had motive to set that office on fire except for Brad?"

"Jessica."

I paused. That consideration didn't occur to me.

"My God, Marcus, you can't be serious. Jess would never endanger anyone at the day program. She loves everyone there. She would never—"

"I agree totally. I'm simply afraid that the fire chief may consider Jess a suspect. He may focus on her daily presence at the facility. Her closeness to Brad. She even has a key to the building."

"Man. What's Tim have to say?"

"Tim thinks Jessica is involved with the fire."

"What?"

"Tim asked Jess if Brad made her destroy the sheets!"

"What's this? Tim suddenly distrusts his college bud Ramsey?"

"Tim said that the timing of this fire, the day after Brad was refused access to the sheets, couldn't be just coincidence. You should have seen him, Dave. He kept bringing you up. He's starting to believe all your allegations."

"Well, I wish I was gratified by that, but look at what we've lost. A key forensic link to what happened to Huey."

"Perhaps more than that."

"Don't tell me you're becoming a Shroudie, Marcus."

"Hard not to be, considering all that's been going on."

On that note, Brad's Jaguar pulled into the driveway. My heart sank. Both he and Jessica stepped out. Jessica looked distraught. Brad had a strange smirk on his face. As Jess walked over, Ramsey paused by the car mirror and smoothed out a few stray follicles.

"Marcus, Dave. Good to see the both of you," Jess murmured between sobs. Tears ran down her cheeks.

"Hey, Jess," Marcus waved, "and Brad."

"Hello, gentlemen," Brad nodded.

"What can I do for the two of you?" my friend asked.

"Marcus," Jess whispered, wiping her face with her sleeve. "I'd like you to vouch for me with Tim tomorrow. Tell him how I was with you all day today. I would never set any fire! What do they think I am? Some sort of psycho?"

"Wild accusations can be aimed at the most undeserving targets, hon," Brad angrily hissed, glaring in my direction.

I gave him a sarcastic smile in return.

"I already pled your case," Marcus replied. "I told Tim how you didn't have either opportunity or incentive to do such a thing. You were with the work crew all day."

"Still, I'm on administrative leave while they investigate this fire. Both Brad and I. How could they think we had anything to do with this? The papers on Tim's desk ignited while he sat there!"

Brad positioned himself in front of me. "You must be enjoying the irony, huh Sparky? Me on administrative leave! How did you get Tim to turn on me? Where were you today?"

"I was at work all day, Brad," I glared back. "I was with Jonah Rubenstein."

"Oh yes, dear Jonah. How is the poor man? How's his heart?"

"He is fine," I murmured.

"Well, that's good. I don't wish the man any ill health."

The four of us stood quietly. It was a tense, awkward moment. Jess gave me a tentative look and quickly averted her eyes.

"Jess, I'm sorry to hear about your situation," I offered.

"Thanks, Dave," she smiled. "Day program seems empty without you."

"Yeah," I nodded. "I suppose I was a good *work* friend."

"You were a good *friend,*" she replied.

"I'd still be, Jess, but that's a risky friendship. Your boyfriend here may body slam me on my car hood again and molest my unconscious body."

"David!" Jess yelled in disgust.

"And you might lunge at me with a peeling knife again, Sparky."

"Brad, stop it," Jess ordered.

I paused. What was this about a peeling knife? I had the intention of attacking him with such a knife on Halloween night, but had lost the utensil. How could he have known this? Goose bumps crawled on me, as I recalled my discussion with Claire Monroe.

"Marcus, perhaps you can bring some sanity between these two," Jess suggested.

"Sorry, Jess, I side with David."

"Arrrggghhh!" she growled in exasperation. "David, can we speak…privately?"

"Sure."

We walked toward the Pattyson's mailbox. Marcus shot me an uncomfortable look, knowing he would be left alone with Brad. Ramsey then walked back to his Jaguar, causing my friend to visibly relax. Once out of earshot, my former coworker gave me her undivided attention. A few strands of long hair blew in front of her face. She looked vulnerable. More than anything, I wanted to embrace her. I resisted the urge.

"David, I don't know how to convince you that you're wrong about Brad. Have you considered the possibility that jealousy is clouding your judgment?"

"Jess, who cares how I feel? I'm not working with you two anymore."

"I care, David! Why become strangers? Marcus is also adopting your attitude! What has happened to you? How'd you go from sweet guy to insensitive buffoon?"

"If I'm an insensitive buffoon, then you shouldn't care about my friendship."

"Okay, fine! If that's how you feel. Meanwhile, both Marcus and Tim are swayed by your hatred. Both of them are now against Brad."

"I have nothing to do with that. They have minds of their own. They realize things that could incriminate Ramsey mysteriously disappear, including Huey's body. Huey's sheets. Coincidence goes so far."

"C'mon Dave! The sexual abuse investigation was over when Huey's body disappeared. Brad was exonerated. Poor Huey was not abused. Also, Brad wanted Huey's sheets given more attention! He wanted the *Humanist Inquirer* to study them!"

"No, Brad wanted the *Humanist Inquirer* to debunk them. To explain away Huey's image, so it doesn't lend credence to the Shroud of Turin."

"Don't tell me you agree with Jonah Rubenstein concerning the Shroud and Huey's sheets!"

"Not at all. But Jonah's Yale friend isn't some nutty Christian or skeptical debunker. He's an objective scientist. If anyone had the potential to find clues on those sheets, it was he. Not the *Humanist Inquirer*."

"Clues?"

"Yes, clues. Like semen stains. DNA. Skin cells."

"Dave, would you stop beating that dead horse? Brad is not a molester!"

"What makes you so sure? You claim that I'm not objective. But what about you? Doesn't Brad excite you? Make your heart beat faster? Charm you? Pleasure you?"

"You've been hanging around those Christians too much. Now you're condemning me for having a sex life."

"I'm not condemning you, Jess. I'm illustrating your lack of objectivity, as you did with me."

"Okay then! I maintain that my hormones do not influence my judgment. I dumped Kyle, didn't I? Kyle was even better looking than Brad!"

"Yes, you dumped Kyle. After six years."

Jess sighed. "The past few years, I opened up to you as a close friend. And here you use this information to judge and criticize me!"

"I don't want to. I still consider you the most warm, caring woman I've ever known. You have a heart of gold. What I am is worried about you."

"Don't! Brad is the warmest, most caring man I've ever known! You should have seen him the night Jonah had his cardiac crisis. He worried. He paced. He called Winsted Memorial several times trying to find out if your friend was all right."

"I'll be sure to inform the Academy about his performance."

"Dave, I didn't know you were such a narrow-minded pig!"

"Oh please! Your boyfriend has threatened me, framed me, beat me up, and confessed his sexual abuse of Huey. After all this, you call me the *pig*?"

At that moment, Tamika pulled into the driveway. Her SUV roared loudly as she parked alongside Brad. She leapt from her vehicle and charged toward Ramsey. I held my breath. Jessica and I ran back toward the commotion.

"What are *you* doin' here?" Tamika yelled at Brad. He looked surprised.

"'Mika," Marcus replied. "Calm it down. Don't do anything nutty."

She walked up to within an inch of Brad's face.

"I know what you did to Jonah Rubenstein," she hissed.

"How I called for the paramedics? No reason to thank me, Mrs. Pattyson."

"Your lies won't work on me, serpent. I know who you serve," Tamika exclaimed.

Jess stepped into the face-off, her arms separating Brad and Tamika.

"Marcus, would you please control your wife? We don't need to see any fundamentalist fanatic going nuts today!" she exclaimed.

Marcus looked stunned.

"*Fundamentalist fanatic?*" Tamika shrieked. "At least I'm not the devil's *little whore!*"

Brad laughed. "Oh, now I'm the devil."

I looked at Marcus with concern. Tamika was making a spectacle of herself. My friend took Tamika's arm, but she yanked her arm back.

"*I cast you out, demon!*" she intoned in a loud voice.

Brad laughed so hard, he bent over and held his stomach. Jess stood there confused.

"Do you hear me, demon?" Tamika continued. "I've been given the power to tread upon serpents and scorpions! You are no match *for me!* I command you! *Begone!* Depart from this person, your human servant! A perfected apostle commands you!"

Brad stopped laughing long enough to salute Tamika. "Yes, ma'am! I recognize your authority! Let's go, Jess."

Jessica took Brad's arm and glared at the three of us.

"You guys need help," she murmured.

They drove off, tires spinning on black ice. I stood with the couple, not knowing what to say. Tamika trembled. Marcus rubbed her back.

"'Mika," Marcus soothed. "I understand your passion. Still, you're not a pastor."

"Hon, don't be ignorant! The apostles weren't ordained as pastors either. They cast out demons, simple because they were close to our Lord."

"I don't know, 'Mika. This encounter doesn't feel right."

"Don't worry, Marcus. The Spirit led me to do this. I doubt you'll be having trouble with this character Ramsey again."

"Tamika," I finally spoke up. "If that were true, I'd join the First Church of Tamika Pattyson."

"No, don't do that hon. Any glory I exhibit is just a reflection of my Lord and Savior."

Marcus put his arm around Tamika. "Let's go inside, hon. I'm starved. Want to sup with us, David?"

"No thanks, guys. I better be shoving off."

"Oww!" Tamika exclaimed.

"What's wrong, hon?"

"Get your arm off of me, Marcus. The left side of my neck is sore."

"Sore spot? Let's see."

Marcus pulled her collar down a few inches.

"Hey, David, come look at this."

I saw three red welts running down her neck. They looked like scratch marks.

"What's this, 'Mika?" Marcus asked. "Did some patient attack you today?"

"No. Why you ask?"

"This looks like someone scratched you. With three fingers."

"No one touched me!"

Marcus looked pensive. Worried.

"My God, 'Mika. Dave. What if Ramsey is responsible for this?"

"Showing psychic ability is one thing," I offered, "but physically marking someone without touching them is another. Let's not let our imaginations run away with us. I always find scratches I don't remember getting."

"Yeah, so do I," Marcus considered.

"Relax, guys," Tamika laughed. "No demon would dare touch me. I've already been touched by our Lord!"

"Sure you won't change your mind?" Marcus asked me again.

"No, I think I need a nap. That exchange with Jess has me drained."

"Okay, Dave. I'll call you tomorrow."

"Bye guys."

During the drive home, I felt embarrassed. I was unrelated to Tamika or her spiritual gyrations. Even though Jess attached herself to the most obscene character I'd ever met, I still didn't want her associating me with fundamentalist performances.

At eleven that night, my phone rang. I knew late night calls were never a good thing. I reluctantly picked up the receiver.

"Dave!"

It was Marcus.

"Yeah, Marcus? What's up?"

"I need Jonah's new home phone number. He changed it last month."

"Sure. But why would you need his number in the middle of the night?"

"It's 'Mika, man. Something pushed her down the stairs, something she couldn't see! Jonah may know what to do...or Claire Monroe. We're really afraid."

I gave him the number. Was this all pious imagination? I suspected it was.

# CHAPTER 20

▼

# BEAR MOUNTAIN

Jonah closed his office two Saturdays a month and I looked forward to sleeping late on this particular day. My depression had gone from insomnia to excessive sleeping. I didn't mind the oblivion of slumber. It allowed a temporary respite from Brad and Jess. Given that I was free from nightmares, that is. This Saturday featured pleasant dreams. I woke up and looked at my alarm clock. Since it was still early, I turned over and pulled the blanket over my head.

The phone rang with unnatural volume. As if shocked by electricity, my body jerked awake. After fumbling around, I picked up the receiver.

"Yeah?"

"Hello, David, it's Jonah."

"Hi, Jonah. No work today, right?"

"I'm over at Marcus' house. Tamika had a rough night and Marcus needs you today."

"Needs me? An agnostic skeptic? C'mon, Jonah. You're a counselor! Can't you help them shed their medieval superstitions? Brad may have some mind reading ability, but he's not possessed."

"You're wrong, David. Tamika has suffered paranormal assaults. What I'd like you to do is take Marcus out today. Go for a hike, or to a movie. Anything."

"You want Marcus to leave Tamika alone?"

"No. I'll spend the day with Tamika. Can you come over around eight?"

"Okay. I'll be there as soon as I can."

I pulled my lethargic body off of my foldaway bed. Shuffling to the bathroom, I longed for the hermit's life.

On schedule, I pulled into Marcus' driveway at eight. My laziness had worn off. I looked forward to spending the day with Marcus. I would try to liberate him from these Christian superstitions. As I exited my Chevy, Jonah opened Marcus's front door. Wisps of smoke drifted from his pipe.

"Good morning, David."

"Good morning."

"Marcus was up until two, I'm letting him sleep. Tamika fell asleep around three."

As I walked into the house, Jonah presented me with a steaming mug of coffee. The scent of hazelnut was welcome.

"So, Jonah," I started. "What's all this about a paranormal assault?"

"As you may know, Tamika felt something or someone push her down the stairs. Marcus was in the garage at the time. After their frantic phone call, I came over. Under my supervision, I watched three defined scratches form on her forehead. Her hands were in her lap the entire time. I've seen this type of phenomena before. The air within twelve inches around her body was frigid. A putrid stench filled the living room. In the name of Jesus Christ, I verbally commanded the presence assaulting her to depart. After three knocking sounds on the ceiling above us, the air returned to normal."

"So Jonah, you consider your Christian faith a defense against this type of attack?"

"Yes, I do."

"Then how come Tamika's Christian faith didn't automatically protect her?"

"That's a good question. I believe Tamika had a vulnerability, one many Christians possess. Her weakness was pride. Spiritual pride."

"Spiritual pride?"

"Yes. Through the years, she boasted of her spiritual gifts. She believes herself to be superior to most people. Including her Christian friends. Including her husband."

"Yes, that's Tamika all right. As a matter of fact, that's most Christians."

"That's a negative stereotype. As a Christian counselor, I know most Christians are keenly aware of their shortcomings. The very basis of the Christian faith is that all mankind is weak. Humanity is incapable of living up to the most basic of behavioral standards, such as the Ten Commandments. Because of our inherent weakness, which some define as the legacy of 'original sin,' man needs God's grace on a continual basis. Through a faith connection with the Almighty, such grace is freely given. This humility is in direct contrast with most organized religions."

"How so?"

"Most religions are focused on how men earn their way into salvation or enlightenment. They obey 'thou shalt' and 'thou shalt nots.' They practice ritualistic disciplines, sacrifices, and meditations. Through their own efforts, they become 'saved.'"

I laughed. "How's this differ from Christianity, with its moralism and ritual?"

"Christian morals and ritual are not agents of salvation. The one and only agent of Christian salvation is the Messiah Jesus. The loving sacrifice of his cross. Jesus was abused for our iniquities, and through his efforts, our failings are erased. His blood washes us clean. Our good deeds are dirty rags in the eyes of God, but Jesus' good deeds are sufficient for all. We are clothed and protected by Jesus' righteousness."

"Then what's to prevent a Christian from believing in Jesus, then feeling free to do whatever evil he wants to do?"

"The Holy Spirit."

"Come again?"

"The Holy Spirit is a gift from God, the only part of God we can take within ourselves. When we believe in, and worship God's only begotten Son, the Holy Spirit is the power that strengthens us to do good. To please God. Yet these 'fruits' of Christian life are not agents of salvation. Nor do they come from ourselves. These fruits are the ramification of salvation, not salvation itself."

"So who's to say what Christian is saved and what Christian is just a pretender?"

"These concerns have divided Christians since the beginning. Jesus spoke of knowing his followers by 'the fruit' they exhibit. Even this can get dicey. Thus, we have different Christian denominations, each emphasizing different tenants. My attitude is that only God can clarify who is saved."

"Haven't you violated this concept by labeling Tamika as spiritually proud?"

"I haven't said that Tamika isn't saved, or that she isn't a Christian. What I did say is that Tamika has vulnerability through the failing of pride. Are you familiar with the New Testament, David?"

"A bit."

"Then you know that Jesus embraced most of whom he was exposed to, even adulteresses, prostitutes, and tax collectors. Only one group of people received harsh judgments from Christ."

"The Pharisees?"

"Yes, the self-righteous. Certain Pharisees, Sadducees, and Scribes were spiritually proud. They considered themselves above the common man. Yet, keep in mind the New Testament didn't condemn all Pharisees, nor is it anti-Semitic. The protagonists, Joseph of Arimathea and Nicodemus were Pharisees. The Rabbi Hillel is honored by Jesus, as he reinterpreted Hillel's teaching as the Golden Rule."

"What about the Gospel of John illustrating how 'the Jews' conspired against Jesus? Isn't that wording anti-Semitic?"

"Jews in this literary context is in reference to Judean Jews and their leaders in the Temple."

"Judean Jews?"

"Yes. On one hand, the common working Jews of the country were receptive to Christ. The Jews in Jerusalem were *initially* receptive to Jesus. They believed in an earthly Messiah who would defeat the Romans. As they realized that Jesus had no intention in opposing the Romans, they turned on him. Thus, the bitterness the gospel writers have toward Judean Jews is understandable. Unfortunately, it's interpreted by modern scholars as anti-Semitic."

"I'll take your word on that. But let's not get too sidetracked here. We were talking about Christian salvation and Tamika in particular. You say that you don't begrudge Tamika of her salvation, yet she has this vulnerability to a supposed demonic attack. How come?"

"As I understand the situation from Marcus, she attempted to exorcise Brad yesterday. Exorcism is a tricky business. It has to be done just right, and performed by a specific cleric. Even in the gospels, two disciples fail at an exorcism because they didn't practice enough prayer and fasting. Based upon Marcus's memory, Tamika tried to exorcise Brad on her own authority. She never used the name of Christ. No human being has authority over the demonic, only through the name of God is authority found. Another catching point would be that the possessed individual has to want deliverance as well."

"Allow me to be blunt, Jonah. Tamika is a religious fanatic. I've seen her go emotionally ballistic over nothing. Isn't it true that hysterical people often break out with marks and rashes? Some even go blind! Fanatical Catholics develop the 'stigmata' through their obsession with the wounds of Christ and his suffering."

"Yes, hysterical people can develop rashes and wounds. Still, the cold and stench surrounding Tamika departed upon using the name of Jesus. Temporarily departed, but departed nonetheless. Three knocks in the ceiling were heard. The number three is in mockery of the Trinity."

"Cold and stench? That's pretty subjective. Perhaps a draft blew through. Perhaps someone farted."

Jonah broke into a hearty laugh. "God bless your humor, David. You be sure to make Marcus laugh today. Don't argue with him, or attack his beliefs. Just be there for him."

"Wouldn't it comfort Marcus to understand that his wife isn't under demonic attack?"

"You can't prove that she isn't. All you can do is be there for him."

"You're tying my hands, Jonah."

"No, I'm being practical. You're just as likely to dissuade Marcus from his beliefs as he is in persuading you."

"Since you put it that way."

"I called Claire Monroe this morning. She is vacationing in England, but will be back in one week."

"Well, this stuff is certainly what she gets off on."

"I confess though, the immediacy of all this is atypical."

"Huh?"

"Tamika challenged Ramsey, and that very instant she exhibits evidence of an attack. That very night she is oppressed! The speed of this infestation is shocking. Usually this process is gradual. Like a slow growing tumor. It can take months or years."

At that moment, Marcus emerged from his bedroom. He came shuffling in wearing a bathrobe. Dark rings bordered his eyes.

"I thought I smelled hazelnut coffee. Thanks for staying, Jon—hey, David! What are you doing here?"

"Uh…after your phone call, I was concerned about you guys."

"Good to see you. Hopefully things will become normal around here."

"If they don't, Marcus, you know the appropriate prayers to use."

"Yes, I do. Thanks, Jonah."

"How did Tamika seem when you got up?"

"She's out like a light. At least the scratches on her face are fading."

Jonah gave me a look. A visual prompting.

"Hey, Marcus, how about a hike up Bear Mountain today? You up for it?"

"I'd love to, Dave, but I don't think I should leave Tamika. Also, I was going to call Tim on Jess's behalf."

"Don't worry about Tamika," Jonah responded. "I'll keep an eye on her."

"Jonah! You were up all night. You've done enough, really."

"Nonsense. I'm fine."

"You're a saint."

After a quick breakfast, Marcus and I loaded a daypack and left for Salisbury. The air was frigid. Early snowflakes drifted in random directions. The ride to the northwestern corner of Connecticut took one hour. It was a scenic drive, winding through the rural towns of Norfolk and Canaan. Marcus and I chatted about the scenery, football, and other trivial matters. I took Jonah's advice to heart. Theological debates were avoided.

The small parking area for the Bear Mountain trail was filled with vehicles, even on this wintry day. We were forced to park on the side of Route 41. The trail ahead looked like an exercise in misery. My initial laziness upon waking tried to reassert itself. During the first hundred yards of our hike, a group of pretty college-age girls came down the trail. With bright smiles, they greeted us. We smiled in return. I turned to look at their backsides, a fact Marcus teased me about.

"Hey, single guy!" he laughed. "Why don't you go get a phone number or two?"

"Yeah, right. That's how to do it. Turn around right here and stalk them."

"I see your point. This is the era of distrust, especially of men. I don't know how well I'd do as a single man these days."

"You'd do better than me, Marcus."

"We may soon find out."

"What?"

"Let's just say that 'Mika and I haven't been too happy."

Tamika's aggressive personality put me off, but I never suspected that Marcus had problems with his wife.

"Jeez, Marcus, I'm sorry."

"So am I. This fast-food exorcism attempt of hers yesterday is the latest straw on the camel's back. Her attitude isn't limited toward non-Christians. I get the worst of it. It seems I can't do anything right. I never eat right, sleep right, dress right, or worship right. She keeps trying to remake me in her own image."

"Did Tamika behave like this when you were dating?"

"Not at all. She was supportive. Even flattering!"

The trail's incline started to increase and we talked around the necessity of heavy breathing.

"Have you two tried marriage counseling?"

"Not yet. But Jonah has been offering his services."

"Hmm. I'll have to admit, I respect Jonah's skills as a counselor. Oh sure, I've been butting heads with him about his views on Huey's sheets. About Brad's supposed possession. He's too eager to embrace the outlandish. But his ability to discern people and their burdens, this I can't deny. The man knows his stuff. He empathizes with people, he cares about them."

"Are you surprised by this?"

"Yeah, I guess. I expected him to be some critical Christian fundamentalist."

"Like Tamika?"

"I never said that."

"You didn't have to. I see your face drop whenever 'Mika appears."

"Well, I know that your wife isn't fond of me. I feel condemnation radiating off of her."

"Don't take it personal. She likes you. She's critical of everyone, even herself."

"Herself?"

"She often mopes around the house, filled with self-loathing. She hates her weight. She hates her face. She hates her hair. She believes she has never done enough for people, or prayed enough to God."

"I had no idea! I believed Tamika thought of herself as perfect."

"Far from it, Dave. Her Holy Roller persona is an overcompensation."

The climb started to take its toll. Marcus and I sat on the trail's edge for a brief rest.

"So, is divorce in your future?"

"I hope not. Divorce is an evil thing, but if we do split, it's better that we do so before we have kids."

I took a swig of water from my canteen and passed it to my friend.

"I'm sorry to hear about this, Marcus. I've been so self-absorbed lately. I didn't think you had any problems of your own."

"We all get self-absorbed. I'm always reminding myself that everyone has his or her cross to bear. We are usually unaware of what burdens weigh on our friends."

With a grunt, we lifted ourselves off the log and started the climb again. Eventually we reached a fork in the trail. The Undermountain Trail continued off to the right. Having hiked it before, I knew it was a long semicircle that culminated in a steep, hand-over-foot climb. The trail continuing uphill resulted in a gradual climb up the mountain. Marcus and I looked at each other. No words were needed. On this day, the easy trail was the obvious choice.

"So, Marcus, are you flying south for your traditional Thanksgiving reunion?"

"Not this year. Thanksgiving at home, watching football on the tube. What about you?"

"Ahh, I have grand plans. A frozen turkey dinner and a healthy dose of self-pity."

"Why don't you dine with us, Dave?"

"I'd love to Marcus, but I don't want to upset Tamika. She has enough trouble without bearing my presence on a holiday."

"She won't mind. She secretly adores you. Don't you know that?"

"Adores…me?"

"That's right. She tries to convert you because she cares about you. She worries about you."

"I had no idea."

"So 'Mika won't have any problem with you coming over. This may possibly be our last turkey day, as man and wife. Perhaps we'll invite Jonah. Just don't ever, ever mention that theory that dogs and crows consumed Jesus' remains."

"Oh no! I wouldn't do that again."

"There may be hope for you yet, Davey-Avey."

At Marcus's comment, I stopped walking. A wave of sadness moved through me.

"Oh God, Dave. I'm sorry. I didn't mean to remind you of Huey. You really miss him, don't you?"

"Yeah. I do."

"I'm sure he's looking down on you with a smile, Dave."

"Looking down on me? I wish that were true."

"Well, 'down' may be a misnomer. Heaven was once thought to be in the sky. It's more likely a parallel dimension."

"Then Rod Serling must guard the pearly gates."

"Maybe he does!"

"Dooo do dooo do." I sang, mimicking the *Twilight Zone* theme song.

"Don't sing that," my friend laughed. "Last night spooked me enough, thank you very much."

"Sorry. Did you see anything…supernatural, Marcus?"

"I saw several scratch marks form on 'Mika's neck, back, and face."

"Did you smell anything foul? Feel unnaturally cold air?"

"Yes. It was focused where 'Mika was sitting."

"Hmm."

I wanted to provide Marcus with rational alternatives. Yet I promised Jonah. No debates.

After an hour of hiking up a gradual grade, we reached the summit. Directly below us were the Twin Lakes. The rolling hills of northwestern Connecticut. A group of hikers were sitting on the base of a stone monument. It used to be higher, but time and erosion collapsed the structure. Low-bush blueberries scattered along the ridge under the shade of wind-sculpted scrub pines.

Marcus sat by me, looking over the vista. A tear rolled down his left cheek.

After the drive back home, Marcus didn't know what to expect with Tamika. Would the unusual phenomena be present? Would Jonah be up to the task of reassuring his wife? With anxiety, we entered his house.

Much to our surprise, Jonah and Tamika were talking in the kitchen. Laughing about something. As she saw Marcus, she ran over and gave her husband a tight embrace.

"'Mika! Everything okay?"

"Everything is fine, Marcus. Jonah and I had a great day, and we cooked up a feast. Get Davey to stay, there's plenty!"

"What about the attacks? Anything unusual?"

"Not at all. No odd sounds, smells, or chills. No scratches."

"Phew! Praise the Lord."

Jonah sported a broad smile. The atmosphere in the house was different—lighter, more cheerful. Eventually, we all sat down and ate dinner. Tamika herself made a point to invite us back for Thanksgiving.

# CHAPTER 21

▼

# THE JOURNAL
# CONTROVERSY

Comparatively, the next few weeks were uneventful. Jonah and I ate Thanksgiving dinner at Marcus's house. Tamika made turkey with all the trimmings. They even displayed Christmas lights around their front door.

The Pattyson household was free from unusual activity during this time. Claire Monroe suspected that Tamika challenged a real demonic presence and supposedly experienced the ramifications of that confrontation. Claire warned that more attacks were likely. As the days passed, Ms. Monroe's warning seemed less likely. Marcus was even getting along better with his humbled wife. All seemed well.

Brad quit his job at RAI. He was deeply offended by the arson investigation. Naturally, no evidence of foul play was found. Both Brad and Jess were cleared of suspicion. Jess returned to her position working under Tim Gould. Upon hearing the news, I was happy for the remaining Elm residents. They were now free from the sexual predator who had been their manager.

Brad's community access television show called *Rational Humanist* was popular from the start. The station moved Jonah's show from its favorable time slot to give Brad more airtime. They reran Brad's broadcast with regularity. Being that Ramsey had connections with the *Humanist Inquirer*, he managed to get high-profile guests into the small-scale studio. Prominent scholars from the

Christ Convention were guests. New England senators showed up. Professors from Quinnipiac and Yale appeared.

Systematically, Brad illustrated the perceived fallacies of America's religious right. He also highlighted stories of reported Israeli oppression, interviewing Palestinians from the occupied territories. He interviewed a doctor shot by an anti-abortion protester. He ran a profile on an elderly woman, bilked of her life savings by a television evangelist.

Brad's show caused big waves for being in a small pond. State newspapers covered Ramsey's splash in the northwest corner. Within two weeks of Brad's debut, his *Rational Humanist* broadcast was picked up by other community access stations across the state. Brad quickly became a local celebrity. I waited anxiously for Dr. Boyington's report on Huey's sheets. Scandal would hopefully visit this local icon.

On December 13, my long wait ended. Dr. Boyington published his findings in the journal, *Microanalysis.* His study was titled, "A Modern Equivalent to the Turin Shroud."

In this article, he basically repeated the findings of his preliminary analysis. The Huey sheets, anonymously identified as "sample A and B," were altered in a manner identical to the Shroud. The tape and patch samples contained surface fibrils, discolored by dehydration. Photographs of Huey's sheets validated the fact that the number of fibrils discolored determined the image intensity. No skin oils or urine were detected in significant quantities. All man-made processes were dismissed. The article ended with a question: What was the process that recorded both a recently deceased, retarded man and an ancient crucifixion victim on linen? Dr. Boyington argued that the process had to be natural. He implied that Huey's sheet weakened the Shroud's dematerialization collapse theory. It was obvious that this twentieth-century man was not raised from the dead, or brought to heaven in a chariot. Jonah fumed at his friend's conclusions.

As I read Boyington's article, I asked Jonah if he had been in touch with his friend. He had. I anxiously asked whether they detected semen on the patch samples. They had not.

I brooded. Somehow I would prove that Ramsey sexually abused my vulnerable friend. Perhaps I could get him to confess once more and secretly record his statement. Even if the recording was legally inadmissible, it would still ruin Brad's rising popularity.

A few days later, Jonah received a phone call from Brad. It was the first time my employer heard from Ramsey since their disastrous first meeting. With a pale face and a tense voice, Jonah sat by my desk and shared the conversation.

"Mr. Ramsey isn't happy with the Boyington report, David."

"Oh? What did the scum have to say?"

"He accused us of hoarding evidence, now that the sheets are ash. He even suggested that we stole the linens and burned Tim's office as an afterthought!"

"Well, Jonah," I laughed sarcastically. "He's on to us. Super sleuths that we are, we steal and destroy whatever we want."

"Also, Mr. Ramsey has invited me on his Christmas broadcast. Actually, it was more of a challenge than a friendly invite."

"Christmas broadcast?"

"Yes, a program to air on December 19. The theme is, Who was Jesus? He invited two professors who seek to redefine Jesus. Transform Jesus from Judaic Savior to political insurgent. It's up to me to defend the traditional Christ of Christianity."

"You're not going to accept his invitation, are you?"

"Yes."

"What? Have you forgotten your experience last time?"

Jonah rubbed his forehead. "No, I haven't. But it is my duty to combat the lies undermining the gospel message."

"Doc, your precious gospel message has been forced down throats for two thousand years. You don't need to do anything."

"Academic distortions have never been as popular as they are now. This very day."

"What about your heart? What if you get overwhelmed again?"

"My heart is fine. Just as yours is. What we experienced had no somatic cause."

"Okay. Let's pretend you're right. Let's assume Brad Ramsey is empowered and possessed by demonic forces. Do you really wish to go against that?"

"Now I know what I'm facing. Before I wasn't certain. Three days before the debate, I'm going to start a strict fasting and prayer regiment."

That will do the heart real good, I thought to myself.

"I will also have Claire Monroe accompany me."

"That may be a good idea! All Claire has to do is flirt with him…he'll run for the hills."

"This is no laughing matter, David."

"Sorry."

"Will you and Marcus attend?"

"Arrrggghhh, Jonah. To see Brad and Jess again. I get sick just thinking about it. I'm sure Marcus would go."

"Okay. I understand."

I felt guilty for wimping out, but I was not a member of Jonah's little Christian task force. It was hard to get over Jess if I was forced to continually see her.

December 19 arrived. I sat in front of my television and prepared for the spectacle. Claire and Marcus were in the studio audience. They were Jonah's support group. My support group was a six-pack of beer.

Brad's show started with dramatic music and a photomontage. Ramsey's voice narrated the introduction.

"Jesus of Nazareth. Who was he? The holiday season brings this question to the forefront. Are generations of supernaturalists and religious adherents correct about this first-century rabbi? Or do they misinterpret and distort the true Jesus of history? Tonight, we search for answers."

The introduction faded and four seated men appeared silhouetted by a backlight. Potted plants flanked the gathering. As each man was introduced, a spotlight lit the man in question.

"Tonight, the *Rational Humanist* is honored to have three scholars, here to discuss this very issue. First on the panel is Dr. Wallace Brody, distinguished professor of history and religious studies at Maryland's Stratton Academy. Next we have Jonah Rubenstein, fundamentalist author and social worker with Christian Family Services."

As Brad said fundamentalist, Jonah cringed. He knew what negative preconceptions that word had with the general audience.

"And certainly not least, we have Dr. Rudolf Jeffries, the editor in chief of the magazine, the *Humanist Inquirer*. Welcome, gentlemen."

The panel nodded.

"In this show's tradition of being direct," Brad smiled, "I ask the three of you directly…in a nutshell, who was Jesus of Nazareth? Dr. Brody."

"Thank you, Brad. In a nutshell, Jesus was not much different than other wandering, Jewish mystics and insurgents we find in first-century Palestine. Honi the Circle Drawer was a miracle worker, and Hanina ben Dosa was an effective healer and exorcist. What makes Jesus different is the accumulation of mythology, added incrementally, that transformed a fairly typical Jewish Hasidim into a Roman substitute for Apollo and other sun deities. Indeed, this Christian movement even took the idea of 'divine kingship' from the Romans. The true Jesus of history is buried under centuries of legend. It's doubtful we'll ever meet him as he was. Only about twenty percent of the gospels are based on historic truth. The rest is religious poetry.

"The earliest, complete gospel accounts in our possession are as late as the fourth century. They are not reliable accounts. Thankfully, we have some manuscripts found at Nag Hammadi, Egypt. Among these we have a 'pearl of great value,' that being the 'Gospel of Thomas.' This gospel contains the words and teachings of Jesus, separated from silly miracle stories and resurrection accounts. Jesus the rabbinical teacher is now revealed to us, a man instructing his followers to seek the kingdom of heaven within themselves!

"So what's my answer to who Jesus was? Jesus was a virtuous man who taught people to find divinity within themselves. He was persecuted for opposing the greed and wealth of the Sadducees. The Romans were none too happy with his popularity. He was a disruption, like so many other would-be 'messiahs' we read about in the works of Flavius Josephus. He was executed, thrown on a common grave, possibly consumed by wandering dogs and carrion crows. A creative community of Jesus followers then proceeded to elaborate, exaggerate, and deify this man who remains a symbol for all. The Jesus of faith is valid in a theological sense, but he is *not* to be confused with the actual Jesus of history."

"Wow, thank you, Dr. Brody! Next, Jonah Rubenstein."

I noticed how Brad failed to address Jonah as 'doctor.'

"Thank you, Mr. Ramsey," Jonah smiled. "I'm delighted to have this opportunity…the opportunity to restore Jesus from the wandering dogs and carrion crows of academia."

The small crowd mumbled at this comment. The men next to Jonah visibly bristled.

"The question is not who Jesus was, but who he *is*," Jonah continued. "Jesus is the fulfillment of my heritage, of Judaism. He fulfills centuries-old prophecies which implied that 'Messiah king' would be sinless, would be divine, would be the sacrificial lamb, would be all that Christians claim he is."

Giggles were heard in the background. Jonah continued unfazed.

"No, Jesus was not deified by gentile mystery religions; these had their source in seasonal cycles. Some church traditions and holiday dates have pagan sources, but that's irrelevant to this discussion. Jesus of Nazareth is the Divine Messiah who died for all sin. Thankfully, the story didn't end there. He is risen and reigns as Lord. History attests to his empty tomb. History attests to his Resurrection. His earliest followers died for this conviction, the very same conviction I now share with you."

"Thank you, Mr. Rubenstein," Brad snickered. "Last but not least, Dr. Jeffries."

"Hi all, I am the editor in chief for the *Humanist Inquirer* magazine. This publication doesn't waste too much time with hypothesis and conjecture. We deal in science. We deal with fact. When it comes down to 'who Jesus was,' in truth, who the hell cares?"

The small audience laughed. They clapped.

"I don't mean to be indelicate, but Jesus was a man. As are we. So it's not really a matter of what we hypothesize about this person, it's a matter of what science tells us. Science tells us that men don't walk on water. Men don't multiply loaves of bread. Men don't heal paralytics. Men certainly don't cast out demons, since demons don't exist to begin with."

More laughter.

"Obviously, the Jesus of religious doctrine is fantasy. Beyond this, I think he is a great symbol. A symbol of advocacy for the poor. A symbol of defiance, especially against any religious powers that be. Jesus was a humanist, and if one wants to find him—avoid the church. Get enlightened, get educated, and join your humanist brethren in a little thing we like to call *reality!*"

With this, most of the small audience gave a standing ovation. Brad stood to clap as well. Dr. Brody looked a tad confused, but went along with the gesture. Jonah remained seated.

"Well, we're off to a good start!" Brad exclaimed. "Mr. Rubenstein, how do you respond to Dr. Jeffries's comments?"

"I say that there is more to heaven and earth than dreamt of in your philosophy."

"Is that so, Mr. Rubenstein?" Jeffries asked.

"Please, gentlemen, I'd like to be addressed as you are—as doctor," Jonah smiled.

"Oh, forgive us…doctor," Brad laughed.

"Christianity is all about forgiveness," Jonah replied. "Anyway, as I was saying, the parameters modern humanism has placed on reality are not accurate. Millions of people, each and every year, have experiences that remain undefined by modern science."

"Anecdotal nonsense," Jeffries replied. "If I claimed I saw a unicorn in my yard, you couldn't disprove it."

"The extraordinary experiences I refer to transcend mere anecdotal evidence."

"Oh? How so?"

"Many paranormal experiences leave physical, measurable evidence in their wake. Photographs. Electronic voice phenomena. Video footage. Some faith healings are verified by the medical community. The Shroud of Turin still confuses the scientific community."

"Such phenomena have naturalistic explanations. If you'd like a subscription to the *Humanist Inquirer*, my friend, I can provide one. Our magazine deals with such hooey," Jeffries grinned.

"No thank you," Jonah laughed. "There is a difference between honest investigation and debunking. Debunking is a business where an investigator assumes a certain claim is a fraud before he investigates. Then as self-fulfilling prophecy, he casts doubt on whatever claim is at hand. If one wanted to debunk the moon landing, all one would need to do is arrange arguments and innuendo in a unilateral fashion."

"Ahh, thank you, Dr. Rubenstein. Now we know the modus operandi of men like you and Dr. Ray Boyington. You two are as one-sided as they come."

"Excuse me?" Jonah raised his eyebrows.

"That's right. Dr. Ray Boyington is a friend of yours, is he not? Your buddy just made the news with his claim in the journal *Microanalysis*. Tell us, 'Mr. Christian,' where is your touted modern equivalent to the Turin Shroud?"

"Sadly, it was lost in a fire," Jonah replied, staring at Brad.

"How convenient," the skeptic Jeffries snorted.

"No, it isn't," Jonah replied.

"Well, I happen to know from an unnamed source that the sheet in question belonged to a developmentally challenged individual named Huey Riiska. Mr. Riiska's body disappeared from his group home, a crime that remains unsolved. Isn't it a fact, Dr. Rubenstein, that you hired a former employee of Residential Associates to be your personal assistant? Isn't it a fact that this man has a criminal history? Isn't it a fact that you and he had motive and opportunity to perpetrate this fraud, for the purposes of promoting your silly Christian-Shroudie books?"

Jonah knit his brow.

As the scene played out on my television, I dropped my beer can. I was getting dragged into this?

"The innuendo you're constructing is not fact," Jonah calmly replied.

"Well, I think the public can judge for themselves," Jeffries continued. "Next month in the *Humanist Inquirer*, we will directly address the claims of Dr. Ray Boyington. We will make it evident that this former RAI employee, who shall remain nameless, probably stole Mr. Riiska's body. Both Dr. Boyington and you could have chemically treated his bedsheets and made linen images of Huey Riiska via a camera obscura. Just as Dr. Nicholas Allen has duplicated the Turin Shroud image. Before the *Humanist Inquirer* had a chance to analyze your forgery, the sheets mysteriously went up in flames. All but a few fabric samples remain, viciously guarded by none other than Dr. Ray Boyington. If I had my way, this article would be titled 'The Shroud of Hooey.'"

Jonah smiled.

"Thank you for proving my point, Dr. Jeffries. Your mudslinging was just demonstrated for all to see. Your conspiracy theory sounds good, but it falls apart upon analysis. The police took the sheets in question the very night this disabled man died and disappeared. The police discovered the faint images that were imprinted on the linens. Now, did the evil conspiracy I supposedly orchestrated unfold at the speed of light?"

I shuddered. If Tim Gould was watching, he was sure to be throwing a fit. The incident RAI sought to conceal was exposed. Was this Brad's revenge on Tim and Scott Fullman?

"Uh, what's all this have to do with our discussion about Jesus?" Dr. Brody asked. Apparently, he wasn't part of the set-up orchestrated by Brad and Dr. Jeffries.

"I'm sorry," Rudolf Jeffries replied. "I just had to expose this recent attempt to legitimatize the Turin Shroud."

"I understand," Dr. Brody nodded. "That linen is obviously medieval. All who think otherwise…are medieval themselves."

The audience chuckled.

"Okay," Jonah responded. "Let's ignore the Turin Shroud for now. Viewers can research for themselves the mountain of scientific…yes, scientific evidence that supports the linen's authenticity. Let's now discuss the historical Jesus."

"Bravo," Dr. Brody said.

Jonah leaned forward.

"Dr. Brody, you claim that Jesus was thrown in a common grave…a pit exposed to scavengers. What about the consistent testimony that Jesus was buried in a rock-hewn tomb…in a garden near Golgotha? A sepulcher owned by the wealthy Pharisee, Joseph of Arimathea?"

"Yes," Dr. Brody replied. "That story was invented to fulfill a specific Old Testament prophecy. This prophecy is found in Isaiah fifty-three nine. It reads, '…they made His grave with the wicked, but with the rich at His death.'"

"Very good, doctor," Jonah nodded. "Yet let us not forget, the gospels and epistles were all written in the first century. Creeds and hymns as well. They repeatedly mention how Jesus was buried. If anyone were going to lie about Jesus, would they risk a lie so easy to expose? If Dr. Brody's theory is accurate, some in Jerusalem must have witnessed the public decomposition of Jesus' body—supposedly flung in a common grave. But no, history doesn't record such an argument to combat the resurrection. The only apparent explanation offered was that the disciples stole the body from the tomb."

"What sources are you quoting from?" Dr. Brody asked.

"Well, first I'm quoting the Gospel of Matthew, an account written as early as fifty AD. Matthew mentions the rumor that the guards slept while the disciples stole Jesus' body. The rumor was still in circulation as he composed his gospel account. Around the same time of this writing, Claudius issued a decree in Nazareth warning of the death penalty for any violation of sepulcher. At that very same time, Claudius expelled Rome's Jewish population because they had some new superstition or belief he disliked. It all ties together."

"Maybe for someone with a pious imagination," Dr. Brody commented.

"Amen to that," Dr. Jeffries laughed.

"Also," Dr. Brody continued. "The idea that Matthew wrote his gospel as early as fifty AD is not widely accepted."

"But Dr. Brody, you do admit that most scholars date that gospel between fifty and eighty AD?" Jonah asked.

"Yes, most do. I don't," Dr. Brody replied.

"That's fine," my employer laughed. "Also, let's not forget the early creeds, memorized and recited by the followers of Jesus before the gospel accounts were written. These creeds are often repeated in the New Testament epistles. In First Corinthian's fifteenth chapter, Paul repeats one of these creeds as something he 'received,' and then 'delivers.' He quotes the standard gospel message, narrating Christ's death and Resurrection. It's noteworthy that within this creed, Paul repeats that 'Christ was buried.' This creed predates all the gospels and is part of an oral tradition that goes back to thirty something AD."

"Nonsense,' Dr. Brody replied. "There is no evidence this creed goes that far back."

"On the contrary," Jonah replied. "First of all, Paul's words 'delivered' and 'received' are indicative of Judaic holy tradition. Next, several terms within the creed are 'primitive.' Not normally used by Paul. Terms such as 'the twelve,' 'the third day,' and 'for our sins.' Also, the creed refers to Peter as Cephas, his Aramaic name. The poetic style of this creed is Hebraic."

"Yes, those clues do indicate how the creed predates the gospels," Dr. Brody replied. "But they don't prove your thirty AD allegation."

"But this creed is definitely early, right, doctor?" Jonah pressed on.

"Possibly…only possibly," Dr. Brody grudgingly admitted.

"Let's not forget recent discoveries at the Church of the Holy Sepulcher," Jonah continued. "Underneath the edifice, evidence of a first-century rock quarry has been discovered. Being located just outside Jerusalem's walls during Jesus' time, this quarry was used as a trash dump…and a place of execution. Sometimes, the bodies of the crucified were heaved on the refuge. It was a vile, smelly place filled with scavengers such as wild dogs."

"Ah-ha!" Dr. Jeffries added. "This supports the idea that Jesus' remains were consumed by scavengers!"

"But the discovery didn't end there," Jonah responded. "Also located in these excavated depths were first-century, rock-hewn tombs. It's likely that the traditional site for Jesus' tomb is accurate. That Joseph of Arimathea had an unused sepulcher not far from the quarry…not far from the more common tombs.

"There are further evidences that Jesus was entombed. Around the fifth century, the Jewish community circulated a booklet mocking Jesus. It was titled 'Toledoth Yeshu,' meaning 'The Life of Jesus.' In this account, the 'sorcerer' Jesus was 'hung on a cabbage stem' on the eve of Passover. Even in this fable, Jesus is buried, but a gardener removes his body.

"Then we have the gospel Resurrection stories. If the Jewish gospel writers were inventing the story of Jesus' burial, they would have never promoted the idea that women were the first witnesses to the empty tomb! Women were considered unreliable witnesses. They couldn't even offer legal testimony in first-century Judea. The fact that women are the first witnesses proves that the disciples are reporting fact, not fictional imaginings."

"Dr. Rubenstein, don't think you're going to control this debate," Dr. Jeffries added. "You have poor Dr. Brody here on the defensive, so let's put you on the defensive."

Brad leaned back with a grin.

"Within the Nag Hammadi manuscripts," Dr. Jeffries started. "A previously unknown gospel came to light. It's the so-called Gospel according to Thomas. No miracle stories were within. No bloody redemptive deaths and glorious resurrections. Instead, we have the teachings of a rabbi and mystic, a promoter of enlightenment. Many prominent scholars these days date the Thomas account before the traditional gospels. How do you handle this uncomfortable fact?"

"The earliest copy we have of Thomas is dated to the fourth century," Jonah answered. "It is suspected that this account was written around one hundred-fifty AD by most scholars. Only the far left fringe of biblical scholarship dates it earlier. Gnosticism influences this manuscript, along with a belief that 'secret knowledge' was the key to salvation. Like the Buddhist belief that the physical world is illusion, Gnostics believed the physical world was evil incarnate. Their Jesus was never made of flesh and bone…he was a pretender to the physical world. He secretly taught people how to liberate themselves from the material universe. The book contains many gospel teachings, but usually conforms them to Gnostic thinking and terminology.

"Scholars have suggested that the 'Q' manuscript—the source of similarities between Matthew and Luke, and an earlier form of Thomas—preserve an uncorrupted portrait of Jesus. A portrayal free from titles like 'Christ' and 'Son of God.' Yet this school of thinking is terribly hypothetical. It lays on the foundation of naturalism. They arrive at their conclusion first, then they uncover evidence that supports their presuppositions."

"Right," Dr. Brody responded. "As if conservative scholars don't approach this study with their own preconceptions."

"Sure they do! But in the case of conservative scholarship, our manuscripts are not hypothetical. They are extant. They are the canonized gospels and the epistles complete with primitive creeds. They have a fragment of John's Gospel dating to one-twenty AD, or possibly earlier. This indicates a dating to the first century for the Gospel according to John and this was the last gospel account written. Conservative scholars have papyri with a solid trail to the first century. The Gnostics have a paper trail to the mid-second century, at the earliest! There is no doubt that traditional Christianity predates Gnostic Christianity."

"Oh, there's doubt," Dr. Jeffries snickered. "One cannot deny that 'proto-Thomas' and 'Q' present us with a Jesus liberated from mythological embellishment. Then the later Gnostics did the same as mainstream Christians— they adapted Jesus to whatever theological worldview they embraced."

"Dr. Brody! Do you happen to have the ancient manuscripts called 'proto-Thomas' and 'Q' with you? Even a fragment from them? I'd love to look at them," Jonah asked.

"Of course not. These records are extrapolated from later, corrupted manuscripts."

"My point exactly," Jonah nodded. "You folks on the far-left fringe of biblical scholarship have appointed yourselves as 'editors.' You have nothing to go on, but hypothetical manuscripts of your own creation. But unlike the early church compilers of the canon, you find yourselves two thousand years removed from the time and events described! Your Jesus is a Woodstock hippie, protesting Rome as if it were the Vietnam War. Your Jesus is a modern, antiestablishment protester of 'the man.'"

Brody, Brad, and Jeffries all laughed.

"I couldn't have put it any better!" Dr. Jeffries chuckled. "Hippie Jesus is certainly more believable than miracle worker and risen God Jesus!"

"Bravo, Dr. Jeffries," Dr. Brody smiled. "Mr. Rubenstein…I mean, doctor, you cannot deny that your precious Christian scripture was shaped by a creative community. A community influenced by pagan myth. A study of parallel gospel accounts shows the evolution of narrative. For example, in Mark, sixteen, two through five, the women who discover the empty tomb also discover a young man in a simple white robe. A few decades later, as Luke reports the event, the one man in a white robe becomes two men wearing 'brilliant cloths.' By the time Matthew writes this story, we have a dramatic earthquake and an angel descending from heaven. Matthew's angel has a face 'like lightning,' and his robe is 'white as snow.' Obviously, this narrative became sexed up over time!"

Jonah leaned forward before speaking.

"Your synopsis is dependent on presumption, Dr. Brody. It is not proven that Mark is the earliest gospel. It is suspected that it is, due to the fact that material in Mark is also found in Matthew and Luke, and differences in Matthew and Luke generally aren't found in Mark.

"My personal opinion is that Mark's verbal style complicates the issue. Writing to a Roman audience, Mark's style is abrupt and direct. This makes the gospel seem primitive. It's primarily an issue of style. Luke's approach is Greek; he gets more visual in description. Matthew's style is Judaic and he makes ample use of Old Testament drama and hyperbole.

"My point is, even if Matthew or Luke composed their gospel before Mark, John Mark, disciple of Peter, still would have been simple and direct in style! As for this so-called 'evolution of narrative,' let's look at the last gospel written—John's. In John, the narrative focuses on Mary Magdalene. She discovers the empty tomb and later encounters two angels simply described as being 'in white.' John omits angelic descents from heaven. Omits dramatic earthquakes. Adjectives such as 'brilliant' or 'as snow' are not used by John."

"Look at all the contradictions you've listed!" Dr. Brody exclaimed. "Your supposedly accurate gospels can't even agree if there was one angel *or two!*"

"Yes," Jonah nodded. "If one judges the gospels like they are reports for CNN, they are lacking. If one gives these first-century authors some elbowroom, let's look at *how much* they agree on! As mentioned before, women discovered the tomb, and it was not impressive to first-century Jews to have females as the first witnesses. So obviously, they didn't make up this account, they reported it as it happened. Angels in white were encountered, be they one or two. The rock was rolled back or pushed flat. The tomb was empty. Peripheral details can get lost, be they in ancient writings or in a modern news story. Is the core truth preserved? This is the *relevant* question!"

"Come now, Rubenstein," Brad sighed. "Can't you just admit that these gospels are fables, like the legends we find in Greek and Roman mythology?"

"Mr. Ramsey, it is your right to believe the gospels are myth. But do not try to imply that the gospels are reliant on pagan mythology. Be they myth or fact, they are totally dependent on Judaic belief. Not Roman or Greek 'mystery religions.' How well Christianity fulfills Judaism is as wondrous as a miracle itself!"

Brad smiled. "Christians are famous for being anti-Semitic. They persecuted Jews as 'God-killers.' The gospels themselves are anti-Semitic."

"The first Christians were Jewish," Jonah responded. "The liberal idea that the persecution of Jesus was misrepresented by anti-Semitism in the gospels is fallacy. Roman historian Josephus recorded a parallel persecution. A first-century Jew named Jesus ben Ananias spoke of the fall of Jerusalem while in the temple. He was arrested and beaten by the Jewish authorities. He was handed over to the Roman governor. He refused to answer the governor's questions and was scourged. Believing him simply mad, Governor Albinus released him. Unfortunately, a stealth assassin stoned this freed prophet.

"The gospels are Judaic and their foundation is unadulterated Judaism! Christians who historically persecuted the Jews were totally ignorant of this fact. Dr. Brody suggested that the empty tomb story was invented to fulfill a prophecy from Isaiah. Well, Christianity fulfills an infinite amount of Judaic prophecy, symbol, and type.

"Genesis three-fifteen tells us that the 'seed of woman' shall wound the serpent's head and the serpent shall wound his heel. Jesus is considered the 'seed of woman,' since he has no biological father. During crucifixion, the Romans routinely pierced the heel, as evidenced by the bones of a first century crucified Jew. Bones discovered in the 1960s. Coincidence? No, it's fulfillment.

"Isaiah seven-fourteen reads that a virginal maiden shall conceive and have a son named 'Immanuel,' meaning 'God is with us' in Hebrew. Jesus is the only Jew in history considered Divine.

"Micah five-two has the Judaic Messiah king being born in Bethlehem, and his 'going forth' shall be from eternity. The only Jew in history who claimed pre-existence was Jesus of Nazareth, born in Bethlehem. More fulfillment.

"Isaiah thirty-five tells us the Messiah shall be a healer. Other first-century Jews were considered healers, such as Hanina ben Dosa, but only one healer was born in Bethlehem, born of a virgin, considered 'God with us,' and proclaimed his own preexistence. Jesus again fulfills Judaic prophecy."

"Jonah. I don't think this is all—"

"Excuse me, Mr. Ramsey, I'm not quite finished."

Brad looked angry.

"Psalm sixteen-ten states that God's 'Holy one' will not see death and decomposition," Jonah continued. "Only one person in history is reported to rise from the grave. Yet another Judaic fulfillment.

"Isaiah, chapter fifty-three tells us that Messiah would be 'wounded for our transgressions, abused for our iniquities.' We also find healing through his 'stripes.' 'Stripes' are a description of flogging wounds. Again, Jesus fulfills this prediction.

"The most dramatic prophecies are contained in the twenty-second psalm. At the beginning of this psalm, we find the verse Jesus quoted from the cross: 'My God, my God, why have you forsaken me?' But the correlation doesn't end there. This psalm goes on to describe a man 'despised,' a man whose strength is 'poured out like water,' a man with 'bones out of joint,' a man with a dry mouth and an intense thirst, a man with 'pierced' or bound hands and feet, a man whose garments are claimed by 'the casting of lots' and a man whose bones are all seen and counted. Those who have studied crucifixion tell us that dislocated shoulders, bound or pierced hands and feet, nudity, intense sweating, dehydration, and acute thirst mark its agony. This psalm was written long before crucifixion was in common use. Coincidence? No. Once again, Jesus fulfills Judaic proph—"

"Brad, this is getting *silly!*" Dr. Brody interrupted.

"You men insist that the Christian Jesus is derived from pagan myth," Jonah answered. "Are you afraid of how well Jesus emerges from prophetic Judaism?"

"Judaism, Roman myth…it's all the same to me," Dr. Jeffries laughed.

"As I was saying," Jonah continued. "We also have Psalm sixty-nine…a verse that details the offering of gall and vinegar. Psalm thirty-four tells us that the Messiah will not have a single bone broken. Zechariah twelve-ten reads '…they will look upon Me whom they pierced.' Amos eight speaks of the day when there will be a 'noontime darkness.' This could go on. The Old Testament stories also mention a messianic forerunner, the betrayal of a friend, thirty pieces of silver, spitting and mocking…and the pulling out of beard hair. Coincidences go just so far! The foreshadowing of Christ's person, passion, and Resurrection found in Judaism is simply overwhelming."

"Your pious imagination is overwhelming," Dr. Brody responded. "Most of those so-called prophecies you just listed could be applied to most anything and anyone. You're just reading meaning into vague scriptures."

"Vague? That judgment will be left to our viewers," Jonah smiled. "But as I was saying, one need not look to Zeus, Apollo, and Mithras to find the foreshadowing of Jesus. Let's simply look at the religion Jesus was born into and fulfilled—Judaism!

"Even the major Jewish feast days have direct correlations to the life of Jesus of Nazareth. The Bible indicates that John the Baptist was born around March and Jesus was born six months later in September. It is likely that Jesus was born near the Feast of Trumpets. Scholars debate, but I believe that rare astronomical conjunctions during the year three BC caught the attention of the Magi. The lunar eclipse, the historian Josephus associates with the death of Herod the Great, probably occurred in January, one BC. Revelations chapter twelve illustrates an astronomical event—that being the constellation Virgo—positioned with the sun in 'her' middle, the new moon under 'her' feet, and a crown of twelve stars over 'her' head. This configuration announces the arrival of the Messiah king. This very arrangement of sun, moon, and stars happened to occur on September eleventh, three BC, the very date of the Feast of Trumpets! The trumpets announced the Jewish New Year and the arrival of the Messiah king."

Jonah then leaned forward, with a look of determination.

"We all know the Passover story, that the blood of a sacrificed lamb protected God's people from the angel of death," Jonah continued. "Death passed over the household whose wooden lintel and side posts were stained with blood. On the feast of Passover, Jesus died on his bloodstained, wooden cross. He protects his faithful from sin and death. What more appropriate day was there for the Lamb of God to save his people with his blood?

"The end of Passover started the feast of unleavened bread. This feast ended at the first day of the week.

"On Sunday arrived the feast of Firstfruits. Unleavened bread was baked in haste because of the Israelites' exodus out of Egypt. The bread is unraised. Jesus also remained unraised, as he inhabited the sealed oven of his tomb. At the start of Firstfruits, Jesus was resurrected and transformed. Paul taught that all of Jesus' faithful would also receive resurrected, transformed bodies. He instructed Christians that Jesus was their 'Firstfruit.'"

"Gee, can't I get a transformed body as well?" Brad whined. Brody and Jeffries broke into hysterical laughter. Jonah continued without acknowledging them.

"Fifty days later, we have the Feast of Pentecost. This very day Jesus' disciples are empowered by the Holy Spirit and start their evangelistic mission."

"Okay, okay," Dr. Brody responded. "We get it. Jesus fulfills Judaism. It really doesn't concern me whether Jesus was exaggerated by Jewish myth, or Gentile myth. Myth is myth!"

"Someone once said, 'If the gospel is an imagined myth, I would worship the author,'" Jonah responded. "Coincidence goes just so far. If fiction, who wove this brilliant story? The common fisherman Jesus selected as his inner circle? Not likely. Yet these common men authored the first accounts. Church elders in the next generation detailed the evangelistic missions and martyrdom of the apostles. All were murdered save John, who was exiled. These men died for their faith, thus it's illogical that they were imaginative promoters of myth. They died for proclaiming Jesus as the risen Son of God!"

"Your myth is layered," Dr. Brody answered. "Not only was Jesus misrepresented, the disciples/apostles were no doubt misrepresented as well. Each successive Christian generation compounded the string of deception."

"For what purpose?" Jonah replied. "To what avail? Prestige? Hardly! Jerusalem's Sanhedrin and the Roman Caesars persecuted these early Christians! No one will die for a lie—this movement believed in the faith they died for. If they devoutly believed in their doctrine, who would dare amend or corrupt such doctrine? This is not how it's done!"

"Well, unfortunately, we've run out of time," Brad murmured. "I apologize to our audience that one of these guests monopolized the discussion. In a future episode, I will invite back Dr. Brody and Dr. Jeffries, and they will have ample opportunity to have their say. For the *Rational Humanist*, I'm Brad Ramsey. Good night."

The lights went dim and credits for the show scrolled upward.

The broadcast discussed topics I was unfamiliar with. I thought about Jonah's evidences. Suddenly, I wasn't sure of my agnosticism. What if Jesus did fulfill prophecy? Jonah was right when he said coincidence goes just so far. Sitting there with chips on my shirt, my mind engaged in a battle.

# CHAPTER 22

▼

# IT RETURNS

Work the next day started normal enough. I congratulated my boss on making Brad sweat. He laughed. Jonah then informed me that the rest of the evening went smoothly. While everyone was packing up, Claire snuck up behind Ramsey's back with consecrated anointing oil. She dabbed some on her finger and lightly touched the back of Brad's dress jacket. He instantly turned around. With flashing eyes, he told her to get away from him. She knew. Brad Ramsey was definitely possessed. All signs indicated that it was a symbiotic possession.

Intellectually, I started to sway toward a traditional view of Jesus. This man believed himself a Divine Messiah. Obviously, the miracle stories were myth. I also refused to believe in pointy tails and pitch forks. That is, until that afternoon. It was around one o'clock when Marcus called Jonah. He was panicked. Jonah mumbled a few instructions to him, then threw on his coat.

"The Pattyson household is experiencing pandemonium," Jonah sighed. "Marcus received a call from Tamika and drove straight home from work. There, he found his wife cowering in the corner. Glasses and dishes apparently flew around the kitchen shattering everywhere. Spirits are manifesting and a stench has filled the house. I'm going over."

"I'm going with you, Jonah," I insisted. "It's time for me to witness for myself just what is going on."

"Very well. But don't do or say anything without my direction. This is a volatile situation."

"Yes sir, boss!" I saluted.

"Keep your humor going full gear, David. You're going to need it."

The sober tone in Jonah's voice gave me pause. Whatever we were going to encounter, Jonah was convinced of the danger.

As Jonah's SUV pulled up to the Pattyson house, I saw Marcus and Tamika sitting on the stoop near the front door. They were motionless. Heads bowed. The doctor and I exited the vehicle and slowly approached the couple. Only after Marcus felt Jonah's hand on his shoulder did he acknowledge our arrival.

"Jonah. Dave. Thanks for coming."

"Are you two all right?" Jonah asked with a concerned look.

"Been better. My wrist is hurt. It may be broken."

"Your wrist?" I exclaimed. "What the hell happened?"

"Something lifted me off the floor and threw me against the wall."

"Something?"

"Yeah. Something we couldn't see."

"It's all my fault," Tamika murmured. "My fault."

Jonah put his arm around the sobbing woman.

"It's all right, Tamika," the elderly scholar whispered. "The Lord is your strength."

"The fetus…my baby. It hissed. *My baby!*"

Jonah paused. "Tamika?"

"Back when Tamika was sixteen," Marcus explained, "she was pregnant. After spending an intoxicated evening at a keg party, she slipped and fell down a stairwell. She miscarried not long afterward."

The doctor rubbed Tamika's back.

"I'm sorry to hear about this tragedy," Jonah replied. "But, what does this have to do…with the spirit?"

"I saw it," Tamika monotoned.

"I'm sorry?" Jonah asked.

"My baby. My premature baby. I saw it."

I frowned. Apparently, Tamika was more psychologically disturbed than I had imagined.

"What did it look like?" Jonah inquired.

"It didn't look like a spirit at all," Marcus answered.

"Wha—? Marcus, you saw it too?" I asked.

"It was…a grotesque thing. It…crawled around the floor, little arms and legs moving like…a spider's legs. Its head jerked around like how a bird moves its head. Its eyes were dark. Like sockets. Its skin was translucent, veins pulsing. It…it hissed like a snake. That was the final straw! We're not going back inside that house."

"What was happening before you saw the…thing?" Jonah inquired.

"The house was putrid by the time I arrived home," Marcus replied. "It smelled like a septic tank. It was frigid. Cold enough to see your breath. The thermostat was set at seventy degrees! Anyway, Tamika was cowering in the living room. A few dishes flew at her head. The walls had loud thumping sounds. A dark shadow moved through the kitchen. It was at that time I called you, Jonah."

"What happened next?" I probed.

"A scratch formed on Tamika's right cheek. I commanded whatever was there to depart, in the name of Jesus. I was immediately thrown against the wall. Not long after…the thing crawled across the floor in front of us."

"Holy! You two are really experiencing this stuff, aren't you?" I exclaimed.

No one replied.

"Whatever is haunting you two is brazen," Jonah observed. "It's unpredictable. Defiant. And…unusually powerful."

"Hey!" Marcus laughed. "How 'bout some good news?"

"The Lord is on our side, Marcus. Believe it."

Jonah tapped my shoulder and stood to enter the house. My heart raced. I was actually scared…me! Level headed, sensible, skeptical me! With hesitation, I followed Jonah through the front door. The house was cold. A faint stench filled the air. Everything was quiet. Dead still. The only sound was our breathing. Slowly, we started to walk through the living room. The couch was turned over. A broken lamp rested in the fireplace.

"Do you smell something foul?" Jonah asked.

"Yes," I replied.

As we entered the kitchen, we stepped over the shards of a plate. Other fragments of dishware were scattered across the floor.

"Jonah!" I gasped. There, imprinted on a patch of spilled flour, was a handprint. A miniature hand—smaller than a baby's.

"My Lord," he whispered. Jonah took a small digital camera out of his pocket. The camera's flash lit up the kitchen making me jump. I feared that the light would attract the attention of…whatever.

We walked into the hallway. Small spots of flour led a trail to the stairs. Jonah photographed these as well. He started up the stairs.

"Damn him," I growled. Then followed.

One third of the way up the stairs. Halfway up the stairs. I counted the steps trying to get my mind off whatever could be waiting for us.

A loud noise came from the bedroom above. I jumped. Two other noises followed.

My friend held out his arm in front of me to stop my movement.

"A series of three. Typical pattern," he whispered.

He advanced again.

"Uh, Jonah. Are y…you sure this is a good idea?" I stammered.

"Stay behind me."

We arrived at the bedroom door. It was closed. Slowly, my elderly friend grabbed the knob and turned it. Hinges whined as the door slowly swung open.

"Shh!" I responded, immediately feeling silly about trying to silence an inanimate object.

We peeked into the bedroom. It was immaculate. Neat. Nothing was out of place. I exhaled in relief.

"Stay out here," Jonah ordered as he walked into the bedroom. He looked around. Everything seemed normal.

"David, why don't you—"

"Jonah! Behind you!" I yelled.

A bulge appeared from underneath the bedspread. By the time the doctor turned around, the bed covering stood five feet high.

"In the name of—" Jonah intoned in a loud voice, but he was not able to complete the sentence. Something shoved him backward. He crashed into the wall."

*"Jonah!"* I yelled, running into the room.

The bedspread was now levitating off the bed and moving into the middle of the room. It looked like some tacky Halloween ghost hung on a wire. The ceiling vibrated. Two other poundings sounded on the far wall.

I grabbed Jonah as he leaned against the wall. I helped him regain his balance.

The bedspread slipped off the form, collapsing into a pile on the floor. What remained is hard to explain. It was a dark form, gray on the edges and deep black in the middle. It pulsated. Swirls of foggy mist circled the form. A canine growl rattled the windows.

I froze. Shocked. A sense of unreality permeated my mind. My thoughts raced, searching for a rational explanation. I felt cold fingers on my neck. An eerie groaning replaced the growl. The flash from Jonah's camera woke me from a trance.

I turned to see my friend walking toward the form! I couldn't believe my eyes!
"Jonah! What are you doing?"

His hand moved slowly and deliberately, making the sign of the cross.

"In the name of Jesus Christ," he ordered loudly. "I command you to *depart!*"

The form shook, then approached closer. It made a low growl, sounding like a lion.

"Do not defy the *Lord!*" Jonah continued. "It is by *his* name, *his* power, *his* spirit, and *his* blood that I command you. Begone!"

It was bizarre. I half expected to see some Hollywood director crouching in the closet, soon to yell "Cut!" The dark swirl pulsated, then backed off. Three feet. Eight feet. Slowly, the black fog collapsed into its center until nothing remained. Jonah slumped to his knees.

"Jonah, my God! Are you okay?"

Again, I helped him to his feet.

"Yes, David…thank you," he gasped. "I…just need to catch my breath."

"Me t-too," I admitted. "Jonah, you are a brave man."

"Hardly," he laughed. "I've seen this sort of…thing…many times, but I'll never get used to it."

"You've…seen energies like this before?"

"Yes. They are black and heavy. They are inhuman, demonic entities."

"At this point," I sighed "I'm willing to believe you."

Three knocks sounded from the attic. Jonah grabbed my arm and led me out of the room.

"We're still not out of danger," he whispered. "Let's get out of here."

"Doc, didn't you just 'exorcise' that thing?"

"No, I'm not an exorcist. The Lord and I have protected us from immediate harm. This type of job is best suited for a clergyman. Someone of exceptional devotion to the Lord. God's power is the force, but God's men are the conduits. The better the conduit, the more effective the exorcism will be."

We quickly descended the stairs.

As we walked through the living room, something grabbed my ankle! I stumbled. Jonah grabbed my arm, but I continued to fall to the floor.

It charged me! A blur rushed across the floor and stopped two inches from my face. Even to this day, I have trouble describing this thing. It was hideous. A glowing baby, deformed and decaying. No eyes. Veins and capillaries moved from under its cellophane-like skin. A maggot twisted from under its right cheek. Mucus ran from its nose, drool trickled from its mouth. Breath tainted with the scent of feces hit my face. I froze. I heard Jonah's voice, I knew he was trying to vanquish the entity. A thin, snake-like tongue wormed out of its mouth and touched my cheek. It felt like an icicle. I screamed with horror.

I don't remember much after that, I blacked out. Jonah later told me what had happened. I actually yelled "Jesus, save me!" The entity backed away and dissolved into luminescent streaks of energy. My elderly employer found the strength to lift me off the floor and walk me outside. Marcus took over from there, using his good arm to walk me to Jonah's SUV.

The next hour was a blur. I remember bits and pieces. The sun flickering through the trees, through the vehicle's windows. The vibration of the truck. The sound of Marcus, Tamika, and Jonah talking. Tamika crying. The next thing I clearly remember, I was lying on a gurney at Charlotte Hungerford Hospital. A doctor was talking with Jonah and Marcus. Marcus's left hand and wrist were in a cast. A heart monitor beeped behind me.

"Hey, could I have a cup of water?" I asked.

Jonah went to the water cooler and filled a small cup. The others rushed to my side. The ER doctor took my hand.

"Mr. Paul, you are at Charlotte Hungerford Hospital. I am Dr. Lee. How are you feeling?"

"Weak. Shaky. What happened?"

"You suffered some sort of mental trauma. Don't think about it, just relax. You're going to be fine."

Jonah handed me the water. I gulped it down.

"Mental trauma?" I asked. "What are you…?"

In a flash, it came back to me. The face. The breath. The tongue. The beeping behind me sped up.

*"Oh God, Jonah! Did you see it? Did you see it? Jonah!"*

My elderly friend took my hand and talked slowly and deliberately.

"Yes, David, I saw it. You thought you drove over a boy. It wasn't a boy, David, it was a dog. It was a dog. You didn't kill anyone."

"Yes, Mr. Paul," Dr. Lee continued. "Mr. Rubenstein explained to me how you thought you killed a child. But you didn't. Try to relax."

"What are you guys talking about? There was no accident, I thought I saw—"

*"David!"* Marcus interrupted. "Take my word for it, we know what you saw."

As Jonah and the doctor walked out of the cubicle formed by a curtain, Marcus sat down beside me.

"I know you saw the entity, David," he whispered. "I saw it too. But don't go sharing this story with the doctors or nurses. They'll admit you to the psychiatric ward. They'll think you're hallucinating. Do you understand?"

I choked. I started to sob. "Marcus, how do I know that I don't belong in the psychiatric ward? Maybe I've flipped! Maybe I was hallucinating!"

"You were not hallucinating, buddy. I saw the thing. Tamika saw it. Jonah saw it. It was real. But don't panic, you did a good job. Your prayer protected you, David. Yours!"

"Mass hallucination, that's it. It was mass hallucination! Shared delusion!"

"Come on, David! Think! Brad Ramsey. His psychic ability. His power over people. The psychic attacks those who oppose him."

"It can't be. It can't be!"

"It can, friend."

The beeping of my heart monitor slowed down.

"This is nuts. Reality is reality. This isn't rational. This isn't scientific."

"This is reality, Dave. Science won't acknowledge it, but that doesn't disprove it."

"My God," I wept. "My God, this is all real."

"Yes. But don't fear, David. The Lord is real too. He is our strength and our protection. When you were at the crisis point, you knew this too. You asked Jesus to protect you. He did, Dave."

"Jesus?" I asked. "The same Jesus who didn't help me expose Brad? The same Jesus who allowed Huey to suffer and die? He protected me?"

"Yes. Sometimes his ways are hard to understand. His timing is difficult to accept. This hasn't all played out yet, the Lord will ultimately win. Brad's defeat is assured…his and the one he serves."

"Somebody should light a fire under God's butt," I snorted.

"I think he just lit a fire under ours," Marcus laughed.

The doctor and Jonah returned through the curtain.

"Okay, Mr. Paul, how are you feeling? Have you accepted what your friends told you?"

"Yes, doctor," I answered. "Apparently, I just ran over a dog. I didn't kill the boy who was chasing him. And even the dog is expected to recover."

"Accidents happen. You are a sensitive person. A caring person. Your first impulse wasn't to flee the scene, but to tune out the world. You'll be fine."

"Thanks, doctor, I think you're right."

"I'm discharging you, Mr. Paul. For a few days, I think it would be wise for you to rest. Perhaps you can stay at Mr. Pattyson's residence."

"Yeah, Marcus, I'd love to. Your couch free?"

"Very free," Marcus laughed.

"Excellent," the doctor commented. "Just sign some papers at the reception desk and you're free to go."

"Thank you, doctor."

As the three of us walked to the waiting room, Tamika sprang from her seat and rushed over. She gave me her routine bear hug.

"David, you're all right!" she squealed. Then hugged me again.

"Yes," I offered through physical pain. "I'm fine, Tamika, thanks."

"'Mika, let's not hurt the guy now," Marcus suggested.

"Sorry, Davey," she laughed.

As we walked into the parking lot, Jonah stopped.

"Dave," he murmured. "I'd like you to stay at my house for a few days. Tamika and Marcus, I don't think it's a good idea for you two to return to your home. Perhaps you can call your pastor, Reverend Wyland. He has dealt with demonic infestation before. He'd probably offer you room and board at the rectory."

All three of us nodded silently.

"Tamika, Marcus, I want you to know something," Jonah continued. The tension was thick. Even birds in a nearby tree stopped singing. "This haunting is not limited to your house," he sighed. "This is personal. It is directed at all of us, but you two are in the most jeopardy due to Tamika's verbal challenge. She unwittingly opened a door for evil. It will come after you again. Any time. Any location. Be prepared."

# CHAPTER 23

▼

# MY NEW REALITY

Boarding with Jonah was pleasant. His guest room had a bed, couch, and television. Each room was adorned with a wooden cross. Instead of being annoyed with the religious symbol, I felt relief. If these things helped to keep that vile spirit away, more power to them.

Marcus and Tamika stayed at the rectory. After a few days of peace, Tamika was awakened one night by the sensation of a cold hand groping under her nightgown. She screamed and Marcus commanded the presence to depart in the name of Christ. The prayer worked. Still, the couple lived in constant apprehension. They continuously wondered what bizarre experience was going to happen next.

Marcus's pastor was youngish, around thirty-five years of age. His name was Wallace Wyland. An obese and balding man. When he spoke, it seemed he was perpetually out of breath. Still, he was a man of conviction. He seemed anxious to confront the forces that plagued Marcus and Tamika.

The reverend went to the Pattyson house to perform a blessing. He chose a selection of prayers he found effective. He returned to the rectory confused. Nothing unusual occurred. The cold spots, the smells, the pounding in the walls, and the manifestations were all absent. "Hide and seek hauntings are the most aggravating," he told Marcus. He also knew that the Pattysons didn't experience a gradual build-up of activity, the pattern usually unfolds. Instead, they suffered two occasions of an all-out attack. "This is all very atypical," the reverend observed.

As I recovered from my mental shock, Jonah found new confidence in me. I adapted well, considering my entire worldview came crashing down that horrific day.

Late one evening, I went grocery shopping for Jonah. It was my last evening at his house. As a thank you, I wanted to restock his refrigerator and cupboards. While at the checkout counter, in my peripheral vision, I saw a woman approaching. I met her eyes, then quickly averted my gaze. I didn't feel up to talking to her, of all people. It was too late.

"David, how are you? I'm glad I bumped into you."

"Really, Jess? Our last meeting was…less than pleasant."

"I know. I want to extend an olive branch. I know Brad has his faults and I understand how some people can be threatened. Brad can be overbearing. Frankly, I disliked how he and his friends ganged up on your friend Jonah Rubenstein last week, as deluded as the old man was. And, what they said about you was nonsense."

"Yes, it was. And Jonah was certainly outnumbered."

"Not that it held him back any," Jessica laughed.

"No, it didn't."

"Anyway, I'm dying to ask you, how's Marcus? He hasn't been to work in days! I would have called him, but I know how his wife feels about me."

"Marcus is fine. He's just taking a few days off."

"Oh good. I was afraid something was wrong with him."

"No, he's fine."

I paused. This was vintage Jessica Kim. She was so caring. I felt the old tug on my heart. The longing.

Jessica turned away from me for a second. She grabbed a tissue from her purse and wiped her eye.

"Hey, what's wrong?"

"It's nothing. It's just that…Brad and I had a fight."

"Oh. Sorry to hear that."

"He can be so…disingenuous! Damn him. Why does he wear so many masks? Why can't he be himself?"

"Uh, you're asking me?"

"Yeah, I know. Look who I'm asking."

"I am who I am, Jess."

"As wrong as you are about Brad, he does have some faults. You know how he's this skeptical, 'rational humanist' on his television show? That's not how he is in his personal life. He believes in a higher power. 'The god of the cosmos,' he calls him or her. 'The god of nature.' 'A bringer of light.' He prays continuously. He even speaks in tongues."

"Jess, now, don't get mad, but do you think Brad may be some type of…devil worshipper?"

"Devil worshipper? *Oh please!* Who gave you that idea? Jonah?"

"Lucifer was called 'light-bringer,' according to Jonah. He also said that Jesus called Satan 'the god of this world.'"

"Oh, now you're quoting the Bible?"

"Not really. I don't have a defined belief. Yet, Brad may be intentionally worshipping some Christian-defined devil concept."

"No way, David. No way. Brad doesn't put stock in anything those silly scriptures say. Satanists and devil worshippers are usually Christians who switch sides. Brad never held a Christian worldview to begin with."

The two of us stood silently. It was awkward. More than anything, I wanted to share the horrific, paranormal experiences I had. But I knew she would never believe me.

"Okay, Jess. Go ahead and check out in front of me and I'll help you put your bags in your car."

"Thanks, David. You don't have to help me. Brad is waiting in the car."

My adrenaline surged. Hopefully, I could get this task done without seeing Ramsey.

Jess quickly finished at the register and leaned over to kiss my cheek.

"You take care, Davey."

"What's going on here?" I heard a deep voice boom behind me. My neck hairs stood on end. Sure enough, it was Ramsey. He loomed over me, glaring.

"Oh!" Jess smiled. "I was just saying good-bye to David."

"How sweet," Brad hissed. "I'm sure Sparky enjoyed that gesture of affection."

"C'mon, Brad," Jessica rolled her eyes. "Don't break into that jealous guy routine."

Ramsey snickered. "Jealous of *what?*"

"Knock it off," Jess reprimanded him.

"Did you tell your former pet here the good news?" Brad asked.

"No, hon. I haven't made my mind up yet. You know that."

"Well, Davey has the right to know. I was offered a chance to take my talk show into syndication! I'm moving to California next week."

I smiled.

"Well, isn't that wonderful! Bon voyage, big guy."

"Don't celebrate just yet. Your unrequited love here is moving with me."

"Maybe," Jess corrected him.

"Oh," I nodded.

I had mixed emotions. On the plus side, I wouldn't see the two of them on a continual basis. I could get Jess out of my system. On the negative side, she was moving away with a dangerous person. She was in jeopardy.

"Be sure to tell Marcus your decision. Okay, Jess?" I said.

"Sure. I'll let you guys know."

The happy couple started to walk away when Brad turned and smiled.

"Oh, David! Tell Marcus that I heard about his house party last week! My friends had the greatest time."

I stiffened. Jonah's view of Brad continued to solidify in my mind. I could no longer embrace a rational view of the situation.

"Will do," I said, glaring back at him.

I paid the cashier. Soon, the grocery bags were in the backseat of my Chevy. With reluctance, my old car started. I began the short drive home.

While driving past a country cemetery, my car sputtered. Then stalled. Repeatedly, I tried to start it. Soon, the engine wouldn't even turn over. The battery was weak.

"Damn!" I cursed, while slamming the car door.

I figured the nearest house was a mile away. I buttoned my coat and prepared for a long hike. Generally, there wasn't any traffic on this back road. It was quiet. Eerie. My boots crunched through the thin layer of snow and ice, sounding intrusive. I didn't have a flashlight to illuminate my journey. Fortunately, the first quarter moon was bright enough to paint the landscape in pale blue. I persevered, feeling half blind.

The cemetery along the road was long. I walked fast, trying to pass this frightening field of tombstones. Limbs from tall elm trees cast finger-like shadows. Being an unusually warm December evening, fog cloaked everything.

After a few minutes, I cleared the cemetery. This provided temporary comfort. Too temporary. Soon, the woods seemed as threatening as the cemetery. Branches inexplicably snapped around me. Shadows darted from tree to tree. It sounded like someone was behind me, crunching the snow like an echo. I stopped and turned around. All I saw was an empty road.

My nerves pulsated. My mind flashed images of the spirits I saw at Marcus' house. This brought me to the verge of panic. My brisk stroll tuned into a jog. My jog grew into a run. The loud pounding of my feet, wheezing gasps for air, all sounded too loud. I would slow down in order to make less noise. Perhaps if I were quiet, the shadows would keep away?

Light glowed over the hump of the road ahead. It was an approaching car! I held my hand in the air. The headlights approached, then passed by. I felt like a passenger on the *Titanic* watching the last lifeboat sail away. I resumed my long walk.

There was a dim illumination over the next knoll. It was the closest house. Finally! Again, my pace quickened. I jogged. Then ran. Suddenly, an eerie, sickly breathing sounded in my left ear. Something was behind me! Closer and closer, the lighted horizon promised safety.

I felt a grab at the back of my coat collar! I was pulled backward! My lower back hit the road first, then my head. Both made a sharp sound. While lying there stunned, I saw a fallen branch within reach. I grabbed the stick and got to my knees.

No one was there. Instead, a gnarled tree branch reached into the roadway. I laughed.

"*It was a branch!* My coat snagged on a branch!" I sighed loudly.

I walked the remaining yards giggling to myself. With a relaxed demeanor, I knocked on the door. An elderly woman hooked the chain and opened the door a crack.

"Hello?" she cautiously announced.

"Hi, ma'am," I responded. "My car broke down a mile from here. Can I use your phone?"

"Oh dear, *no!*" she answered. "One can't be too careful these days."

"Okay. Ma'am, could you make a phone call for me? I'll stay out here."

"All right. Do you have a number?"

"Yes. Dial four eight nine, one three three one. Ask for Jonah. Jonah Rubenstein."

"Oh! Dear Dr. Rubenstein, from Christian Family Services?"

"Yes, that's him! I'm his assistant and currently his houseguest. Could you dial him for me? Tell him David Paul needs a ride and give him your address."

"Oh nonsense, young man," she laughed, unlatching the door. "Any friend of Dr. Rubenstein is a friend of mine! Come in, young man, come in! You make your call."

"Thank you, ma'am," I nodded politely. I stepped into the house and saw a living room cluttered with antique furniture and cats. There must have been twenty cats, lying around, roaming, meowing. The aroma of soiled cat litter was overpowering.

"Never mind my darlings," she laughed. "They won't bother you."

As I turned to shut the door, the woman gasped.

"Oh my!" she exclaimed. "What happened to your coat?"

"Yeah," I chuckled. "I snagged my coat on some branch."

"Thank goodness. I thought you were mauled by a bear!"

"Excuse me?"

I took off my coat and looked at the backside. Four rips were near the collar, a couple inches long. Parallel to each other. Claw marks! I shivered from an unearthly chill. Something did grab me.

# CHAPTER 24

▼

# THE SCIENTIFIC
# APPROACH

I was at a crossroads. A very real phenomenon was occurring. Whether one called it supernatural, paranormal, or metaphysical, I had no explanation for the events of the past several days. No explanation other than the theological, that is. Such rationales went against the very grain of my being. On a gradual basis, I felt myself gravitating toward the mindset of Jonah, Marcus, and Tamika. I was adopting a Christian worldview.

I never told Jonah about my coat. He was good enough to pick me up at the cat lady's house and drive me to my car. Inexplicably, the car started right up. This was the last night I lodged at the doctor's house.

It felt good to move back to my studio apartment. I felt like myself again, not some Christian intern being chased by demons. At this time, a thought occurred to me. An epiphany. What if there was a scientific, rational explanation for what I had been experiencing? What if Jonah, Marcus, and Claire Monroe were blinded by their faith? What I needed was a more objective view.

At the local community college library, I logged onto the Internet. I typed the words "Connecticut" and "parapsychology" into a search engine. Several links appeared. Ms. Claire Monroe, parapsychologist was listed. "No," I laughed to myself. I continued looking. The fourth link down, I paused. Who was this? Dr. Richard Clarkson, professor of psychiatry at Danclift University. His parapsychological research had been published in peer reviewed journals. Studies authored by him traced the influence electromagnetic fields had on human perception. His theories were plausible. That evening, I called the university and left a message for the professor. Much to my surprise, he called back one hour later. He was familiar with Dr. Boyington's recent research on Huey's sheets. Ray Boyington had told him to call Jonah or Mr. David Paul if he wanted to know more about the enigmatic linen. He jumped at the chance to talk with me. I had an appointment to meet at his office in two days.

Upon arriving at Danclift, I noticed how small the campus was. With trial and error, I eventually discovered which building hosted Dr. Clarkson's office. I entered the room to be greeted by an attractive intern at the reception desk. She looked up from her magazine and beamed a smile.

"Good morning, sir."

I flinched. I hated how college students referred to me as "sir." I was only slightly older than she!

"I'm David Paul. I have an appointment."

"Yes, the professor is expecting you. Go ahead in."

The office was cluttered. Piles of magazines, newspapers, and books occupied all but one chair. Behind a messy desk sat Dr. Clarkson. He weighed at least three hundred pounds, his face was red. I estimated his age to be around forty. He was bald on top and wore a groomed goatee. Only after finishing the last bite of his glazed donut did he acknowledge my presence.

"Ahh! You must be Mr. Paul!" He smiled and held out his right hand in greeting.

"Yes, I am. Thanks for seeing me, professor."

"My pleasure."

I shook his hand. It was hot and sticky.

As the rotund scholar sat back in his chair, he reached into the donut box.

"Care for a snack?"

"No thanks."

"Good for you, these things will kill ya," he sighed.

He bit into a jelly donut and white powder coated his mouth. With some loud smacking, he started our conversation.

"So, you work with Jonah Rubenstein and met with Ray Boyington."

"Yes."

"And, you can confirm that there was a modern equivalent to the Turin Shroud in their possession?"

"Apparently so. It looked like the Turin Shroud, but only Dr. Boyington can confirm how identical those two cloths actually are."

"Fascinating! Ray Boyington is an honest man, there's no reason to doubt his findings. I find this utterly fascinating."

I nodded politely. I wasn't interested in rehashing this topic, but it was what got me through the door.

"What do you know about this modern Shroud?"

"Well, a mentally challenged man died one night from a grand mal seizure. As the group home staff signed some paperwork with the paramedics, his body disappeared from his bed. An image of the front of his body was left on the top sheet and his back was imprinted on the lower sheet. No pillowcase was involved. No one ever found his remains."

"Intriguing," Clarkson responded, "and sad."

"It is."

"I wager that Jonah believes your friend dematerialized? That the cloth was imprinted by some sort of radiation?"

"You know Jonah well."

"Indeed I do! The man is keenly intelligent, despite his Christian imagination."

"You don't subscribe to Jonah's Shroud theory?"

"I should say not!" Clarkson snorted. A bit of jelly donut shot out of his mouth and hit my right cheek.

"Interesting," I nodded. "How do you explain the odd images left on linen?"

"I cannot, entirely. I believe the Turin Shroud was treated with an ancient preservative called 'Saponaria officinalis.' Soapstone. A unique chemical reaction occurred between the traumatized corpse and the chemically treated shroud. Body vapors may be involved. In regard to your modern linen image, who can say?"

"So you believe that the Turin Shroud is genuine, but does not indicate some resurrection process?"

"Certainly not! Resurrections aren't good science, they're theological symbols."

I liked the man. If any scholar could cut away my growing Christian tumor, it was he.

"I'm glad to hear you say this, doctor. I have other things to share with you."

"And these things involve haunting phenomena?"

"Yes."

"Good ol' Jonah," Clarkson laughed. "His demons follow him around like some sort of paranormal paparazzi."

"So, you know how he has an affiliation with Claire Monroe, demons, and exorcisms?"

"Oh yes. The man has spent too much time with that English quack."

"It's refreshing to hear someone say that," I sighed.

"I take it you have been immersed in Jonah's social circle?"

"To say the least!"

"You have my sympathy," Clarkson laughed.

"Doctor, it's to the point where…well, I uh…I've questioned my sanity."

"You seem like a together young man. What would make you say that?"

"I have experienced this…haunting phenomena myself."

"I see. David, you have nothing to be ashamed about. Millions of people have experienced haunting activity. Now tell me, what have your experiences involved?"

"Well, a personal friend of mine was experiencing odd things in his Torrington home. He and his wife left their house one day and called Jonah to tell him what was happening. They are both extremely religious. Anyway, his wife kept saying how she saw her baby. A premature infant she miscarried while she was a teenager."

"Interesting. Is this woman highly emotional? Turbulent?"

"Very much so!"

"I thought so. Please continue."

"Anyway, I won't bore you with the details. Jonah and I toured the abandoned house and experienced…odd things."

"Please, be specific."

"Well, the temperature in the house was cold. The air smelled foul. There was a dark, misty form, seen by both Jonah and I. It threw Jonah against a wall. Later, we saw something else. Leave it at that."

"Please, I want to hear about everything."

"I'd rather not talk about this."

"If you want a comprehensive analysis of this situation, you *will* share everything."

I sighed loudly. "Okay, don't say I didn't warn you. And don't try to institutionalize me after hearing this."

"David, I've heard just about every bizarre experience the paranormal can offer."

"Well, while Jonah and I were walking through the living room, intending to get out of that place, something grabbed my ankle. I fell to the floor."

Clarkson leaned forward with interest.

"And uh…something rushed across the floor toward me. It scurried. Like…a spider. Doctor, I swear, it was physical! It looked like an underdeveloped baby. Like a fetus. Its skin was transparent. It…it scowled with rage. Its tongue looked like a lizard's. The tongue t…touched my face. Jonah told me it later dematerialized. I don't remember. I blacked out."

I started to experience anxiety. Clarkson reached into a small refrigerator he kept near his desk and handed me a bottle of mineral water. "Mineral water goes well with Hostess cupcakes. Soft drinks are unhealthy," he informed me.

"Thanks, doctor."

I gulped down the cool liquid.

"David, have you experienced anything else since that day?"

"Yes. While walking on a dark road at night, something grabbed my jacket and pulled me backward. Whatever it was, it left four rips in the fabric."

"I see. What was your emotional state that evening? Were you tense? Anxious?"

"Yes."

"Uh-huh," the professor scowled. He stood. Donut crumbs tumbled off his belly. He strolled over to a window and peered out at the courtyard.

"Well," he sighed. "Your experiences go beyond the norm. But don't despair. There is a rational, scientific explanation for everything you have experienced."

He shoved a small pile of paperbacks off a chair next to me and sat in a controlled collapse. I started to take hope. This man didn't think I was crazy after all!

"David," he started to explain. "I'm sure you've heard of the poltergeist phenomena. Poltergeist is translated as 'noisy ghost.' When certain adolescents reach puberty, their stress levels skyrocket. Sexual tensions occur within them for the first time. They are like…low pressure systems on the Weather Channel.

"Combine adolescent turbulence with an area containing high electromagnetic fields, chaos can result. Bedrock and tectonic stresses create a good deal of magnetic energy. Especially in Connecticut. The ground has a high concentration of iron ore. Certain houses are built near high power lines. Near power plants. Our homes are charged with all sorts of energy fields, thanks to modern technology. Through a process we have yet to fully understand, psychological conflict can manipulate the external world around us. The stress of puberty can throw dishes in an empty kitchen. The psychiatric dynamics of deep-seated guilt, of religious fanaticism…these are also powerful influences on the environment.

"For example, the shared psychodynamic energy at Catholic shrines causes people to hallucinate. To manifest external illusions. Some see apparitions. Others see the sun move, spin, or blink. UFO buffs go through abduction experiences. Buddhists relive past lives. Natives have vision quests. The recipient's state of mind determines the experience!"

"Do you mean that all of this is merely hallucination?"

"No. Sometimes, a person's internal conflict manifests in a very physical way. Especially in areas with high amounts of electromagnetic energy."

"You're saying people create their own ghosts, demons, visions, and so on?"

"Exactly."

"I like your theory doctor. You have no idea how much I like it! But I'm not religious. I am a devoted, rational agnostic. Why should I see these things?"

"Two reasons for this. First, the psychological dynamics of your group manifested in an external fashion. The wife of your friend, a turbulent woman, who probably feels some guilt about a miscarriage. Jonah's expectation to encounter a demonic force is its own catalyst. David, you were just caught between these two psychic generators."

"You know, doctor, now that you mention it, Jonah has something he feels guilty about! One paranormal experience weeks ago involved a vision associated with his guilt!"

"So, you see the logic of my position?"

"Most definitely. Still…"

"Yes?"

"Well, I was alone that evening on the dark road. Neither Tamika or Jonah were there to generate any psychic manifestations."

"This experience you had—this was after the horrific experience you had in your friend's house?"

"Yes."

"Why were you walking on this dark road?"

"My car quit on me."

"You were upset?"

"Yeah."

"What was your mind on during your walk?"

"Well, it was spooky. I broke down by an old country cemetery."

"So, you almost expected to see a ghost!"

"Well, yeah, that's true!" I laughed with vigor. "Still, doc, I've never been what you would call a psychic generator. I never experienced anything paranormal while growing up."

"You never had the state of mind that you have now. The sensitivity."

"I see what you're saying."

"And, David, forgive me for getting personal, but I suspect there are other stresses in your life. Extraordinary stresses."

"I suppose so."

"This mentally challenged man who died and left behind those enigmatic sheets. Do you feel at all responsible for this man's death?"

"Yeah, I do. I was suspended from my job at the time. If I had been at work, I might have noticed a few petit mal seizures. Seizures often missed by others."

"I see. And again, forgive me for getting personal, but do you have problems with your love life?"

Mineral water sprayed out of my mouth as I laughed.

"Uh yeah, my love life is nonexistent!"

"There is someone you have strong feelings for, correct?"

"H…how did you know that?" I asked in amazement.

"It follows a classic pattern. Sexual frustration can be the most powerful psychic generator there is. Take the poltergeist phenomena, for example. It involves puberty."

"I see."

"Were you thinking of your unrequited love before your car broke down?"

"I *just* bumped into her at the supermarket!"

"And it was not a pleasant encounter for you, was it?"

"Dr. Clarkson, you don't need to press on," I said, sighing. "I'm convinced. It's as if all these loose, bizarre puzzle pieces suddenly formed a picture."

"Glad I could be of assistance," he smiled. "I wonder though, would your friend be open for a scientific investigation of his house?"

"Marcus and Tamika just moved back into their abode this week. They're at peace. I don't want to shake the beehive. I'm hoping they will get beyond all this."

"I understand perfectly," Clarkson grinned. "You're a good man, Mr. Paul."

"No, Dr. Clarkson," I smiled. "You're a good man. You have restored the universe for me. Thanks for not letting me slide into illusion. Jonah's reality was becoming my reality!"

"Glad I could be of service. Now, perhaps you can help me with something?"

"Name it."

"Do you have access to the fabric samples Dr. Boyington studied? I'd love to introduce these fibers to my microscope!"

"Sorry, doctor. Those samples are the official property of Residential Associates Incorporated. I don't even work there anymore."

"*But*, you could get them from Ray Boyington."

"No. A Dr. Scott Fullman, the president of RAI, gave Dr. Boyington permission for his study. You might want to ask Fullman. His number is in the book."

"I see."

The professor stood up. I took the cue and stood with him.

"Well, it was a pleasure meeting you, David. You let me know anytime, if I can be of further assistance."

I shook his hand.

"Thank you, doctor."

"Anytime."

I visited the restroom in the hallway. When I walked back into the waiting room to retrieve my coat, I heard Clarkson's voice talking on his phone. He sounded angry.

# CHAPTER 25

▼

# A MEDIA CIRCUS

During the next few days, the Pattyson household was comparatively docile. Marcus and Tamika celebrated the Christmas holiday without incident. On occasion, cold spots were felt. Knocking sounds were heard in the walls and attic. This phenomenon was tame.

I had a solid tradition. I avoided Christmas. My reasons were twofold. I didn't have a family, and held an aversion to Christian tradition. Jonah invited me for dinner that holiday, along with the Pattysons. I politely declined.

The Saturday proceeding, Jonah arranged an appointment with Claire Monroe. She recently toured the Pattyson's house and discerned the type of supernatural infestation that was occurring. She was bringing a friend of hers, a Catholic priest and exorcist. He planned to cleanse the house. I decided to accompany the crew, but would refuse to enter the residence. I hoped to stay in the yard. I would provide company for Marcus if he needed moral support.

It was a warm December afternoon. Icicles dripped steadily. As Jonah and I drove onto Marcus's street, I noticed a line of four vans parked in front of the Pattyson's house. One was from a local television station. Cameramen and reporters gathered on the yard.

"Good Lord, you think something terrible has happened?" I asked.

"I don't know," Jonah answered with concern.

We pulled up behind a van and parked. The reporters jogged toward our vehicle. I rolled down my window.

"Hey!" I yelled. "What's going on here?"

In response, a man stuck a microphone in my face. "Are you acquainted with Marcus and Tamika Pattyson?"

"Yeah! And why are you people here?"

"Have you witnessed any ghosts or apparitions, sir?"

"Oh nooo," Jonah sighed. "Here we go again."

"And what is your name, sir?" the man asked Jonah.

"I have no comment," the doctor answered. "David, let's get inside."

I froze. "Jonah," I murmured. "We agreed that I wouldn't have to go into that house."

"Right now, this yard is more dangerous than the Pattyson living room."

"I'm not going inside," I insisted.

"Young man, if you don't accompany me inside, I will have no further need of your services."

I paused. Was Jonah actually threatening to fire me? I couldn't believe it. This wasn't like the gentle therapist at all.

"I resent this," I growled. Jonah left the SUV and turned to look back at me. With a moan, I stepped from the vehicle and followed my elderly friend. After a gentle knock on the door, Marcus peered out the crack. The chain was still attached.

"Yeah?" he asked cautiously.

"Marcus! It's Jonah and David."

"Thank God!" he exhaled, then closed the door and quickly unhooked the chain. He opened it again, exclaiming, "Get in here! Quick!"

We slipped inside and a reporter managed to get his arm and microphone through the opening behind us.

"Marcus Pattyson! Can I get a comment about—"

Marcus pushed the arm back and slammed the door. He quickly locked it.

"Jonah," Marcus sighed. "How did these locusts find out about our experiences?"

"I have no idea," Jonah answered. "Both Claire and myself are very careful. Your pastor wouldn't have said anything."

"Well, somebody leaked our story," Tamika added.

"Oh man, I just remembered," I mumbled. "I had the misfortune of bumping into Brad at the supermarket. He said he heard about your house party, Marcus. His quote was 'My friends had the greatest time.'"

"My word!" Jonah exclaimed. "I've never encountered such a blatantly evil force!"

A loud sound vibrated through the ceiling above us. Two small knocks then sounded in the kitchen.

*"Aw gawd, get me outta here!"* I panicked.

"It's okay," Jonah reassured. "I believe this activity has been weakened by Pastor Wyland's efforts, albeit, not driven out. Have you two been attacked recently?"

"Not at all," Marcus answered. "Just some benign stuff. Noises and cold spots. That last sound was the loudest we've heard all week."

"Not surprising," I murmured. "You were expecting some activity, Jonah."

"What's that, Dave?" Jonah inquired.

"Oh, I've done some research on this paranormal stuff. Anyone know of Dr. Richard Clarkson?"

"Unfortunately, yes," Jonah replied. "That man has been a thorn in my side for years. How do you know of him, David?"

"I met him two days ago."

"You what?" the doctor asked.

"I wanted another perspective on what's happening to Tamika and Marcus. To us."

"Of all people," Jonah sighed.

"What's so bad about him?" I asked. "Ray Boyington corresponds with him."

"Yes, I know. Ray hasn't seen the side of Clarkson that I've seen."

"What side is that?"

"Clarkson is a sensationalizer. A publicity seeker. Oh, you didn't tell him Marcus's name and address, did you? This man will do anything to sell his unpopular books."

"I…think I mentioned their first names, but nothing beyond that."

"You didn't tell him what town they lived in, right?"

"I might have."

"Oh Lord," Jonah rubbed his neck.

"Why would Clarkson alert the press? Is that what you're thinking?"

"Yes, it is. First, he enjoys making life hard for me. He would love it if my reputation were tarnished. Second, he makes himself very available to reporters. He provides commentary on situations he isn't involved in. He'll do anything to be on television."

"I didn't know. I'm sorry, he seemed like a professional researcher. Much of what he said made sense."

"You mean, how the human subconscious influences the environment, through natural electromagnetic energy?"

"Something to that effect."

"David!" Jonah shook his head. "You should be able to recognize that what assaulted us was sentient. It had purpose, it wasn't some free floating energy field."

"Yeah, it had the purpose we ourselves gave it."

"No. The purpose it demonstrated was to break us down, the oppression of our spirit, through the exploitation of past trauma."

"Jonah, the emotional turmoil of past trauma could be all *'it'* is! 'It' could be nothing more than a waking nightmare, brought to life through whatever energy fields are available."

"Mmm. I see Clarkson managed to recruit a new disciple," Jonah murmured. "Eventually, you will see what motivates this man. As a matter of fact—"

The elderly sage stopped, then walked to the nearest window and slowly moved the drape a few inches. He peeked into the yard.

"I knew it!" he exclaimed. "Marcus, come over here quickly!"

Marcus peered out the window.

"What am I looking for?"

"Do you see that rather rotund man standing in the midst of three reporters? That's Richard Clarkson, the ambulance chaser of paranormal research."

"You're kidding!" I laughed. "Let me see!"

Sure enough, the professor was standing by the front walk. The reporters scribbled notes as he spoke and gestured.

"Jonah, Marcus…I'm sorry. I never thought this man was a bloodhound. Look at him out there. They probably believe he's been directly involved with our situation. Still, the fact that this man is unscrupulous doesn't dismiss his theory."

"Okay, David, let's assume that collective trauma, belief and expectation causes the haunting phenomena. Then why would any exorcism ritual work at all? Internal conflicts aren't healed on a dime. Also, why would this type of haunting follow a predictable pattern? They always begin with some type of invitation, be it deliberate or accidental. Ouija boards are the most common doorway. In this case, it was Tamika's challenge to Brad Ramsey."

Tamika moaned.

"I'm sorry, Tamika, I didn't mean to throw that in your face again," Jonah apologized.

"That's all right," she smiled weakly. "The truth is what it is."

"Next," the elderly sage continued. "We have the infestation stage. Sounds, smells and temperatures indicate the presence of something unusual. The oppression or obsession stage comes next, where these entities work to break down a person's will. If they succeed in weakening a person, possession can occur. If possession goes unexorcised, death is sure to result…be it the death of the possessed or the death of someone involved in their lives."

"You're saying that Brad was possessed through this process?" Marcus asked.

"No, with Ramsey, this is called a 'perfect possession.' This occurs when a person willingly offers himself to the demonic. They work in symbiosis, thus the will and the personality of the possessed is not subdued. It's ever present and delights in the power the demonic spirits provide him or her. This is a negative imitation of the Christian and his or her symbiotic relationship with the Holy Spirit."

I laughed. "Once again, you have your theological ducks in a row."

"Shut up, David, or *I'll shut your mouth for you!*" Marcus growled.

His eyes were dark. I stepped back in shock. This wasn't the Marcus I knew.

"Uh, sorry, Marcus. My sarcasm was uncalled for."

"And are you sorry for bringing those *wolves* to my door?" Marcus snarled as he approached me. He grabbed the top of my shirt. I flinched. Marcus was a big, powerful guy! I was a weed compared to him.

*"Marcus!"* Jonah yelled

My friend ignored him. I felt his fist slam into my stomach. With a gasp, I bent over in pain. My diaphragm was paralyzed. I couldn't breath.

*"Marcus!"* Jonah yelled again. "Look at what you're doing! This isn't *you!*"

Marcus looked confused. Suddenly, the dark expression left his face.

"Oh my *God!* Dave, are you okay? Man, I'm sorry!"

My friend leaned down and offered his hand. Coughing, I stood again. My breath slowly returned.

"It's okay. I think I had that coming."

"Once again, it's the pattern," Jonah nodded. "The demonic inspires fear, rage, and violence. The oppressed act in atypical ways."

"You don't think I was just possessed by something, do you, Jonah?" Marcus asked with fear.

"Absolutely not," Jonah reassured him. "Normal reactions are magnified by this environment. Annoyance becomes rage, for example."

"I see."

Marcus peered out the window again. "What's that Clarkson character doing now?"

Jonah walked over to look.

"Oh no," the doctor sighed. "Richard has his TriField EM meter out. He is taking electromagnetic field measurements. Look at the reporters still hovering around him."

"This is BS," Marcus moaned. "I'm going out there."

"I'd recommend against that," Jonah warned. "Anything you say in the presence of the media *will* be held against you. I know from experience."

"I'm going to at least invite Clarkson in," Marcus growled. "So I can kick him out!"

"You've been under enough stress," I offered. "Besides, I don't want you to punch him and end up with a lawsuit on your hands. I'll get rid of him."

"Thanks, Dave. Considering what I just did, you're a true friend."

"I'm the one who caused this circus. I'll bring down the big top."

I quickly slipped out the front door. Ten reporters heard the noise and ran over with cameras, microphones, and tape recorders.

"Sir! How are you connected to the Pattysons?"

"Did you experience anything unusual in there?"

"Can you confirm or deny that demons are haunting this family?"

I ignored them and marched straight toward Richard Clarkson. He looked up from his meter.

"Mr. Paul! I didn't know you were here today!" The professor smiled.

"And Dr. Clarkson, who invited you? I never gave you this address!"

"Well, you did tell me about Torrington residents that go by the names Tamika and Marcus. Only one couple in Torrington fits the bill."

"So you went snooping, like some sort of investigative stalker?"

"Not at all. We have a mutual friend."

"Oh? Who's that?"

"Mr. Brad Ramsey, host of the soon to be syndicated talk show the *Rational Humanist*. Although the man is extremely skeptical of everything paranormal, he was good enough to recently interview me."

"What?"

Reporters stood around us, writing in pocket notebooks.

"Mr. Paul, you are the undisclosed caretaker of Huey Riiska alluded to in the *Humanist Inquirer*," Clarkson grinned. "You were fired just after that poor man died, and shortly after those mysterious sheets were discovered. Why is that?"

"I have nothing to say about that. What I am concerned with is that you're hovering around the Pattyson's house. Did you tell the media something supernatural was going on here?"

"And were you behind those imprinted sheets, recently covered in the publications *Microanalysis* and *The Humanist Inquirer*?"

"No."

"And is this why Residential Associates and Ray Boyington prevent other researchers from studying these linen fibers?"

"Clarkson, I'm trying to keep my cool here. Don't push it," I hissed.

"Or what?" he laughed. "I suspected that you're volatile, Mr. Paul. Did you do something to that poor Riiska fellow?"

"No."

Clarkson held up his TriField EM meter. "Notice, folks, the EM readings are significantly greater in the presence of this volatile man." Reporters peered over his shoulder.

"I wonder how strong the EM readings are up your butt," I growled.

"Careful, Mr. Paul. Ramsey warned me of your aggressive nature. You have a criminal history, correct?"

"Nothing but juvenile misdemeanors. Not that it's any of your business."

"Just be sure not to attack me in front of all these witnesses," he warned.

I stood there, speechless. Suddenly, a practical approach occurred to me. A dishonest approach.

"Ladies and gentlemen," I addressed the small gathering. "You all know how popular Brad Ramsey's show has become here in Connecticut. Soon, this show will be aired nationwide. Brad…"

I choked on my words before continuing.

"Brad Ramsey is a sharp, astute man. He doesn't lend credence to hooey or nonsense. Obviously, this man's public opinions were damaged by Mr. Ramsey and you folks are being duped."

The reporters started to murmur. The blood drained from Clarkson's face.

"Really, folks. Electromagnetic fields? Paranormal activity? This stuff is fit for the tabloids, not respectable news providers. There's nothing going on at this house."

The reporters nodded in agreement and started to walk away.

"Please, folks!" Clarkson called after them. "This man is involved in a cover-up. A scandal that involves a dead retarded man! This deserves your attention, I'm sure! Two fine publications have already touched upon this mystery! Either this man or the people inside know more than they're sharing!"

Still, half the reporters got into their vehicles and drove away. The other half meandered around their vehicles, conferring with each other. I directed a sarcastic smile at Clarkson.

"Let he who lives by skepticism, die by skepticism," I chuckled.

"You made a mistake, not wanting to share those fabric samples with me," Clarkson glared.

"Apparently not," I smiled. "You were just going to pass them off to Brad Ramsey, weren't you?"

"To the fine researchers of the *Humanist Inquirer,* yes."

"You're a fool. That publication would dismantle your theories, just as they did with Claire Monroe and Ray Boyington. You think they approve of your paranormal research, just because it's secular?"

"Not only will they cover my research favorably, they will actively promote my publications! I have Brad Ramsey's promise."

"Well!" I laughed "Brad Ramsey is certainly a man of his word!"

"You don't understand the ultimate mission of Ramsey and *The Humanist Inquirer,* David. It's not their goal to dismantle anything paranormal and mysterious. What they want is to liberate our culture from the shackles of organized religion! This is a goal I wholeheartedly support."

"This includes throwing slanderous allegations about me in front of reporters?" I asked with hostility.

"Whatever it takes to get you onboard. Come now, Mr. Paul. You don't belong with those medieval promoters of hellfire. I know you don't."

"I should sue you for what you said about me."

"I doubt you want much media attention. Your lawsuit would bring just that."

At this point, a black Audi pulled into the driveway. To my dismay, a Catholic priest arrayed in ecclesiastical robes stepped out. This caught the attention of the few remaining reporters. They ran back to the yard. As if things weren't bad enough, Claire Monroe stepped out of the driver's side.

I groaned. I had forgotten about those two.

One reporter nudged me. "Nothing goin' on here, eh? Liar. Perhaps your role with the disappearance of Huey Riiska's body should be investigated!"

"I didn't believe any respectable reporter would be interested in Claire Monroe and her religious cohort," I responded.

"Of course it's all nonsense, but it's the type of nonsense the public enjoys," he answered, while approaching the small mob.

They thrust a few microphones at Claire Monroe and the priest.

"Are you two here to exorcise this house?"

"Father, do you believe this residence is haunted by demons?"

"What do you two know about the Pattysons and their connection to that new Shroud image?"

Claire and her partner didn't respond. They approached the front door.

"Hey, Claire! Claire! Over here!" Clarkson yelled.

Monroe paused and turned around. Her face grimaced when she spotted Clarkson.

The reporters turned to give the professor renewed attention.

"Richard!" Claire yelled back. "Why are *you* here?"

"I'm the guest of Mr. Paul!" he gleefully announced.

I looked at Claire and shook my head in denial.

"Folks," Clarkson addressed the reporters. "Here you see some classic Christian behavior. If anyone dares challenge their precious little belief system, such people are excluded from viable investigations."

"Ms. Monroe? I know this guy's a manipulative, lying, ambitious scumbag, but he does have a point," I admitted.

"First we'll have to ask the Pattysons," Claire answered.

Marcus let the pair inside. After a few minutes, Jonah opened the door a crack.

"Dave, you can bring Clarkson in," he sighed with resignation.

# CHAPTER 26

▼

# THE EXORCISM

As I followed Professor Clarkson into Marcus's living room, stares of disapproval penetrated me like lasers. I was embarrassed. I didn't know how unscrupulous this investigator was. I felt used.

I still embraced the hypothesis Clarkson promoted. The past guilt and current expectations of this group was powerful. Their faith seemed to border on fanaticism. Claire set a video camera on a tripod. Silently praying, the priest sat by himself. Tamika and Marcus held each other. I believed these people were setting up psychic bowling pins, soon to be knocked down by their personal demons.

"Uh-huh," Clarkson nodded, while looking at his hand-held, electromagnetic meter. "I knew it! The energy fields in this house are powerful. Three times normal levels! This house is probably situated over a unique concentration of iron ore and quartz."

"Richard, I hope you realize," Jonah glared. "You cannot write about, or report any events within this house without the written consent of Marcus and Tamika Pattyson."

"Of course, Jonah. I'm here in the interest of science, not profit."

Claire Monroe walked over to the two men.

"The infrared is on," Claire reported. "The video should pick up orb or vortex activity unseen by the naked eye. Prepare yourselves for the exorcism. The paranormal poopy is gonna hit the fan."

"Do you plan to share any video taken here today?" Clarkson asked her.

"Only if Marcus and Tamika wish it, love."

"Now, now Claire. Don't start flirting with me again."

"I'd do anything to get you to leave," the English woman laughed.

"I'm sure you would!"

"It's almost time to begin," Jonah commented. "Let's be seated."

Everyone found a chair. I sat on the couch to the right of Marcus.

"If I knew Clarkson was an opportunist, I would have never sought his opinion," I whispered to my friend.

"It's okay, Dave. Jonah says that Clarkson can't exploit our situation without direct permission."

"And what about Claire Monroe?"

"Claire and Jonah have worked together before. Only ten percent of people in supernatural situations give permission for their case study to be discussed or written about. With the other ninety percent, these two have a stainless record. They honor confidentiality."

"Hello, friends," the priest started to speak. He stood at the front of the room, to the side of the fireplace. He was an elderly man with a full head of gray hair and a lean build. Deep facial crevasses indicated a hard life.

"My name is Father Jacob Lorias. I have participated in exorcism rituals across our globe, from Africa to Albany. I will be using a modern language version of the Roman ritual. Shall we begin?"

The gathering nodded in agreement.

"Let us pray."

Everyone in the room bowed their head, all except Clarkson and me. He rolled his eyes and gave me a sarcastic smile.

"Heavenly Father, we are gathered today in your name, seeking deliverance from powers and principalities. May your Spirit strengthen us. Your presence is assured. We are certain that where one or two are gathered in your name, you are there as well. We beseech you, Lord Jesus, deliver us from the enemy. Amen."

"Amen," the gathering responded.

The room filled with a stench as powerful as an open septic tank.

"The enemy is announcing its arrival," Claire murmured. "Father, continue to use direct provocation."

"In the name of *Jesus Christ*," Father Lorias loudly announced. "Come forth and show *yourself!*"

A loud rapping echoed through the house. Upstairs. In the basement.

"In the name of Jesus Christ, make your presence known!"

Something smashed in the kitchen. Four books flew out of a bookcase. One hardcover propelled across the room and hit Jonah in the head. My employer picked it off the floor and grinned at the selection. It was *The Two Towers* by JRR Tolkien, one of his favorite books.

Professor Clarkson sprung out of his seat and rushed over to the bookshelf with his electromagnetic meter.

"Sit down, Richard," Claire sighed.

Clarkson ignored her.

"Our Father," Lorias continued, "Who art in heaven. Hallowed be thy name. Thy kingdom come, thy will be done…"

The coffee table levitated two inches off the floor, then dropped.

I desperately wanted to leave the house, but didn't want to seem cowardly. With pounding heart and sweaty hands, I forced myself to stay seated.

"…on Earth as it is in heaven. Give us this day our daily bread, and forgive us our trespasses as we forgive those who trespass against us. Lead us not into temptation…"

"…but deliver us from the evil one," Claire finished.

The prayers continued, with Lorias starting and Claire concluding. I knew that Lorias must have been unconventional, allowing Claire to participate in the ritual.

"Save Marcus and Tamika, your servants, from oppression…"

"For they place their trust in you."

"Be a tower of strength for them, O Lord…"

"…In the face of the enemy."

"Let the enemy have no victory over them…"

"…and the Son of Iniquity not succeed in harming them."

"Lord, hear my prayer,"

"And let our cry reach you."

"May the Lord be with you."

"And also with you."

"Let us pray. God, it is an attribute of yours to have mercy and forgive. Hear our prayer, so that your servants may be mercifully freed by the compassion of your goodness. Holy Lord! All powerful Father!"

A low, growling sound vibrated around us. I looked at Jonah in fear, who reached over and squeezed my shoulder. A wheezing breath sounded in my left ear.

"Eternal God! Father of our Lord Jesus Christ! You who destined that recalcitrant and apostate Tyrant to the fires of hell; you who sent your only Son into this world in order that he might crush this roaring Lion."

A guttural giggle filled the room.

"Look speedily and snatch from oppression and from the devil this couple who were created in your image and likeness."

"Nah nayah nah nayaaaah nah." A child's voice taunted from the ceiling.

"Remarkable!" Clarkson smiled. He seemed to actually enjoy the goings on. I wanted to run. Everyone else ignored the sounds, their heads bowed in prayer.

"Throw your terror, Lord, over the beast who is destroying what belongs to you. Give faith to your servants against this most evil serpent, to fight most bravely. So that the serpent not hold in contempt those who trust in you and say—as it said through the Pharaoh—'I do not know God, and I will not let Israel go.' Let your powerful strength force the serpent to let go of your servants, so that it no longer oppresses them whom you designed to make in your image and to redeem by your Son, who lives and reigns with you in the unity of the Holy Spirit, as God, for ever and ever. Amen."

At this moment, a light bulb in a lamp to the right of the couch exploded. Little shards of glass flew in a ten-foot radius. Everyone shielded their face.

Clarkson walked over to the lamp, taking more measurements.

Father Lorias moved to the part of the room that had exhibited the most activity.

"*Unclean spirit!* Whoever you are and all your companions who oppress these servants of God—by the mysteries of the Incarnation, the sufferings, death, Resurrection, and ascension of our Lord Jesus Christ, by the sending of the Holy Spirit, by the coming of our Lord into the last judgment, I command you—"

"You command *meeee?*" A shrill, squeaky voice announced.

I startled. With panic, I looked around the room. Nothing unusual was visible.

"Tell me, with some sign, your name."

"I'm meeee!" the shrill voice giggled. "I'm your *child,* eunuch!"

Clarkson walked over to me.

"It is his child," the professor whispered to me. "It was born of his subconscious."

"Shh!" Claire responded.

The sound of a baby crying replaced the shrill voice. This affected Tamika, who leaned against Marcus and sobbed.

"Obey me in everything, although I am an unworthy servant of God," Lorias announced loudly.

"Scope out any cute choir boys lately, Lorias?" a deep, gravely voice asked from the ceiling.

"Do no damage to these people, or to my assistants, or to any of their goods," Lorias responded.

A painting flew off a wall and crashed against the front door. Tamika cried out in pain, as three red welts appeared on her throat. The rapping noises were continuous.

Lorias looked angry. Infuriated.

*"Unclean spirit!"* he yelled. *"It is not men who you are defying, it is the Lord!"*

"Mea culpa," the shrill voice giggled.

"Hear the word of God, serpent," Lorias responded. "'And he said to them, go into all the world and preach the good news to the whole human race. He who believes and trusts in the gospel and is baptized will be saved. But he who does not believe will be condemned. And these attesting signs will accompany those who believe. In my name they will drive out demons…'"

The giggling continued.

"'…they will speak in new languages. They will pick up serpents, and if they drink any poison, it will not harm them. They will lay their hands on the sick and they will get well.'"

The rapping and giggling suddenly ceased. The air became lighter.

"Lord, hear my prayer," Lorias continued.

"And let my cry reach you."

"May the Lord be with you."

"And also with you."

"Let us pray. All powerful God! Word of God, the Father! Christ Jesus! God and Lord of all creation! You gave power to your apostles to pass through dangers unharmed. Among your commands to do wondrous things, you said to 'drive out evil spirits.' By your strength, Satan fell like lightning from heaven. With fear and trembling, I pray and supplicate your Holy Name. Pardon all the sins of your unworthy servant. Give me constant faith and power so that, armed with your holy strength, I can cast out this cruel evil spirit in confidence and security. Through you, Jesus Christ, Our Lord God, who will come to judge the living and the dead and the world by fire."

"Let us now stand and form a prayer circle," Claire suggested.

Everyone stood except for Clarkson and me.

"I would advise you two to join us," Lorias prompted.

"I'd be a hypocrite if I did," I replied.

The circle held hands, heads bowed forward.

"I exorcise you, most unclean spirit!" the priest started again. "*Invading enemy!* All spirits! Every one of you! In the name of our Lord *Jesus Christ,* be uprooted and expelled from this residence. He who commands you is the same who threw you down from the highest heaven into the debts of hell. He who commands you is he who dominated the sea, the wind, and the storms. Hear, therefore and fear *Satan!* Enemy of the faith! Enemy of the human race! Source of death! Robber of life! Twister of justice! Root of evil! Warp of vices! Seducer of men! Traitor of nations! Inciter of jealousy! Originator of greed! Cause of discord! Creator of agony! Why do you stay and resist when you know Christ has destroyed your plan? Fear him who was prefigured in Isaac, in Joseph, and in the Paschal Lamb. He who was crucified as a man and who rose from the dead!"

"Amen."

"Lord, hear my prayer."

"And let my cry reach you."

"May the Lord be with you."

"And also with you."

A low, mournful wail was heard upstairs.

Clarkson started for the stairwell, but Claire grabbed the back of his shirt.

"You can't go up there without permission," she whispered to him. In response, the professor gave Marcus a pleading look. My friend shook his head "no."

"Let us pray," Lorias announced with irritation. He didn't appreciate disruptions.

"God, Creator and defender of the human race! You who made man in his own image! Look down in pity, on your servants who are assaulted by the cunning of an unclean spirit. Repel, oh Lord, the power of the evil spirit!"

With an abrupt motion, the couch flipped backward. The noise made everyone startle. The room became dark, as if a gray mist surrounded all things. The stench of feces made everyone gag and cough. Moans came from the walls.

"Dissolve the fallacies of its plots! May the unholy tempter take flight. May your servants be protected in soul and body! May the residence and belongings of this couple be liberated from the presence of the unholy!"

One by one, each book in a rather large bookcase was thrown at the group. People ducked. Some protected their heads with their arms.

"I enjoin you under penalty, *ancient serpent!* In the name of the judge of the living and the dead! In the name of our Creator! In the name of him who has power to send you to hell! Depart from this residence and *plague these servants of God no more!*"

The gray fog condensed toward the middle of the room. Father Lorias gestured for everyone to step back. I needed no such prompting, ducking for cover behind the overturned sofa. The fog was becoming a figure! I didn't want to watch. I tried to look away, to concentrate on something else. I couldn't. My eyes were sealed on the horrific spirit.

Most everyone cowered away from the scene. Jonah and Claire stood behind the priest. Father Lorias was resolute. His expression remained unchanged. Not one indicator of fear could be seen on his face.

A deep, coarse voice came from the figure.

"We are Minus, Baalus, Tamarius."

"Devils," Lorias announced with victory in his eyes. "You have identified yourselves to the Lord. Leave therefore now!"

The figure was a mass of swirling mist. Slowly, a pair of legs manifested. Cloven, goat hoofs. Burned, dark flesh covered its upper body. Its head took the form of a pig, with ram horns curling backward.

*"Fascinating!"* Clarkson exclaimed. "A traditional, medieval form!"

The beastly form turned to look at the skeptical professor, and the pig's head transformed into a duplicate of Brad Ramsey's head. Its eyes were hollow. A disproportionate grin stretched from ear to ear.

"I…likes 'em *fat and cushy!*" The ghostly image squealed, moving toward the now frightened parapsychologist.

*"Get out of here, Richard!"* Claire yelled.

The rotund scholar didn't need further prompting. He unlocked the front door with frantic, shaky hands and ran into the front yard. Tamika closed and locked the door.

The figure then molded into a young girl. She wore a blue dress covered in blood. Her torso hovered, no legs were visible. "Tha' man killed me," she whispered, pointing at Jonah. "Where's my mommy? Mommy! Tha' man let me die!"

Jonah grimaced, then looked away from the spirit. Tamika buried her face into her husband's shoulder. The manifestation slowly faded away.

"The time cannot be put off," Lorias continued. "Behold the victorious Lord is near and quick. The fire is burning before him and devours all his enemies—"

Tamika screamed! She collapsed onto the floor with Marcus breaking her fall.

"It's in me!" Tamika shrieked. "It's moving inside me!"

Marcus held his wife's hand.

"Honey, don't let it get to you! Don't let it scare you!"

Tamika reached down and lifted her sweater. Her stomach was rising and falling as if something were pushing from the inside.

"Tamika, the demon is a liar!" Lorias offered, before continuing the ritual. "Even though you have deceived men, you cannot make a mockery of God! From his eyes, nothing is hidden! *He has ejected you!*"

Tamika jumped to her feet and ran toward the kitchen with a scream. Marcus followed closely. By the time the group caught up with the couple, a horrifying scene was unfolding! Tamika had a large carving knife and was holding it to her stomach!

"'Mika!" Marcus yelled, while wrestling with her arm. "Put that thing down, 'Mika!"

"I'm gonna cut it out of me!" she shrieked. "I'd rather die than feel like this!"

The bulge pressed harder against Tamika's stomach. A defined shape appeared; a small head with two apparent horns! Two rounded knobs on either side! Tamika screamed with horror and then collapsed. As her body went limp, Marcus grabbed the knife from her hand and threw it across the room.

"All things are subject to his power!" Lorias yelled, sprinkling holy water on Tamika. "He has expelled you! The living, the dead, and the world will be judged by him with complete discernment. He has prepared hell for you and your angels. *Return to it now, in the name of Jesus Christ!*"

Every piece of furniture, every object in the house vibrated and shook. Tamika's bulge appeared to deflate. A high-pitched shriek made everyone hold their ears when the front windowpane in the Pattyson's living room shattered! Glass and wood flew outside. At the same moment, the air warmed. The putrid scent of feces left, replaced by a floral odor.

Everyone stood silent. Marcus cradled his unconscious wife. Was it over? The environment in the house changed so suddenly, no one knew how to react. It seemed too good to be true.

"Praise God," the priest sighed.

Jonah and Claire hugged and Tamika slowly regained consciousness. Marcus hovered over her. I was numb. Peeking out the broken front window, I saw that Clarkson hadn't left. He remained on the yard speaking with two individuals. Possibly reporters?

The priest was unsteady, so I grabbed one of the overturned chairs and brought it to him. He whispered a thank you and collapsed into the seat.

"*Oh, Jacob!*" Claire exclaimed. "I'm so sorry, you must be spent! Let me get you a glass of water."

"That would be appreciated," Lorias smiled.

Jonah approached and knelt down next to the priest.

"Jacob, did anything distinguish this cleansing from others you've participated in?"

"I should say," he murmured. "I've never felt such a vile, powerful presence. If this infestation had become entrenched, if possession occurred here, I shudder to think of the resistance we would have encountered."

"How could that be?" I asked. "This exorcism lasted only about fifteen minutes!"

"Fortunately, these entities had a mere toehold in this place. This doesn't diminish the vile power of these spirits, rather this reflects on the faith of those who live here."

"Thank you, Father," Marcus smiled. "Thank you for the compliment, and for what just occurred."

"You're quite welcome. Thank God most of all."

Claire came back into the room and handed the priest a glass of water. With trembling hands, he gulped it down.

"What did you experience, Jacob?" Claire asked.

"Every sadness, every loss in my life was replayed before my eyes," he answered. "I've never experienced such a mental assault, save for a few exorcisms of those in the later stages of possession."

"I knew these spirits were powerful, but I never expected this much activity. I should had given you prior warning," Claire sighed.

"Every situation has its own unpredictability," Lorias nodded.

"Those manifestations, those images. I'm afraid that every time I close my eyes, I'm going to relive this," Marcus whispered.

"And did anyone see an apparition of Brad Ramsey?" I asked.

"Yes!" Marcus cried. "I did! Did you also notice—"

"It's best, dear friends," Lorias interrupted, "that everyone here try to forget the imageries you saw today. Erase them from your mind. Do not speak of them. Mental and verbal recognition will empower the very entities that were just expelled."

"Eh…" Marcus grimaced.

"You just hold on to your faith," Jonah smiled, grabbing his arm. "You and Tamika were blessed by God today. Let us all give thanks for the next several days. Making a donation to a charity or church would be a great way of thanking the Lord."

"Speaking of imagery," Claire whispered. "Shall I go check my video camera?"

"Oh God! I forgot! You think you captured any of the bizarre manifestations?" Jonah inquired.

"Probably not," the demonologist answered. "If I did, it would be a first."

She peered into her view piece and held down the rewind button. After a few minutes of anticipation, she looked up with disappointment.

"Well, as usual, I managed to film some psychokenisis. Some objects flying about. Around the time the spirits took form, the electrical disturbance was too great for the videotape. All we have is static. Interference noise."

"Just as well," Lorias smiled. "The imagery should be forgotten, as I advised before."

"Still, how dramatic this footage would had been, presented to a disbelieving world," Claire sighed.

"It wouldn't have proved a thing," Jonah laughed. "Right, David?"

"Well, it may have reinforced Clarkson's theory," I admitted.

"David," Claire responded, "Clarkson knows the process of the phenomena. Yes, paranormal occurrences draw energy from earthly sources, be they high-tension wires, iron ore, lightning storms, or even human beings. They are energy conduits, not a source unto themselves. There is intelligence behind the phenomena, intelligence more organized than the human subconscious. It has intention. It has cunning."

"So do men," I murmured, looking out the window. "Excuse me folks."

I marched out the front door and approached Richard Clarkson who was still chatting with two bystanders.

"Look at that window! The collective, pious imaginings of those people have created a paranormal snake pit in there!" The professor was exclaiming to the men.

I ran toward the professor and grabbed his shirt.

"Clarkson! You weren't given release to talk to any media, you bastard!"

"Calm yourself," he laughed. "These two men aren't reporters. They are undergraduate interns who assist me."

"Still, watch yourself. You better not spread any stories about my friends, or we'll sue you, regardless of the attention that would come back to me."

"Okay, okay," the professor smiled. "Don't worry now. I won't even attempt to explain what we both saw today. Those individuals are generating so much psychic energy, I never thought it possible that anyone could manipulate the environment as they just did."

"Be that as it may, these people have a right to privacy."

"And privacy they shall have, Mr. Paul."

# CHAPTER 27

▼

# PARTINGS

The exorcism was a success. Marcus and Tamika were free of intrusive sights, sounds, smells, and cold spots. Were real entities expelled, or were subconscious energies tamed by the power of suggestion? Everyone involved, except Clarkson and I, believed in the power of exorcism. This had to factor in.

New Years came and went. After the sound and fury of the last couple of months, I found myself wrestling with the same old problems. I was lonely. Marcus distanced himself from me and I couldn't blame him. I betrayed his trust. I couldn't share his worldview.

Jonah's office returned to normal. Family counseling dominated once again, instead of parapsychological investigations and bizarre field trips. The realm of relationship trouble and child rearing were again the focus.

Brad's talk show was syndicated. His move to California certain. The big question remained. Would Jess accompany him? I was conflicted. Here was a woman who rejected me, who was involved with a pedophile and a rapist. She was his defender. His apologist. Still, she was Jess. A sweet woman who deserved happiness and security. If only I could convince her of the danger she was in. I wanted to call her, but I was too timid.

It was a Thursday, about ten minutes before Jonah's office closed when I received a phone call. To my surprise, it was Marcus. He wanted me to drop by when I got off work. I agreed. What did he want? Did he finally forgive me for exposing his story to Clarkson? Perhaps he had news about Jessica. My palms started to sweat.

When I arrived at the house, Marcus was sitting on his front step. I tensed. The last time I saw this scene, the house was a terror trap. Did the haunting activity come back?

I walked up to my friend slowly. Reluctantly.

"Hey, Marcus. What's going on?"

He looked up and gave me a weak grin.

"Relax, Dave. Nothing supernatural is going on."

"That's a relief. Still, something must be troubling you."

"I'm sorry I haven't been in touch, Dave."

"No need to apologize. I don't deserve your forgiveness."

"We all make mistakes."

"Yes, some of us more than others."

"Well, I do have news."

"Shoot."

"Tamika left me."

"What?"

I sat next to Marcus. It took me a minute before I thought of a question.

"Did she give you any warning? A good-bye?"

"She did leave a note. Here, let me read it."

Marcus pulled out a wrinkled, tattered piece of paper. It looked like it had been handled for about a year.

"Dear Marcus, first I'd like to tell you how much I love you. You've been a wonderful husband. Still, the last month revealed many things to me. I believe I married you for the wrong reasons. You were nice. Perhaps *too* nice. My arrogance, my pride had invited Satan into our home. I even felt it within my body. I shudder to imagine if we had any children. Honey, you deserve better. I'll eventually send you some divorce paperwork. Whether you go along with the proceedings or not, I will not return. You will always be in my prayers. Love, 'Mika."

"I'm sorry, Marcus. Just when it seemed you two had finally caught a break."

"When the crisis ended, this is when she became introspective. Too much so."

"I can see how that would happen."

Marcus stood up and straightened his coat.

"I need to walk. You up for a stroll?"

"Of course."

The road was frozen. The hard-packed snow had traction, but black ice could catch a person unawares. Marcus and I walked quietly for a few minutes, looking at our feet. My friend finally broke the silence.

"My God. What am I going to do?"

"I don't know. Why don't you ask Jonah?"

"I'd hate to do that. The man put himself out for us during our crisis. He needs a break."

"This is true."

"So, what is your opinion? What should I do?"

"I think if you try to get her back, she'll resist."

"So I should wait?"

"I think so. She may change her mind, after some time alone. But hell, look who's talking? Mr. Strikeout. What do I know about women?"

"Yeah. There's another bit of news I need to share with you."

"What's that?"

"Well, Brad and Jess married last weekend. They had a civil service. They're moving to California on Saturday."

I stopped walking. Fighting back a few tears, I simply shook my head.

"Shh…she's only known him for four months," I choked.

"I know."

"I'm afraid for her."

"So am I."

"Marcus, look at us. Your wife left you and Jess married a pedophile rapist."

"It would make quite a soap opera, wouldn't it?"

"We'll call it 'As the Stomach Turns.'"

Marcus didn't smile, or acknowledge the joke. I decided to keep pushing the humor.

"My character should be called Stone Braddock. You can be Steel Carson."

My friend remained expressionless.

"I'll be the doctor *you* can be the lawyer."

"Wait a minute," Marcus frowned. "Why do I have to be the lawyer? Doctors save lives, but lawyers are considered bloodsuckers!"

"Still, considering the cost of malpractice insurance these days, you'll have more money."

Marcus's brief smile evaporated. "That's good, Dave. I alone can't afford the payments on our house."

"Oh."

Again, we walked in silence. The crunching of snow under our shoes was hypnotic. I enjoyed its rhythm. It distracted me from the depression hanging over us. As a neighbor's mailbox came into view, Marcus held out his arm to stop me.

"We should turn back here, Dave."

"Why here?"

"Percy."

*"Percy?"*

"Yeah, you don't want to meet Percy."

"Who's this? Some difficult neighbor? Well, hell with him. I refuse to be intimidated."

"Suit yourself. I'm standing right here."

"Marcus, you confuse me. You can stand in the midst of ghostly activity and remain calm. But some neighbor has you nervous?"

"Yup."

"Well, let me see if anyone is home."

I advanced. Just as I reached the mailbox, I noticed the names painted on the side: Pat and Judy O'Halloran. I turned to yell at Marcus who stood about one hundred feet away.

"Hey, Marcus! There's no Percy who lives here!"

I heard a low growl. Slowly, I turned around to see an animal, perhaps from the Jurassic Period. It was a Great Dane. He stood as high as I did. Drool dripped from the corner of his mouth as he growled again. The dog was walking toward me.

"Nice doggy," I soothed. "Good doggy."

Its bark was comparable to a sonic boom. Making sure not to make eye contact, I slowly backed away. The dog followed. I had backtracked about ten feet from the O'Halloran mailbox before the creature broke off pursuit. It returned to its kingdom.

As I rushed back to Marcus, he was bent over laughing. This was the final straw.

"Sure, you won't laugh at my jokes. But putting me in mortal danger, this you consider *funny!*"

"'Cause it is funny!"

*"Is not!"*

"Relax, Dave. I knew Percy stays near the driveway. He hasn't bitten anyone."

"Well, with my luck I'd be the first."

"With our luck," Marcus giggled.

"Yeah. Think about it. This world is full of horrible, despicable people who have it made. They are media moguls, CEOs, celebrities, politicians, and execs.

They have beautiful women, summer homes, and private jets. They live the good life. Then there are people like you and me. Decent and unassuming. We care for the disadvantaged, we work hard. What kind of lives do we live?"

"Dave, I never compare myself to others."

"How can you not?"

"Okay, you live in an apartment. Soon, I will as well. We have few possessions. Few luxuries. We reside on the bottom of the employment ladder. Women generally yawn around us."

"Hey!" I protested.

"It's okay, Dave, I'm going somewhere with this."

"Try to go there quickly."

"I will, I will. As I was saying, we have our personal crosses to bear. Yet in the grand scheme of things, do we really have it so bad? Think about it. In Africa, starvation is common. In other nations, people live under dictators. Under oppression. Some people have disabilities, diseases, and disfigurements."

"Oh, I see. We're not starving, diseased, or disfigured. Alleluia!"

"No, Dave. Just look at your life. You are blessed!"

"Me? Surely you jest!"

"Not at all. I know that God works in your life!"

"If God goes by the name of Satan, I'd agree with you."

"Think, Dave. You told me how you brought a peeling knife with you to Elm the night Huey died. You wanted to murder Brad. Thankfully, the knife disappeared from your back pocket. If it didn't, you could be serving a life sentence right now! Someone named 'hacksaw' could be calling you 'honey.'"

"That's true. On the other hand, Jess would be free from Brad. She'd be safe."

"Okay, let's consider something else. The very day you lost your job at RAI, you were offered a new job for more money!"

"True."

"Now, please don't be offended by my next observation. But you and Huey were close. He had a bond with you. After enduring Brad Ramsey's abuse for a month, Huey was delivered from his situation."

"Delivered? You call an untimely death delivered?"

"No, no—hear me out. Huey could have died of a seizure at any time. We knew this was part of his condition. He may have died the exact same way, the exact same time whether Brad was in his life or not. After Huey passed away, he disappeared and a miraculous image was left. Don't you see? Huey—and the Lord—left this image for you!"

"For me? You really believe this?"

"Yes. This image was left to comfort you. To reassure you that there is a God…a heaven. You are blessed!"

"Blessed," I murmured. "Yeah, that's me."

Loose snow started to blow in all directions. Our faces were bombarded by small ice particles making them sting. I zipped my coat.

"This weather is perfect," Marcus sighed. "Good weather for a man whose wife just left him."

"Yeah, and good weather for a man whose unrequited love is leaving him."

"Yes, about that," Marcus responded. "Jessica asked me to tell you her news. She also said you could call her. That's only if you were comfortable with it."

"She did?"

"Yup."

"Think I should call her, Marcus?"

"We both know that you can't dissuade her from leaving. Still it might bring some resolution to your heart, just to say good-bye."

Marcus and I returned to his house. With reluctance, I asked to use the phone. Marcus nodded and left the living room. As I dialed Jess's number, I looked around the room. At the corners. The floor. The exorcism still haunted my memory. It caught me off guard, how quickly my beautiful friend picked up.

"Hello?"

"Uh, hi, Jess. It's David."

"David! I'm so glad you called!"

"Yeah. Marcus told me about the news."

"Brad and I are so happy! I never thought I'd find anyone who made me feel so alive. I wish the same happiness for you, David. I really do!"

I felt the sting of her words. Her wish for me sounded like pity.

"Well, yes, about that. Do you really have to move with him, Jess?"

"No, Dave, don't. Don't do this."

"I'm sorry, but I'd never forgive myself if you were hurt out there. If you were in jeopardy and I never said something."

"What? Brad's going to hurt me?"

"I think he's capable of hurting you."

"Capable?"

"Yeah. You told me how he has different faces."

"Damn. I knew you would end up using that comment against me!"

"Not against you, Jess. Against Brad."

"Anything said against Brad is against me."

"Even if it's from your own mouth?"

"David, where the hell are you going with this?"

"You are aware of how Brad is disingenuous. How he has different personas for different forums. For example, in your study group he's some sort of new agey, 'find your higher power' guru. Yet on his show, he's a scientifically minded skeptic and agnostic."

"Okay…so this makes him dangerous?"

"No, this makes him deceptive. Don't you think it's possible that the man you fell in love with is just another mask? What if Brad is not the man you think he is?"

"Well, I know him. You don't. You still think he's some sort of perverted sexual predator. I know the real Brad Ramsey. A sensitive, caring man who weeps for people. Who cares about them. He is a tender man and the most considerate lover I've ever had."

An awkward silence ensued. I didn't know what to say next. Jessica was the first to speak.

"David, once again we wasted time arguing about Brad. Get this through your head; I will never change my mind about my husband."

"Okay, Jess. I am convinced of that," I sighed.

"Let's put that behind us. I just wanted to say to you Dave, that…I love you. You are like a brother to me. A special friend. Work would not have been the rewarding, enjoyable experience it was…if you weren't there."

A lump formed in my throat.

"Thank you, Jess," I coughed. "You know how I feel about you."

"Yes. I appreciate your caring. You want good things for me. I know this is why you continue to attack Brad. I understand it. Perhaps you and I can speak on the phone on occasion? I'd like to know how you are. I…won't forget you."

"Sure. We'll keep in touch."

Even as I said this, I knew it was unlikely we would ever speak again.

"Good-bye, David. No, I'll say 'until next time.'"

"Until next time, Jess."

I hung up the phone. It felt like a chapter had ended in my life. Marcus walked into the room and patted my shoulder.

"Well, Marcus," I sighed. "I'll never exert any influence on her."

"It's very hard for men to influence women. Look at Tamika and I."

"Unless the man's name is Brad Ramsey. Now Jess is leaving with Brad. It's as if she's walking toward a cliff while ignoring my voice."

"Have faith, David. You'll see Jess again."

# CHAPTER 28

▼

# THE SPEARHEAD

The next several years defined a new life for me. Gradually, I managed to get Jessica Kim out of my mind. Unfortunately, her residency within my heart was permanent. I never called her. She never called me.

On a rare occasion, I stumbled across Brad's syndicated talk show while channel surfing. Ramsey wasn't the next Oprah or Larry King. Instead, he enjoyed a small cult following who set their VCRs to record his show broadcast on private stations. At odd hours. Brad's *Rational Humanist* became increasingly political. He ranted and raved about Christian conservatives, the moral majority and other right-wing organizations. On occasion, his editor friend from *The Skeptical Humanist* would discuss paranormal issues. They routinely deconstructed all claims of the supernatural. There were rumors that Ramsey wanted to run for prominent political office. His following were devout, but weren't yet large enough to launch him into power.

The hubbub about Boyington's paper, Marcus's haunting, and Clarkson's intrusion all died out within a few months. Yes, Richard Clarkson did attempt to give a firsthand account of the exorcism in one of his books, but Jonah, Claire, and Marcus got wind and threatened legal action. The professor backed down.

Tamika never returned to Marcus. She moved to North Carolina to live with her mother. Their divorce was finalized within one year. My friend was heartbroken. He became a hermit for a solid year, seldom leaving his apartment. I would visit him once a week. We would watch sports, or rent a movie. Marcus used to be the one to cheer me up and suddenly our roles reversed. At the very least, Marcus never heard anything "go bump in the night" again.

After his mourning period, I suddenly had a bachelor friend. We gradually started to circulate among the singles' clubs and peruse the personal ads. Our social life became a running joke. A parade of mismatched dates marched through our lives. Now that I was in my early thirties, most women I dated were bitter divorcees. Marcus had it harder, being older. How we tired of hearing ex-husband horror stories. We tired of their disapproving children.

The year 2000 came. Computers continued to function, despite a paranoid fear of a societal collapse labeled "Y2K." That New Year's celebration featured spectacular fireworks. The anticipated apocalypse would have to wait.

Jonah remained active as ever during these years. My job became more demanding. When the good doctor was off on his frequent field trips, the office still kept me busy. Where did Jonah go? He journeyed twice to Israel. One archeological dig lasted a month. Another involved the tomb of a first-century leper. The find confirmed the fact that leprosy did exist during New Testament times, regardless of what skeptics alleged. Another trip involved the exorcism of an English farmer. This man came to Claire, plagued by voices. The infestation lasted months.

My story resumes in the late summer of 2001. Nearly six years had passed since the horrible days of Brad Ramsey. While I didn't consciously think of Jess often, she had the most annoying habit of appearing in my dreams.

August 27, 2001. It was a hot morning. I threw my legs over the side of my foldout bed hoping the rest of my body would take the hint. It didn't. I laid in a stupor. Since Jonah was at a Christian revival in Boston, I contemplated just sleeping in. My work shift was on the honor system, since neither the good doctor nor his patients would be in the office for several weeks. My job was to organize Jonah's filing. Conduct some Internet research. Run a spell check on his new manuscript. The Christian advocacy in his writing still annoyed me. After finding alternative explanations for the paranormal experiences I witnessed, I abandoned my brief flirtation with Christianity.

In the bathroom, I splashed cold water on my face. Damn my nagging conscience. Yeah, I would have to go to the office. I couldn't let Jonah pay me for services not rendered. The elderly man had been a real friend, after all.

Over the past six years, Jonah's health noticeably faded. His speech became slower. A gaunt and pale appearance overtook his face. None of this held him back. Between his archeological trips to the Middle East, Christian seminars, revivals, paranormal investigations, and normal social work, the man made my life look sedentary.

I was dwelling on this very thought in Jonah's office when the phone's ring startled me. It was my friend and employer. He ran into Claire at a revival and she wanted him to fly out with her to Los Angeles in a week or two. They were going to investigate a bizarre haunting, in which the occupants of a certain household witnessed the manifestation of a crawling, demonic-looking fetus. A small, premature infant with transparent skin and empty eye sockets. The similarity to Marcus's haunting was unsettling.

I wished Jonah and Claire well. I suspected that Claire herself was generating this apparition, her subconscious memory and fear manipulating available electromagnetic energy.

The daily work tedium ensued. After staring at the flickering computer screen for hours on end, I would become dizzy. Or develop a gripping headache. Small breaks from the monitor were needed. It was during such a hiatus that another phone call caught me off guard. Jonah's patients knew he was away. Who could this caller be? With a moan, I picked up the receiver.

"Christian Family Services."

The other end was silent.

"Hello, this is David Paul at Jonah Rubenstein's office."

More silence, then a click. I assumed it was a wrong number.

Ten minutes later, the phone rang again.

"Hello. Jonah Rubenstein's office."

Silence.

"Okay," I groaned. "Either speak up or stop calling!"

"Dave?"

I paused. It was a very weak voice. Female.

"Yes, this is David Paul. Who?"

"Dave, it's Jess. Jessica Kim."

I froze. Jess was calling me? After six long years? Something wasn't right.

"Jess! Uh, wow. Good to hear your voice. How's sunny California?"

"I'm...actually calling from the Ramada Inn near Bradley Field."

"You're in Connecticut? What brings you here?"

"I need to see you."

"Uh, okay. Do you know where Jonah's office is?"

"Could you meet me here? When your shift is over?"

"Certainly. Jess, is something wrong?"

"I'll tell you later. I'm in room two forty-four."

"Got it. I'll see you around five thirty."

"Thanks, Dave. Thank you so very much."

"No problem. See you soon."

"Bye."

How strange it seemed. How surreal. It was as if a part of my life I had buried, rose again. It didn't have me shouting "Alleluia." It resurrected painful memories.

The rest of the work day dragged. My mind kept drifting. I worried. What could Jessica want with me? Was Brad with her? Was she in danger?

These concerns plagued me as I drove through rush hour gridlock. Interstate 91 North was glutted with Hartford commuters returning home. Gradually, stop and go driving transformed into a crawl. By the time I reached Windsor-Locks, it was six in the evening. I pulled into the Ramada parking lot with apprehension. What bizarre stories awaited me in room two forty-four?

The pounding in my chest dwarfed the knock on the door. I could hardly believe I was about to see Jess again. It seemed as though a century passed since the last time our eyes met. The door slowly opened.

At first, I didn't recognize the wisp of a woman standing in front of me. Jess was always slender, but this woman was anorexic. Her hair was tied behind her. Dark circles rimmed her once bright eyes. She weakly smiled.

"Dave. Thanks for coming."

I held my hand out, but she made an awkward step forward for a hug. I lowered my hand and followed her prompt. The embrace was gentle and cautious. Jessica giggled nervously.

"Come in, Dave. Have a seat."

I looked around tentatively.

"Brad isn't here," she reassured me.

I sat on the plush couch and Jess sat in a chair opposite me.

"Can I get you a beer, Dave? A soda?"

"No thanks."

An awkward silence ensued.

"Sooo," I started. "Six years!"

"Has it been six years? I didn't realize."

"Yeah. Yes sir, six years," I nodded. "Where does the time go?"

"Mmm," Jess acknowledged.

More silence.

"Yup. Tempus fugit," I prattled on, feeling stupid.

"So, how are you, Dave? I see you're still at Jonah Rubenstein's office."

"It's been good work."

"Good to hear. How is Marcus?"

"Well, he and Tamika ended up divorcing. Officially."

"That's terrible. I plan on calling him."

"I'm sure he'd love to hear from you."

"Does Marcus still work at RAI?"

"Hmm-mm. Tim is still his manager!"

"Tim is still there?"

"Yeah, Tim's still going strong. His day program is about twice the size it was."

"Really! Nothing ever stays the same, does it?" she sighed.

More silence.

"So, Jess, have any kids of your own?"

"No, no children. What about you? Have you found Mrs. Right? Are you working on a family?"

"Naw. I'm as lucky at love as I used to be."

"So, both you and Marcus are bachelors?"

"That's right. We get a group rate at the local supermarket. Fifty percent off all the TV dinners."

"I'm sure you're wondering why I asked you here."

"I was surprised by your call."

Jess pulled a tissue from her pocketbook and dabbed at her tears.

"It's over between Brad and I. I've left him."

"Oh," I acknowledged. "That must be hard for you."

"It's more than hard, Dave. The Brad I knew…the man I fell in love with…he's gone. I don't know who my husband is now."

"Sorry to hear that." I was dying to remind her that this was the exact scenario I warned her about, but I knew it would be insensitive.

"As a matter of fact," Jess hesitated. "Well, I'm sort of on the run."

"On the run?"

"Brad hit me a few times. Once he broke my wrist."

"My God!"

"I left him several days ago. I'm looking for a battered woman's shelter, a place to help me disappear for awhile. I seem to remember your friend Dr. Rubenstein used to promote a shelter during his broadcast. I remember Brad ridiculing it saying how it was nothing more than a Christian reprogramming center."

"That's right. Jonah works with such a center in Torrington. Do you want the number?"

"I'd appreciate it."

"When I get home, I'll call you back."

"Thanks. I know Brad will come looking for me. Torrington will be the first town he'll comb through."

"Perhaps you shouldn't have returned here."

"I had to touch base. My brother lives here, I need to see him. Marcus, yourself—you guys. I needed to see you."

"How violent is Brad? Do you fear for your life?"

"Nooo," Jess insisted. "No. Not that bad. But he would manhandle me, force me to return with him. I'm tired of being treated like a possession. An object."

"I see."

"Yes. Nine people from our study group followed us to California. There, Brad recruited two more. They—*we*—are Brad's disciples. At first, he was a gentle seeker of truth. Slowly, he started to change. We owned a large mansion and his flock moved in with us. Everyone pooled their resources, their income. We were like a commune from the sixties. We were happy."

"Were you happy, Jess? As his wife?"

"At first. But things changed."

"Things?"

"Yeah, just things."

Jessica became flushed.

"Okay. If you don't want to talk about it."

"You know, Dave, I always could talk to you. Remember?"

"I remember."

"So, why not now, right? Right. Here goes."

Jess breathed in deep before continuing.

"Brad loved to experiment. Sexually."

"Oh."

"At first, I went along. Anything to keep Brad happy. Little by little, our lifestyle started to repulse me. Partner swapping. Group sex."

I sighed.

"Each year, Brad became different. More erratic. We grew apart. He often seemed to be closer to some of his flock than to me. Eventually, we stopped sleeping together. He was closer to those who blindly obeyed him."

I nodded quietly.

"Brad also started to claim that he was channeling messages from elsewhere. From 'inter-dimensional beings.'"

"You're kidding!"

"I know. The rational, skeptical Brad on television is a far cry from the Brad at home."

I still wanted to remind Jess of my warning six years prior.

"Anyway, his messages were entitled 'revelations,'" she continued. "He predicted news events. To our astonishment, he was always right. He predicted that the House would impeach Bill Clinton. That the Senate would protect the president. That NATO bombing would destroy the Chinese embassy in Belgrade. That the USS *Cole* would be attacked by terrorists. That the presidential election in two thousand would involve recounts in Florida."

"He predicted all that? I knew Ramsey had an uncanny ability to read minds, but this!"

"A few weeks back, Brad became excited. He said a 'new age was coming.' That 'the reign of the Jew and Christian would end.' He knew he had an important role to play in the future, but first he needed something. He needed what he called a 'precious scepter.'"

"Precious scepter?"

"I know. That was his term. I feared that he finally snapped. Are you aware that his publisher father was mentally ill?"

"Yeah, I heard something about that."

"I begged Brad to seek psychiatric help. He laughed, saying that the medical community was comprised of enemy Jews. Worse yet, he started to speak more and more of Adolf Hitler. He spoke in glowing, respectful terms of Nazi Germany."

"Oh God."

"Brad said Hitler had a scepter and that he needed the same prize. In the Hofsburg Treasure House, there is—was—an artifact called the Spear of Destiny. The weapon which supposedly pierced Jesus' side after he died on the cross."

"Yeah, right."

"I agree. That's all bunk. What isn't bunk is the fact that both Kaiser Wilhelm and Adolf Hitler possessed this relic. It's rumored that Hitler believed it carried power. Whoever possessed the spear was destined to rule. Among those who supposedly owned the spear were Constantine and Charlemagne the Great. Napoleon supposedly wanted to possess it as well."

"What do historians say?"

"It's all conjecture. One odd coincidence, though, ninety minutes after US soldiers discovered the spear in one of Hitler's vaults, he committed suicide."

"Hmm."

"Brad's obsessed with the spearhead. One of his followers actually traveled to Vienna, and somehow managed to steal the thing. Brad stares at it. Talks to it."

"Why not just report him to the police? No need to go into hiding!"

"His flock is devoted. You have no idea. They would murder me, I'm sure of it."

"Good Lord."

"Brad continues to say that something big is coming. He's not precise, but a major world event is about to occur. He says it will precipitate the downfall of Israel and the United States. The Jew and the Christian. He told me that all I have to do is read the second installment of *The Lord of the Rings* trilogy."

"Sounds like insane rambling."

"Yeah, I know. Still, he's been right so many times before."

"Since he's nonspecific regarding this prediction, I doubt he's on to anything."

"Probably. His 'inter-dimensional beings' are supposedly the same small, gray aliens people report being abducted by."

"No way."

"I know, I know. Calling doctor straightjacket. STAT!"

"Sooo, Jess. I hate to even bring this up, but it must be. Remember what I said many years ago? Brad Ramsey admitted to me, Jess! He told me that he sodomized Huey with his religious statuary."

"Daavvee—"

"After telling me about Ramsey's perversions, delusions, and criminal activity, you still think he had nothing to do with Huey's abuse and disappearance?"

"Dave, it was never established that Huey was abused."

"And what about me? I'm making up what Brad said to me?"

Jess started to sob. "I don't know, Dave! I don't know what to think!"

I walked over and put my arm around her. She leaned against me.

"Dave, Huey was so…innocent! So helpless! I can't allow myself to believe what you say! It can't be! It just can't be. It can't."

I started to rock her body slowly, back and forth.

"Not Huey. No. No. He was such a sweet, childlike man. No, not him."

"It's okay, Jess."

"Don't make me accept what you say. Don't. *I can't handle it!*"

"Okay, Jess. Okay."

The evening sun started to come through the hotel window. A pink shaft of light illuminated the top of Jessica's head. Silver and red highlights danced across her hair. My friend continued to cry violently. Her turmoil had been bottled up for too long. Her pain became my pain.

# CHAPTER 29

▼

# AT THE BAR AND GRILL

I called Jess and gave her the number of a woman's shelter. She thanked me and promised to go there immediately.

Jessica's conversation weighed heavy on me. Jonah's perspective would have been appreciated at a time like this, but I didn't want to discuss it on the phone. My employer was in Boston, soon to be headed for Los Angeles. Marcus and I had a plan to meet at TGI Friday's in West Hartford, so I saved the topic for my friend.

As usual, Marcus was sitting at the three-sided bar when I arrived. The restaurant was swarming with beautiful young women. A dull roar of conversation filled the eatery. Many were college students, attending a local campus in New Britain. Occasionally, older women would drop in after shopping at the nearby West Farms Mall. They would arrive with several shopping bags and multiple friends in tow. In the past, whenever Marcus or I gathered enough courage to talk to one of these ladies, the collective stare of their judgmental posse would eventually chase us away.

A beautiful young lady was chatting with Marcus when I approached the bar. Not wanting to cramp his style, I silently sat to his other side. They murmured and giggled, then the woman stood up and walked back to her table of friends.

"So, Marcus!" I smiled. "Doin' pretty well without me, I see."

"Yeah," he laughed. "She came over to settle a bet. She wanted to know whether it was Mario or Luigi who was featured in the first *Donkey Kong* video game."

"That's odd. What made her ask you?"

"I just have that geek look, I guess."

"She wasn't familiar with *Donkey Kong*?"

"Dave, she was born in nineteen eighty-three."

"Oh man. She's younger than *Donkey Kong*."

"You know, on retrospect, who was that little guy running up the girders and jumping over barrels?"

"Mario! Man, I don't know you, Marcus."

"What, just because I wasn't a nerd who hung out in arcades?"

"Who needed arcades? The orphanage had an Atari and a Colecovision."

"Well, la-dee-da."

I ordered a Coors Lite. My friend and I assumed our scan-the-crowd posture.

"Well, Marcus, I have news. That's assuming that you don't know already."

"Hmm. I don't know anything new, I don't even know video game trivia."

"Any phone calls lately?"

"No."

"Well, hang onto your Mario hat. Jess has returned."

"What?"

"That's right. Jessica Kim called me from the Ramada near Bradley. It turns out that she's left Brad."

"Aha! I knew it! It was only a matter of time! Good for her."

"Still, she's afraid. She wants to go into hiding, via a battered woman's shelter."

"Battered? Did that Ramsey crud beat her?"

"Not only that, he's behind a newsworthy theft."

"You're joking. No way."

"Have you heard of the Spear of Destiny?"

"You mean the relic stolen in Vienna? He did that?"

"Technically, one of his flock did the legwork."

"Flock?"

"Yeah, flock. Cult. Coven."

"He still has followers?"

"Followers—sex slaves—what have you."

"Please, I just ate some beer nuts. Stay down there, little 'uns."

"My reaction exactly."

"So, what on earth does Brad want with the Spear of Destiny?"

"Shh, Marcus. Let's keep it down."

"Okay," my friend whispered. "What does he want with the pointie thingie?"

"Apparently, a coming world event may topple Christian and Jewish world power. This relic supposedly empowers the one who possesses it. Brad's hoping to become a political or religious leader."

"Oh no! I better call my pastor!"

"I know, it sounds stupid. Still, he has predicted world events with accuracy, according to Jess. Something is bound to happen."

"I suppose it's possible. Brad is possessed. Satan imitates. Prophecy is one of the gifts of the Holy Spirit."

"Okay, if that's the avenue you choose to take Brad seriously, that's fine."

"It's more than an avenue, Dave. You saw Brad's minions in my house. They infested my home the very night Tamika challenged Ramsey."

"We've been over this before, Marcus. You and Tamika have a certain zealous theological view and this psychology lends itself into an external manifestation."

"Then explain why we never, ever experienced anything odd before Tamika challenged Ramsey."

"I can't. Perhaps Ramsey is like a power generator and people experience their subliminal conflicts through his presence. Maybe an alien buff would see UFOs after spending time with Ramsey."

"And what, precisely, would make Brad a power generator?"

"I have no idea."

"Well, right or wrong, I have an idea," Marcus smiled.

"Fair enough. Anyway, Jess said she'll call you soon."

"That's nice. I'd love to hear from her."

"Unfortunately, you may end up hearing from Brad as well."

"Oh gawd, no."

"Yes, it's a guarantee. Brad Ramsey will be here."

"I'll pray about it."

"Also, watch your back. Don't go down any dark alleys."

"Will do."

A cute waitress walked in front of us. A few napkins blew off the platter she was carrying. Marcus bent low, and with a smile, handed them back to her. She grinned nervously and quickly moved on.

"See her fear, Dave? Women don't like middle-age men."

"Perhaps she's had a few too many butt grabs, Marcus."

"Perhaps. So, what event could possibly affect the world and undermine Christianity and Judaism?"

"Good question. Jess said the only clue Brad offered had to do with *The Lord of the Rings* trilogy. Particularly, the second installment."

"Hmm. That would be *The Two Towers*. Oh man! I just remembered! Did you know that during the exorcism, the one book that flew and hit Jonah was *The Two Towers*!"

"Ew, that's creepy. What on earth made you remember what book hit Jonah?"

"Jonah had me in stitches afterward. He said the demon was rather considerate, throwing one of his favorite books at him."

"So, what occurs in this book? I presume it has the standard hobbits, dwarves, dragons, and the like."

"If memory serves—I read it years ago—it's mostly a go-between story. It connects *The Fellowship of the Ring* and *The Return of the King*. It features a creature called Gollum, who becomes a guide for the two main characters seeking to destroy an evil talisman—a ring."

"A talisman. Hmm. Much like how Hitler supposedly saw the Spear of Destiny."

"That could be significant."

"Do you think Ramsey is forecasting the return of Fascism? After all, Hitler despised both the Jewish and Christian religions. He sought to erase the Jewish race. Jess said he's becoming more anti-Semitic. That Brad is idolizing Hitler."

"Sick freak."

"Marcus, if Jonah was around, I'd warn him about Ramsey. Jonah represents everything Ramsey despises."

"That's right. Good thing Jonah is in Boston. How is he doing up there, anyhow?"

"He's fine. But Claire is dragging him to Los Angeles. Apparently, there are spirits plaguing a certain household. Things that resemble the type of manifestations that occurred in your house."

"Those poor people, whoever they are! I wonder. Brad lives in San Francisco. Do you think these LA people crossed paths with him as well, with this result?"

"Considering the zillions of people who live in California, I'd say that's rather unlikely."

"The unlikely becomes commonplace around Brad Ramsey."

I laughed loudly causing a few patrons to stare.

"Someday, they're going to ban us from this place," Marcus grinned.

"Might as well," I sighed. "Two aging bachelors like us are out of our element here. I did spy a senior center a few miles back."

"That's an idea," Marcus laughed.

"What should we do when Ramsey comes looking for his wife?"

"We protect Jess at all costs. We need to also protect Jess with prayer. We should pray that she remain hidden from Brad."

"I mean what do we do if Brad threatens us? Attacks us?"

"Hmm. Neither of us own a firearm and the waiting period to get one is quite lengthy."

"Marcus! A Holy Roller like you? You want a gun?"

"Being a Holy Roller, as you say, doesn't mean being a pacifist."

"Oh? What about all that 'turn the other cheek' stuff?"

"Yes, some can interpret that teaching as pacifistic. I tend to subscribe to a more literal reading. If someone literally slaps your cheek, turn the other, and prove to him that you will not descend to his level. In first-century Judea, a slap often came in the form of a backhand; a Middle Eastern gesture of disrespect. Turning the other cheek also made the aggressor, using the same hand, employ a forward slap. He would use the front of his hand, rather than the back. So the lesson is twofold, a Christian is to demonstrate his control by not sinking to his attacker's level. The Christian is also demanding some respect from his attacker."

"Interesting perspective. Who would have thought anyone could regard a forehand slap as respectful?"

"Let's just say that the forehand slap is the lesser of insults."

"I see. What about the 'love thy enemy' teaching?"

"Yes, we are required to pray for those who persecute us. God wants all men to come to him, regardless of their past. God's hope is that an active demonstration of love and forgiveness will lead to the repentance and conversion of his lost creation."

"So, how could you, as a Christian, ever be justified in using violence as self-defense?"

"Just imagine if any nation with a Christian majority decided not to have a national defense. Their resources, their very lives would be at the mercy of any aggressor or invader. Any Stalin or Hitler to come along would initiate a persecution, a holocaust. I don't believe that Jesus wants his followers to relinquish their rights as human beings. We are to pray for our enemies. At the same time, we shouldn't let such aggressive, oppressive individuals have their 'will be done' on earth."

"Marcus, you have actually prayed for Brad Ramsey?"

"Yes."

"How could you? A vile, abusive man you believe to be demon possessed through his own choice?"

"David, evil is more than the small, frail creatures it manifests through. 'We wrestle not with flesh and blood, but with principalities and powers.'"

"So people aren't accountable for their choices?"

"Ultimately, everyone is accountable for their choices."

"How could they be, if evil is an external power that manipulates?"

"Evil may be an external force, but we still have freewill. We succumb through willful sin or through weakness. God understands how vulnerable we are. One biblical interpretation for sin is 'falling short.'"

"Falling short? Not deliberate wrongdoing?"

"Well, much of our sin is deliberate. But at our core, human nature is weak. Even the most kind, the most well-intentioned human being has a weak inner core. The human ego seeks glory. The human will is seduced by pleasure."

"Thus, your religion refuses to recognize good people. It condemns everyone with one broad brush," I said.

"Not completely. Many people qualify as good soil. They have the ability to grow close to God, regardless of their weakness. Others are considered poor soil—they have no hope."

"But you believe that all of humanity is sinful, don't you?"

"Yes."

"This is where I can't agree with you. Let's consider someone like myself. I'm a good person. I don't lie, steal or hurt people. I do my best every day. Yet your theology would put me in the same boat as Brad."

"In the same boat, but not on the same deck."

"Still, it's the cruise ship to hell, correct?"

"Yup."

I gestured with disgust. "A decent person like me—hell bound. Nice, Marcus, real nice religion you got there."

"Yes, Dave, you are a decent person by all earthly standards. That's why you're my friend. Still, you flunk the righteousness test. As all humans have."

"The righteousness test?"

"Consider the Ten Commandments. Have you honored them your whole life?"

"Yes."

"Have you ever taken the Lord's name in vain?"

"Hmm, yeah, if you define the Lord as Jesus."

"The Bible calls this blasphemy. Have you ever lied?"

"Nothing huge, no."

"But you've told small lies, right? Lies designed for convenience? For ego?"

"Yeah, I've done that. As has everyone."

"My point exactly. Have you stolen anything?"

"Small things. When I was a juvenile delinquent."

"But now you never steal anything, correct?"

"Yup. Well, not counting that pen I pocketed from the bank last week."

"Yeah, even that counts."

"Oh brother."

"Have you ever slept with a married woman?"

*"C'mon Marcus!* You know the answer to that!"

"Jesus said something very revealing. He said that if a man lusts in his heart after a woman, he has committed adultery with her. Have you lusted after center-folds, models, or actresses—like the women of *Baywatch*? Many of these women are married."

"Guilty as charged."

"So, according to the Ten Commandments, you are a blasphemer, a liar, a thief, and an adulterer."

"Aw c'mon! No one alive could pass that anal-retentive test."

"You may call that test anal-retentive, but it's God's basic guide for humanity. Paul said the Law is our 'schoolmaster,' its purpose is to educate us. To show us how we need God's forgiveness."

"So, according to you, no one passes God's test. Not even Orthodox Jews who dedicate their lives to obeying moral laws?"

"Jews have always known that moral perfection is unattainable. This is why Jews of antiquity gave animal sacrifice and burnt offerings. These were for forgiveness. An offering for past sin. Christians believe that the blood of animals have no intrinsic value unless it's a symbol for the perfect Lamb of God, the Messiah Jesus. Christ obtained that perfection we couldn't. He kept God's law perfectly."

"I seem to remember Jesus breaking Judaic law like when he healed on the Sabbath, or when he ate without ritual washing. Or when he touched those considered unclean."

"Yes, Jesus broke the Law as it was defined by the Pharisees and Sadducees. Jesus said these teachers distorted God's true Law. Apparently, Jesus fulfilled the commandments as God the Father intended them to be."

"That's convenient."

"Yeah, convenient *for us!* Even with the most liberal, non-restrictive interpretation of God's Law, even then, we fail to measure up! *All of us fall short!*"

"Real convenient. According to you, I'm headed to *hell* along with Brad Ramsey."

"Personally, Dave, I don't see hell as hellfire and pitchforks. It's simply a realm defined as separation from God. With this segregation, all intrinsic pain and misery is related to two things—the pain of being separate from our Lord, and the pain inflicted by other lost souls. I was on that same cruise you and Brad are on until I noticed that huge life raft floating alongside."

"Nice God. Sending all of humanity on the cruise to hell just because they are imperfect."

"No, God doesn't want humanity on that cruise. He littered the deck with flyers telling them of his life raft."

"Why make it so hard? Why doesn't God march through the ship and force everyone into his lifeboat?"

"Dave, Dave. Let's say that you woke up tomorrow as the supreme dictator of the United States."

"Awesome!"

"No, hear me out. You wake up tomorrow and your word is Law. Whatever you say goes. Would you *force* Jessica to love, honor, and obey you?"

"Maybe," I smiled.

"No, think about it! She would be with you, but you'd never see her eyes light up when she looks at you. You might catch her crying when she stole private moments. After months or years, she would resent you. Hate you. This is inevitable when you force anyone to do anything against their will."

"Hey, we're talking God here! He could make us love him or her!"

"Then we'd be nothing but some robot or computer program. Some toy like a Furbie. God gets no relationship from the bargain. When the Bible says we were created in God's image, it means we were created with the gift of freewill. An autonomy that separates us from the animals. A freedom that is divine in nature!"

"I suppose that makes sense. So to get back to my original question. You actually pray for Brad Ramsey?"

"Dave, I despise Brad as much as you do. Still, he's just a fragile, weak human who is caught in evil's rip tide. Just think! He was once some cooing baby in a cradle. Some tot giggling on his swing set. As was Hitler. Somewhere on their journey, they tethered themselves to evil."

"It's hard for me to call Brad weak, I still remember him body slamming me on the hood of my car."

"Our true enemy isn't that bag of flesh, it's the spiritual force that empowers him."

"And now, Claire and Jonah are off to investigate another case of a demon-baby manifestation."

"Yep. And we're left with Jess and Brad," Marcus sighed as he swallowed his beer. "Be prepared, Dave. We're on our own this next week or two."

That sentiment frightened me. Why did I suddenly wish that Jonah Rubenstein were sitting with us? I had always been Mr. I don't need anyone! Had I grown to see him as the father I never had? Did he make me feel safe somehow? Maybe it was a combination of the two. Strange that I would have this emotional reaction to a man I never agree with.

# CHAPTER 30

▼

# VISITATIONS

Another workday was upon me, another lonely exercise in filing. Still, solitude has its advantages. It relaxes the senses. One doesn't need to adorn the polite and smiling mask the public expects. As much as I missed Jonah, I was starting to enjoy this isolation.

The main office door opened. Its noise woke me from my meditative trance.

"What the?"

I knew I locked that door. Jonah's patients knew he was on hiatus. As I walked from Jonah's office to investigate, I froze. Standing in the waiting room was Brad Ramsey.

"My Sparky," he sneered. "It has been a long time. Too long, wouldn't you agree?"

"I think you know my answer to that Brad. What brings you from sunny California?"

"You know very well what brings me here. Where is she?"

"She?"

"Jess. I know you've seen her. I can smell her on you."

His sunken eyes gleamed with a fierce determination. The last six years had not been kind to the talk show wannabe. Deep lines carved his face. His hair thinned. Still, he was as tall and brawny as ever.

"As you used to gloat about, Brad, no scent of any female is on me. Now, you actually lost track of your wife?"

"Not really. I know she was in touch with you. If you know what's good for you, you will share all you know."

Just as Brad finished his threat, a nearby bookcase shifted an inch. Several books fell to the floor.

"What the?" I paused. "What are you Ramsey? Some sort of *freak?*"

"I am a man with friends. Powerful friends. Not that I need them to deal with you. Once again, where is Jess?"

"How should I know? She chose to live happily ever after with you, not me!"

I sat down at my desk and faked a casual tone. "Jess rejected me for you. For all I care, she can be in a gutter somewhere."

"Hmm, very good, David. I see you may have developed a spine these last few years. You actually don't care about Jess anymore?"

"No, I don't. The best thing to happen to me was when you and your pet moved to California."

"Yes, she is my pet. She's my personal, bought and paid-for whore. Don't you forget that, little Davey."

My blood boiled. My knuckles itched.

"Brad, you haven't seen me for six years. Isn't that proof enough for you? I'm over her."

He leaned in toward me, stopping about four inches from my face.

"Uh-huh," he skeptically sneered. "You are a weakling, David Paul. A gutless, limp little noodle. Once you fall for some slut, I suspect that you're hopelessly incapable of escaping your emotional dependency."

I cringed. He was right. I couldn't turn off my feelings for Jess like a light switch. Even after six long years! I forced a laugh in response to Brad's observation.

"Believe what you want, Ramsey. I don't give a crap."

"I'm watching you. My friends are watching you as well. Sleep well, Sparky."

With a smirk, Brad turned and left the office. I ran over and locked the door again. Apparently, I needed to hang garlic and wolfbane to keep my nemesis away.

It had been six days since I talked with Jess on the phone. I knew it would be a mistake to check up on her. If Ramsey claimed that I was being watched, it wasn't an empty threat.

I didn't feel comfortable with the work shift ending. Paranoia was overtaking me. Was Ramsey waiting for me in the parking lot? At my apartment building? What if Jess did call or visit me, would this be enough to drive Brad over the edge? Not only was the man a criminal, he also had followers.

On the way home I decided to stop at a local Ames department store. While browsing, I noticed a display of security items. Pictures of frightened women graced the packages. One item was a small air horn, meant to call attention to an assault or mugging. The other was a small pepper spray gadget. With sheepish embarrassment, I purchased the spray. The only thing I was missing was a purse and some lipstick.

The parking lot at the Clock Shop Apartments was dark. The few working streetlights cast long shadows. With trepidation, I approached the side door to the building. So far, so good. No suspicious figures or shadows. The stairwell was clear. I peeked through the second floor hallway door. No one. With relief, I unlocked the apartment door and entered my private domain. My left hand never left the pepper spray tucked in my coat pocket.

Thankfully, my small studio apartment was empty. I knew locked doors were no insurance against Ramsey. Still, something wasn't right. Something was off. A dim, red glow illuminated the counter top. A blinking glow. It occurred to me, this is what the indicator on my answering machine looks like when it has a message! This was the first time I had a message in years! I hoped it wasn't Jess. Or Brad. Anyone else would be preferable.

I pressed the "play" button. A static noise ensued, then a dial tone. Another message. More static. What was this? A bad connection? Maybe Jonah?

I turned on the television. Some cookie-cutter situation comedy was on, complete with a laugh track. A group of good-looking yuppies were sitting around the workplace, teasing the one character who couldn't "get any."

"Shaadduup," I growled at the television before changing the channel. "Where can I find Andy Griffith or the Beav?"

The telephone rang. I answered, expecting a long distance call from Jonah.

"Hello?"

The same static hissed.

"Hello, Jonah? Jonah? Is that you?"

This time, I heard an electronic sounding noise. It was monotone.

"Jonah, I can hardly hear you. Say again?"

The sound articulated louder.

"Avveeyy."

"Hello? Who is this?"

"Avveeyy. Ewy goo boy."

My blood chilled. It sounded like a weak, electronic version of Huey!

"Ramsey, is this you? You're not funny, you sick freak!"

"Bra bad. Bad. Bad."

The voice was stronger.

*"My God, Huey! Is that you?"*

A click, then a dial tone.

My heart raced. What if Huey was alive? The grand mal seizure report came from Brad's staff—they were under his control—like Ramsey's so-called followers. Still, the paramedic report confirmed Huey was dead. What if Brad had conned the paramedics? What if Huey is held hostage somewhere? Would Ramsey put him on the phone and tease me? On the other hand, if Brad had done something so sickening and had actually gotten away with it, he would have rubbed my face in it long ago. He knew when it was my word against his he always won.

The phone rang again. I quickly picked it up.

*"Huey!* Is that you?"

"Huey?" Marcus answered. "What are you talking about?"

"Marcus?"

"Why did you answer the phone like that?"

"I just had a phone call. *It sounded just like Huey, Marcus!"*

"It couldn't be. His body was examined by paramedics."

"I'm telling you…it sounded exactly like him! He said 'Avey,' 'Ewy goo boy' and 'Bra bad, bad.'"

"It's gotta be a sick joke!"

"If it's a joke, it must be someone we know. And the only person we know who's this sick is Ramsey. And guess who paid me a visit at Jonah's office today?"

"No…you actually saw Ramsey? Today?"

"Yeah. He tried to get information on Jess. He assumed, and rightly so, that Jess would come to me for help. I played it callous. I let him believe that I was too hurt by Jess to ever talk to her again."

"Good idea."

"Marcus, he went on to say he'd be watching me."

"Dave, bunk out on my couch tonight. With that maniac in the area, I think a united front is best."

"Normally, I'd agree. But, what if Huey is alive? It's best that I stay here for future phone calls."

"Let's assume that by some slim chance, Huey is alive. You think Huey Riiska is dialing your number? Calling you? He never had that ability. He couldn't recognize numbers or letters, or control his finger."

"What if Brad is holding him somewhere? What if Brad dialed and held the receiver?"

"Dave, you're not thinking clearly. Brad and Jess are married. Jess recently told you about Ramsey's dark little secrets. Do you actually think Ramsey could have kept Huey a secret from Jess all this time?"

"Still, through all that static, it sounded just like his voice. Some of the suspicious static is on my answering machine."

"Static?"

"Yeah, first there were two calls on my machine. Just static. Next, a weak voice came through. It sounded electronic. Like a voice through a synthesizer."

"Hmm. Static and electronic. Dave, have you ever heard of EVP, electronic voice phenomena?"

"Electronic what?"

"It's something Jonah shared with me once. He and Claire were analyzing recordings on regular cassette tapes. Recordings made in a supposedly haunted cemetery. Apparently, at a very low frequency, voices can be heard. Voices below the human ability to hear."

"Voices? Did they ever say anything?"

"Yeah. They said many things, some of which made sense. One female voice demanded that someone 'replace my stone.' Next to where they recorded this message, teenage vandals had recently shattered an old tombstone."

"Sounds compelling. But Jonah and Claire may have projected those voices themselves, through some mental abilities. Or they were picking up obscure radio or televised broadcasts."

"A broadcast that specifically said 'replace my stone?' You don't believe that, Dave."

"No, I guess not."

"All I'm saying is that this Huey voice could be an electronic voice phenomena from beyond the grave. Some of these communications have been known to come through phone lines. Do you still have those recordings of static?"

"Yeah, I do. What about it?"

"Take the tape out of your machine. There may be a message on there that you can't even hear. I'm not saying it's Huey. It could be demonic."

"Marcus, I think you've been hanging around Claire Monroe too long."

"That may be, bud. But humor me. Save that cassette. I'll bring it to one of Claire's students. He has a computer that analyzes audio frequencies. He's Claire's number one EVP guy and happens to attend the University of Hartford."

"What do you expect to find through the static?"

"God only knows. Now come on over. I insist. My couch awaits."

"Jeez, Marcus. You boss me around like you're my wife or something."

"I've been married. Believe me when I say I don't come close to how a wife behaves."

"That's good. You're not my type anyhow."

"No need to insult me."

I laughed.

"Okay, Marcus. See you within the hour."

"I'll save some cold beer and pizza for you."

I hung up the receiver, a bit comforted that Huey was not a prisoner somewhere. Within five seconds, the phone rang. With reluctance, I slowly picked up the receiver.

"Hello?"

The only response was that same hissing static.

"Ramsey, if this is you—"

"Avey, listen. Listen."

"Damn, this isn't funny anymore. Whoever this is, get a life."

I hung up the receiver. Immediately, it rang again. I ignored it. The phone rang continuously as I threw some clothes, towels, pajamas, a bathrobe, and a toothbrush into a backpack. I turned off the television, the lights.

As I exited my apartment, the ringing suddenly stopped. This was an odd coincidence. I locked my door and stood in the hallway for a few minutes. The phone was silent. What if I stepped into the apartment again? I held my breath, then unlocked the door. The moment my foot crossed the threshold, the phone started ringing. I withdrew my foot and the phone stopped in mid-ring. I waited ten seconds and placed my foot into the apartment a second time. The phone rang again.

With frantic speed, I quickly shut the door and locked it. The apartment was silent. Goose bumps crawled up my back. Whatever was behind those phone calls was not of this world.

# CHAPTER 31

▼

# SEPTEMBER 11, 2001

Jonah was glad to have a small child sitting next to him on the airline. She was a pretty girl, about four years of age. Her mother sat in the seat behind her. She was fascinated with Jonah's briefcase and laptop. "What's that?" she continuously asked him. "Is that a 'puter? We're way, way up in the air!" He didn't mind the interruptions. The therapist delighted at her curiosity.

Suddenly, Jonah noticed that they were unusually low over the city. The buildings were close.

*"We're gonna crash!"* someone yelled two seats ahead of Jonah. *"We're headed for a tower!"*

*"Mommy!"* the girl yelled. *"Mommy!"*

Her mother didn't answer. She crouched low, breathing with panic.

Jonah looked at the frightened child. His eyes glinted with recognition. He reached for her and held her tight. They both crouched low.

"It's okay, angel," Jonah soothed. "We'll be fine. We're all going home."

I jerked awake from my vivid dream, wet from perspiration. With a sigh, I picked myself off Marcus's couch and waddled into the bathroom. Even after splashing cold water on my face, I couldn't shake the feeling. Something was going to happen to Jonah. His flight to Los Angeles was this morning. Claire was already on the West Coast waiting for him. I decided to call him. Maybe I could get him to delay his trip. Normally, I didn't put too much stock in dreams foretelling the future, but this eerie business with Brad Ramsey demonstrated the reality of psychic phenomena.

I called his cell phone. No answer.

"Morning, Dave," Marcus said as he emerged from the bathroom. He was towel drying his hair.

"Morning."

"You all right? You look spooked."

"Just a nightmare. I dreamt that Jonah's airline flew into a building. No biggie."

"Ooookaaay. Grab the shower while you can. The water is still warm. I'm off to the day program."

After a quick shower and breakfast, I was on my way to the Exchange building. It was warm. I cracked the window down and the air against my face was welcome. Some of the leaves were starting to turn color. It was a beautiful day.

While approaching the Route 10 intersection in Farmington, my cell phone rang. I answered the phone and propped it between my head and shoulder.

"David, I just wanted to wish you a Merry Christmas!"

"Jonah?"

"Yes, it's me. En route to Los Angeles. I'm in the air on United, flight one seventy-five."

"Oh."

"You sound disappointed?"

"Well, I had a vivid dream. I wanted you to postpone your trip."

"You, David? Mr. Skeptic…believing in prophetic dreams?"

"You've been rubbing off on me."

"You should be so lucky, young man."

"Okay, Jonah. Merry Christmas back at ya, even though this September eleventh date for Jesus' birthday is far from recognized."

I heard a child's voice in the background. Jonah murmured something to him or her.

"Jonah, who are you talking to?"

"The most delightful little girl is sitting next to me. Her mom is in the seat behind us. She is so adorable…asking questions about my laptop and my cell phone."

Cold hands wrapped around my neck.

"I see. Well, you take care of yourself, Jonah."

"Will do. I'll call you from LA."

I tried to shake off the dread. So Jonah was sitting next to a young girl. What of it? That isn't rare on airliners. I brooded for the remainder of the drive.

As I walked into the waiting room, the phone was ringing. I ran over and answered it.

"*David!* I've been trying to reach you! Here at the day program, we have the television on for Teddy. You know how it calms his nerves. Anyway, it appears that some sort of plane malfunctioned and *crashed* into the North Twin Tower in New York City! I immediately thought about your dream. Do you think it was Jonah's flight?"

"A crash into the North Tower? My God. I was just talking to Jonah on his cell phone. He seemed fine. He was kidding around with a little girl sitting next to him. When did this happen?"

"Uh, let's see. It's almost nine now. The crash happened about ten or fifteen minutes ago."

"I was talking to Jonah around then. I don't think it's his flight. Do you know what type of plane hit the skyscraper?"

"Uh, let's see. I'm watching some news guy and there's an information scroll on the bottom of the screen. Uh, yeah, there it is. Atlantic Airlines. They may have had some sort of engine failure."

"Thank God. Jonah is on United Airlines, flight one seventy-five."

"Phew. You had to share that nightmare with me, didn't you, Dave?"

"Sorry. What a coincidence!"

"Perhaps more than a coincidence."

"Come now, Marcus. If I were some psychic, I think I would know by now."

"Perhaps someone communicated that information to you. Through your dreams."

"Who, Huey? Come on, give it up already."

"Tonight, Jason will return your answering machine tape. Who knows what kind of electronic voice phenomena he found?"

"I'm sure it's nothing. The whole thing was probably a sick Brad Ramsey joke."

"We'll see, Dave. *Oh, God!*"

"What?"

"*Guys, come over here!*" Marcus yelled to his coworkers.

"*What?* What is it, Marcus?"

I heard Marcus's coworkers talking in the background. Someone was calling for Tim. Another person turned up the television, hissing in the background.

"*Marcus!*"

"Sorry, Dave. I had to get everyone to see this. Another airliner just flew into the other Twin Tower!"

"What?"

"I'm not kidding! While the news camera was fixed on the smoke billowing out of the North Tower, another airliner just crashed into the South Tower!"

"Another…crash?"

"The plane seemed to steer right into the skyscraper! *It crashed with a big fireball!* Now the two World Trade Center towers are on fire!"

"God, it can't be accidental. Both of these collisions had to be *intentional!*"

"Had to be! Why would anyone want to fly a plane into the Twin Towers?"

"Remember that basement bombing?"

"That's right! Some terrorists tried to bring down one of the towers around nine years ago. This could be another act of terrorism!"

"I bet. It has to be terrorism. Hijackings."

"The news crew on the tube is stunned. They're looking for answers."

"You don't think that last plane was…Jonah's flight?"

"Dave, don't even think it."

"I don't want to."

"Do you have a television in the office?"

"I think Jonah has one somewhere."

"Tim's making us get back to work. If this is a widespread coordinated attack on this country, we may have to drive these guys back to the group homes."

"Okay, Marcus. I'll try to find Jonah's TV. We'll be in touch."

I discovered a small, black-and-white TV with rabbit ear antennas in Jonah's supply closet. I plugged it in near my desk and kept an eye on the news while typing Jonah's field notes from Israel. The news was slow. Frustrating. It seemed that no one could confirm any facts. First, the US Federal Aviation Administration shut down all New York airports. Next, all the bridges and tunnels leading into New York City were closed. By nine thirty, *all* domestic flights were grounded. It was nightmarish. I kept thinking about Ramsey's prediction. He told Jess that a major event was soon to take place, something orchestrated to undermine Christian and Jewish world power.

Most hijackings I could recollect involved radical Muslim sects. According to Islamic doctrine, both Christians and Jews were defined as infidels. I was scared. How far could this go? What further carnage would occur? Were we on the edge of World War III? Would nuclear weaponry be deployed? I tried to concentrate on Jonah's field notes.

The news kept getting worse. Next it was reported that an airliner crashed into the Pentagon. Clearly, this was an organized strike. I kept watching the information scroll at the bottom of the screen.

Eventually, the scroll read "United Airlines flight 175 from Boston to Los Angeles flew into the South Twin Tower around nine a.m." Now I knew. Jonah's plane *was* the hijacked airliner that flew into the second tower. With a shaky hand, I reached for the phone. Marcus should know. As my fingers touched the receiver, it rang. I slowly picked it up.

"Hello?"

"Dave," Marcus's voice choked out. "There's something I need to tell you."

"I know," I murmured. "Jonah's flight crashed into the South Tower."

"I have to pull it together. I'm at Elm Street right now. We brought the residents home."

"That's good. Keep alert."

"I…can't believe this," Marcus gasped out. "Oh God. Jonah."

"None of this seems real."

"Well, it's after ten. I have a few meds to dispense," my friend sighed.

"Okay. I'll keep in touch. Oh no. Look at the television again."

"Wha—?"

On the television, being broadcast live, was a scene of horror. The South Tower at the World Trade Center collapsed. A plume of smoke and cement ash made the site look like an erupting volcano. News cameras captured the chaos from all possible angles. Panicked pedestrians ran down city streets, keeping ahead of the wall of smoke and dust pursuing them.

"Dave," Marcus finally spoke after several minutes. "I think you should go back to my apartment. Jonah would have sent you home, I'm sure of it. Who can say what public buildings are safe?"

"God, Marcus! Like a zombie, I continue to type Jonah's field notes. What's wrong with me?"

"We just need time to let this all…sink in. I'll meet you when, and if, second shift takes over."

"Okay. I'll see you soon."

I turned off the portable television, unplugged it, and returned it to Jonah's closet. As I grabbed my coat, I turned around and looked back into Jonah's office. The kind man's coffee mug sat on his desk. Several journals were bookmarked, pages waiting for Jonah to revisit. I strolled back to his desk and gently picked up the mug. It had a Christian fish embossed on the side. Reverently, I put the mug into one of my coat pockets. As I turned to walk out, I stepped on a hard-covered book on the floor. I picked up the edition and read the title.

*The Two Towers* by JRR Tolkien.

The ride home from the Exchange building was a blur. I turned on the local radio news station. Reporters spoke of the White House being evacuated. The president was on a secret flight, leaving a school in Florida. Another airliner went down in Pennsylvania. Apparently, several of the passengers learned of the suicide missions and rose against their hijackers. By the time I reached Marcus's apartment, the North Tower had collapsed in the same manner as the South Tower. The news stations were repeating the scene over and over. After placing Jonah's cup on a counter top, I simply curled up on the couch. I didn't nap. I just watched the news dispassionately. Like a zombie.

Hour after hour passed. It was uncertain who or what group was responsible for the attacks. It was certain that thousands were dead. The airline passengers. The workers trapped on the upper floors in the Twin Towers. Other workers unaware of the imminent collapse of the buildings. Some leapt to their death from high altitude windows. Rescue workers died. Pentagon employees perished. Bystanders died.

I spent the rest of the day glued to the television. Replay after replay showed the United Airlines collision into the South Tower. The collapse of the South Tower. The collapse of the North Tower. The debris-strewn field in Pennsylvania. The Pentagon on fire. Over and over. Slowly, the reality of Jonah's death grew on me. I had considered Jonah more than a good friend and employer. I saw him as the father I never had. Now, the universe had denied me even this relationship. If any God did exist, he or she was obviously a sadist who enjoyed depriving me of familial connections. "No parents for you," he ordained from on high. "And while we're at it, no wife for you as well."

Poor Jonah. He had lived his life in service of his Messiah. Now, in the end, he would perish in a senseless act of violence. So much for guardian angels. So much for Divine blessings.

Around four in the afternoon, Marcus dragged himself through the door. He looked tired and tense. Without taking off his jacket, he sighed and collapsed on the couch next to me.

"Lord Dave. I still can't believe this. Jonah. So many people."

"I know."

"I suppose Ramsey was referring to this. A major world event."

"It does fit the bill. Also, and I even hate to bring this up, but Jess said that Brad alluded to Tolkien's book *The Two Towers*."

"Aaa! *That's right!*"

"And Jonah usually celebrated this day. He considered it Christmas, due to the theory about the Feast of Trumpets in three BC."

"So, Dave. You recognize the signs? Satan does exist."

"You know, Marcus, I'll grant that. The devil is real. There's no God or Divine Jesus, but there *is* a pointy-tailed power in the cosmos."

"There can be no darkness without light," my friend replied.

"And, where was this light today?"

"Today, the light was eclipsed. Although, some glimpses of that light can be seen. The passengers who rose against the hijackers. The rescue workers."

"Okay, Marcus. I agree with that. Still, Jonah was abandoned by your God today."

Marcus didn't respond. He simply stood and walked into his bedroom. The door slammed with violence. I immediately felt ashamed for attacking Marcus's faith once again. On this day, of all days.

The phone started ringing. Since Marcus didn't have a receiver in his bedroom, I answered it.

"Hey, Marcus."

"I'm sorry, this is David Paul, Marcus's friend. He's not available right now. Can I take a message?"

"Oh, David! This is Jason Marino, Claire Monroe's intern. I'm unable to come over tonight, as promised. I was just calling to tell Marcus about that answering machine tape of yours. Is this a bad time? Today's events have everyone reeling and all that. Claire is quite traumatized. Survivor guilt, I guess. She was supposed to be on that flight, but she decided to fly out before Jonah to assess the situation."

"Yeah, Marcus and I were quite…traumatized ourselves today. You might as well share your electronic voice phenomena results now, no reason not to."

On cue, Marcus emerged from his room. He looked curious.

"Marcus, it's Jason Marino," I whispered. "You want to speak to him?"

"You can talk to him instead," he sighed.

"Go ahead, Jason. Shoot."

"Okay. The first EVP, located on a very low frequency, occurs four seconds into the recorded static. It sounds like 'find my sheets.'"

I swallowed hard. "Okay, Jason, go on."

"The second EVP, eleven seconds in, sounds like 'good boy today.' The third, fourteen seconds in, sounds like 'Mary pretty.' The forth, twenty seconds in, is rather strange. It sounds like 'no dark without light.'"

I broke into a sweat. I looked at Marcus.

"Uh, thanks Jason. Those all mean something. Very much so."

"Would you like a CD copy of these EVPs? I can burn one for you. Both you and Marcus can hear them for yourselves."

"That would be appreciated. Thanks."

"Don't mention it, Dave. I'll be in touch. Bye."

"Bye."

I slowly put the receiver back on the charger. I looked at Marcus with teary eyes.

"Marcus, I apologize. We're dealing with the loss of Jonah and I can only see darkness."

"I understand. What did Jason have to say?"

I grabbed a chair and sat down.

"He said the EVPs were of low frequency. They must have been from Huey, or someone otherworldly. Must have been!"

"What were the messages?"

"'Find my sheets.' 'Good boy today.'"

"Those are certainly things Huey would say. Although, of course, Huey's sheets were lost in that fire."

"It gets more specific. He said 'Mary pretty.' This was one of his observations at the Lourdes Shrine in Litchfield. There's no way Ramsey could had known about that! Even Jess didn't know what Huey said since I routinely took him on a tour of that grotto by myself."

"So it was a Huey quotation that only you would know!"

"The last comment was…rather prophetic. He said what you just said! He said 'no dark without light!'"

My friend's eyes grew wide. He too had to sit down.

"Marcus, my attacks…my cynicism. I'm just an idiot. As the message said—if there are dark forces—there must be light…somewhere."

My friend grinned. "Jesus said, 'I am the light of the world. He that believes in me shall not dwell in darkness, but will have the light of life.'"

"I can't accept that. I've spent my whole life as a rational person. I just can't abandon who I am."

"Dave, did you consider Jonah a rational person?"

"That's an unfair question to ask today, but the answer is yes and no."

"That's clear."

"Okay, I considered Jonah a brilliant man with theological bias."

"We all have our biases, Mr. Paul. Be they philosophical, religious, political, or whatever."

"Perhaps."

"So the question is, what's your bias of choice, Dave?"

"To tell you the truth, I'm not sure I have one anymore."

"Do you believe something extraordinary created the images on Huey's sheets?"

"Obviously it wasn't a process researchers can duplicate. Not yet at least."

"The same enigma applies to the Shroud of Turin, correct?"

"Correct."

"Let it all sink in, Dave. Brad Ramsey and his abilities. The paranormal phenomena you've bore witness to. Jonah's apologetic research. Huey's signs…sent for your benefit."

"I…I used to think I had it all figured out. I know…nothing."

"You know, Dave, people often assume that we Christians are know it alls who have all the answers. Actually, while we are devoted to our faith tenants, we recognize our limitations. The Apostle Paul himself said that we are currently 'looking through a mirror, darkly.' The greatest mysteries concerning God, humanity, and eternal life will be revealed to us after this life. This existence."

"Okay, Marcus. Tell me what you believe about God. My mind is open."

# CHAPTER 32

▼

# THE GATHERING

On September fourteenth, Marcus and I attended a memorial service for Jonah Rubenstein. Colleagues, former and current patients, and other affiliates of the gentle social worker wept openly. Me included.

Tamika traveled north to attend, but refused to sit with Marcus and me. She walked past us for a seat in the front. When the service was over, she made a hasty retreat through the crowd before Marcus could talk to her.

The parish house next to Saint Paul's Episcopal Church in Farmington was large. Yet with the gathering crowd, there was barely enough room for the refreshment table. Bagels, cold cuts, salads, and a large punch bowl remained untouched. Eating or drinking was the last thing people wanted to do. Each corner and crevasse of the fellowship hall was filled with a multitude of bereaved friends and family. The sound was deafening. A roar of voices. Eventually, I heard someone calling my name. I figured it was my imagination. The voice became louder and recognizable. Jessica, sober and pale, approached. She gave Marcus and I a quick hug in succession.

"Marcus, Dave, I'm so sorry for the loss of your friend."

"Thank you, Jess," Marcus nodded. "It's good to see you again."

She rubbed Marcus's right arm. "I've missed you, buddy. I really have."

"Jess, forgive me for ruining the moment, but is it wise for you to be here?" I interjected.

"I know. Brad could be in this mob."

"Primarily, he'd be here stalking me in hopes of locating you. He told me he'd be doing just that."

"You saw him?"

"He visited me at Jonah's office. In his typical, threatening posture."

"I'm sorry you've been dragged into the middle of things once again, Dave."

I started to say that it was all right, but caught myself. It wasn't all right! If Jess had respected my judgment, neither of us would be in our current position. My bitterness was obvious.

"Jess, is it true that Brad anticipated this terrorist strike?" Marcus asked.

"He sure did," she sighed. "His reference to Tolkien's *The Two Towers* is still bugging me. He also implied that some event would be directed against Jewish and Christian interests. The fact he didn't include Muslims in his list is telling."

"Many American Muslims died in that attack as well," Marcus corrected her.

"I don't think Brad was referring to individual lives," Jess continued, "but to nationalistic symbolism. America is a melting pot, but it's still called a Christian nation by many. Also, if it weren't for American effort and support, there wouldn't be any modern nation of Israel."

"Perhaps," Marcus murmured.

"Who knows what's to come?" Jess exclaimed. "When the stock market opens again, will it crash? Will other hijackings, bombs, or attacks come? I shudder just thinking about it!"

"So do I," my friend nodded.

"Are you somewhere safe, Jess? You still in Torrington?" I asked.

"No, I'm up in Springfield. The shelter advised me how I can live incognito."

"Glad to hear it," I sighed.

My eyes continued to dwell on the crowd. The top of someone's head was cutting through conversational circles, walking in our direction. To my relief, it was a bald scalp—it wasn't Brad. Given that Brad hadn't shaved his head in the last few days. As the bald head emerged from a forest of faces, I flinched. Richard Clarkson, the professor and parapsychologist who betrayed my confidentiality six years before, approached.

"Ahh, here are a few familiar faces," Clarkson smiled. "I'm glad that Rubenstein has such an incredible send-off. What a turnout!"

"This is the memorial one receives when one is honorable," I murmured.

"Come now, Mr. Paul," the parapsychologist chuckled. "Honorable men let bygones be bygones." Clarkson's eyes grew large as he spotted Jess. "Well now, Mrs. Ramsey! What a surprise! Is your husband here as well?"

"I wouldn't know."

"Oh. Trouble in paradise?"

Marcus was within an inch of Clarkson's face. He dwarfed the pudgy professor.

"I don't see how that's any of your business," my friend growled.

"Mr. Pattyson, if your intent is to intimidate me, you will not succeed."

"Oh?" Marcus exclaimed, as his body tightened.

"Marcus," I interjected. "C'mon man. He's not worth it."

"You are volatile, Mr. Pattyson," Clarkson sneered. "It's no mystery how and why your house became a paranormal hellhole."

"I've had no problems since your buddy Brad Ramsey left the area."

"That's irrelevant."

"No, it isn't, Richard," a woman's voice answered from behind the rotund scholar. We all turned to see Claire Monroe, her face pale and tear stained.

"Ms. Monroe!" I exclaimed. "You made it back from California in time!"

"I had to be here. And again, never mind this Ms. Monroe malarkey, it's Claire. You're making me feel ancient."

"Sorry, ma'am."

"Ma'am? David, stop that! Anyway, I'm heartened to see all of you here," Claire grinned. "I feel Jonah is with us right now. I believe that our loved ones have the ability to watch us at any time. Even when they transition to the next level. The hereafter is with us. It surrounds us. It isn't discerned by the five senses."

"Claire," Clarkson inquired. "Have you published the events in Mr. Pattyson's house…in any of your infinite paperback releases these past five years?"

"Of course not, Richard. Marcus can verify this, he wants privacy on this matter."

"That's right," Marcus growled.

"A shame. You have some good video evidence of telekinesis during that exorcism," Clarkson sighed.

"What on earth are you folks talking about?" Jessica inquired.

"Ignore it," Marcus advised.

"Perhaps we should clue Jess in on what we've been experiencing. It may be…illuminating…for her," I suggested.

"Maybe. You'll excuse us Claire, Clarkson," Marcus sighed.

"Certainly," Claire smiled.

The three of us left the crowded building and found a private corner in a courtyard. The mid-September air was welcome. I unbuttoned my tight collar. Apparently, I had gained weight since the last time I wore my one suit.

"Jess," Marcus started. "Do you remember the embarrassing confrontation 'Mika had with Brad? In my yard six years ago?"

"Who could forget?" She chuckled.

"'Mika tried to exorcise Brad. Cast out the demonic spirits she believed inhabited your husband."

"Uh-huh…" Jess knit her brow with concern.

"Well, we're all in agreement. Her makeshift ritual was ill-conceived. Embarrassing."

"It sure was."

"Here comes the hard part. 'Mika was right about Brad. Demonic spirits possess him. Empower him."

"Marcus!" Jess exclaimed. Then she laughed.

"I know, I know, this sounds nutty. But, hear me out."

"C'mon guys! My husband is unbalanced, yes. Psychic, yes. But possessed?"

"Not Hollywood's version of possession, Jess. It's more of a symbiotic relationship. Brad has displayed powers that go beyond any run-of-the-mill psychic."

"Like what?" Jess wheezed out between giggles.

"The evening 'Mika tried to cast the demons out of Brad, she developed red welts and scratches. On her neck, her face."

"Hysterical people often develop rashes and skin irritations," Jess answered.

"I thought exactly the same thing," I added. "But more phenomena occurred."

"Oh? Like what?"

"Cold spots, knocking and banging noises in the walls and ceilings, physical attacks, foul smells, and…ghostly manifestations."

"Manifestations?"

"That's right, Jess," Marcus answered. "Dark, shadowy forms. Some hideous."

"Guys," my former heartthrob commented while shaking her head. "I can't swallow this stuff. You've been hanging around Claire Monroe too long."

"I've always been a rational, naturalistic thinker," I added. "You know that, Jess! Yet, I have seen too much. I can't deny the theological implications."

"Okay, Dave, say you're telling the truth. Why blame Brad for this haunting?"

"Tamika challenged Brad without calling on the name of God," Marcus replied.

"*God?*" Jess questioned. "What God is that? The same God that just *allowed* three thousand innocent people to die?"

"The same God that allows his children the freedom to choose good and evil. The same God that allowed his only begotten Son to be tortured and killed," Marcus replied.

"Nice God ya got there," Jess sneered. "Dave, are you buying into this sidewalk pamphlet religion?"

"Only recently, Jess. But yes, I've seen and heard so much. I'm now a Christian believer."

"Okay. So Tamika exorcised Brad in her improper way, and that Amityville crap started to happen. It's a leap of faith to imply that Brad caused that haunting."

"Is it a leap of faith to say that Brad predicted the tragedy that occurred three days ago?" I asked.

"Well, not as much as one," she admitted.

"Is it a leap of faith to say that Brad has many contrasting personalities?" I continued.

"No. But that hardly means—"

"Is it a leap of faith to say that Ramsey has beaten you, has sexually abused his followers, has honored Hitler, has the Spear of Destiny in his possession?"

"Dave!" Jess exclaimed, while nervously looking at Marcus.

"Is it a leap of faith, Jess," I challenged, "that Brad Ramsey sexually and ritualistically abused Huey?"

"*All right!*" she yelled back. "*You win!* You were right, I was wrong! Is that what you've been wanting to hear?"

Marcus stepped between the two of us.

"Jess, this isn't about who was right or wrong. This is about you in danger."

"And it's also about worldview," she sighed in response.

"Yes it is," Marcus continued. "Think about the evidence, Jess. Think! Brad desecrated Huey's icons, while sexually abusing Huey. He manipulated the workplace, making people distrust Dave here. Huey dies and his body vanishes. An unexplainable image is left on his sheets, identical in nature to the Shroud of Turin. Brad is denied access to the linens. Immediately thereafter, a mysterious fire spontaneously combusts in Tim's presence and this miracle on fabric is lost forever. Except for the photos and fiber samples Dr. Boyington gathered beforehand. Now what does Ramsey need to do? Debunk Boyington's findings! Debunk the Turin Shroud! Adopt naturalistic attitudes on his broadcast. Attitudes that he doesn't actually possess."

"Wait a minute," Jess frowned. "Marcus, slow down."

"No, Jess, you're an intelligent woman. Absorb all this together! Don't compartmentalize each scene and judge it separately. This is a puzzle you need to see assembled!"

Jess stiffened.

"A charismatic leader destroys and debunks the image this helpless man left behind. Exhibits psychic awareness of future events and private lives. Causes Jonah Rubenstein to see nightmarish images from his past. Punishes Tamika with paranormal attacks. Has multiple personalities. Is sexually uncontrolled. Is abusive, even with delicate women like you. Arranges the theft of a medieval relic. Honors Hitler. Predicts the terrorist attacks like it was a positive event. Now, remember when you asked how we could believe in a God who allows last Tuesday to happen? How can you, a rational, intelligent woman that you are, love and believe in the man I just described?"

"I…don't k…know," Jess stammered. "I suppose I fell for an illusion of Brad."

"So, if you were so deceived, so deluded by this powerful character, isn't it possible that you are also deceived in regard to God? Isn't it possible that God is real? The devil is real? And Ramsey serves the latter?"

"I don't know. Maybe. At this point, I'm just accepting hearsay."

"Hearsay?" I yelled in frustration. "Hearsay? That's it, the gloves are off! Are you calling us liars? I was right about Ramsey! I was right then and I'm right now! I accepted all you had to say when you came for my help! You are so blind, so—"

"Dave," Marcus interrupted, "Don't lose it. Jessica needs time. As you did."

The observation put me in my place. Jess sat on the bench, face in her hands.

"My, what's all this?" a deep voice taunted from behind Marcus and me. "It's a reunion! A party! And here, I wasn't even invited."

We didn't need to turn around. We knew who it was. The hairs on my neck stood on end. Ramsey walked over to Jess and put his huge hand on her shoulder. She jerked away from him.

"Don't worry, hon," he said softly. "Their verbal assault on you is over. I'm here."

"Brad," Jess hissed. "That's rich. You're going to protect me?"

"I know I've made mistakes. Jess, I'm so sorry. You know about my upbringing. The abuse. After you left me, I immediately admitted myself into the Bayside Behavioral Health Center. I'm now in an outpatient recovery program."

I looked at Marcus with concern.

"Babe, don't listen to these religious nuts," Ramsey continued. "If you catch a flight back with me, I've arranged for a beautiful hotel suite you can stay in. No need for you to go slumming up here. I'll give you your space for as long as it takes. Until I get better."

"That would be a long wait indeed," Marcus murmured.

"Don't test my patience, boy," Brad hissed.

"Who are you calling boy?" Marcus shot back.

"You see any other 'darkie' around here?"

*"Darkie?"*

Marcus rushed at Brad, but the crud dodged my friend's tackle. Before Marcus could react, his arm was twisted behind his back. He grimaced in pain.

*"Brad!"* Jess yelled. *"Let him go!"*

I ran over to help Marcus, but with little effort Ramsey pushed me away. I flew backward to the ground.

"Okay, hon," Brad grinned, while releasing Marcus. "I won't sink to their level."

Marcus rubbed the feeling back into his arm. Where Brad had grabbed his flesh were dark red marks. The beginning of bruises.

"Our level?" I asked. "Jess, did you hear him bait Marcus?"

"I sure did!" Jessica answered. "Brad, I don't know who you are anymore."

"I'm who I've always been. I have some anger issues. I'm working them out."

"I wish I could believe you," she sighed.

Marcus quietly prayed, and then withdrew a vial from his pocket. With a quick gesture, he popped the small cork and threw droplets of water at Brad.

Brad looked shocked. Where the water hit his face, blisters formed. Large, red blisters.

"You…flea," Brad hissed with red eyes. "I could *squash* you without trying."

Ramsey reached for Marcus, but quickly drew back. He was visibly shaking. He looked weak.

"What have you done to me, *boy?*" he exclaimed. "What did you *throw* at me?"

"Simple water," Marcus smiled. "Blessed and consecrated. It's not the water you're reacting to, but what power the water represents. Rivers of living water."

*"Water my ass,"* he whined. "The fanatic just threw *acid* on me!"

*"Marcus!"* Jess yelled. *"You didn't!"*

"He probably mixed anthrax in there as well," Brad moaned.

"Jess, hold out your palm," Marcus offered.

*"Don't hon!"* Brad exclaimed.

Jessica slowly held out her hand. My friend poured some water into her palm. She visibly relaxed.

"He's right. It's just water."

"He probably switched vials!" Ramsey protested.

"How could water do that?" Jess asked.

"It's what we've been saying," Marcus answered. "Think about it!"

Even in his weakened condition, Brad had enough energy to match Marcus's strength. The behemoth tackled my friend! They rolled down the small hill behind us. Jess and I ran after them. Brad ended up on top. He wrapped his hands around Marcus's throat and started choking him. This time, Marcus had strength enough to counter. He thrust his knee into Ramsey's groin. With pain, the demoniac rolled off. Marcus stood to walk away, but Ramsey reached out and grabbed his ankle. My friend fell once again. Brad quickly stood and raised his foot over Marcus's head.

The foot never landed. This time, I would finally have retribution. I stuck Ramsey across the jaw. Even though I was small, the blow knocked the weakened Brad off his feet. As he struggled to get up, I kicked him in the stomach. He groaned in pain. All my fantasies were coming true! I kicked Ramsey again. And again. He rolled in pain. I laughed with glee. Images of Huey flashed through my head. I kicked him once more as he moaned and gasped. Brad's life was mine for the taking.

Suddenly, an arm wrapped around my midsection and pulled me back. I jerked around, clenched fist ready for a new battle.

"David, can't you hear me? *David!* Snap out of it!"

It was Marcus. I was literally deaf while I beat Brad. It was an altered state of consciousness. Trembling, I became aware of tears streaking down my face.

"Dave! Are you okay? *Snap out of it!*"

"Marcus?"

My friend was bleeding. Over his right eye was a nasty cut.

"Yeah, I'm okay. How about you?"

"I'll live."

Jessica bent over the injured Ramsey, face wet with tears.

"Is he okay?" she asked. "You didn't kill him, did you?"

"Him?" I exclaimed. "How about concern for us, your protectors?"

Before she could answer, an arm wrapped around her middle. Brad was on his feet once again.

"Enough of this," he groaned weakly. "Come on, Jess. Let's go home."

She tore away from his embrace. "No, Brad! Not this time. You are dangerous. I can't trust you."

"Babe!" he answered. "Hon! You don't mean that! Who just beat the crap out of me? I'm dangerous?"

"You provoked and attacked them."

Jess stood between Marcus and me. I gave Brad a huge smile. The giant, still bent with pain, trembled with rage. His eyes were red. The muscles in his cheeks and forehead trembled and twisted. He looked inhuman.

"Very well," he growled. "I hope you two enjoy her. Just remember, she's leftovers. *Sloppy seconds.*"

"*Bastard!*" she yelled back.

Ramsey slowly dusted off his clothes. "You can keep the whore. I just want the disc."

"What disc?" Jess asked innocently.

"I know what you did. You downloaded my private information. If you hand over that disc, you won't have to ever, ever see me again."

"I have no idea what you're talking about," she murmured.

He growled and ran toward her. Marcus blocked Ramsey's charge. Brad bounced backward and fell.

"You know, Marcus, I'm starting to enjoy this day," I laughed.

"Laugh while you can," Brad giggled. "Just remember…that Jew friend of yours was reduced to ash. *Burned in a blaze of glory!* Who needs Auschwitz ovens in this day and age?"

"You filthy piece of…" Marcus growled, as he grabbed Ramsey's throat.

"Do it, Marcus," I prompted. *"Make him pay!"*

"No," my friend sighed. He released his grip on Ramsey's throat. "God will deal with him. 'We fight not against flesh and blood, but against principalities and powers.' Satan hates God's chosen people almost as much as he hates God."

The three of us started to walk back to the fellowship hall. Ramsey turned and limped toward the parking lot.

"This isn't over," he laughed. "Not anywhere near over!"

# CHAPTER 33

▼

# JESSICA'S PLAN

I was fortunate. Christian Family Services allowed me to keep my office position. They replaced Jonah with a kind, but humorless pastor. He immediately changed Jonah's office and decor. I considered it disrespectful.

Days passed. To everyone's cautious relief, no other terrorist attacks occurred. Nor was Brad Ramsey an immediate threat. After his humiliation at the hands of Marcus, I suspected Ramsey wouldn't be seen for a long time.

One day at work, I received a mysterious e-mail on the office computer. It was an invitation to a picnic from a woman nicknamed Lotus. The location was the Lourdes Shrine in Litchfield. I knew who sent it. There wasn't any picnic. Jess wanted to meet at our old haunt.

On the scheduled day, the autumn morning was crisp. A cool breeze rustled the changing leaves. As I sat on the picnic table waiting for my old friend, the scene reminded me of the other September day six years prior. The day Jess told me of the childhood abuse she suffered.

Across the small brook and ravine, I saw a car pull into the parking lot. Sure enough, Jessica emerged from the Hyundai. Her head darted side to side, nervously scanning the area. She continued to look around as she approached.

"You can relax, Jess. Brad isn't here."

"I wouldn't be so sure."

"Well Jess, where did you park the company van? Remember, you're the one feeding Rich," I smiled. "I don't care to look at that pureed gunk today."

"These past six years have been very, very long, haven't they? An eternity."

"Yeah."

"And look how different we are. Those two coworkers, so comfortable and open with each other, they no longer exist."

"Well, a glimmer of what those two shared is still alive. You have something new to tell me?"

"You know what I'm going to share with you?"

"The CD-ROM from Brad's computer. You want to tell me about it."

"Again, you're right. I have the download Brad mentioned. Believe me, this information is very damning."

"Does this info refer to the stolen Spear of Destiny?"

"Yes. It details the whole operation. The theft plan. I prefer…that Brad be arrested about this…rather than about other dealings."

"Other dealings?"

"Brad has corresponded with a few hate groups. Groups of radical Muslims and Fascists who share an intense hatred for Jews. Although the Muslim extremists on the Net haven't disclosed any knowledge concerning the recent attacks, they do admit definitive ties with al-Qaeda and Hamas. Some have detailed their plans to mail anthrax to prominent politicians and Jewish leaders."

"Whoa. Anthrax in the mail is a current threat."

"Exactly. This could put Brad away for a very long time."

"Why didn't you share this with me before?"

"Dave, you have to understand how hard this is for me. I love Brad. He's troubled. Perhaps he's clinically paranoid or schizophrenic. I don't know."

"But, you're sharing this with me now."

"Things have changed. Radicals have attacked this country. Anthrax is in the mail system. I can't allow Brad to get further involved in all this. Have you heard the gossip? The rumor that thousands of Jewish World Trade Center workers called in sick on that dreadful day? The underground buzz is that Israel either secretly arranged the attacks, or knew about the attacks and purposely kept silent. Well, Brad is currently posting this conspiracy hooey on his Web site. I've seen it. In time, he'll rant about Jews and American policies on his broadcast. It won't be long before the Feds start investigating any and all extremists. They may discover that Brad was predicting an attack. Psychic predictions aren't a viable explanation. They may consider Brad a conspirator!"

"So you want Brad arrested for theft now, before his risky elbow rubbing with terrorist groups catches up with him? You're still concerned for the maniac!"

"My love for him is unconditional."

"Said the doormat to the boot."

"Dave, Brad's father did unspeakable things to him. Especially after the old man became a religious fanatic. I know what it's like to be sexually abused. You couldn't possibly know. I pity him."

"I understand sexual abuse. This is why I risked myself and my job trying to protect Huey. I can also sympathize with the child Brad was. Ever since, he has chosen evil wherever he can. Through freewill. He chose to molest and abuse Huey. He chose to beat you. He chose to promote anti-Semitism at every opportunity."

"But his choices weren't truly free. His father and the abuse made them."

"If this was true, Jess, every person with an abusive childhood would turn out like Brad. They don't."

"But they are more likely to be abusers themselves. Demographically."

"Yes. But this doesn't erase personal accountability."

"That's an insensitive attitude!"

"On the contrary, Jess. I'm very sensitive, when one considers the big picture. If we continue to make excuses for people like Brad, those who ultimately pay for our attitude are people like Huey."

On that point, Jess went pale. Tears started to steam down her face. I gave her a side hug and she leaned her head on my shoulder.

"It's my fault, Dave. My fault. I was blind."

"Jess, I understand how we transform people into what we want them to be."

"Poor, poor Huey. Now he's gone. Lost forever."

"I wouldn't say that."

"No, Dave, don't feed me any of that heaven malarkey."

"I may have heard Huey just recently. Through the phone."

"What?"

"It's true, Jess. I received several phone calls, a few days before September eleventh. A faint, electronic sounding voice."

"Could have been some technical glitch."

"The voice said 'Ewy goo boy,' 'Avey,' and so on. It even repeated certain things he used to say at this grotto. Comments no one else would know."

"You can't be serious."

"It's recorded on tape. One of Claire Monroe's students analyzed it for us, Jess."

"Claire Monroe? Aw, gawd."

"She's legit."

"Dave, I hate to see you lose perspective like this. Marcus and his circle have—"

"Jess," I interrupted. "I wish I could make you witness the things I have. I've seen spiritual manifestations. Hideous forms, like one that resembled a decaying infant. All these things infested Marcus's house, Jess. Right after Tamika confronted Brad. An exorcism ritual expelled the phenomena. Just last week, you saw Brad's skin blister when holy water was sprinkled on him. Simple, normal water! There's more going on here than a man disturbed by his abusive past."

"Dave, I don't know what you saw. I know what you think you witnessed. Yet I refuse to intellectually travel to the Dark Ages."

I felt a surge of anger and frustration. I stood and looked down the ravine. Jess walked up behind me and put her hand on my shoulder.

"Dave, I'm sorry. I'm hardly one to preach about perception and reality."

"No, you're not."

"Perhaps I can rectify some of my mistakes."

"You're really going to turn Brad in?"

"Right away. After Brad is in custody, I plan to move back to California. But I want you to know, that despite our differences, I appreciate everything that you and Marcus have done for me."

She then embraced me. Tightly. A cool, fresh breeze lifted her long hair. I momentarily felt an old pang. A wish that we could stay like this. I swallowed the affection down, as a child would swallow castor oil.

# CHAPTER 34

▼

# IN THE WILDERNESS

The visit with Jess still weighed on me as I unlocked my apartment door. I encouraged my delicate friend to betray her very dangerous husband. Now I worried that Brad would try to kill her before he was caught.

I tossed my leather jacket on the couch and walked into the small kitchenette. My mouth dry from anxiety. As I filled a glass, a shadow crept over my shoulder and onto the wall. Suddenly, a pungent cloth was pressed against my mouth and nose! I struggled. The room went dark.

My vision returned slowly. It was twilight. I could make out a few details. A leafy branch hung over my head. A few bright stars were visible. Crickets chirped loudly. Apparently, my attacker had dumped me in the woods somewhere. With a sigh, I attempted to sit up. At this time I noticed being anchored to the ground somehow. In the dim blue light, I saw that my arms were tied to a beam or to a log. Ropes held my upper forearms to the wood. A flashlight illuminated the ground in front of me.

"Now don't struggle, Sparky. You have no hope of freeing yourself."

"What do you want with me, Ramsey?"

"I wanted to take you on a field trip, kiddo. An educational adventure. We happen to be in a very historic place. We're in the colonial settlement of Devonshire."

"Devonshire? We're in Kent?"

"I see you're familiar with the place."

"Yeah. You've made a big mistake, Brad. These woods have the reputation of being haunted, and teenage curiosity seekers caused a fire a few years ago. The cops now patrol all access roads onto this hill. If they see your car, they *will* search the trail."

"No worries, mate. A good friend of mine dropped us off. I entered the Black Path Forest up the dirt road, the loonngg way. I carried you and my backpack for miles. I believe you are familiar with Richard Clarkson? He'll be returning come morning."

"*Clarkson* is helping you?"

"He's a good disciple, yes. A faithful servant."

I snorted with disgust. "What do you plan to do to me? Why here?"

"I don't want to reveal our docket, David. Why ruin it? Not just yet. As for 'Why here?' Well, I have a flair for the dramatic. As you know, this colonial village was wrought with misfortune. Little by little, people moved away or died. Now all that remains are stark cellar holes and a charcoal pit. Thanks to certain authors and researchers, this location grew an image. A famous mystique. These woods are a symbol of despair and madness. Demonic forest creatures supposedly frolic here. Occultists come here, conjuring candles in hand."

"That's certainly up your aisle, Ramsey. Despair and demons."

"Be that as it may, what better location is there for my interrogation of you?"

Fear flooded me.

"Interrogation?"

"Now, now, little boy. Don't fret. Consider this an interview. Better yet, we're having our own round of *Jeopardy*. Now, let's have 'missing persons' for one hundred, Alex. The answer is Jessica Ramsey."

"What are you rambling about?"

"You know where Jess is hiding. I need to talk to her without you or your bodyguard in tow. Where is she residing?"

"I have no idea. She just happens to pop up on occasion."

I mentally suppressed the word Springfield. I feared that Ramsey could psychically read my mind.

"I sense your stress level is rising, child. Your breathing…your heart rate."

"That may have something to do with being abducted and tied to a log."

"No, it doesn't. You're hiding the truth. You know where she is."

"No, I don't. Why not just ask your demon friends where Jess is?"

"They want me to get the information from you. 'More fun that way,' my spirit guides tell me. Now, I just want to talk with my wife. I'm even willing to grant her the divorce she wants."

"How reasonable of you! You are indeed a reasonable person. *Except* for how you abduct people and tie them up in the woods, that is."

"Let's call this a special circumstance."

"And what circumstance inspired you to abuse Huey?"

"Let's not flog that old horse again."

*"Burn in hell, Ramsey."*

Brad started to walk around me. Slowly. In a circular fashion. Dry leaves crunched under his feet. The crickets went silent and a cold breeze blew. Hoots from an owl sounded in the distance.

"Hear that owl, Davey? This town used to be called Owlsbury as well. Did you know that?"

I ignored him.

"Still, your bad attitude continues. I hear you recently found the Lord, didn't you? Well, praise the Lord."

I turned away from where Ramsey was standing. He then walked around to my other side.

"As a new Christian, I'm going to provide you a spiritual service. As you know, the deified Jew known as Jesus went into the wilderness after he was baptized. There, he fasted for forty days. Satan appeared to him. Tempted him. Your Messiah survived the ordeal and his life thereafter earned him entry into the hall of mythical heroes. All bull crap, of course. But potent mythology. Joseph Campbell fodder."

"I hope you're entertaining yourself, Brad. Because I'm not impressed by your rhetoric."

"Now, now. Give me a chance. Let me finish. Your Messiah had the desert as a wilderness. We have a forest. Trees. Yes, David Paul, welcome to your official temptation."

"Oh brother," I laughed.

I heard a few clanking sounds behind me. The sound of metal. I started to worry. I imagined the worse case scenario. My fear quickly grew to terror! A sharp point was pressed against my right wrist! I turned my head just in time to see a large hammer rise into the air.

*"Oh God, Ramsey—don't do it!"*

With one blow, a large spike was driven through the space at the base of my palm where the thumb crease is. The spike exited through the back of my wrist.

I screamed in agony. An anguished cry that hurt my throat as much as the spike pained my hand. Spasms traveled down the arm into my shoulder, neck, and head.

"Shut up, wuss," Ramsey hissed. "There's no one within earshot." He grabbed another spike and drove it through my left hand. The trauma knocked the air from my lungs. My heart raced. All the muscles in my upper body knotted, tensed, and convulsed. After what seemed an eternity, I finally inhaled. My legs kicked and curled.

"Look at you," Ramsey laughed. "What a pussy! The Nazarene was flogged with metal pellets—his entire body—back and front. He was shredded and blistered. Sharp thorns pierced his scalp. He carried his crossbeam for quite some distance. When it came time for his hands to be pierced, he took it better than you!"

*"Oh God,"* I gasped. *"God, h-help me."*

*"God?"* Ramsey giggled. *"God?* Give me a break. You used to be a man I secretly admired, Sparky. Someone I could *relate* too."

"Wh...what an...honor," I hissed.

Just as the torture was transforming into an agony to be endured, Ramsey walked behind me. With superhuman strength, he lifted the wooden beam off the ground with me attached! He continued to lift, while climbing a small stepladder. Apparently, he had prepared two metal hooks on a tree to support the beam I was nailed to. He reached into his pocket, pulled out a pocketknife, and cut through the ropes on my left arm. With the added stress, the pain in that wrist tripled in intensity. He descended the small stepladder and walked over to my right side. There, he removed the ropes on my right arm. Now my arm, shoulder, and chest muscles were supporting all my weight. I tried to brace my feet against the tree to lessen the pull on my hands, despite the fear that Ramsey could now nail my feet against the trunk. Ramsey then provided what seemed to be an act of mercy. He placed the small stepladder under my feet.

"Go ahead, David. Stand on the ladder. I won't nail your feet."

I stood. With my body weight on the ladder, the pain lessened considerably.

"Now," Ramsey started as he paced in front of me. "Tell me. You are experiencing a fraction of the agony that deified Jew experienced. How do you like it?"

"L-let me down."

"In time. Now, what do you think of a God who would ask his own supposed Son to endure something like this? Imagine your current pain multiplied many times! Is that God-loving?"

"I...I...I don't know."

"Come on, my logical friend! That God concept is *not* a loving God! That God is a *sadist!*"

"Jesus...sacrifice for us."

"*For us?* Come now. You're now a believer in sin? Your sadist God wants to punish a race for being what he created them to be? He wants to punish them for being human?"

"He...doesn't want to punish. He bore o-our penalty."

"Uh-huh. Through his supposed Son, with which he shared his essence."

"Y-yes."

"Three people with a shared substance. Three persons who comprise one God. So, David, apparently God is *schizophrenic!* He has a multiple personality disorder! Or perhaps he's a *conjoined triplet!*"

"Being n-nailed to a tree doesn't lend itself to t-theological discussions, Ramsey."

"You will talk," Ramsey threatened. "Or—"

With a quick kick, Ramsey knocked the stepladder from under my feet. All weight shifted down on throbbing wrists. Again, I screamed with pain.

"Now, let's see how you like hanging this way."

I writhed in agony. Kicking. Convulsing. I tried to brace my feet against the tree and alleviate the pressure on my wrists and upper body. It didn't work well. My body knotted with muscle cramps. Fire traveled up my arms, up my neck, into my head. After several minutes, a new problem developed. My diaphragm started to cramp. Breathing became an effort. Any breath I managed to take was shallow and insufficient. Streams of sweat ran down me, even though it was cold enough to see my breath. After another ten minutes, my clothes were completely saturated. I felt woozy. I was drowning. Unconsciousness approached and I welcomed its arrival.

"Oh no, you don't," I heard Ramsey say. I felt the stepladder under my feet once again. Despite my desire to pass out, the compulsion to stand on the platform couldn't be denied.

"Now, how was that? A pleasant experience, wasn't it?"

I coughed. A burning acid filled my throat. After some more coughing, my breathing returned to normal.

"Go back to h-hell."

"Be nice, pup. Otherwise, your ladder may disappear again."

"*I don't k-know where Jess is!*"

"Never mind that. I just want to talk. Discuss. Share metaphysical concepts."

I threw up. Vomit dripped down my chest.

"Forget the whore for now, Davey. If our conversation goes well, some dry clothes are awaiting you. Sure, there'll be some nerve damage in your hands and wrists to live with, but you'd be surprised how well wounds like this can heal."

"N-not…f-feeling chatty."

"Too bad. I'd love to hear how that Jew Rubenstein warped your perceptions. Don't you want to know who the real, historic Jesus was? Yeshua Ben Pantera, known as Jesus of Nazareth, was the son of a Roman soldier. Jewish writings preserve this tradition. Or perhaps he was Herod's son himself! Anyway, this Mary woman was knocked up! Obviously! She missed her period and had to make up a story! What could be better than an angelic visitation? An Immaculate Conception?"

The thought of enduring another unsupported hanging overwhelmed me. I decided to try and debate with Ramsey and play his game. Even though it was hard to talk. Meanwhile, perhaps a cop or nearby resident would detect Brad's campsite—somehow.

"The fact this miracle was recorded sixty years later, B-Brad, supports the account. The m-miracle gave an a-appearance of indiscretion."

"Uh-huh. A packaged and processed Rubenstein response. Back on topic. Jesus studied Greek and Far Eastern mythology. He faked a death on the cross, through the use of 'mandrake' which was mixed with vinegar and offered to him on a Roman spear. Maybe this very spear!"

Brad held up a long, wooden shaft with an ancient-looking metal head. The spearhead had two sections.

"The S-Spear of Destiny?"

"Ah-ha! Jess did share much with you, didn't she!"

I reprimanded myself. The agony compromised my judgment. Conceivably, Brad could eventually get the name Springfield out of me. Suddenly, I worried more for Jessica than for myself.

"No. I…I guessed."

"Don't even presume to deceive me, David."

Again, the stepladder was kicked out from under me. This time, I didn't have the strength to yell in pain. The sudden jerk on my wounds was unbearable. I felt some flesh on my right wrist give way. Perhaps a ligament. My legs kicked and searched for the tree trunk once again. My diaphragm was paralyzed. Within one agonizing minute, the stepladder was under me again. I gasped, wheezed, and coughed uncontrollably.

Ramsey walked directly in front of me. Giggling.

"Damn, this is fun!" he squealed. "Anyway, Jesus was drugged. Through certain followers, he was taken from his tomb. He healed, relocated with Mary Magdalene, and had children. All secret societies know this!"

"First-century C-Christians were dying. They s-should have known if gospel was untrue. Disciples…died m-martyr's deaths."

"Nonsense. There's no viable account of these martyrdoms. Only the writings of church historians who also lied about Jesus."

"Christians lied…just to be p-persecuted, tortured, and killed?"

"According to who? Church historians?"

"Even Roman historians. Nero's time. F-first century."

"But no Roman reports concerning those twelve disciples. Right, Dave?"

"They…wandering p-peasants. Not newsworthy."

"I see Rubenstein indoctrinated you well. You have an answer for every logical objection."

"Logic, Brad? Logic? I'm *nailed* to a t-tree!"

"What's wrong with you? Can't you see I'm trying to save you from that Jewish mystical *bull crap?*"

"Save m-me? What for?"

"Because, *no blood relative of mine will serve that deified Jew!*"

I hung there, trembling in pain. His claim didn't sink in immediately. It took a minute.

"R-relative?"

"Yes, Sparky. You're blood! After my—our father—died rotting in his prison cell, I cleaned out his old estate. I found boxes of papers. Photo albums. Behind one framed photo, I discovered an envelope. Inside, my—our mother—had scribbled out some sort of confession. Details of a year I suppressed in my memory. I was around twelve years old when Mother was pregnant. With you. She saw what dear old Dad was doing to me every night. In secret. In the dark. You were her precious, lovely little runt! A drooling rug rat adored far more than I ever was! She called you Sparky! While she allowed the old pervert to have his way with me night after night, she found it necessary to protect your precious little ass. She abandoned you at an orphanage. Dear Pappy demanded to know where she hid you. Where your bulrushes were. She refused to say. He murdered her."

Hanging there, engulfed in waves of agony, I finally knew who I was.

"Somehow, the rumor mill found out that Mother had some illegal abortion in her youth. This explained why the religious zealot murdered his wife. The press never found out that it was about you. Dear ol' Dad encouraged the false story, hoping to gain support with right-wing militants. So, I traced you through the orphanage Mother mentioned in her letter. I then tracked you through the foster homes. The last home to reject you was the Paul family. Why on earth did you assume their name, you needy little jellyfish? Anyway, I moved to Torrington just to assure that you didn't get off scot-free. Mom had no reason to protect you over *me!*"

"B-Brad, y-you need help."

"I need help?" Brad yelled. "Me? *Ha!* I'm powerful! No one can hurt me again! I'm one with the true god! The light bringer! No one can hurt me! Not our *Christian* Daddy! Not our negligent Mother! And not *you,* brother! Who were *you,* little Abel? Who were *you* to escape my hell? You took my family! So, I took your heartthrob, your job—even your favorite retard from you!"

Brad moved erratically. His voice quavered. He started to cry like a little child. He stomped his foot. He pulled his hair. I suddenly didn't see him as a possessed villain. I saw him as a pathetic, warped, and traumatized human being.

"Brad, our f-father was evil. We'll get you help."

"You understand?" Brad trembled. His eyes were wide, like a child's.

"Yes, Brad. You're ill."

Brad's eyes flashed. His pupils narrowed. The muscles in his forehead swelled and lowered. It gave him a Neanderthal appearance.

"What are you doing, *butt muffin?*" a coarse voice asked through Brad.

Before my eyes, Brad seemed to be shifting personalities. Normal to demonic.

"He's my *brother!*" child Brad whined. "Let's deliver him from the Nazarene cult and protect him!"

"Protect him? Look at *him!*" the demon responded. "Hanging there like that Nazarene bastard. That God-man who made your father abuse you. Look at *him!* Doesn't he look like dear old *Dad?*"

"He's not Dad."

"He's your father's demon seed. He even adopted your father's religion! Little Christian bastard, hanging there and judging you! What better help for him is there than to *force* him into disavowing his silly faith! If he won't disavow, *he will die!* He caused the death of your mother! Look at him look down on *you!* Him!"

"Yeah! He is looking down on me!"

"No," I gasped. "I want to h-help you!"

Brad bellowed like a bull. His eyes grew wilder.

"Hear that, butt muffin?" the coarse voice asked. "He wants to help you! *You!* A powerful, strong god among men! You, who will achieve world greatness, Spear of Destiny in hand! The die is *cast!* The Muslims are at war with the Christians! The Jews will get caught up as well! When the smoke clears, only the enlightened will remain. You will lead them, my son! *In my name!*"

In my haze, I remembered how Jonah handled the demonic manifestations.

"In the name of Jesus Christ, *leave!*" I bellowed with as much strength as I could gather.

"Shut *up!*" Brad shrieked. He then dropped to the ground, trembling.

"In the n-name of Jesus," I repeated. "In the name of Jesus, depart from my brother."

Howls and shrieks surrounded us. Dark forms and shadows darted tree to tree.

"Through t-the blood of Jesus. By the cross of J-Jesus!"

Demonic Brad writhed on the ground.

"No-no-no-no! Stop-stop-stop-stop-stop."

Unexpectedly, with Brad squirming ten feet away, something kicked the stepladder out from under me. Everything went gray. When my vision partially cleared, Brad was standing in front of me. His eyes narrow.

"Nice try," he giggled, sadistically.

# CHAPTER 35

▼

# DARK NIGHT OF THE SOUL

Whatever remnant of humanity left in Brad was completely buried. The person in front of me didn't look human. The muscles in his forehead rippled and thickened. His cheeks were higher, his eyebrows arched. Thin, feline pupils darted from side to side. The voice, while still his, was considerably more coarse. The only light available was from his flashlight, which lit everything from below.

The stepladder was denied me. My right foot found a small knot on the tree trunk, which I used as a support. It was inadequate. The throbbing, searing pain from my wounds became a secondary concern. I needed to breathe. Muscle cramps paralyzed my diaphragm. Sweat poured off of me. Shallow breaths were all I could manage.

I remembered the static portrayals of crucifixion in all those classic Hollywood movies. Like statues—Jesus Christ, Spartacus, or whomever—they would hang still and passive. Real crucifixion was squirmy. Undignified. The body keeps searching for the position that will allow it to breathe. Muscles tremble and shake.

"Well, Davey-Avey," Brad taunted. "Consider where you are. Hanging there, like some ancient Jew bastard. For what reason? Because you won't renounce that fictitious god Rubenstein introduced you to? Because you want to protect that little whore wifey of mine?"

"'Cause of you," I gasped.

"Au contraire, little brother. Renounce the Nazarene. Tell me where Jessica is. I'll end this. I'll even drop you off at the Sharon Hospital."

"Y-you're crazy."

"Throughout history, great men have been considered crazy. I'll take that as a compliment."

"Yeah. You're g-great."

"*Flea!* Look at you, suffering for your god. Your unrequited love. So where *is* your false god? Is he here? Heelllooo, Jesus! Ya here, Jesus?"

Guttural laughter surrounded us.

"The answer is *no!* He's not here! As a matter of fact, your false god wants you to *suffer!* He wants you to carry your own cross! Heh. Look at what your drooling moron friend experienced, at my hand. Did Jesus rescue him? Deliver him? Not at all. Only after his death did your friend mysteriously dematerialize. If Rubenstein was right, if your fictitious god 'translated' your friend into some spiritual existence, why couldn't he have done this before he suffered?"

"God isn't cause. *Y-you* are."

"And your god is responsible for *me,* dear boy! Have you read the book of Job? Your god dares his partner, called Satan, to steal the faith of a simple man. Your god allows him to torture the poor soul. Take away his loved ones. His wealth. His health. While enduring the torment, your god wants this man to sing his praises. How *reasonable!*"

"No l-light without darkness."

"Ah-ha. A profound pearl of wisdom from little brother. It does my heart well, to see you stretching your philosophical wings. Let me put it this way, your false god of light wants you to suffer in the dark!"

"Jesus bore my suffering."

"Did he? Then why, pray tell, are you in your current situation?"

"Because of you."

"Myopic fool. God can rescue you at any time. He *chooses* not to."

"Ahh. Y-you forgot to say 'your false god.' My God is the *true* God?"

"*Shut up!*" Brad squealed in a shrill voice.

"T-touchy!"

"The Nazarene is not the true god! He's the deified bastard son of a Roman murderer and a Jewish *slut!*"

"If true, he can't save me. No power to."

"Oh, he *has* the power! It doesn't compare to the true God's power, though."

"Y-your light bringer?"

"The light bringer. The morning star. Neither male nor female. Neither moral nor wicked. My god is *power!*"

Brad's eyes rolled back in his head. He appeared to be entering a trance, moaning and rocking back and forth.

With Brad in an altered state of consciousness, I dug my right foot into the previously mentioned knot in the tree. I pressed with all my remaining strength. A sharp piece of bark cut the sole of my foot. Slowly, the wooden beam started to lift off the metal hooks. I prepared myself for the pain to come.

Brad growled as he regained consciousness. He walked over and grabbed my supporting foot. The wooden beam slid back down and the jolt made me wail pathetically.

"I'll allow you to support your weight on that knot, but don't even consider leaving your perch!"

Despair engulfed me. Bitterness. My life had been a waste. I was a loner. I was poor. Women shunned me. Now I was going to die in this desolate ghost town. In torment.

"Ahh," Brad giggled. "I can see it in your eyes. You're starting to see the truth of things. Life is all sound and fury, brother. It signifies nothing. In the immense, cold, stark emptiness of space, there exist a few billion galaxies. Within these galaxies, exist billions of stars. Around these stars, billions of planets. Among this almost infinite number of planets, we have an insignificant piece of debris called earth. On this speck, this molecule, species live and die. Evolve and disappear. One of these insignificant animals came out of the trees and adapted into mankind. Now with this proper perspective, you actually believe the absolute Creator of all this cares about you? A mere microbe? One of billions of organisms, residing on one of billions of planets, orbiting one of billions of stars, existing in one of billions of galaxies?"

I let the logic of what Brad said sink in. My heart sank.

"Ahh, *you see!* I can tell! You are *nothing!* Life is *nothing!* It's a cosmic *joke!* A random accident! There's *no* meaning! There's *no* divine love!"

"*Jesus!*" I gasped.

"Yeah, now we have your Jesus. A man. Just another insignificant organism among billions. In our rampant denial of life's futility, we have our god myths. Zeus. Odin. Isis. Sol Invictus. *Jeeezzzuuus.*"

"W-what about your l-light bringer?" I asked.

"My father is the lord of meaningless, dear boy. He knows that death and annihilation are inevitable. The ultimate truth. Within this cosmic joke called existence, power is the only virtue. Morality? Good and evil? A loving, personal

Creator? Please. Disneyland fantasies. My supernatural father came into my pathetic life and granted me power beyond all comprehension."

"If he's a spirit…then d-death isn't final?"

"Only a few souls have enough power to exist as energy. I have this power. Ultimately, even these energies will die—as the universe expands and fades into nothingness. We're in on the joke, brother. We're enjoying this cosmic accident while we can."

"You have p-power, Brad? What power?"

Suddenly, the shirt on my left arm went up in flames. Despite the fact that it was saturated with sweat, a hot inferno seared my flesh. I screamed. After about twenty seconds, the flame slowly died out. I shuttered with pain.

"See that, Davey-Avey? Don't ever doubt me. By the way, that flame was a perfect illustration of our universe. It starts, it burns brightly, then it dies. Pain is the only meaning behind it."

"Lord God, help me," I prayed.

"Still, the speck clings to his delusion."

"Jesus. W-why aren't you helping me?"

"*Silence!*" Brad ordered. "Don't mention that name! Don't *think* that name!"

Three scratches slashed down my right cheek. Cold fingers touched my body. Poked. Pinched.

"W-why does the name of Jesus a-annoy you? He's supposed to be insignificant."

"Now I know why you loved that drooling moron named Huey. You share his developmental limitations. Okay, I'm going to grant you a mercy. You don't have to renounce your mythical god. Go ahead and cling to your psychological crutch. All I ask of you is that you tell me where Jessica is. Just the city or town. That's all I need."

"Go back to h-hell."

"Idiot. You'd suffer for a woman who rejected you? You'd die for her?"

"I couldn't l-live with myself if you hurt h-her."

"Let me enlighten you about a few things, little brother. When I first started dating Jessica, she told me about your attraction to her. Oh, she felt guilty. She admitted how she playfully flirted with you, but thought you understood the context. You were a friend. You weren't a man to be desired, you were a *boy!*"

The words hurt. They cut deep.

"That's right, you scrawny imitation of a man. Obviously, you didn't have the tools to please her. She knew it. And hooo man, she has a sexual appetite that will not be denied! As a matter of fact, she has slept with just about every man she had a friendship with! Every man except you, runt!"

"Vulgar f-freak."

"Ahh, I'm getting through! I can tell! You believe that Jessica liked you? She simply felt *sorry* for you! And who wouldn't? You're some little Charles Dickens orphan, carrying a 'poor me' sign on his back. Aw, pooorrr little Davey. 'No wun luvs da little boy.'"

My despair started to turn into anger.

"Shut up, B-Brad."

"Hitting home, aren't I? You're a shadow of a man. A wisp. Self-pity is your religion, not that Nazarene crap. Be a man now. Let that skank Jess know that you're no longer her pet. Tell me where she is."

I lowered my head.

"Don't you know, Sparky? She laughed at you! Laughed at how you would ask her out as friends. She knew you wanted her, little horn toad. She kept talking about her boyfriend just to let you know. You weren't *worthy* of her."

More and more, a rage gathered strength within me.

"L-look who's talking!" I snarled.

"My, look at the hit bird flutter," Brad giggled.

"Look at *you*," I gasped with emotion.

*"Okay!"* he laughed.

"You're s-scared of life. Father raped you. Demon is doing same thing."

"My god empowers me."

"What was exchange b-before? You arguing with y-yourself?"

"Sometimes, my lord needs to straighten me out. Sometimes I lose perspective."

"No, Brad...you have glimmer of conscience. Demon is erasing it!"

"He's my mentor. My guide."

"Demon called you butt muffin. W-what did Father call you?"

*"Shut up!"* Brad screamed. "You shut up! *Shut up!"*

More scratches appeared on my chest. An unseen hand slapped my face.

"Lord Jesus," I prayed. *"Please."*

"I am my lord's willing concubine," Brad snarled. "He can use me for any-thing. I willingly offer my entire being to him! You dare to demean *him?"*

Brad again grabbed my supportive foot. With another length of rope, he tied both my feet against the tree, below the knot. My pierced wrists bore all weight again. I was groggy with pain. Multiple muscles cramped with intensity. Slowly, the cramps worked their way to my diaphragm. I couldn't move. I couldn't take in air. I started to lose consciousness.

"Die," Brad hissed.

All pain left me. I floated in darkness. If this was annihilation, I welcomed it. It was peaceful. Like a dark lake to float in. One star appeared above me. A pin-point of light was approaching me, or I was approaching it. Soon, the star became a brilliant sun, blazing with every color of the spectrum. It was so beautiful. So warm. I almost felt like thanking Brad for sending me to this place.

A comforting, authoritative voice permeated me. Words beyond all language. To this day, I can't fully translate the flood of love and knowledge I received. Any attempt demeans the experience.

My eyes jerked open. The pain returned. I was lying on the ground, free from the spikes. A stranger was looking down at me. A distant flashlight illuminated his features.

"Is he alive?" someone behind me asked.

"Yeah, but he's in bad shape," the face above me responded.

I looked at his pale blue shirt. I saw a shining badge. Apparently, the police had noticed Brad's light in the woods.

"Can you speak, Mr. Paul?"

It's at this time I noticed the man leaning over me was Officer Mullady. I tried to speak, but started coughing on a bitter liquid in my throat. He turned me on my side and I continued to cough. I spit out cups of foaming fluid.

"Take it easy, Mr. Paul. Take your time. We need to know who did this to you."

I wheezed. "Rh-rha-rha."

"Take your time," he repeated.

"Rha-my. Ramsey."

"Ramsey? Brad Ramsey?" Mullady asked.

"Yes."

At that very moment, a scream sounded behind us. Mullady sprung to his feet. I turned my body the best I could to see what was happening. Brad suddenly dropped out of a tree, from a high limb. He landed on all fours, growling.

*"Watch it, Jay,"* Mullady warned. "The guy's either insane or doped up!"

Like a cat on the prowl, Brad lunged off his hands and feet and flew ten feet in the air at the officer named Jay. The demoniac, foaming at the mouth, landed on top of him.

"Ramsey, don't move," Mullady announced. "Or *I'll shoot!*"

Brad wrestled with the officer. He pinned his arms with no effort.

Mullady pulled the trigger. It clicked. He quickly checked the chamber and saw the pistol was loaded. He pulled the trigger again, to no avail.

Brad looked like an animal in the moonlight. He hissed, then bent low and bit into the officer's neck! Apparently, he hit the jugular. Blood spurted like a fountain, pulsing out with each heartbeat. Brad's face was covered. He licked the blood off his lips.

Mullady charged at Ramsey and knocked him off his partner. The two wrestled in a bush. I reached for Brad's flashlight. My hands and wrists felt useless. Using my forearm, I knocked the light closer.

With a scream, Mullady flew through the air. Apparently Brad tossed him like a toy. The officer impacted against a tree and crumpled to the ground.

Finally, I managed to weakly hold the flashlight. I looked at the other officer. He was applying direct pressure to his neck, trying to limit the profuse bleeding.

"Lord," I prayed with a wheezing, weak voice. "I know you are with me. Please, save us."

With a maniacal laugh, Brad walked through the bushes toward me.

"You still alive, maggot?"

"Jesus Lord," I wheezed.

"The more you use that name, the more I'll make you suffer," Brad warned.

"Please, Jesus."

"I smell a piggy for the roast," he snarled. Ramsey reached and lifted me by my shirt.

With a lunge, Mullady tackled Brad again. This time, he was Brad's equal. The two wrestled in the leaves. The officer reached for something, I think it was his club. Ramsey grabbed Mullady's hair and hit his head against a rock. It made a loud, cracking sound. Somehow, the agile cop managed to bring his foot under Brad and throw him off with his leg. Ramsey tumbled backward.

Mullady scrambled on the ground and located his partner's gun. He aimed and pulled the trigger. A pathetic click sounded again.

Brad returned to his hands and feet and then scrambled into the bushes. Mullady cautiously illuminated the thick brush with a flashlight.

*"My God,"* Mullady shrieked. "What the hell *is* this guy?"

"He's strong. Be c-careful," I urged.

Snarls and growls sounded everywhere. Mullady looked around with confusion. The bushes rustled on all sides.

*"This is bizarre!"* the officer hissed.

Mullady's partner managed to crawl over to my side. Blood continued to ooze out from under his hand on his neck wound. He appeared to be semiconscious. I helped him apply direct pressure on the wound, using my traumatized hands.

With a shriek, Brad lunged from the bushes and knocked Mullady over. Drooling and snarling, Ramsey bit his left ear off. The flesh stuck out of his mouth, as he chewed on it. Mullady swore as he tried to get Brad off of him.

"Please, Jesus," I continued to pray. "Our strength, our d-defender."

With a snort, Brad spit out Mullady's ear and leapt like a cat toward me.

"I warned you, baby brother!" he laughed. "Still, you insist on calling on that deified Jew bastard for help. I think I'm going to *skewer* you, piggy."

Brad stood over me, holding something in his hand. As he raised it higher, I shuttered. It was the Spear of Destiny! My body was weak and helpless. I needed to stop Brad—somehow. I needed to at least delay the deathblow.

"Brad, Brad, Brad. You are s-still the little butt muffin, aren't you?"

"What? What did you just say to me, flea? You dare speak to me with such disrespect?"

"Respect you? Come on, brother. Why would I respect someone used and manipulated like you are?"

"I already explained this to you, moron. My lord doesn't use me! He *empowers* me!"

I continued debating, relieved that Brad was receptive to this ego challenge. "Please. Don't you know who inspired our f-father, as he molested you night after night?"

"Your deified Jew bastard inspired him. Your false Christian god suppressed his natural sexuality and this led to unnatural outlets."

"Unnatural outlets? I thought children and the mentally challenged were supposed to be introduced by experienced adults to the pleasures of sexuality."

"Shut up. You're just trying to confuse me."

"How can I confuse you—moron that I am?"

"Just as Einstein might be confused by the reasoning of a retard, I am confused by you."

"Brad, come now. T-think about it! Your lord, your light bringer, *he* is the one who wanted father to molest you. Just as he has led you to molest Huey, and whoever else y-you have victimized."

"Not the same! Not the same! Huey, among other lucky recipients, loved it!"

"Just as *you* loved it, Brad? Just as you loved what Father did to you, night after night?"

"Yeah! I loved it. I loved it as well!"

"Then why hate me?"

"Because Mother protected *you* over *me!*"

"Protected me from what? From the *pleasure* F-Father was giving you?"

"Shut up! Shut up! Don't confuse me!"

Brad sobbed heavily, as he lowered the spear. He wailed like a child. "Why, Daddy?" he gasped. "Why did you hurt me? Why me?"

"Because he was evil, Brad. Because he was led by your evil, demonic guide."

"Shut up!" Brad shrieked. "You are evil, just like Dad! You are trying to confuse me, just like Dad! You are a Christian, just like Dad! You took Mom from me, just like Dad!"

"Why do you w-want to find Jess, Brad? Why?"

"Because she *betrayed me!* She needs to pay!"

"Just as Mom betrayed Dad? Just as Dad m-made *her* pay? Can't you see, Brad? The demon has turned you into Dad! You are Dad!"

"No! Not me! Not me! I am great! My lord is great!"

"You're as great as Dad was, Brad."

The guttural, demonic voice reasserted itself. "Are you starting to doubt me?" it asked. "Without me, you're nothing but a child sobbing pathetically in the dark."

"I'm not a child!" Brad yelled at his possessor.

"Don't defy me," it snarled.

"My god, why have you forsaken me?" Brad sobbed.

"Forsaken *you?* It's not about you, flea," the voice snarled back. "It's about me! It's always been about me! Now submit!"

Mullady finally managed to stand up and illuminated the scene with a bright flashlight. The light was behind the tree I was crucified on, and its shadow cast a dark cross onto Brad. My brother stood there, trembling. Finally, his eyes flashed red as he raised the spear into the air once again. I held my breath and waited for the stabbing.

Instead, he stood motionless. Tears streamed down his cheeks. I really don't know how to explain what happened next. Brad grimaced. Then with a quick and deliberate thrust, he drove the metal into his own skull! Wailing, Brad collapsed to the ground. His body convulsed. The spearhead separated from the shaft, impaling his forehead.

I knelt over him, confused and crying.

Brushing off his uniform, Mullady ran to his partner. With a firmer hand than I had, he pressed down on Jay's neck wound.

"Mr. Paul, you have someone to thank out there," Mullady groaned while assisting his partner. The bleeding wound that was once his ear dripped down his neck.

"H-how so?"

"I just got off duty in Torrington and was riding along with my friend here. Apparently, someone called the dispatcher and reported that a man was being tortured in old Devonshire. Everyone thought it was a prank, considering how many loonies obsess on this place. When asked for his name, the caller wouldn't identify himself. He just said 'Help Avey.' Any ideas who that was?"

"You wouldn't believe me if I told you," I responded.

"After fighting this Ramsey guy, I'm prepared to believe anything," Mullady sighed.

I looked down at Brad. He was motionless. What was I supposed to feel? Relief or pity? I was overwhelmed by both emotions. I leaned down and started to pray.

Suddenly, the air grew colder. A stench of decay filled the area. Next to Brad, a dark fog formed. It swirled. It pulsed.

"What in holy hell is that?" Mullady shrieked.

"Subtract the 'holy' from that," I whispered. It was hard for me to stand. I was dehydrated and in intense pain. Still, adrenaline enabled me to back away.

The black fog grew. A transparent leg emerged from the mist. It was bony. Emaciated. The rest of the translucent form revealed itself. It was female, and very old. Thin breasts drooped down to its waist. A full rib cage was seen. Toothless and withered, a grin stretched its skeletal face. The top of the head was hairless, except for one long tuft of hair that hung down its neck. Large, claw-like nails grew from its fingers. Empty eye sockets stared at me. Coarse hair covered the putrid body, dripping with pus and mucus. The form rippled and oscillated, much how one would see something through water.

"Daviiidd Paauull," it seethed with a man's voice. "You'll see me again, *Sparky.*"

The form started to illuminate brighter. With an electronic hiss, it burst into a dozen round globules of light. They twirled and darted about. Soon, even these faded.

Mullady managed to keep the pressure on his partner's neck, despite the terror illustrated on his face. I knelt on the ground next to him. Cricket's chirped again. A warm, refreshing breeze blew over us. The sound of a siren was heard in the distance. We waited with quiet horror.

# CHAPTER 36

▼

# AFTER THE STORM

Two months later.

My wrists and hands healed, but their dexterity would forever be compromised. Pain and numbness would be expected the rest of my life.

Officer Mullady's ear was successfully reattached. His partner recovered. I formed a friendship with both men. They believed my explanations for what transpired that dark, frigid night.

Brad also lived. Due to his injury and subsequent bleeding, he suffered from a traumatic brain injury. His personality reverted to childhood. Innocent and gentle. Ironically, he became a permanent resident in a Torrington group home. Prison time was deemed inappropriate for this shadow of Brad Ramsey. Thankfully, all malevolent, supernatural phenomena that accompanied him were gone.

Claire, Marcus, and I puzzled about Brad's final act. Did Brad recognize how he became our father, and his hatred for Dad became hatred of self? Did the demon punish him for his disobedience? Did Brad, with the sliver of humanity that remained, finally decide to protect me? I'd like to think it was the latter, but I have no way of knowing.

Why did the demonic entity abandon its once willing host? That was another mystery. We figured the spirit had ambition. It wanted to influence society on a grand scale. To discourage faith in Jesus. To spread anti-Semitism. It failed to actualize its ambitions—this time. Anyway, it wasn't interested in possessing a developmentally challenged individual. Perhaps the spearhead actually exorcised the entity? Was it possible that it was the Roman lance that pierced Christ?

The Spear of Destiny was returned to Austria with little press coverage. Various members of Brad's cult were arrested and convicted for the theft. Richard Clarkson was also arrested for his part concerning my abduction. Incriminating evidence was located in his car.

Several weeks passed since I had seen Jess. She visited me once in the hospital and seemed overwhelmed by what had transpired. She needed to go and clear her head. Upon returning, she arranged to meet me at a familiar forum.

This day program was much like our past workplace. Severe developmental disabilities were the norm. Brad was one of the few ambulatory participants serviced at this location. I arrived before Jess and entered the facility.

"Daa-ve," Brad smiled upon seeing me. "Daa-vey! Yeah!"

"Hi, Brad. How are you?"

*"Look!"* he exclaimed, holding up a crayon drawing. It depicted two stick figures holding hands. A sun with a smile face beamed in the corner.

"That's very nice, Brad."

Brad clumsily pointed at the figure on the right.

"Tha you," he giggled.

"I see! Very good work."

At times, it was hard for me to look at Brad's face. My memories were harsh and bitter. Whenever hatred rose within me, I reminded myself that this childlike individual wasn't the willing host for evil. This Brad Ramsey was divorced from his prior life.

"Wan it?"

"Sure. I'd love it."

"You're so good with him," a soft voice complimented me from behind.

"I didn't see you come in," I whispered.

Jess walked over to Brad and kissed the top of his head.

"Hi, Brad, it's me again. Jessica…your wife."

He looked at her with confusion.

"Hi, lady," he replied. He quickly resumed his coloring.

Jessica wept openly.

I took her arm. "Come on, Jess," I said softly. "Let's talk in private."

The late November air was unusually cold. We both shuddered outside the front door. She continued to weep as I put my arm around her.

"Dave, you still don't believe Brad was possessed, do you?"

"Yes, I do. Just ask the officers who saved me."

"Well, perhaps insanity could be considered possession at that," she sighed.

I didn't press the issue.

"Dave," Jess started again with hesitation. "Were you protecting me when Brad tortured you so terribly?"

"No. Brad had issues with me, being that I was his younger brother. The one who escaped the abuse of our father."

"You're lying. Brad wanted to know where I was hiding, didn't he? He knew I had the CD-ROM. He needed to protect himself and pursue his ambitions."

"Yeah, I suppose. A small part of the interrogation had to do with you."

"You were going to die for me, weren't you?" she sobbed. "Even though I never believed you! Even though I never returned your affections!"

"You're giving me too much credit," I smiled.

*"You shut up!"* she yelled before locking lips with me. It was a long kiss. My heart raced. For so many years I wanted this. Now here she was, in my arms! Elation coursed through me.

"Oh, Jess," I sighed, while continuing to kiss her. Slowly, her lips stiffened and tensed. Her chest shook. I could tell she was repressing tears. I stepped back.

"Dave," she spoke mechanically. "I love you. I want to marry you."

I looked in her eyes. They were lifeless. She reached out and held my hand. Her whole body was stiff.

"Jess…you love me?"

"Yes," she answered after a short pause.

My heart ached. My whole being craved her affection. But I couldn't deny what my senses were telling me. This woman did not love me. She was simply grateful and ashamed.

"Jess," I sighed. "Go home. Put this part of your life behind you. Brad. Me. Find a man who will make you happy."

"What are *you* saying?" she protested. "You make me happy! David, my close friend and confidant. I owe you *everything!*"

"You love me as a brother. I accept that. But I cannot accept this gesture you're making. You should find a man who will make you feel as strongly as I feel toward you. Go find him. Be happy for a change."

She weakly smiled and took my hand again.

"On one condition," she answered. "You also find happiness. If there is a God you are one of his or her greatest creations. He or she must love you as well."

"I know, Jess. *I know.*"

She squeezed me with all her strength before wiping her face and walking away. I despaired. What was it with human beings? Why do we only desire what we cannot have? Why would I have traded all the wisdom and revelation I gained, just to see this woman's eyes look on me with romantic love? The heart is a very foolish, very fickle thing. I thanked God that it no longer enslaved me. Despite my sorrow, I was free.

# EPILOGUE

▼

Lisa Branford was a quiet girl. It was hard for her to ask the enigmatic Mr. Paul for his journal. Still, Lisa's term paper was about the turn of the century and she knew the elderly man was at his prime during those years. Unfortunately, time and religious zeal must have distorted his memory. The tale was too wild to believe! The story explained why Mr. Paul hid his hands and wrists behind bulky gloves all year long. He had been crucified, this was certain. As for the demons and the like, this was too hard to swallow. In the year 2045, humanity long since abandoned this silly notion of miracles, hauntings, and demons. Lisa knew that God and Jesus were simply metaphors for charitable living, not objective realities unto themselves. Likewise, the devil was a symbol of man's darker desires. Most churches now taught this. The old man was a throwback to a more superstitious age.

With a sober face, the teenage girl approached her mother. Mr. Paul had been a loving, gentle friend to the family for most of her life. He attended every birthday party, every Christmas dinner. The girl was loath to speak ill of the gentle soul, especially since the man died a few days prior.

"Finished, Mom."

"Wonderful! Did you learn about life at the turn of the century?"

"Well, there was an interesting account regarding terrorism. But beyond that, I'm afraid the thing reads like an old Stephen King novel."

"How's that?"

"Mom, it's a wild tale that involves miracles, demons, and exorcisms."

"Oh dear. I know David was eccentric, but demons? I'm sorry, hon. You can still quote the sections of the journal that focus on world events, can't you?"

"I'm way ahead of you, Mom. I have two pages typed out already. I can't help but dwell on Mr. Paul, though. He must have been very lonely."

Lisa grabbed a tissue and wiped her eyes before continuing.

"He loved this woman very much. He almost died for her. Still, the man was alone his entire life."

"No, dear. He wasn't alone. He had us, didn't he?"

"Yeah, he did."

A few days later, David Paul was buried. It was a moving service, despite the pouring rain. Mr. Paul's headstone was simple. He had no relatives, no children. Still, a few parishioners from Saint John's attended the funeral.

After the service, Lisa lingered at the gravesite. When she turned to leave, she noticed another mourner had also stayed. Under a large black umbrella, a tall, thin figure shivered. Lisa approached with curiosity.

"Hello, young lady," an elderly woman with startling green eyes welcomed. "Did you know Mr. Paul well?"

"Are you…Jessica Kim?"

"Why yes! How do you know that?"

"Mr. Paul described you…in a journal he kept. Your green eyes gave you away."

"He wrote of me? How sweet of him. What a darling man he was."

"Yes, he was that," Lisa wept.

"Now, now honey, don't mourn. He's in a better place now."

"I'm not so sure," Lisa replied, while sniffing.

"He's with the Lord now."

"The Lord?" Lisa asked. "Mr. Paul wrote down some rather imaginative stories from his past. He portrayed you as an atheist."

"Oh, I was!" Jessica laughed. "I was skeptical for so many years. Just a few months ago, I found something I planned to share with David. Something that validates David's thinking. If only I'd flown out here *earlier!*"

Lisa nodded politely.

"I see you doubt this," the elderly woman laughed.

"Don't get me wrong, ma'am. I adored Mr. Paul. But, he was very imaginative. His fables rivaled Aesop."

"I see! Did he write about a developmentally challenged man named Huey?"

"Mm-hmm. He claimed that this man left his own Shroud of Turin after mysteriously disappearing. Do you know about the Turin Shroud? It used to be considered authentic."

"Yes, I remember. And, Mr. Paul wrote of my ex-husband? His brother?"

"Yeah. I'm…embarrassed to tell you something. Keep in mind that I loved Mr. Paul with my whole being. But, he depicted your ex-husband as possessed."

"Oh. Well, I had a hard time accepting that as well. But *now* I believe he was."

Lisa paused. The old woman seemed so reasonable! So together! Apparently, she too was going senile or was another throwback to a more superstitious age.

"Uh, okay. Well, it was nice meeting you, ma'am."

"Don't be frightened, young lady! I'm not off my rocker, as they used to say."

Lisa started to back away. "I'm sure you're not, ma'am."

"Don't leave, honey! Not yet. Am I correct in assuming that Mr. Paul wanted you to read this journal?"

"Yes, ma'am. Just before he died, he promised to let me read it for a term paper I'm writing."

"Then David trusted you! We've written back and forth for a while now, around Christmastime. Ever since my second husband died. Believe me when I say your elderly friend never shared this story. Not with anyone! Not when he was a missionary, not after he retired. You must be special!"

"Mr. Paul watched me grow up. He was like a grandfather to me."

"Then, I think he would have wanted you to have this."

Jessica slowly handed Lisa a plastic bag. Lisa was afraid to look inside. Still, the teenager managed to pull out an old sheet. Slightly yellowed with age.

*"This isn't—"* Lisa gasped.

The girl unfolded the sheet, taking care that her large umbrella shielded the cloth. Upon viewing half the sheet, she paused. A dark yellow, negative image of a man's face was imprinted on the surface.

"Huey?" Lisa asked. The elderly woman shook her head in the affirmative.

"But, Mr. Paul said this was lost in a fire!"

"I thought so too. Recently, a real estate agent discovered a safe deposit box hidden in the floorboards of Brad's California mansion. He guessed that it belonged to Brad Ramsey, the old-time talk show host. Sure enough, the sheets were within. Tightly folded. Apparently, Brad stole the sheets from my old manager's office, before causing the fire."

"Why would Mr. Ramsey have done this? He wanted the sheets studied by his researcher friends!"

"No, hon. He wanted the sheets debunked."

"Then, why didn't he destroy the sheets himself?"

"Perhaps, deep down, he was *afraid* to destroy them. God had touched them. Over the years, Huey's image darkened. In the past, one had to stand eight feet away to see Huey's image. Now we can see it one foot away. And here, by Huey's side, what do you see?"

"What? I can't believe—"

Lisa rubbed her eyes. On the left side of the sheet, an image of a robed sleeve and hand was imprinted, reaching down and grabbing Huey's hand. If they were imprinted on the sheet, the hand must have reached *through* the fabric!

"David trusted you with his story, young woman. Now I'm entrusting you with this sheet. Tell his story. This era needs a sign. You could be the one to provide it."

The tall, elderly woman then placed her hand on David's tombstone and whispered something. Lisa strained to hear, but couldn't. The lean woman then walked away, with the assistance of a cane.

The rain stopped. A warm breeze blew Lisa's long hair across her face. The sun peeked through the clouds, washing everything in orange. Lisa Branford held the sheets closely to her chest.

# Recommended Reading

Antonacci, Mark. *The Resurrection of the Shroud*. New York: M. Evans and Company, Inc., 2000.

Brittle, Gerald. *The Demonologist*. Lincoln: iUniverse Inc., 2002.

Bruce, F.F. *The New Testament Documents: Are They Reliable?* Leicester: Inter Varsity Press, 1943.

Guscin, Mark. *The Oviedo Cloth*. Cambridge: The Lutterworth Press, 1998.

Heller, Dr. John H. *Report on the Shroud of Turin*. Boston: Houghton Mifflin Company, 1983.

Jenkins, Philip. *Hidden Gospels*. New York: Oxford University Press, 2001.

Lewis, C.S. *Mere Christianity*. New York: McMillan Publishing Company, 1943.

Martin, Ernest L. *The Star that Astonished the World*. Portland: ASK Publications, 1996.

Martin, Malachi. *Hostage to the Devil*. New York: Readers Digest Press, 1976.

McDowell, Josh and Bill Wilson. *A Ready Defense*. San Bernadino: Here's Life Publishers, 1990.

McDowell, Josh and Bill Wilson. *He Walked Among Us*. San Bernadino: Here's Life Publishers, 1993.

McDowell, Josh. *The New Evidence that Demands a Verdict*. Nashville: Thomas Nelson Publishers, 1999.

Miller, Kenneth R. *Finding Darwin's God*. New York: Harper Perennial Publishing Company, 2000.

Morison, Frank. *Who Moved the Stone?* Grand Rapids: Zondervan Publishing House, 1958.

Ross, Hugh. *The Fingerprint of God*. Ornage: Promise Publishing Company, 1991.

Strobel, Lee. *The Case for Christ*. Grand Rapids: Zondervan Publishing House, 1998.

Thiede, Carsten Peter and Matthew D'Ancona. *The Jesus Papyrus*. New York: Doubleday, 1996.

Whanger, Mary and Alan. *The Shroud of Turin: An Adventure of Discovery*. Franklin: Providence House Publishers, 1998.

Wilkins, Michael and J.P. Moreland, Craig Blomberg, Darrel Bock, William Lane Craig, Craig A. Evans, Douglas Geivett, Gary Habermas, Scot McKnight and Edwin Yamauchi. *Jesus Under Fire*. Grand Rapids: Zondervan Publishing House, 1995.

Wilson, Ian. *The Blood and the Shroud*. New York: The Free Press, 1998.

978-0-595-35533-4
0-595-35533-1

Breinigsville, PA USA
13 November 2010
249262BV00002B/1/A